Standish O'Grady's
Cuculain

Irish Studies
James MacKillop, *Series Editor*

Select titles from Irish Studies

All Dressed Up: Modern Irish Historical Pageantry
Joan FitzPatrick Dean

Compassionate Stranger: Asenath Nicholson and the Great Irish Famine
Maureen O'Rourke Murphy

The Irish Bridget: Irish Immigrant Women in Domestic Service in America, 1840–1930
Margaret Lynch-Brennan

Israelites in Erin: Exodus, Revolution, and the Irish Revival
Abby Bender

Joyce/Shakespeare
Laura Pelaschiar, ed.

Postcolonial Overtures: The Politics of Sound in Contemporary Northern Irish Poetry
Julia C. Obert

Seamus Heaney as Aesthetic Thinker: A Study of the Prose
Eugene O'Brien

The Snake's Pass: A Critical Edition
Bram Stoker; Lisabeth C. Buchelt, ed.

Standish O'Grady's
CUCULAIN

A Critical Edition

Edited by Gregory Castle

and Patrick Bixby

SYRACUSE UNIVERSITY PRESS

First Edition 2016

16 17 18 19 20 21 6 5 4 3 2 1

∞ The paper used in this publication meets the minimum requirements of the American National Standard for Information Sciences—Permanence of Paper for Printed Library Materials, ANSI Z39.48-1992.

For a listing of books published and distributed by Syracuse University Press, visit www.SyracuseUniversityPress.syr.edu.

ISBN: 978-0-8156-3491-1 (hardcover)
978-0-8156-3477-5 (paperback)
978-0-8156-5389-9 (e-book)

Library of Congress Cataloging-in-Publication Data

Available from publisher upon request.

Manufactured in the United States of America

For Camille, Claire, and Owen,
who already know the meaning of heroism.

Contents

Illustrations

Note on the Text

The text for this edition derives from the two-volume edition of *History of Ireland* (London: Sampson Low, Searle, Marston and Rivington; Dublin: Ponsonby, 1878, 1880). We have also drawn from *History of Ireland: Critical and Philosophical*, which was issued by the same publishers in 1881. Facsimile versions of these editions are available, but the three volumes are unwieldy, somewhat repetitive, and difficult to manage for classroom and basic research purposes. The present edition is designed to make this material readily accessible to contemporary readers.

O'Grady's spelling of proper names in Irish was idiosyncratic, but perhaps no more so than that of other Irish writers in the late nineteenth century. All significant names can be found in the glossary, where we have provided their variant spellings and contextualizing information, sometimes drawn from O'Grady's work, sometimes from contemporary scholarly sources. But because there are so many variants for most names and no clear consensus as to the "best" ones, we have decided not to change O'Grady's spellings in the text (though we have silently corrected obvious errors).

Most prominently, we have preserved the spelling "Cuculain," which O'Grady favored, over Irish spellings and other Anglicized forms of it, such as "Cuchulain." The multitude of spellings reflects not only a loosely codified language but also a tradition of transliteration with no central organizing orthographic principle. John Harvey has noted that O'Grady, upon meeting Pádraic Pearse, pronounced the hero's name "Cutch-ul-ane," whereon Pearse corrected him, explaining that the pronunciation was "Coo-hu-lin." "O'Grady was overwhelmed by the discovery, and after a long pause informed Pearse that he would have written an entirely different book if he had known the correct sound of the name."[1]

Our selection of chapters from the three volumes of the *History of Ireland* was guided by a single consideration: how best to tell the story of Cuculain as O'Grady presented it, a version that enjoyed tremendous popularity in the late nineteenth and early twentieth centuries. To allow the reader to get a sense of the larger scope of O'Grady's story, we have summarized the omitted chapters in separate sections corresponding to these chapters' placement in the original. Many of the included chapters have epigraphs, typically from nineteenth-century poetry, and we have identified the epigraphs' sources in footnotes, save for those few that can be found only in O'Grady—in particular those attributed to an "ancient bard." We have included substantial excerpts from the introductions to all three volumes of O'Grady's *History*, which will help the student understand the bardic culture that informs it.

Citations to *History of Ireland* in the introduction and critical essays are given parenthetically in the text rather than in notes, and they include an abbreviated title (see the list of abbreviations), volume number, and page number from the original three volumes published in 1878, 1880, and 1881. If quotations also happen to be from material included here, we have provided page cross-references to this edition. In addition, we have placed an asterisk next to names and terms in the text that can be found in the glossary.

1. John Harvey, *Dublin: A Study in Environment* (1949; reprint, London: Batsford, 1972), 17.

Acknowledgments

This project began with a suggestion from Jim MacKillop, who thought an accessible collection of Standish O'Grady's historical writings on Cuculain would find an audience among students, teachers, and the general public. I had been frustrated with the lack of access to O'Grady's *History of Ireland* and had to satisfy myself with the materials I could find online through the Colby College Library, so I was eager to take up the project. Shortly after I began work on it, I enlisted my friend and colleague Patrick Bixby as coeditor, and together we designed and completed this volume. Our gratitude goes out to our contributors, whose readings of O'Grady's work have made our own understanding richer and more precise. We thank our graduate student, Scott Icenogle, and the director of the Fletcher Library, Dennis Isbell, for their assistance in researching and compiling the materials presented here. We also thank the anonymous reviewers, whose comments enabled us to highlight and emphasize what we had imperfectly realized, and our editor at Syracuse University Press, Deborah Manion, whose kind attention and steadfast support have helped us to bring the project to a conclusion.

Abbreviations

HI 1 Standish O'Grady, *History of Ireland*, vol. 1: *The Heroic Period* (London: Sampson Low, Searle, Marston and Rivington; Dublin: Ponsonby, 1878).

HI 2 Standish O'Grady, *History of Ireland*, vol. 2: *Cuculain and His Contemporaries* (London: Sampson Low, Searle, Marston and Rivington; Dublin: Ponsonby, 1880).

CP Standish O'Grady, *History of Ireland: Critical and Philosophical*, vol. 1 (London: Sampson Low, Searle, Marston and Rivington; Dublin: Ponsonby, 1881).

1. *Map of Ireland in the Heroic Times*. Frontispiece to Standish O'Grady, *History of Ireland*, vol. 1: *The Heroic Period* (Dublin: Ponsonby, 1878).

Standish O'Grady's

Cuculain

Introduction

"Wild and Improbable Narratives": Standish O'Grady's History of Ireland

Gregory Castle

> They listened to their elders
> relating the deeds of Cuculain,
> which he had performed and forgotten
> in that small theatre of his fame.
> —*HI* 2:319

I

Standish James O'Grady began his career as a historian of Ireland rather inauspiciously at the age of twenty-three, entirely ignorant of Ireland's past—"not through my own fault, for I was willing enough to learn anything set before me, but owing to the stupid educational system of the country."[1] By the end of his career, he was hailed as the "father of the [Irish] Literary Revival."[2] The lack of historical education at Trinity College, from which O'Grady graduated in 1868,

1. Standish O'Grady, "Wet Day," an autobiographical sketch for *The Irish Homestead* (1899), quoted in Ernest Boyd, "Introduction," in *Standish O'Grady: Selected Essays and Passages* (Dublin: Talbot Press, 1918), 3.

2. Boyd, "Introduction," 7. Yeats makes a similar claim. See W. B. Yeats, "Irish National Literature, II," in *The Collected Works of W. B. Yeats*, Vol. IX: *Early Articles and Reviews*, ed. John P. Frayne and Madeleine Marchaterre (New York: Scribner, 2004), 271–72.

reflected the state of affairs generally in Ireland, and he lost no time in reading through the Irish historical tradition, from the ancient *Four Masters* to Eugene O'Curry. His most important contribution to this tradition was the two-volume *History of Ireland* (1878–80), which focused almost exclusively on what many historians would call prehistory or legend. It followed upon the antiquarian and folklore revival that began in Ireland in the early 1800s (with people such as George Petrie and O'Curry) and an upsurge in the academic study of Irish and other Gaelic folk cultures in England and throughout Europe. Matthew Arnold's long essay *On the Study of Celtic Literature*, published in 1867, is a good example of the kind of work being done on Celtic traditions that O'Grady's *History* was meant to counter and correct. Arnold's essay is deeply invested in ethnological fantasies about the Celtic people, which, he believed, offered a feminine complement to the more manly "Teutonic" Britons.[3] Another example would be the historian and cultural critic Thomas Carlyle, whose colonialist attitude toward Ireland (like that of the historian A. J. Froude, his friend) was more vitriolic and condemnatory than Arnold's. Yet O'Grady found in Carlyle a model for the historian who wished to use aesthetic—that is to say, *imaginative*—means to get at the truth of the Irish past. Following Carlyle and the French historian Jules Michelet, O'Grady countered the tendency toward "scientific" or liberal-progressive historiography that otherwise prevailed.[4]

Just as important in understanding O'Grady's idiosyncratic attitude toward the Irish past is his peculiar brand of "Fenian unionism," a political perspective from which he attempted to make a historical

3. See Matthew Arnold, *On the Study of Celtic Literature* (1867), in *The Works of Matthew Arnold*, 15 vols. (London: Macmillan, 1903), 5:vi–xxi, 1–150.

4. On Carlyle and O'Grady, see Geraldine Higgins, "Reviving the Irish Hero," in *Heroic Revivals from Carlyle to Yeats* (New York: Palgrave Macmillan, 2012), 11–35, and Michael McAteer, *Standish O'Grady, Æ, and Yeats: History, Politics, Culture* (Dublin: Irish Academic Press, 2002), 14–35. Roy Foster calls O'Grady a "young Carlylean" in *Words Alone: Yeats and His Inheritances* (Oxford: Oxford Univ. Press, 2012), 77; see also 60.

virtue of his ambivalent relation to his own social caste, the Anglo-Irish Protestant Ascendancy, an ambivalence that all the contributors to this volume attempt to explain, if not resolve.[5] He served as a kind of public intellectual, unattached to any university or public office, writing for publication to a general readership as an independent scholar. In his later work for the *All-Ireland Review*, which he edited from 1900 to 1908, this perspective was more overtly political; the *History*, however, comes from a more patently pedagogical desire to offer the Irish people a *readable* account of its legendary past. He knew well the Irish historical tradition that runs from Geoffrey Keating and Sylvester O'Halloran to W. C. Taylor and O'Curry, but he often found the emphasis laid in the wrong place, with too much attention paid to chronicling and not enough to understanding the ethos of the ancient times and to communicating that ethos to present readers, who stood in need of the chivalric and heroic values exemplified by legendary warriors such as Cuculain. Volume 1 of *History of Ireland*, titled *The Heroic Period* (1878), addressed the needs of a growing number of young men and women who were seeking an alternative to imperial historiography and the nationalist variety of biography and history writing associated with Young Ireland.[6] The latter tradition certainly remained attractive to nationalists well into the twentieth century, but as early as the 1890s both established and emergent writers alike, such as George Sigerson and W. B. Yeats, were looking for a dramatic and visionary alternative, a form of epic history that would be true to the struggles of Ireland's

5. Ernest Boyd reports that "Lady Gregory once described Standish O'Grady, in an appropriate paradox, as 'a Fenian Unionist, for it was his peculiar fortune to have assembled in support of the Imperial relationship precisely those arguments which have increasingly fostered the spirit of independence'" (*Appreciations and Depreciations: Irish Literary Studies* [1918; reprint, Freeport, NY: Books of Libraries Press, 1968], 16).

6. It should be noted, though, that Charles Gavan Duffy, editor of the *Nation* newspaper and leading figure in Young Ireland, was also a follower of Carlyle. See Foster, *Words Alone*, 45–50.

past in the way that Carlyle was true to the French Revolution in his monumental but largely invented history of it.

Like O'Halloran, an eighteenth-century surgeon, medical writer, and historian whose work *General History of Ireland* (1778) begins with an account of the mythical Milesians,[7] O'Grady was interested in prehistorical people. Chapter 1 of the first volume of *History of Ireland* is called "The Prime," a condensed and largely speculative account of prehistoric conquests and shifting populations.[8] Also like O'Halloran, O'Grady ended his history well before the modern era: O'Halloran stops at the twelfth century CE, and O'Grady barely makes it into the first.[9] The second volume of *History*, titled *Cuculain and His Contemporaries* (1880), stops with the death of Cuculain right around the time of Christ, and the third volume of the series, subtitled *Critical and Philosophical*, reframes the entire story within a contemporary meditation on historiography, historical evidence, and the authenticity of bardic literature. In *History*, O'Grady does not marginalize or ignore the ancient legendary past, a tendency we find in progressivist views of history, but rather keeps it in view as a vital part of his readers' thinking about the more recent past and about their future.

Carlyle is a precedent here for precisely the reasons that Michael McAteer and Renée Fox give in their essays in this volume. In a review of Samuel Boswell's *Life of Johnson*, Carlyle gives voice to his desire to prevent the past from becoming *dead time*: "Time shall not

7. Sylvester O'Halloran, *The Pictorial History of Ireland, from the Landing of the Milesians to the Present Time* (Boston: Murphy & McCarthy, 1884); originally published as *A General History of Ireland, from the Earliest Accounts to the Close of the Twelfth Century. Collected from the Most Authentic Records*, 2 vols. (London: Hamilton, 1778).

8. Emily Lawless also understood the value of the prehistorical in establishing a kind of claim to the past that does not make it a conquered land on the road to the future: chapter 1 in *The Story of Ireland* (1887; reprint, New York: Putnam & Sons; London: T. Fisher Unwin, 1891) is titled "Primeval Ireland."

9. *History of Ireland: Critical and Philosophical*, published in 1881, takes O'Grady to the fifth century CE, but the focus is on the bardic literature that constitutes the history rather than on the events of that literature.

utterly, not soon by several centuries, have dominion over us." Like "Naphtha-lamps," the dead move in the general dark surrounding us, burning "clear and holy through the dead Night of the Past: they who are gone are still here; though hidden they are revealed, though dead they yet speak."[10] O'Grady's aesthetic approach to the ancient Irish past, as Hayden White sees it, meant not only giving voice to the dead—"transmut[ing] the voices of the great men of the past into admonitions of, and inspirations for, the living"—but also realizing the past artistically, as a form of "palingenesis, the pious reconstruction of the past in its integrity."[11] But I believe that O'Grady goes further than his predecessor's "pious reconstruction" when he directly (and performatively) addresses the problematic historical authority of bardic literature and asserts the essentially creative agency of the historian. In O'Grady's estimation, the bard's powerful and even supernatural mimeticism, like the historian's objectivity, brings clarity and distinction to "the turmoil and confusion of these antique, obscure times," which become "clear and distinct only when the wonderful mirror of the bards is held up against them" (*HI* 1:47). He argues at length across all volumes of the *History* in favor of the bardic accounts on which he relies (through secondhand sources such as O'Curry), even when he concedes that their authority, if not their authenticity, is threatened by their material textual form: a "loose chaotic mass of bardic story and monkish archive" (*HI* 1:x; p. 50).[12] He was, in short, an anomalous historian who worked comfortably

10. Thomas Carlyle, "Bowsell's Life of Johnson," *Fraser's Magazine* 28, no. 5 (May 1832): 387.

11. Hayden White, *Metahistory: The Historical Imagination in Nineteenth-Century Europe* (Baltimore: Johns Hopkins Univ. Press, 1973), 146.

12. On the social function of the bard (or *fíle*) and the structure and genres of bardic poetry, see Osborn Bergin, *Irish Bardic Poetry*, ed. David Greene and Fergus Kelly (1912; reprint, Dublin: Dublin Institute for Advanced Studies, 1970). Bergin's text was first delivered as a lecture in Dublin in 1912. For an account of the nineteenth-century bards that influenced the Literary Revival, see Lady Augusta Gregory, "Raftery," in *Poets and Dreamers: Studies and Translations from the Irish* (1903; reprint, Cambridge: Cambridge Univ. Press, 2010), 1–46.

and effectively at the confluence of historical discipline and literary epic sensibility.

Throughout the *History*, which relates a "wild and improbable" narrative (*CP* 202; p. 64) and departs significantly from mainstream British and Anglo-Irish historiography, particularly on the issue of what constitutes *evidence*, O'Grady insists on historical *discipline*—that is to say, he insists on the viability (if not always the veracity) of the bardic accounts and his ability to extract historical knowledge from them, no matter how unreliable they might be. In this, he is perhaps more the hermeneutist than his mentor, Carlyle, because he is less concerned with *what the past might be made to say for the present* than with *what it has to say for itself*.[13] Paradoxically, the latter approach yields a more vital connection with the present because the past is not invoked as a key to unlock it. Rather than a teleological orientation along a progressive path, we have a form of romantic dialectics, a recursive and disjunctive historical field in which the past and future are interwoven, neither of them surrendering its singular temporality. The past does not progress *into* the present but coexists with it as one of its cultural expressions—a coexistence that O'Grady's imaginative historiography attempts to capture.

II

O'Grady aspired to write an accurate history of ancient Ireland that was true to the ancient sources who stood behind the *History* and legitimized its assumptions about the past. He resisted the idea that historical knowledge could flow only from the realm of facts; he believed that the old legends had their quantum of historical truth to convey, and *History of Ireland* was an attempt to convey it. It stands at the beginning of a new era of history writing in Ireland and was followed by a reissue of O'Halloran's *General History*,

13. For Carlyle's approach, see *Past and Present*, ed. Richard D. Altick (Boston: Houghton Mifflin, 1965).

retitled *Pictorial History*, in 1884. As was common in Irish history publishing, O'Halloran's book was extended and brought up to date by contemporary authors. The period from the twelfth to the early nineteenth century was covered by "a committee of gentlemen, who [would] endeavour to avoid those partialities and defects which occasionally characterize the productions of individual writers of Irish History."[14] Despite that caveat about individual writers, the 1884 edition ends with A. M. Sullivan's *The History of Ireland from the Rebellion of Robert Emmet to the Fenian Resurrection.* O'Grady, with his singular style and emphasis on heroic individualism, would surely upset such a "committee of gentlemen." We can say the same for the many who followed O'Grady and attempted to write about Ireland's ancient past from a singularly Irish perspective. Emily Lawless published *The Story of Ireland*, which was part of the *Story of the Nations* series, in 1887, and not long afterward, in 1899, Douglas Hyde published *Literary History of Ireland from Earliest Times to the Present.*[15] Like O'Grady, Lawless and Hyde sought to produce accessible and readable historical accounts—not just for scholars but also for anyone interested in Irish accounts of the Irish past. These contributions to popular historiography were part of a larger canon of writing about the Irish past that included Continental Celticists such as Henri D'Arbois de Jubainville and Kuno Meyer, whose work focused on folklore, legend, and myth but who also made very different claims for this material than what we find in O'Grady. Closer to O'Grady's imaginative *History of Ireland* are the productions of

14. "Preface," in O'Halloran, *Pictorial History*, iv. "The text has been compiled from the best authorities; dulness of record is avoided as much as possible; and it will be perceive that, in order to furnish a true and lively narrative, the variations of different writers are noted with discriminating and connecting remarks. In adopting this latter method of construction, we are conscious of having deviated from the rigid canons of historical composition; but our excuse will become more apparent, as the student travels over the dusty road of research where we have laboured" (iii).

15. Douglas Hyde, *A Literary History of Ireland from Earliest Times to the Present* (1899; reprint, London: T. Fisher Unwin, 1906).

other Irish writers: Eleanor Hull's study *The Cuchullin Saga in Irish Literature*, which came out in 1898, and Lady Augusta Gregory's *Cuchulain of Muirthemne*, which followed in 1902; both covered much the same ground, though less extensively, as *History of Ireland*.[16] O'Grady's series of historical novels featuring Cuculain were released about this time, and they reinforced this general trend of readable and popular accounts of the legendary past.[17]

The bardic sources on which O'Grady and many of his contemporaries drew for their historical accounts had previously been studied largely in antiquarian or archaeological terms. To some extent, the earlier study of the materials had done little more than translate isolated portions of the archive. For this reason, O'Grady regarded the archive as an insurmountable problem. In the volume 1 introduction, he writes that "the narration of all the bardic tales and fragments in connection with each hero and heroine" (an idea mooted by O'Curry but left unattempted) would be "physically impossible, or if it were effected, the result would not be satisfactory" (*HI* 1:ix; p. 50). Rather than a complete transcription of the tales, O'Grady wanted to provide a concise account of ancient Irish society, focusing in the main narrative on the heroic age of Cuculain and his contemporaries. But he went a step further than O'Curry when he produced an emphatically historical account based on bardic literature. In this way, he sought to challenge—in a rectifying, revisionist manner—the way Irish history was written and to use imaginative means to tell historical truth of the sort that was lively, speculative, to some degree fabricated, but *true to* the uniquely Irish spirit of the age being narrated. The one thing needful was a readable style that aimed at conveying this truth. The way "historians of neighbouring countries" (*HI* 2:17; p. 48) operated would not do for the Irish public, O'Grady

16. Eleanor Hull, *The Cuchullin Saga in Irish Literature* (London: Nutt, 1898); Lady Augusta Gregory, *Cuchulain of Muirthemne* (1902; reprint, Gerrards Cross, UK: Colin Smythe, 1973).

17. *The Coming of Cuculain* was published in 1894, and *In the Gates of the North* came out in 1901.

believed, for their treatment of the ancient past amounted to "mere history," not the form of historical writing that brings the heroic past back into the national imagination in the form of thrilling stories about "the slow growth of a noble people."[18] Required for the latter form of writing is a certain "readableness" of style and a harmony of views between the historian and the "prevailing humour and complexion of his contemporaries" (*HI* 2:17–18; p. 48). Between historian and reader, there needs to be a general agreement on ideological matters, but there also needs to be a sense of connection, a shared affective or emotional response to the heroic drama of the past. The challenge was clear: produce a popular account of the ancient Irish past that would lay claim to the reader's attention and serve as an influence on the national character.

When O'Grady speaks of "the historians of neighbouring countries," he means people such as Thomas Babington Macaulay, Michelet, and Leopold von Ranke—powerhouse historians (English, French, and German, respectively) who preferred unified and unifying historical narratives and a historical vision rooted in Enlightenment rationality, specifically as it was manifested in modern science and technology, political liberalism and social reform.[19] O'Grady's

18. "There is a pleasure in watching the dispersion of darkness before the rising sun, the gloom changing slowly into the silver twilight, the twilight ripening gradually into the golden day. . . . But there is a pleasure more certain, more human, more sublime, felt by one who contemplates out of the seething welter of warring tribes *the slow growth of a noble people*, the reclamation of a vast human wilderness, the stormful gloom of ignorance and hate growing less and less dense, shot through by the rays of imagination, knowledge, and love—the chaos of confusion and aimless strugglings concentre gradually into the wise and determined action of a nation fulfilling its part in the great national confraternity of the world" (*HI* 1:38–39, my emphasis).

19. Jules Michelet, French historian of France and the French Revolution, was active from the 1830s to the 1870s. He was by temperament a romantic statist who believed, against the Marxists, in the reconciliation of social classes. Leopold von Ranke, German historian in the early to mid-1800s, opposed Hegel and relied on the disciplined use of archives; he is associated with "scientific history." Thomas

imaginative historiography, with its multiple and recursive temporalities, required something other than a narrative of progress of the sort offered by Whig historians such as Macaulay, who believed that the past existed solely to justify and legitimize present social conditions. The past, as O'Grady saw it, did not exist merely to show, by what followed, how thoroughly it had been overcome. O'Grady also required something other than the scientific or empirical model of historical discourse exemplified by Ranke, whose credo, as Lee Benson restates it, was "tell it like it was."[20]

This tradition of historiography (followed by Ranke and Macaulay especially), in which ancient folk culture is ignored or marginalized, offered little to an Irish historian such as O'Grady, for whom that culture and its "bardic organization" (*CP* 453–54) provided the foundation for a truly *national* history. Macaulay's five-volume *History of England*, after a brief summary of the time extending from Roman Britain to the Puritans (sixteen pages), begins in earnest with the time of King James II, whose reign was a decisive turning point for Ireland—the point at which the Irish people became a "subject people," peripheral and subaltern, within an imperial world-system.[21] The Penal Laws, which began in the Elizabethan era and were designed to limit political power among Catholic populations in Ireland, grew more severe in the decades following the fall of James II and the Battle of the Boyne (1690). Certainly, laws forbidding the use and teaching of the Irish language had a devastating effect on bardic literature and practices of transmission (or what O'Grady

Babington Lord Macaulay, English historian and politician, was active in the early to mid-1800s and insisted on the ideal of progress in history, which came to be known as the "Whig" interpretation.

20. Lee Benson, *Toward the Scientific Study of History: Selected Essays of Lee Benson* (Philadelphia: Lippincott, 1972), 175. Thomas Henry Buckle, also known for his scientific historiography, became something of a celebrity when the first volume of his unfinished work, *History of Civilization*, was published in 1858.

21. Thomas Babington Macaulay, *The History of England from the Accession of James II*, 5 vols. (Philadelphia: Butler, 1856).

calls "transmitted traditional evidence" [*CP* 442]), which meant, if we follow O'Grady, a loss of historical knowledge. He believed that the bardic tales enabled a connection between the heroic era and the present moment by way of cultural inheritance, specifically the transmission in an epic mode of traits that he believed embodied the nobility of soul animating the conquering hero. *History of Ireland* was designed to "tell the history of Ireland through the medium of tales, epical or romantic, written with the object of bringing remote times and men vividly before the mind's eye, and within the reach of common human sympathies" (*CP* ii). O'Grady was sensitive to the temporality of passage and transmission, for "[t]he bards were but the abstracts and brief chronicles of their own time, and in their hands the ancient tales and traditions varied from century to century" (*HI* 1:xiv; p. 53). Rather than demonstrate progress *away* from the heroic world depicted in bardic texts—or, worse, rather than mourn the passing of "bardic organizations"—O'Grady brought the reader as close possible *into* that world. An important presupposition for O'Grady is that the past is *not* discretely passed; it does not lie in a remote region, inaccessible and autonomous, but is a living element of modern times. Cuculain would come to symbolize this living element—for better or worse, as Patrick Bixby and Michael McAteer show in their essays in the present volume—and O'Grady would not have been surprised at the conflicting and contradictory responses this legacy has produced.

One way of understanding this imaginative and analogic way of thinking of the past is to see it in terms of a specific form of *Revival.* O'Grady found models for a revival historiography not in the progressivist and empirical traditions outlined earlier, but in the romanticism of Michelet and Carlyle, whose relation to the past was recuperative, reliant on the historian's creative capacity to revive the past in the present moment of the historian's text. As Renée Fox shows in her essay, Michelet's method of "historical resuscitation" was "a form of historicist responsibility, implying an unmediated historiographical mode in which historians shepherd dead men back to life but do not transform them by doing so." O'Grady, however, felt that adopting such an "unmediated" mode of writing in order to guarantee veracity or objectivity was missing the point of what he considered to be the goal of imaginative history—to capture, as Fox puts it, "essential and incontrovertible historical accuracies" and to give "revivifying power" to historical writing in part by "privileging . . . affect over epistemology." The result, as Fox argues, is "an affective historical aesthetic in which the meaning of the past emerges in the historian's ability to make it a felt, living entity in the present moment."

We can read O'Grady's opposition to dominant modes of historiography as an "opposition to any kind of history," as Fox does, or as the foundation for a new form of historical composition. I would like to suggest that both positions converge in the revolutionary climate of Revival thinking about the past. In effect, O'Grady's imaginative historiography combines the two main virtues of nineteenth-century orthodoxy: its romantic commitment to Revival and its faith in objectivity. The latter is especially important if we are to understand O'Grady's historiography as something other than a rejection of history. In the volume 1 introduction, he writes that in the *History* "the heroic period reflects the actualities of the early historic times" (*HI* 1:xii; p. 51), but he insists elsewhere on the historian's role in "realizing" what is actual in the bardic tales. Realization is but a tool to get at what is actual. His account would be credible, disciplined, and accurate to the extent that bardic literature offers us genuine historical knowledge. But above and beyond this, it would be true to the era it recounts—and this kind of truth is often the historian's *to add* to what he finds in his sources.

O'Grady dissents from progressivist and empirical historiography and the triumphalist view of the past that both trends exhibit, yet his *History* accommodates both a vision of progress and a requirement for empirical evidence. In the volume 1 introduction, he argues that the historian's task "is to give a clear and vivid picture of the past" (*HI* 1:iii; p. 42), but he then shows how this task has been split up and redistributed. The realist novel has taken on the burden of providing a faithful narrative account of social and cultural environments, both present and past; meanwhile, the "archæologist" historian (such as Carlyle's Dryasdust) keeps track of minutia: "Nearly every work which one takes up affecting to treat of the past in a rigid and conscientious spirit, is merely archæological. It is an accumulation of names, dates, events, disquisitions, the balancing of probabilities, the testing of statements and traditions, categorical assertions concerning laws and customs. All works of this character are of the nature of archæology; they are the material of history, not history itself" (*HI* 1:iii–iv; p. 42). For O'Grady, names, dates, events—in a word, historical *facts*—are only a starting point: "History is the flower of archæology," he writes; "it justifies, rewards, and crowns the obscure toil of those patient and single-minded excavators into the buried past" (*HI* 1:vi; p. 43). He is after "history itself" (*HI* 1:vi; p. 43), not the authentic fragments supplied by contemporary antiquarian (or "archæological") historians: "In history, there must be sympathy, imagination, creation. The sorry remnants discussed by the antiquarian, do not of themselves supply a picture" (*HI* 1:iv; p. 51), not the "clear and vivid picture" that historians were once able to produce.

To supply this picture, O'Grady uses "the actual language of the bards" to describe the "essential element" of his heroes and heroines and "that order of events which best harmonises with the records and traditions of the poets" (*HI* 1:x). He feels that the "period of which he treats" (*HI* 1:v; p. 43), the radical, sometimes magical *alterity* of ancient Ireland, is both substantially ancient and separate from present concerns but at the same time connected by definite means to the contemporary moment. He articulates something akin to what Frances Dolan calls *presentist historicism*, which "haunt[s] the present as a conceptual structure" and dwells "on the connections between present and past so as to estrange the present rather than domesticate the past."[22] I think we see this kind of estrangement at

22. Frances E. Dolan, *Marriage and Violence: The Early Modern Legacy* (Philadelphia: Univ. of Pennsylvania Press, 2008), 17. Dolan writes of early-modern "marital economies of scarcity" and how they "haunt the present as a conceptual

work in *History of Ireland*, particularly in the accounts of Cuculain and the Red Branch (often called the Ulster Cycle), which can be read as part of O'Grady's attempt to offer to the Anglo-Irish Ascendancy an example of heroic leadership. On this view, O'Grady's Ireland was out of time, and its leaders needed to catch up with the past, as embodied by Cuculain.

Like many of his contemporaries, O'Grady felt sorely the absence of a heroic vision, a "clear and vivid picture of the past" (*HI* 1:iii; p. 42). As McAteer notes in this volume, the *History* can be read as an appeal to its author's own caste, the Anglo-Irish gentry, to make heroic sacrifices at a time when their claim to the land and to their place in history was coming under fire.[23] O'Grady's interest in the heroic era of Cuculain, though enshrouded in "primeval" mists and known primarily through the complex prism of the bards, is never far from his contemporary concerns. It is clear that he sought, much as Yeats would later, to awaken the heroic element of Irish society in both Catholic and Protestant communities against the common enemy: British incompetence and misrule. This aspect of his message would later be repeated in his political writings for the *All-Ireland Review*. It is also clear that O'Grady could not escape the empiricism of his age, which accounts for the rigid disciplinary ground he attempts to occupy in *Critical and Philosophical*, a study of ancient Irish culture arranged in a manner that isolates and defines discrete aspects of that culture, much in the manner of a modern ethnographic account. Unlike the two-volume *History*

---

structure of plot." The "conflict between incompatible models and irreconcilable expectations," a conflict that for her *is* the "history of marriage," leads paradoxically not to rupture but to continuity, which is enacted again and again from early-modern to contemporary times in the form of "presumptive" heterosexuality and the "marriage plot" (ibid., 4, 2, 135).

23. See Gregory Castle, "Nobler Forms: Standish James O'Grady's 'Imaginative History' and the Irish Literary Revival," in *Reading Irish History: Text, Contexts, and Memory in Modern Ireland*, ed. Lawrence McBride (Dublin: Four Courts Press, 2003), 170–76.

of Ireland, this volume is "critical not constructive or imaginative" and grounded in "literal translations supplied by competent scholars" (*CP* iii).

Tellingly, what is at issue for O'Grady is not so much accuracy as authenticity, for although *Critical and Philosophical* covers the same ground as the two-volume *History*, it does so in order "to ascertain to what extent we have been traversing a region of authentic history, and to what extent mere cloud-land, the enchanted world of poetic tradition, and religious or heroic myth" (*CP* 425). The volume concludes with "Verification of the Irish Bardic History; How Far Reliable, Doubtful and Mythical," in which we find the scholarly sources and erudite footnotes that are largely absent in the earlier volumes. Where "absolutely verifiable human testimony does not extend," O'Grady relies on the attestations made by "transmitted traditional evidence" (*CP* 442). The complex process by which the bardic tales found their way into written form involved layers of historical intervention. Christian clerics transmitted and modified the legends, introducing evidence of a foreign cultural sensibility and thereby contributing to "the shifting chaos of obscure epic tale" (*CP* 203; p. 65). But there is also the sense, felt earlier by Carlyle, that the "historical field" was itself a "Chaos of Being,"[24] which a romantic historian could redeem through his essentially aesthetic stance toward the past and its documents or—if the problem is seen from the point of view of the past—which would issue, as Fox suggests in her essay, in an "aesthetic dawn . . . outside of historical time." The perception of chaos and disorder led O'Grady to a mode of reduction that enabled him to pierce through the layers of textual "accidents" to the artistic core of the tales. His method "consists in the reduction to its artistic elements of the whole of that heroic history taken together" (*HI* 1:x; p. 50). In this way, "imaginative" historical accounts "preserved the closest adherence to the authorities" (*HI* 1:xii; p. 51)—that is, the bardic storytellers.

24. On Carlyle and the "Chaos of Being," see White, *Metahistory*, 144–49.

Despite the role of imagination, O'Grady's approach presupposes that bardic literature is capable of generating the "material of history," for "[t]he bardic tales were to our ancestors genuine history, and implicitly believed in. In their genesis there was never anything like conscious creation" (*HI* 1:xix; p. 56). In the long essay on bardic literature that opens the second volume, O'Grady insists on the "general historical accuracy" of the bardic literature and its "acquaintance with the general course of the history of the country, and with preceding and succeeding kings" (*HI* 2:19).[25] Bardic history was reliable history to the extent that it accorded with a larger historical framework. But it also had to be *realized* so that "a living, adequate, affecting representation of the life of our ancestors" could be derived from the historian's "sympathy, imagination, creation" (*HI* 1:iv; p. 43). The historian had to double the force of the bards in an effort to get at the heroic ideal that was limned in the ancient accounts: "Upon the realisation of the bards *I have superadded a realisation more intense*, working closer to those noble forms, whose outlines are more or less wavering and uncertain in the literature of the bards" (*HI* 1:xii, my emphasis; p. 52).

At the basis of imaginative historiography is a moment of creative transformation, for the historian's superaddition *realizes* a profound

25. See, for example, *HI* 1:108, where Emain Macha is described, with geographical features, the system of tribute, martial exercises, and other "everyday" practices. Two more examples: "Cuculain, planting his great spear in the ground, drew his sling and fitted thereto an iron bolt, where thong and timber joined. Into the loop he passed his thumb, and bent the crann-tawl upon his right knee, gazing, as he bent, upon where the remnant of the nations of Cooalney and Murthemney were overborne by the sons of Lon-Cras" (*HI* 2:263; p. 127); and "Like the sound of a gong was the back-springing sling, and like a fierce blast so hissed the twisted thong of the crann-tawl, and the deadly bolt sped afar. . . . Swifter than words can tell was the slinging of Cuculain, nor might man discern the rapid movements of his hands, but ever flashed afar the sweep of that bright sling, and ever hissed the sling-thong through the air" (*HI* 2:263–64; p. 128). Vivid historical details (iron bolt, sling thong, back-springing sling, "crann-tawl") inform O'Grady's imaginative account.

human potentiality, an *epic emotion* that pierces through the obscurity of the narrative and "stirs the spirit":

> Wild and improbable as is the whole narrative, weird with incursions from the supernatural world, with wizardry and enchantments, spurning the laws of nature, of space, and time, dazzling with the wild light of incredible heroisms, loud and agitated with the rush and noise of gigantic shapes writhing in superhuman battles, recalling the fabled wars of gods and Titans, or the Miltonic strife of celestial and infernal powers, *the profound and vital humanity with which the whole is instinct*, touches and stirs the spirit with the strangest and most unapprehended emotions. (*CP* 202–3, my emphasis; p. 64)

Though the historian faces an insurmountable problem in the archive, though the bardic literature is chaotic and duplicitous, and though the tales found in that literature are "wild and improbable," there is throughout all of it a "profound and vital humanity" that O'Grady believes the historian *must* communicate to the reader. The *History* is meant not to replicate the archive, but to reinstate this heroic emotion at the center of Irish national life: "I desire to make this heroic period once again a portion of the imagination of the country, and its chief characters as familiar in the minds of our people as they once were" (*HI* 2:17; p. 48). As Patrick Bixby and Joseph Valente show in this volume, O'Grady's nationalist aspiration aligns him with later historically minded Literary Revivalists, who also sought to invigorate the national imagination by offering it a model for contemporary heroism.

III

In *History of Ireland*, O'Grady lays claim to a portion of the national imagination, and he does so in part, as many intellectuals did in the late nineteenth century, by appealing to the ancient Greeks. He found in "the immense mass of the Irish bardic literature" (*HI* 2:14) something of the Greek heroes' noble struggle against fate. Phillip Marcus asserts that the "choice of [epic] models was a good one" and that the *Táin Bó Cuailnge* (Cattle Raid of Cooley), the central tale in the Ulster Cycle, "shows the direct influence of the great Classical epics."[26] Edward Hagan concurs, noting that O'Grady's *History*, at its best, achieves "a cosmic, epic effect" that makes readers feel "heirs to a great tradition." He adds that O'Grady was "fond of constructing Homeric similes, but many of them were ridiculously inept."[27] More important than his stylistic blunders, however, is the atmosphere he generates, for there are times in the *History* when one feels the light of an epic time fall on the page: "Then there approached the flying scattered battalions of the Red Branch, driven out of Murthemney by the great host of Meave, and Cuculain stayed them, and re-formed their broken bands in the mountains of Cooalney, breathing into them his own unconquerable soul" (*HI* 2:339; p. 182).[28] This sense of unconquerable heroism is paired with a heroic acceptance of fate's inevitable conquest: "It is enough, O school-fellow [Mac Manar], my end is come. I shall perish in this battle, but the high gods of Erin are

26. Philip Marcus, *Standish O'Grady* (Lewisburg, PA: Bucknell Univ. Press, 1971), 28. The account given of Cuculain in *Critical and Philosophical*, part 8, chapter 1, is illustrative of the Irish heroic style; see especially the long sentence (206–8) that describes Cuculain's attributes. Valente, in this volume, points to *Morte D'Arthur* as another model for heroic values.

27. Edward A. Hagan, *High Nonsensical Words: A Study of the Works of Standish James O'Grady* (Troy, NY: Whitston, 1986), 2, 88. For an example of inept writing, consider this description of warfare, which O'Grady usually describes quite well: "Through a field of slaughter dashed then the war-car, and over the mangled bodies of heroes, and the blood bespattered the war-car, and reddened the tires of the wheels and the spokes. But above the head of Cuculain there was as it were a bright circle, so did he with a single hand cause those eight balls [of glittering brass] to revolve, watching warily, nevertheless, lest a spear or a bolt from the men of Meave should smite his charioteer or himself" (*HI* 2:273; pp. 133–34).

28. See O'Grady's note on Achilles (*HI* 2:269). Cuculain is also likened to biblical heroes (on David, for example, see *HI* 2:265). Also note the high biblical style of dialogue throughout the *History*, a style that is as often awkward as it is lofty; see, for example, *HI* 1:151–54.

around me, and I shall die, as I have lived, under their hands" (*HI* 2:322; p. 169).

The Irish and the Greek canons speak of two very different ancient worlds that championed similar heroic values. In *Critical and Philosophical*, O'Grady ranks the bardic literatures higher than the works of Homer and the Attic poets. He invites the reader to find in the Irish legends a *gold more golden*: "massier and more pure, the sentiment deeper and more tender, the audacity and freedom more exhilarating, the reach of imagination more sublime." In the legends, "the depth and power of the human soul more fully exhibit themselves" (*CP* 201; p. 64). Like Yeats after him, O'Grady knew how to seduce readers who wanted to feel the nobility of the past, to feel even the brutality of that nobility, but also to feel that their assent to the epic world—even as *other* as it must appear—was legible in their own cultural moment. The historian's imaginative *mis*recognition of the past (based on an incomplete, inconsistently legible, ambiguous, multifarious archive that offers the "certainty of misrepresentation" [*HI* 1:vi; p. 44]) encourages the reader's authentic recognition of a common humanity, a common "unconquerable" human soul.

Although the warrior ethos of the Irish heroic era shared much with the ethos of classical Greece, the mythological system in which Cuculain finds his place is rooted in Irish traditions that, according to O'Grady and other commentators, predates the classical Greek era. According to legend, Cuculain is the nephew of Concobar, the son of Concobar's sister Dectera, and is thought to have been sired by the solar deity Lu (Lugh, Lu Lamfáda, or sometimes, in O'Grady, Ioldāna). He is raised among warriors and very soon becomes one himself by defeating the fierce guard dog of a family friend, Culain, and then taking its place until a new dog can be found. Henceforth, he is "Cu (Hound) of Culain." He is a precocious warrior—"The strange boy seemed to be a very demon of war; with his little hurle grasped, like a war-mace, in both hands, he laid about him on every side, and the boys were tumbling fast" (*HI* 1:109; p. 73)—who grows up to lead the men of Ulster against those who invade and destroy it. At the center of the *History*, stretching across both volumes, is the *Táin Bó Cuailnge*, an account of Queen Meave's cattle raid at Cooley, in Cuculain's home county (near present-day Dundalk). Early in the account, O'Grady places Cuculain simultaneously in the ancient world and in the pages of the bardic texts that recorded it: "Like a bright star, when the wind is high, revealing and concealing itself, a moment seen, and then again deep-buried in the driving clouds, Cuculain is revealed and hidden, crossing the spaces of the bardic sky, ere attaining the region where he blazes out with surpassing splendour, dimming all the lesser lights in that heroic age" (*HI* 1:130; p. 84).[29] The great warrior is simultaneously revealed and concealed by the clouds—a trickster figure, an early version of the "wood-kerne," Irish irregulars that in the Elizabethan era hid in the dense forests that still covered the island. This seemingly extravagant and playful image, with its Homeric resonance of Helios crossing the heavens in his chariot, gives the reader a sense of Cuculain's invincibility, his ferocity, and his willingness to "blaze out with surpassing splendour," to live purely, *fatefully*, for his reputation in coming times.

In many ways, Cuculain is not a typical hero. He can at various times be silly and weak, overcome by fatigue, or susceptible to the charms of others. He is subject to certain vulnerabilities (he is tricked and kept from battle in part by druid magic), just as he is bound to certain limitations on his power, the *geasa* (*geise* in O'Grady) or prohibition uniquely tailored to each warrior.[30] In the midst of the

29. O'Grady writes elsewhere that Cuculain, like the moon, moves "through the spaces of that bardic sky, so through the shifting chaos of obscure epic tale, and the broken fragments of antique ruined verse, ever flashes on the eye the wonderful glory of this extraordinary hero, till on the plains of Murthemney it sets for ever in enduring night" (*CP* 203; p. 65).

30. Douglas Hyde writes, "It was geis [*geasa*] or tabu to [Cuculain] to narrate his genealogy to one champion as it was also to his son Conlaoch, to refuse combat to any one man, to look upon the exposed bosom of a woman, to come into company without a second invitation, to accept the hospitality of virgins, to

campaign against Meave, he feels that the Red Branch has forsaken him. "[H]e saw faces that moved amongst the trees mocking him, and horrid things, formless and cold . . . and there was laughter in the hollow chambers of the forest" (*HI* 1:229; p. 108). Even when he is beaten, he is never *beaten down*: "his countenance was hollow and wan, dull were his splendid eyes, and there was a wound in his hand and in his leg and in his left side, and his noble breast was mangled, and all his body black with dried gore. . . . Then arose Cuculain, the unconquerable, striding through the forest" (*HI* 1:230–31; p. 109). This heroic indomitability appealed to Yeats, who later transformed it into the sublime recklessness of the Irish airman, whose "lonely impulse of delight"[31] is as mad as it is noble. It would also inform Yeats's Cuculain plays, in particular *The Green Helmet* (1910), in which the hero readily volunteers his head to settle a dispute with that "juggler from the sea, that old red herring," Manannán mac Lir, but ends up with a crown instead.[32]

A crucial point for understanding O'Grady's imaginative historiography is that the "presence or absence of the marvellous" is no suitable criterion for determining the "general truth or falsehood of the tale" the historian tells (*HI* 2:14; p. 46). For in the legends, principles of causality and temporal linearity simply do not hold. What we find

---

boast to a woman, to let the sun rise before him on the fields of Emain, he must when there rise before it, etc. . . . [A]s each geasa is broken, Cuchulain loses a corresponding power. Finally the last geasa broken signals the end of Cuchulain's career" (*Literary History*, 301).

31. W. B. Yeats, "An Irish Airman Foresees His Death," in *The Collected Works of W. B. Yeats*, vol. 1: *The Poems*, 2nd ed., ed. Richard J. Finneran (New York: Macmillan, 1997), 135–36.

32. W. B. Yeats, *The Green Helmet*, in *The Collected Works of W. B. Yeats*, vol. 2: *The Plays*, ed. David R. Clark and Rosalind E. Clark (New York: Scribner's, 1989), 251. Manannán mac Lir is the Irish sea god. See my discussion of Yeats's Cuculain plays in "'The Age-Long Memoried Self': Yeats and the Promise of Coming Times," in *Yeats and Afterwords: Christ, Culture, and Crisis*, ed. Marjorie Howes and Joseph Valente (Notre Dame: Univ. of Notre Dame Press, 2014), 137–44.

instead are magical events and multiple temporalities—including the timeless time of the gods and fairies, the mystic time of druid priests, and the histories and chronicles of the bards—braided together, reinforcing each other, in conflict with each other, forming parallel worlds with shared imaginative geographies. Cuculain is constantly set upon by specters and revenants who occupy an *otherworld*; at one point, he and his charioteer Læg see a "druidic mist covering the province like a great fleece, and he marvelled what it meant" (*HI* 1:148; p. 94). The chariots themselves are haunted, for "the great car brayed and shrieked as the wheels of solid and glittering bronze went round, for there were demons that had their abode in that car" (*HI* 1:126; p. 80). Just as in Homer the gods are a constant presence in the days and ways of mortals, these otherworldly beings constitute a permanent and parallel force that is by turns a source of protection *and* a source of great danger for "unconquerable" warriors like Cuculain.

Cuculain's vulnerability to the *otherworld* is offset by sexual aggression and a masculine ethos that grows only bolder when he comes up against women as powerful as he is—preeminently Queen Meave, Eefa (or Aoife, an early teacher and lover who bears him a son), and his wife, Emer. Cuculain's wooing of Emer is a set piece in Lady Gregory's account and was dramatized by Yeats in *The Only Jealousy of Emer* (1919). In O'Grady's *History*, the love story of Cuculain and Emer is sung by the "son of Buan" but serves mainly as a plot point, a device to showcase Meave's all-encompassing hatred of Cuculain. Meave, whose cunning is both matched and undermined by her emotional exuberance, fears no man but Cuculain. She sets friend against friend and engages druid priests to enchant the warrior who threatens her the most. From him alone do she and her host retreat: "Loud then pealed the voice of the Hound. . . . Then sprang Queen Meave from her chariot, and fled away upon her feet" (*HI* 2:267; p. 130).

One aspect of the bardic canon that frustrates most translators and compilers is the "warp spasm"—the battle fury (Ir. *ríastarthae*) that possesses Cuculain in a way that renders him gigantic and supernatural, well beyond the bounds of the human frame.[33] Jeffrey Gantz's modern translation retains something of the zesty vulgarity of the original. When Cuculain's "ríastarthae came upon him," "[y]ou would have thought that every hair was being driven into his head. You would have thought that a spark of fire was on every hair. He closed one eye until it was no wider than the eye of a needle; he opened the other until it was as big as a wooden bowl. He bared his teeth from jaw to ear, and he opened his mouth until the gullet was visible. The warrior's moon rose from his head."[34] Compared to this, Lady Gregory's and Eleanor Hull's accounts of Cuculain are quite tame.[35] And although O'Grady was prone to abstractions such as Panic and Terror to describe Cuculain's "countenance" (*HI* 2:267; p. 130), he retains something of the hero's feral savagery once Cuculain is in the frenzy of battle. Cuculain "laughed in the fierceness of his wrath, for not like a mortal fighter was the hero that day, but like a genius of war," and "around his lips there was a foam, and from his forehead down upon his neck the great veins had swollen out like ropes" (*HI* 2:267, 276; pp. 130, 136). Even near the end of his life, "a fiery wrath" possessed him and "a fierce tide of angry blood raced through his veins, and he started forth with a cry" (*HI* 2:320; p. 167). The barely suppressed fury, the masculine body near the point of rupture, the savage engagement with other men, and the indifference with which he treats women when he is not trying to woo

33. Hence the parodies of heroic figures in James Joyce's *Ulysses* (1922; New York: Vintage, 1990), 293–97, and Flann O'Brien's *At Swim-Two-Birds* (1939; New York: Penguin, 1976), 10–11, 16–25.

34. "The Boyhood Deeds of Cú Chulaind," in Jeffrey Gantz, trans., *Early Irish Myths and Sagas* (London: Penguin, 1981), 136. One had to be careful around Cuculain off of the battlefield as well. Later, with the women of Ulaid, we discover that "it was Cú Chulaind's gift, when he was angry, that he could withdraw one eye so far into his head that a heron could not reach it, whereas the other eye he could protrude until it was as large as a cauldron for a yearling calf" (ibid., 156). On the warp spasm, see Valente's essay in this volume.

35. See, for example, Gregory, *Cuchulain of Muirthemne*, 25. On the relationship between these authors and O'Grady, see the essays by Valente and Fox in this volume.

them—all of these affects congeal into a heroic figure of great charm, hardheartedness, and strength of body and resolve.

But these same affects also give shape to another kind of hero, as Valente points out, one who violates the ancient code of Fir Fer, "the truth of (a) man," which demands fairness in combat. In scholarly versions of the legends that include the "warp spasm," we find Cuculain routinely violating this code with the Gæ-Bolg, his fearsome spear, which, Valente tells us, "does not just kill but debases and even dehumanizes its victims." Fir Fer thus becomes "the site of a momentous ideological contradiction: the highest ethical concept of Gaelic warrior culture admits of the most treacherous violation of its terms," all to ensure Cuculain's fame as a warrior. As if in counterpoint to this diabolical side of his hero, O'Grady reminds us that Cuculain possesses the weaknesses of heroes who thrive on outlandish expectations and outlandish rewards, including a superhuman sense of responsibility, for he must save *all of Ireland*: "Not alone for the Red Branch shalt thou now fight," Ioldāna tells him, "but for all the nations of Eiré," so that Éire does not become a land of bogs where dragons dwell "and slimy unnameable monsters, and all manner of foul creeping things," a land where "few and base shall her people be" (*HI* 2:278; p. 138).

A chief value of O'Grady's *History* is that it shows how the heroic world of Cuculain's time (itself always at risk of sinking back into a primeval state) existed within a much larger world-system. On a visit to Ath-a-Clíah (Baile Átha Cliath, present-day Dublin), the hero finds out much about the customs of a cosmopolitan town ("at this time a city of timber") and its people. "The trade of Dublin with the Continent must have been considerable at this time," O'Grady writes in a footnote. "In the second century the division of the dues of this port caused a great war" (*HI* 2:290 n. 3; p. 146). Cuculain and Læg, on their perambulations through the city, pass windows "in which were exposed mantles and lēnas of wool, linen, and silk" and "rolls and leaves of parchment in which men's thoughts were inscribed." They notice works of art and other evidence of high culture. Læg, in fact, purchases a toy chariot ("small images of horses cut in timber . . . the head of the fighting man nodded as the wheels went round") and pays for it with a "small silver weight, for uncoined gold and silver were then used instead of money." Amid this welter of social activity and cultural detail comes the information that a fair amount of this "uncoined" wealth has found its way to Cuculain's "rechtairé," or agent who manages the sale of "the wool which his estates produced abundantly" (*HI* 2:291; p. 147). Cuculain is also something of an imperial master: "Now before that, there came tributes to him even from the isles of Ore, where Cuculain Mac Sualtam had broken the power of the native races, and established the authority of the king of Ulla" (*HI* 2:283; p. 141).

Cuculain clearly plays a part in this global economy, which in the heroic era was heavily dependent on a handful of well-traveled routes and well-known ports. The "city of timber" would have seemed to him an outpost of urban sophistication and cosmopolitanism precariously huddled on Dublin bay, its back to a hostile interior. He is fascinated by the courts and the regalia of men in power, even the fat *ollav* (a member of an elite class), who is "uncomely to look upon, but a bright and nimble spirit illuminated his unheroic visage" (*HI* 2:292; p. 148). Cuculain's fascination turns to despair, however, when he discovers that his visit to Dublin is part of a scheme to keep him from the heat of battle. For, as Læg tells him, "throughout Eiré there is not a household in which thy name is not like a curse, for there are not many tribes in Fohla out of which thou hast not at some time slain a son, or a father, or a brother" (*HI* 2:286; p. 143). Cuculain realizes that heroism has come at a great cost, but he is not the kind of hero to be prevailed upon to retreat from "a tide of vengeance": "I, when I die, shall be slain in battle, breathing forth warlike breath, defending the Red Branch" (*HI* 2:286, 288; p. 145). He returns to Emain Macha, where the central lesson of the warrior culture—to "love law and hate lawlessness"—is learned through "noble exercise." Amid boys learning "the management of steeds and chariots" and how "to hurl the spear when the steeds galloped" (*HI* 2:316; p. 164), Cuculain regroups for his final battle against Meave.

O'Grady's account of Cuculain's near-lawless final exploits is as gripping and well told as any adventure novel of the late nineteenth century. Cuculain "defeated the host of Meave in seven great battles on the plains of Murthemney, and the tombs of those he slew are scattered over all that land" (*HI* 2:339–40; p. 183). O'Grady links the historical battles with monuments in what McAteer calls a "living landscape": "The ancient raths and cairns to be found throughout Ireland were all-important to O'Grady because they functioned as the remnants of ancient historical episodes that survive in the fragments of stories that make up Irish mythology, fragments that he attempted to work into 'epic proportion and reasonableness'" (*HI* 1:48). In this case, the tombs remind Cuculain of his own fate. A tragic hero, one who goes "to war like one who has devoted himself to death" (*HI* 2:339–40; p. 183), must fall, and his death is, in a way, a final defiance of even this noble "truth." For he literally does not fall. Wounded, knowing he is about to pass on to the other side, he is allowed by his slayer to prop himself up on a milestone, "tying with languid hands a loose knot, which soon was made fast by the weight of the dying hero." O'Grady leaves Cuculain still fierce in his "death-pangs, a terror to his enemies, and the bulwark of his nation"—"'mild, handsome, invincible'" (*HI* 2:344, 346; p. 188).

IV

O'Grady's understanding of the heroic past as an ethical template for the cultural needs of the present did not emerge at the expense of the past's temporal singularity. If we follow Dolan and see O'Grady as a presentist historicist—one whose thinking about the past "haunt[s] the present as a conceptual structure"—we see that the singularity of the past is defined and guaranteed by its agency, its ability to *haunt* and thereby alter the way we think about our contemporary moment, which in turn alters how we think about the future. O'Grady's claims about it are based on the creative potential of the hero's engagement with destiny, with what Yeats called "coming times." Cuculain's heroism—an impossible intensity of human aspiration—harmonizes, in O'Grady's presentation, with the "aesthetic striving" that Bixby, in the present volume, sees in the high Revival era, a kind of heroism that "gives rise to cultural, spiritual, *and* political transformation" (emphasis in original). Pádraic Pearse, for example, recognized that the cultural authority behind a hero such as Cuculain rested largely on his sense of futurity, of the creative potential of those who would learn from his example, and for that reason he used Cuculain's words as the motto of Scoil Éanna (St. Enda's School): "I care not though I were to live but one day and one night, if only my fame and my deed live after me."[36] Like O'Grady before him, Pearse turned to Cuculain as a fit emblem of nationalism and its triumphant future.

Indeed, as Bixby shows in his analysis of Oliver Sheppard's statue of Cuculain in the Dublin General Post Office, Irish nationalism was well into the 1930s determined in myriad and conflicting ways by this Iron Age warrior. "More than any other example in the Irish tradition," Bixby writes, "Sheppard's sculpture embodies the heroic ideals that had been explored in poems and plays of Irish Literary Revivalists and in the educational rhetoric of the Gaelic Revivalists such as Pearse, all of whom sought to restore a lost cultural vitality that might transform present social and political conditions." Like Yeats's Cuculain plays, which dramatize the hero's fundamental ambivalence—fierce individual and loyal champion, exemplary hero and heroic exception, soldier and saint, killer and lover—Sheppard's statue renders Cuculain's last moments, tied to a post and awaiting death. It is not his weakness and mortality, however, that appealed to so many revivalists and nationalists, but his indomitable spirit, his "unconquerable soul," which seemed to live for the future even as it was vanquished on the battlefield.

O'Grady's legendary and imaginative conception of history elevated heroes such as Cuculain in a way that enshrined certain values of heroism, masculinity, loyalty, and tragic self-knowledge that he, like Yeats, his most ardent supporter, felt were central to an authentic Irish national identity. Yeats accounts for O'Grady's popularity by

36. Pádraic Pearse, "Murder Machine," In *Collected Works of Padraic H. Pearse: Plays, Stories, Poems* (Dublin: Maunsel, 1917), 381. Education must "lead Ireland back to her sagas" (382).

pointing to his anti-English sensibility and his imaginative method. O'Grady's texts, he argued, avoided the partisan political skirmishing that characterized conventional history. "In Ireland, we are accustomed to histories with a great parade of facts and dates, of wrongs and precedents, for use in the controversies of the hour." Yeats believed that "a conventional patriotism had killed honest research and overthrown imaginative freedom."[37] He found just this combination of research and imagination in *History of Ireland* and praised its author as "the first historian who has written Irish history in a philosophic spirit and as an imaginative art."[38] O'Grady's historical vision was meant to appeal to all of Ireland, but it was focused through the extraordinary exploits of a singular hero, one whose self-sufficiency, bravery, and self-sacrifice provided revivalist and nationalist writers with a standard of heroic chivalry.[39] Both McAteer and Valente make this point in their essays, for chivalric discourse and chivalric affect constructed masculinity in complicated contestatory fashion in the Revival period. The expected gender norm of hypermasculinity (apish and brutal, a colonialist vision of the sexuality of the colonized) confronts an alternative in the more liberating and dignified concept of *manhood* exemplified in warrior culture and preeminently in Cuculain. "O'Grady set the tone," Valente writes in this volume, "and provided the discursive means for effecting this ideological 'translation' of Cuculain the hypermasculine specimen into Cuculain the paragon of manliness." O'Grady's desire to rewrite Cuculain's story in the manner of the Arthurian legends, Valente

37. Yeats, "Irish National Literature, II," 272, 294.

38. Ibid., 342.

39. This motif is picked up by the "committee of gentlemen" who continued O'Halloran's *General History* and noted in "Observations," appended to the new material, that "[t]he rules of chivalry protected all ranks of people with a bond of independent and yet social reliance, which diffused a general happiness among all the individuals, each in the appointed degree" (in O'Halloran, *Pictorial History*, 4). Would that this were so.

notes, was in part an attempt to veil the savagery and bloodlust of warrior culture that the bards themselves took pains to represent in a critical light. But rather than see O'Grady's rewriting as a maneuver to whitewash the Irish past, we might see it instead as part of a larger Revival effort to reappropriate that past from imperial and Anglo-Irish historians. If this view is plausible, so too is the idea that O'Grady followed the bards in offering a critical perspective on ancient warrior culture—albeit one that purged some elements in order to *realize* others.

O'Grady's imaginative historiography would prove influential in the formation of Revival historicism, not least because it provided Revivalists—and many other cultural nationalists—with an iconic hero. For them, Cuculain represented the virtues of an ancient, chivalrous warrior culture, but he also embodied the tensions, contradictions, and anxieties of Irish colonial culture—anxieties that lay at the foundation of modern Irish decolonization. This is nowhere more evident than in Yeats's Cuculain plays, especially the first one, *On Baile's Strand*, in which the hero's struggle with his king and his own son (borne to Aiofe and unknown to him) underscores the dynamic ambivalence of the warrior's greater struggle with fate, for although he can accept the young man who challenges him ("I'd have you for my friend"), he must fight him (and, of course, win) *because* he has been challenged. The massive misrecognition that leads to filicide is compounded by Cuculain's dissociation from the young man's relation to him: "I had rather he had been some other woman's son."[40] The denial of paternity masks his emotional complicity with Aiofe and his ethical responsibility to his son. The play ends with the spectacle of Cuculain entering into combat with the sea. This indomitable quality, this reckless working out of contradiction and tension appealed to Revivalists such as Yeats, who, like O'Grady, sought to *realize* in the present moment the heroic world of Cuculain in

40. W. B. Yeats, *On Baile's Strand*, in *Collected Works*, 2:172.

ways that sustained its temporal singularity. This imaginative vision neither preserves the past nor privileges the present but encourages their entwinement in the formation and consolidation of the Irish nation. As McAteer shows, O'Grady's historiography leads to a kind of practical inhabitation of the past in present social practice in the Free State, particularly in education. "After Irish Independence in 1921, O'Grady's tales of Cuculain became part of the curriculum in the Irish Free State primary schools. To this extent at least, he succeeded in fulfilling the desire he wrote about in the second volume of *History of Ireland*: to 'make this heroic period once again a portion of the imagination of the country'" (*HI* 2:17; p. 48). By focusing on heroic values, O'Grady hoped to awaken familiarity with them in the present so that they might help shape new kinds of social and cultural responsibility.[41]

Cuculain's heroism, by turns fiercely individualistic and recklessly loyal to his community, is the paradoxical heroism of the outlaw who lives to protect the law, often at the risk of his own life: "I am he who was called the Hound of Ulla. I was not a Hound for the guarding of cattle, but a Hound for the protection of territories and the defence of nations" (*CP* 204; p. 66). This boast was backed up by the willingness to sacrifice everything, a willingness that is often vocalized by the hero and is part of the warp and woof of his epic self-fashioning. As Bixby points out, "Cuculain came to stand for an ideal of heroic self-sacrifice" that was "essential to the struggle for Irish independence from the United Kingdom." Sheppard's statue of Cuculain conveys something of the marmoreal turbulence of this struggle, in which savagery and rage commingle with the noble destiny of a nation. The nationalists who chose Cuculain as an icon of their own heroic struggle were not always as aware as Sheppard was of Cuculain's all-too-human suffering and his all-too-human joys. Nor could they have predicted the consequences of their choice, for

41. In 1916, Yeats summed up this sentiment in the epigraph to *Responsibilities and Other Poems*: "In dreams begins responsibility."

not everyone agreed that a man so fierce and so fiercely individualistic was the appropriate symbol of Irish self-determination.

Like O'Grady's contemporaries, we may find ourselves in disagreement with his claims or his aims, but what is undeniable is the extent to which his imaginative historiography resuscitated or revived what was most needful: a new attitude toward and responsibility to the Irish past. This attitude became part of a *messianic* tradition in Irish Revival (the temporality of "coming times"), but it also anticipated the kind of fully developed Revival historiography we find in Daniel Corkery's cultural study *The Hidden Ireland* (1924).[42] Corkery's approach to history, though less pronouncedly "imaginative" than O'Grady's, accepted the underlying premise his predecessor had set out: that imaginative records of historical events—such as those found in bardic texts—are reliable as historical documents and, although possibly erroneous in many points, are nonetheless capable of yielding historical knowledge. O'Grady sought "[t]o work back into the elder vein of thought and feeling" (*HI* 1:xviii; p. 55), to realize through his imaginative misrecognition of the archive the sensibilities and values of Ireland's heroic era. And having decided that a true recognition was impossible, the effort too immense for any one historian, O'Grady took on the bardic mantle himself and tried to find imaginative expression for the "profound and vital humanity" that he believed was native to the Irish people and within their grasp in the modern world.

42. Daniel Corkery, *The Hidden Ireland: A Study of Gaelic Munster in the Eighteenth Century* (1924; reprint, Dublin: Gill and Macmillan, 1967).

PART ONE

From Standish O'Grady's History of Ireland

History of Ireland

Introductions

I

Scattered over the surface of every country in Europe may be found sepulchral monuments, the remains of pre-historic times and nations, and of a phase of life and civilisation which has long since passed away. No country in Europe is without its cromlechs and dolmens, huge earthen tumuli, great flagged sepulchres, and enclosures of tall pillar-stones. The men by whom these works were made, so interesting in themselves, and so different from anything of the kind erected since, were not strangers and aliens, but our own ancestors, and out of their rude civilisation our own has slowly grown. Of that elder phase of European civilisation no record or tradition has been anywhere bequeathed to us. Of its nature, and the ideas and sentiments whereby it was sustained, nought may now be learned save by an examination of those tombs themselves, and of the dumb remnants, from time to time exhumed out of their soil—rude instruments of clay, flint, brass, and gold, and by speculations and reasonings founded upon these archæological gleanings, meagre and sapless.

For after the explorer has broken up, certainly desecrated, and perhaps destroyed, those noble sepulchral raths*; after he has disinterred the bones laid there once by pious hands, and the urn with its unrecognisable ashes of king or warrior, and by the industrious labour of years hoarded his fruitless treasure of stone celt and arrow-head, of brazen sword and gold fibula and torque; and after the savant has rammed many skulls with sawdust, measuring their capacity, and has adorned them with some obscure label, and has tabulated and arranged the implements and decorations of flint and metal in the glazed cases of the cold gaunt museum, the imagination, unsatisfied and revolted, shrinks back from all that he has done. Still we continue to inquire, receiving from him no adequate response, Who were those ancient chieftains and warriors for whom an affectionate people raised those strange tombs? What life did they lead? What deeds perform? How did their personality affect the minds of their people and posterity? How did our ancestors look upon those great tombs, certainly not reared to be forgotten, and how did they—those huge monumental pebbles and swelling raths—enter into and affect the civilisation or religion of the times?

We see the cromlech with its massive slab and immense supporting pillars, but we vainly endeavour to imagine for whom it was first erected, and how that greater than cyclopean house affected the minds of those who made it, or those who were reared in its neighbourhood or within reach of its influence. We see the stone cist with its great smooth flags, the rocky cairn, and huge barrow and massive walled cathair*, but the interest which they invariably excite is only aroused to subside again unsatisfied. From this department of European antiquities the historian retires baffled, and the dry savant is alone master of the field, but a field which, as cultivated by him alone, remains barren or fertile only in things the reverse of exhilarating. An antiquarian museum is more melancholy than a tomb.

But there is one country in Europe in which, by virtue of a marvellous strength and tenacity of the historical intellect, and of filial devotedness to the memory of their ancestors, there have been preserved down into the early phases of mediæval civilisation, and then committed to the sure guardianship of manuscript, the hymns, ballads, stories, and chronicles, the names, pedigrees, achievements, and even characters, of those ancient kings and warriors over whom those massive cromlechs were erected and great cairns piled. There is not a conspicuous sepulchral monument in Ireland, the traditional history of which is not recorded in our ancient literature, and of the heroes in whose honour they were raised. In the rest of Europe there is not a single barrow, dolmen, or cist of which the ancient traditional history is recorded; in Ireland there is hardly one of which it is not. And these histories are in many cases as rich and circumstantial as that of men of the greatest eminence who have lived in modern times. Granted that the imagination which for centuries followed with eager interest the lives of these heroes, beheld as gigantic what was not so, as romantic and heroic what was neither one nor the other, still the great fact remains, that it was beside and in connection with the mounds and cairns that this history was elaborated, and elaborated concerning them and concerning the heroes to whom they were sacred.

On the plain of Tara*, beside the little stream Nemanna, itself famous as that which first turned a millwheel in Ireland, there lies a barrow, not itself very conspicuous in the midst of others, all named and illustrious in the ancient literature of the country. The ancient hero there interred is to the student of the Irish bardic literature a figure as familiar and clearly seen as any personage in the Biographia Britannica. We know the name he bore as a boy and the name he bore as a man [i.e., Cuculain]. We know the names of his father and his grandfather, and of the father of his grandfather, of his mother, and the father and mother of his mother, and the pedigrees and histories of each of these. We know the name of his nurse, and of his children, and of his wife, and the character of his wife, and of the father and mother of his wife, and where they lived and were buried. We know all the striking events of his boyhood and manhood, the names of his horses and his weapons, his own character and his friends, male and female. We know his battles, and the names of those whom he slew in battle, and how he was himself slain, and by whose hands. We know his physical and spiritual characteristics, the device upon his shield, and how that was originated, carved, and painted by whom. We know the colour of his hair, the date of his birth and of his death, and his relations, in time and otherwise, with the remainder of the princes and warriors with whom, in that mound-raising period of our history, he was connected, in hostility or friendship; and all this enshrined in ancient song, the transmitted traditions of the people who raised that barrow, and who laid within it sorrowing their brave ruler and defender. That mound is the tomb of Cuculain, once king of the district in which Dundalk stands to-day, and the ruins of whose earthen fortification may still be seen two miles from that town.

This is a single instance, and used merely as an example, but one out of a multitude almost as striking. There is not a king of Ireland, described as such in the ancient annals, whose barrow is not mentioned in these or other compositions, and every one of which may at the present day be identified where the ignorant plebeian or the ignorant patrician has not destroyed them. The early History of Ireland clings around and grows out of the Irish barrows until, with almost the universality of that primeval forest from which Ireland took one of its ancient names, the whole isle and all within it was clothed with a nobler raiment, invisible, but not the less real, of a full and luxuriant history, from whose presence, all-embracing, no part was free. Of the many poetical and rhetorical titles lavished upon this country, none is truer than that which calls her the Isle of Song. Her ancient history passed unceasingly into the realm of artistic representation; the history of one generation became the poetry of the next, until the whole island was illuminated and coloured by the poetry of the bards. Productions of mere fancy and imagination these songs are not, though fancy and imagination may have coloured and shaped all their subject-matter, but the names are names of men and women who once lived and died in Ireland, and over whom their people raised the swelling rath and reared the rocky cromlech. In the sepulchral monuments their names were preserved, and in the performance of sacred rites, and the holding of games, fairs, and assemblies in their honour, the memory of their achievements kept fresh, till the traditions that clung around these places were inshrined in tales which were finally incorporated in the *Leabhar na Huidhré** and the *Book of Leinster*. Pre-historic narrative is of two kinds—in one the imagination is at work consciously, in the other unconsciously. Legends of the former class are the product of a lettered and learned age. The story floats loosely in a world of imagination. The other sort of pre-historic narrative clings close to the soil, and to visible and tangible objects. It may be legend, but it is legend believed in as history never consciously invented, and growing out of certain spots of the earth's surface, and supported by and drawing its life from the soil like a natural growth.

Such are the early Irish tales that cling around the mounds and cromlechs as that by which they are sustained, which was originally their source, and sustained them afterwards in a strong enduring life. It is evident that these cannot be classed with stories that float vaguely in an ideal world, which may happen in one place as well as another, and in which the names might be disarrayed without changing the character and consistency of the tale, and its relations, in time or otherwise, with other tales.

Foreigners are surprised to find the Irish claim for their own country an antiquity and a history prior to that of the neighbouring countries. Herein lie the proof and the explanation. The traditions and history of the mound-raising period have in other countries passed away. Foreign conquest, or less intrinsic force of imagination, and pious sentiment have suffered them to fall into oblivion; but in Ireland they have been all preserved in their original fullness and vigour, hardly a hue has faded, hardly a minute circumstance or articulation been suffered to decay.

The enthusiasm with which the Irish intellect seized upon the grand moral life of Christianity, and ideals so different from, and so hostile to, those of the heroic age, did not consume the traditions or destroy the pious and reverent spirit in which men still looked back upon those monuments of their own pagan teachers and kings, and the deep spirit of patriotism and affection with which the mind still clung to the old heroic age, whose types were warlike prowess, physical beauty, generosity, hospitality, love of family and nation, and all those noble attributes which constituted the heroic character as distinguished from the saintly. The Danish conquest, with its profound modification of Irish society, and consequent disruption of old habits and conditions of life, did not dissipate it; nor the more dangerous conquest of the Normans, with their own innate nobility of character, chivalrous daring, and continental grace and civilisation; nor the Elizabethan convulsions and systematic repression and destruction of all native phases of thought and feeling. Through all these storms, which successively assailed the heroic literature of ancient Ireland, it still held itself undestroyed. There were still found generous minds to shelter and shield the old tales and ballads, to feel the nobleness of that life of which they were the outcome, and to resolve that the soil of Ireland should not, so far as they had the power to prevent it, be denuded of its raiment of history and historic romance, or reduced again to primeval nakedness. The fruit of this persistency and unquenched love of country and its ancient traditions, is left to be enjoyed by us. There is not through the length and breadth of the country a conspicuous rath or barrow of which we cannot find the traditional history preserved in this ancient literature. The mounds of Tara, the great barrows along the shores of the Boyne, the raths of Slieve Mish, and Ratherōgan, and Teltown, the stone caiseals* of Aran and Innishowen, and those that alone or in smaller groups stud the country over, are all, or nearly all, mentioned in this ancient literature, with the names and traditional histories of those over whom they were raised.

There is one thing to be learned from all this, which is, that we, at least, should not suffer these ancient monuments to be destroyed, whose history has been thus so astonishingly preserved. The English farmer may tear down the barrow which is unfortunate enough to be situated within his bounds. Neither he nor his neighbours know or can tell anything about its ancient history; the removed earth will help to make his cattle fatter and improve his crops, the stones will be useful to pave his roads and build his fences, and the savant can enjoy the rest; but the Irish farmer and landlord should not do or suffer this.

The instinctive reverence of the peasantry has hitherto been a great preservative; but the spread of education has to a considerable extent impaired this kindly sentiment, and the progress of scientific farming, and the anxiety of the Royal Irish Academy to collect antiquarian trifles, have already led to the reckless destruction of too many. I think that no one who reads the first two volumes of this history would greatly care to bear a hand in the destruction of that tomb at Tara, in which long since his people laid the bones of Cuculain; and I think, too, that they would not like to destroy any other monument of the same age, when they know that the history of its occupant and its own name are preserved in the ancient literature, and that they may one day learn all that is to be known concerning it. I am sure that if the case were put fairly to the Irish landlords and country gentlemen, they would neither inflict nor permit this outrage upon the antiquities of their country. The Irish country gentleman prides himself on his love of trees, and entertains a very wholesome contempt for the mercantile boor who, on purchasing an old place, chops down the best timber for the market. And yet a tree, though cut down, may be replaced. One elm tree is as good as another, and the thinned wood, by proper treatment, will be as dense as ever; but the ancient mound, once carted away, can never be replaced any more. When the study of the Irish literary records is revived, as it certainly will be revived, the old history of each of these raths and cromlechs will be brought again into the light, and one new interest of a beautiful and edifying nature attached to the landscape, and affecting wholly for good the minds of our people.

Irishmen are often taunted with the fact that their history is yet unwritten, but that the Irish, as a nation, have been careless of their past is refuted by the facts which I have mentioned. A people who alone in Europe preserved, not in dry chronicles alone, but illuminated and adorned with all that fancy could suggest in ballad, and tale, and rude epic, the history of the mound-raising period, are not justly liable to this taunt. Until very modern times, history was the one absorbing pursuit of the Irish secular intellect, the delight of the noble, and the solace of the vile.

At present, indeed, the apathy on this subject is, I believe, without parallel in the world. It would seem as if the Irish, extreme in all things, at one time thought of nothing but their history, and, at another, thought of everything but it. Unlike those who write on other subjects, the author of a work on Irish history has to labour simultaneously at a two-fold task—he has to create the interest to which he intends to address himself.

II

I had intended at first to let my book [volume 1 of *History of Ireland*] explain itself, but as I reflect on the unusualness of its form and character, I feel the advantages which would be derived from some introductory matter. If I appear sometimes to travel over ground covered by the text itself, this must be my excuse.

It is a common-place that the true function of the historian is to give a clear and vivid picture of the past; but, although the principle is recognised in theory, it is practically set aside, and pure historical composition relegated to the novelist and romancer, whose audience, as they desire merely amusement, make no very stern demands on the veracity and historical faithfulness of the writer. In fact, the province of archæology has so extended its frontiers, as to have swallowed up the dominion of pure history altogether. Nearly every work which one takes up affecting to treat of the past in a rigid and conscientious spirit, is merely archæological. It is an accumulation of names, dates, events, disquisitions, the balancing of probabilities, the testing of statements and traditions, categorical assertions concerning laws and customs. All works of this character are of the nature of archæology; they are the material of history, not history itself.

Upon the foundations laid, with the materials provided, by the archæologian the historian builds. When he has acquainted himself with all that the patient toil of archæological investigation has amassed, he is equipped for his work, and not till then. But surely, no mere accumulation of facts only, no matter how profound or exhaustive may have been the search whose results he has laid up in his mind, is by itself to be dignified by the name of history. Out of the sad leavings of the past, how can even the most cunning mechanical arrangement evolve a living, adequate, affecting representation of the life of our ancestors?

In history, there must be sympathy, imagination, creation. The sorry remnants discussed by the antiquarian, do not of themselves supply a picture. All these the historian will study attentively, after which, in proportion to his strength and truth of imagination, a more or less faithful and vivid picture of that life of which they are the relics, will impress itself on his mind.

History is the flower of archæology; it justifies, rewards, and crowns the obscure toil of those patient and single-minded excavators into the buried past.

In the department of Pre-Norman Irish Archæology, a generation of workers has passed away. The time has come for an embodiment in a fitting form of the results of their labours. The facts which they have accumulated, the obscurities which they dispelled, the amount of antique Irish literature which they have translated, the pregnant passages which they have collected out of the bardic writings, the number of forgotten heroes, events, characteristics—legal, social, and political—which they have brought to light, furnish such a mass of antiquarian knowledge as can supply the historian with ample materials for the reconstruction by imaginative processes of the life led by our ancestors in this country. Until this mass of information is popularised, and by popularised, secured and appropriated, it is unlikely that any new surge of antiquarian enthusiasm will again ruffle the tranquil mind of the intellectual classes in Ireland. Until this mound of ore is smelted and converted into current coin of the realm, who will spend a lifetime in adding to those heaps which, as they stand to-day in their gaunt uselessness, almost justify the apathy with which they are regarded?

But how can the historian escape the introduction of elements into the period of which he treats, which it did not really contain, but which are only factors in his own mental and moral temperament, and of the age of which he himself is a part? Will not his own complexion colour all he writes? This is certainly the case. The most strenuous efforts will not keep his own age and his own character altogether out of his work. Even amongst the historical writers around me, who affect to aim only at archæological results, and the lucid arrangement of what has been discovered, I perceive their work dyed deep with the hues of their own individuality. There is this danger, indeed, this certainty of misrepresentation; but alas, there has yet been discovered no photographic agency by which may be depicted the actual life of our ancestors other than that fallible and feeble instrument, the human imagination. Yet this objection will lose some of its force by a consideration of the nature of that period, which will be represented in the present and succeeding volumes.

The forefront of Irish history we find filled with great heroic personages of a dignity and power more than human. The age in which these heroes lived was that which almost alone absorbed the attention of the Irish bards. Century after century the mind of the country was inflamed by the contemplation of those mighty beings whom, too, men believed to be their own ancestors. All the imaginative literature of the country revolved round this period, was devoted to the glorification of the gigantic figures with whom it was filled.

Naturally then, this heroic age was as it were a huge bright mirror, in which were reflected the magnified images of the bards themselves, and of the contemporary kings and heroes for whom they sang. The value of any, even the slightest characteristic of the heroic age, is, therefore, of the highest historic importance. The vastness and populousness of this age, which have been employed for the purpose of pointing derision at this country, are really the best proof of the value of Irish antiquarian research; they indicate the enormous fecundity and force of the imagination of a people whose Pantheon was so great.

Now, it is not to be supposed that the heroes and events of this wonderful period are to be lightly passed over—a period which, like the visible firmament, was bowed with all its glory above the spirit of a whole nation. Those heroes and heroines were the ideals of our ancestors, their conduct and character were to them a religion, the bardic literature was their Bible. It was a poor substitute, one may say, for that which found its way into the island in the fifth century. That is so, yet such as it was under its nurture, the imagination and spiritual susceptibilities of our ancestors were made capable of that tremendous outburst of religious fervour and exaltation which characterised the centuries that succeeded the fifth, and whose effect was felt throughout a great portion of Europe. It was the Irish bards and that heroic age of theirs which nourished the imagination, intellect, and idealism of the country to such an issue. [St.] Patrick* did not create these qualities. They may not be created. He found them, and directed them into a new channel.

III

The pre-Christian period of Irish history presents difficulties from which the corresponding period in the histories of other countries is free. The surrounding nations escape the difficulty by having nothing to record. The Irish historian is immersed in perplexity on account of the mass of material ready to his hand. The English have lost utterly all record of those centuries before which the Irish historian stands with dismay and hesitation, not through deficiency of materials, but through their excess. Had nought but the chronicles been preserved the task would have been simple. We would then have had merely to determine approximately the date of the introduction of letters, and allowing a margin on account of the bardic system and the commission of family and national history to the keeping of rhymed and alliterated verse, fix upon some reasonable point, and set down in order, the old successions of kings and the battles and other remarkable events. But in Irish history there remains, demanding treatment, that other immense mass of literature of an imaginative nature, illuminating with anecdote and tale the events and personages mentioned simply and without comment by the chronicler. It is this poetic literature which constitutes the stumbling-block, as it constitutes also the glory, of early Irish history, for it cannot be rejected and it cannot be retained. It cannot be rejected, because it contains historical matter which is consonant with and illuminates the dry lists of the chronologist, and it cannot be retained, for popular poetry is not history; and the task of distinguishing in such literature the fact from the fiction—where there is certainly fact and certainly fiction—is one of the most difficult to which the intellect can apply itself.

That this difficulty has not been hitherto surmounted by Irish writers is no just reproach. For the last century, intellects of the highest attainments, trained and educated to the last degree, have been vainly endeavouring to solve a similar question in the far less copious and less varied heroic literature of Greece. Yet the labours of Wolfe, Grote, Mahaffy, Geddes, and Gladstone, have not been sufficient to set at rest the small question, whether it was one man or two or many who composed the Iliad and Odyssey, while the reality of the achievements of Achilles and even his existence might be denied or asserted by a scholar without general reproach. When this is the case with regard to the great heroes of the Iliad, I fancy it will be some time before the same problem will have been solved for the minor characters, and as it affects Thersites, or that eminent artist who dwelt at home in Hyla, being by far the most excellent of leather cutters. When, therefore, Greek still meets Greek in an interminable and apparently bloodless contest over the disputed body of the Iliad, and still no end appears, surely it would be madness for anyone to sit down and gaily distinguish true from false in the immense and complex mass of the Irish bardic literature, having in his ears this century-lasting struggle over a single Greek poem and a single small phase of the pre-historic life of Hellas.

In the Irish heroic literature, the presence or absence of the marvellous supplies no test whatsoever as to the general truth or falsehood of the tale in which they appear. The marvellous is supplied with greater abundance in the account of the battle of Clontarf, and the wars of the O'Briens with the Normans, than in the tale in which is described the foundation of Emain Macha* by Kimbay [Mac Fiontann]*. Exact-thinking, scientific France has not hesitated to paint the battles of Louis XIV with similar hues; and England, though by no means fertile in angelic interpositions, delights to adorn the barren tracts of her more popular histories with apocryphal anecdotes.

How then should this heroic literature of Ireland be treated in connection with the history of the country? The true method would certainly be to print it exactly as it is without excision or condensation. Immense it is, and immense it must remain. No men living, and no men to live, will ever so exhaust the meaning of any single tale as to render its publication unnecessary for the study of others. The order adopted should be that which the bards themselves determined, any other would be premature, and I think no other will ever take its place. At the commencement should stand the passage from the *Book of Invasions**, describing the occupation of the isle by Queen Keasair* and her companions, and along with it every discoverable tale or poem dealing with this event and those characters. After that, all that remains of the cycle of which Partholān* was the protagonist. Thirdly, all that relates to Nemeth* and his sons, their wars with curt Kical the bow-legged, and all that relates to the Fōmoroh* of the Nemedian* epoch, then first moving dimly in the forefront of our history. After that, the great Fir-bolgic cycle, a cycle Janus-faced, looking on one side to the mythological period and the wars of the gods, and on the other, to the heroic, and more particularly to the Ultonian cycle*. In the next place, the immense mass of bardic literature which treats of the Irish gods who, having conquered the Fir-bolgs*, like the Greek gods of the age of gold dwelt visibly in the island until the coming of the Clan Milith*, out of Spain. In the sixth, the Milesian* invasion, and every accessible statement concerning the sons and kindred of Milesius*. In the seventh, the disconnected tales dealing with those local heroes whose history is not connected with the great cycles, but who in the *fasti** fill the spaces between the divine period and the heroic. In the eighth, the heroic cycles, the Ultonian, the Temairian*, and the Fenian*, and after these the historic tales that, without forming cycles, accompany the course of history down to the extinction of Irish independence, and the transference to aliens of all the great sources of authority in the island.

This great work when completed will be of that kind of which no other European nation can supply an example. Every public library in the world will find it necessary to procure a copy. The chronicles will then cease to be so closely and exclusively studied. Every history of ancient Ireland will consist of more or less intelligent comments upon and theories formed in connection with this great series—theories which, in general, will only be formed in order to be destroyed. What the present age demands upon the subject of antique Irish history—an exact and scientific treatment of the facts supplied by our native authorities—will be demanded for ever. It will never be supplied. The history of Ireland will be contained in this huge publication. In it the poet will find endless themes of song, the philosopher strange workings of the human mind, the archæologist a mass of information, marvellous in amount and quality, with regard to primitive ideas and habits of life, and the rationalist materials for framing a scientific history of Ireland, which will be acceptable in proportion to the readableness of his style, and the mode in which his views may harmonize with the prevailing humour and complexion of his contemporaries.

Such a work it is evident could not be effected by a single individual. It must be a public and national undertaking, carried out under the supervision of the Royal Irish Academy, at the expense of the country.

The publication of the Irish bardic remains in the way that I have mentioned, is the only true and valuable method of presenting the history of Ireland to the notice of the world. The mode which I have myself adopted, that other being out of the question, is open to many obvious objections; but in the existing state of the Irish mind on the subject, no other is possible to an individual writer. I desire to make this heroic period once again a portion of the imagination of the country, and its chief characters as familiar in the minds of our people as they once were. As mere history, and treated in the method in which history is generally written at the present day, a work dealing with the early Irish kings and heroes would certainly not secure an audience. Those who demand such a treatment forget that there is not in the country an interest on the subject to which to appeal. A work treating of early Irish kings, in the same way in which the historians of neighbouring countries treat of their own early kings, would be, to the Irish public generally, unreadable. It might enjoy the reputation of being well written, and as such receive an honourable place in half-a-dozen public libraries, but it would be otherwise left severely alone. It would never make its way through that frozen zone which, on this subject, surrounds the Irish mind.

IV

The heroic period demands treatment, the very best and fullest that can be accorded to it. There is one mode in which it has been treated, and that I think the worst. All the names, dates, battles, events, births, deaths, geneaologies, &c., have been set down in due order. In this treatment there is absolutely no advantage. One name is as good as another. Abracadabra is as good as Owen Mōr, if we are told naught concerning him than that he had a certain father and mother, fought certain battles, and died. Moreover, the archæological and scientific objections would apply to such a treatment with full force, namely, the unprovability of the statements so made.

The manner of [Geoffrey] Keating* is different from this, and better, but not to my mind the best. Keating, following the old rationalistic compilers of the Irish chronicles, sets down in regular order the kings and heroes of ancient Eiré, and related concerning many of them, one or two of what seemed to him the most important anecdotes. Now, Keating believed that all this ancient bardic lore represented pure historic fact, which caused him to commit many grave errors, artistic and archæological, by which the value of his beautiful treatise is much impaired. Even his anecdotes lose their importance by being deprived of their substance, colour, and life, so that each under his handling has become the mere *residuum* and anatomy of the old bardic tale, whose essential elements he desired to represent. Treating these tales as history, he attached no importance to those qualities which have alone value to me, viz., the epic and dramatic.

But even pursued in this direction, a fuller and more artistic treatment would not be satisfactory. No single tale, however well adapted to the modern literary taste, would form a complete and perfect representation of any of the more important heroic personages or events. Round each of the heroes revolves a whole cycle of literature in prose and verse, and no treatment would be adequate which did not take in this cycle in its completeness.

I now come to that treatment which has been suggested by [Eugene] O'Curry*, but the effect of which he did not fully realise, viz., the narration of all the bardic tales and fragments in connection with each hero and heroine. Such a work is physically impossible, or if it were effected, the result would not be satisfactory. The bardic literature of ancient Erin would fill, perhaps, a hundred volumes such as the present. When completed, the piled up mass would be without harmony, meaning, or order. The valuable and the valueless would be mingled together. It would be utterly incondite, inorganic, and, I think, unreadable, except to archæologians and the philosophical [historians]. A passage illustrating the character of a hero might be imbedded in a tale concerning another, or in a note to a Christian hymn, or in the life of a saint, or in some ancient chronicle, dictionary, or legal treatise. Moreover, the genesis of these tales must be ascribed to peoples separated from one another by wide tracts of country and distances of time, so that contradiction and confusion are inevitable. The result would be a huge literary chaos, not a work of art, and this would be true even if the tales were reduced each to its pure epic elements. For instance, Tierna*, the Abbot of Clonmacnoise, and a man thoroughly conversant, I think, with the heroic history, tells us that the greatest of the Irish heroes [i.e., Cuculain] died young, yet there is extant a celebrated tale in which he is represented as contending in single combat with his own son.

The treatment which I have myself adopted consists in the reduction to its artistic elements of the whole of that heroic history taken together, viewing it always in the light shed by the discoveries of modern archæologians, frequently using the actual language of the bards, and as much as possible their style and general character of expression. The death of Conairey Mōr* is almost a literal transcript from the tale. Through the loose chaotic mass of bardic story and monkish chronicle, I have endeavoured to trace the mental and physical personality of the heroes and heroines in their essential elements, and to discover that order of events which best harmonises with the records and traditions of the poets, and the characters of the heroic personages. Hence it follows, that in order to be faithful to the generic conception, one must disregard often the literal statement of the bard. That the whole should be fairly represented, one must do violence to the parts upon which, indeed, no more violence can be wrought than they inflict upon one another, perpetually diverging in detail, though in unison generally as to the main idea of characters and events.

But there is another element than the merely epic one in this volume, and which represents a great portion of our literary remains with an almost verbal exactitude and precision.

The bardic mind affected a certain fastidiousness in its mode of treating the heroic period. A conventional set of ideas were deemed poetic, and all outside that was unpoetic. We can see how some such traditions clung around the mind of Homer. For instance, he obstinately refuses to allude to writing of any sort, or to horsemen other than drivers of chariots. The same limitations, to a great extent, pervade the heroic literature of Ireland. There are many allusions to Oghams*, and inscribed tablets of wood, but the bards would have us imagine that they never heard of a book or a parchment. In the more ancient literature also they do not allude to the riding of horses, nor to horses at all in connection with Mac Cool and his Fenians. From the bardic literature too, we would imagine that there was not a wolf to be seen in ancient Ireland.

Now, in relating the heroic history, I have departed wholly from the limited range of ideas permitted to themselves by the bards, and have introduced boldly the ancient civilisation of the country. In this part of my work I have preserved the closest adherence to the authorities. In all that relates to the material, social, political condition of the country, I believe that in this and the succeeding volumes will be found an accurate and faithful representation of the civilisation of ancient Ireland. In these volumes the heroic period reflects the actualities of the early historic times. I remember some remark of Horace to this effect, "Hence it happens that we see, as in a picture, all the life of the old man." This has been my object to represent, as in a picture, the state of society which obtained in this country in ancient times, which, though distant in one sense, are near in many others. It is the same sky that bent over them, which shines or darkens over us. The same human heart beat in their breasts as beats amongst us today. All the great permanent relations of life are the same. Therefore, I think I am also justified in treating that old heroic history in connection with the enduring facts of nature and of humanity. I do not like to contemplate that heroic age as vague, shadowy, and remote, and have not so contemplated it. Upon the realisation of the bards I have superadded a realisation more intense, working closer to those noble forms, whose outlines are more or less wavering and uncertain in the literature of the bards.

Nevertheless, the outlines are there, and in many an instance a flash of genius disperses altogether the mist for a moment, and lets us see the real hero. From these outlines I do not depart, where they appear with any consistency and definiteness. Yet when a whole nation is busy realising its heroes, it must follow that many an ignoble thought and tale will find its way into the preserved literature. The tales that are canonical and that are not must be determined. For instance, the tales told [in the penultimate chapter of *History of Ireland*, vol. 1] concerning both Cuculain and Emer strike down deep into the bardic conception of the characters of both. Nothing that interferes with these can be tolerated by the historian of the heroic period. We feel instinctively that they are essential, while we feel that others are not essential or wholly to be rejected. The nobler conception of any character, is, of course, to be preferred to the ignoble.

One of the most interesting features of early Irish civilisation, the religious feature, is also unfortunately the most obscure. In the absence of clear philosophical statements by the monks, we are obliged to fall back upon the tales and poems. The only monkish allusion to the Irish gods with which I have met, excepting another by St. Fiech*, is one in Cormac's Glossary*, where Ana is called the mother of the Irish gods, *mater deorum Hibernensium*. Now, if we had a sufficient quantity of pre-Christian Irish literature, there would be no loss sustained by the unfortunate reticence of the ecclesiastics; but this is not so. The bards were but the abstracts and brief chronicles of their own time, and in their hands the ancient tales and traditions varied from century to century, acquiring more and more a new complexion as the ages ran on. The consequence has been that, although all the Irish bardic tales revolve round the Pagan and heroic period, yet under the stress of the new faith the old distinction between gods and heroes was lost, and it is only here and there that we can see the differences that formerly obtained. For instance, in the battle of Moy Tura*, Mac Erc*, King of the Fir-bolgs, figures only as a mighty warrior, yet in the following ancient rann*, discovered by Professor Sullivan, in what a different character does he appear:

> "Twice during the Treena of Tailteen,
> Each day at sunrise I invoked Mac Erc
> To remove from me the pestilence."

The chronicles follow the later tales, and the Fir-bolgs, as well as the Tuátha De Danan*, are set down with circumstantial births and deaths; yet this single verse shows clearly the true character of Mac Erc as a great and powerful deity.

That the Tuátha De Danan were deities, is perfectly apparent to one who reads carefully the old tales and poems. In the tale called the Sick Bed of Cuculain, the Tuátha De Danan are also termed the Shee*; and in St. Fiech's hymn, in honour of St. Patrick, St. Fiech distinctly states, that in the old times the people used to worship the Shee. The term Fir-bolg has, however, acquired a very definite meaning, which we cannot forego, in the received accounts of early Irish history. It is applied generally to nations not of Milesian descent. The word itself means no more than giant.

When a complete collection and translation of all the bardic literature has been effected, I should not be surprised if we should be in a position to give a clear and intelligible description of all the occupants of the Irish Olympus.

The old heroic history is overlain and concealed, but much of it is still there. In the bardic account of the Milesian invasion, we find a multitude of ancient tales reduced to their essence, or rather their anatomies, and then poured pell-mell together. By looking closely into these relics, we see that the real history was something very different from that which the last redactor desired to represent. The materials which he employs tell a different tale.

There seems to have been a bardic golden age, as well as one of brass, or even earth. The advent of Christianity ruined the bards. The missionaries felt instinctively that the bards were their enemies. The praise of gods and demi-gods, and of heroes who were favoured and helped by these, was the theme of the bards. The degradation of the bardic class was therefore essential to the success of the missionaries. Both could not live in the same country. On the two occasions on which St. Columba* refers to the bards, he speaks of them as *homunculi*, and on one of these he alludes disrespectfully to their art. On a third occasion, he is represented as snubbing the chief poet of Ulster*, when he addressed to him a laudatory poem. In fact, St. Columba silenced him after the first line.

The consequence was that as the missionaries grew powerful, the bards declined, descending in every generation lower and lower in the social scale. The relations at first subsisting between them are reversed. St. Patrick, and his compeers and fellow-missionaries, seem to have been rude, uneducated men. Their Latin is rude, clumsy, and ungrammatical. His own compositions are so bad, that they have been considered forgeries; but his pupil, St. Sechnall*, was quite as illiterate. In the same age, Dûvac Mac Ua Luhair, the chief poet of the King of Leinster, composed two magnificent Irish poems—bold, glowing, energetic, and even sublime. On the other hand, in the time of Adamnan*, three centuries later, the monks had perfected a splendid Latin style, enriched with contributions from the Greek and Hebrew, and giving the reader the impression that they were the intellectual lords of the land. In the bardic literature of this period, we look in vain for anything which might be considered in profane literature the equivalent of "The Life of St. Columba."

In fact, the positions of the contending parties had been reversed. The bards now amused only farmers and tradesmen, while the monks crowned kings, and trained the minds of princes. The consequence was, that secular literature did not flourish, or flourished only in the monasteries, where it was not the chief thing, but an ornament of the monastic mind. The generous tribute paid to the chief hero of the Red Branch* by the Abbot of Clonmacnoise, proves not only the growth of a scientific and secular spirit in the monasteries, but also, I think, the complete collapse and prostration of the bardic class. Otherwise, it is unlikely that the monks would have affected to perceive the grandeur of the heroic period. We perceive, also, traces of an union between the two modes of thought in the statement of St. Fiech, that the Túatha of Erin*, i.e., the gods, used to prophesy the reign of a new faith, and certain stories of favourite personages of the heroic period announcing the approach of Christianity, or in other ways brought into connection with the Christian idea. Cuculain, borne in his fairy chariot over the City of Emain Macha, with his steeds trampling the winds, announces from on high to the weeping people the coming of the Talkend*. Concobar Mac Nessa* is informed of the death of Christ by one Altus, a Roman centurion, and loses his life in the fit of wrath which the account produces.

As we examine closely the bardic tales, we will see traces of the same transformation. There are clearly marked vestiges of a golden age of bardic composition in the existing tales. In the midst of flat wordy prose, vulgar in tone, and barbarous in construction, are embedded perfect gems of bardic verse, clear, noble, and pathetic. To work back into the elder vein of thought and feeling as much as possible, has been my object in the composition of the history.

If it be asked whether the principal characters of the heroic age really existed, I would myself answer that they certainly did. I have the strongest belief in the incapacity of the uncivilised mind to create imaginary characters, or to discover a personality in the various beautiful or sublime aspects of nature. The Wordsworthian notion of the genesis of the gods and fairies, I think quite incorrect. I believe that all the characters in the present volume really existed, and had more or less the general attributes with which they are invested. Hardly was the mighty barrow piled above the charred relics of the hero, than he started forth to run a new career of glory in the imagination of his people; a career whose goal was a serene god-hood; but the first impressions left upon their minds by his actual life, though heightened, were not destroyed. I cannot help thinking that whether the local hero became a national hero, or advanced to the dignity of a god, depended very much on the size of the barrow that concealed his bones. But, indeed, such a notion one ought to be ashamed of entertaining; yet, too, the mound of Achilles is the highest of those that cluster upon that ancient cemetery called Ilium.

I desire to qualify considerably those passages in which I speak of the old bardic tales as romances. They are by no means correctly so designated. Romance is a product of civilisation, and belongs to a luxurious and leisured age. The bardic tales were to our ancestors genuine history, and implicitly believed in. In their genesis there was never anything like conscious creation.

A considerable number of strange words will be found whose meaning, I think, will be generally discovered by the context.

I have taken the great liberty of spelling proper names in the way in which an ordinary reader would best arrive at the correct pronunciation.

History of Ulster, *Tempore* Cuculain

A rapid superficial sketch of the character and chief personages of an age so remarkable will be desirable at this point—a sketch unencumbered with many names or minutiae for which the more curious inquirer must consult the authorities or those books in which I have endeavoured epically to set forth what I here cursorily glance over.

At first, Fergus mac Roy* was king of Ulster; but by stratagem, or by a cabal of the chieftains, was supplanted, and his cousin Concobar mac Nessa installed in his place. Thus, Concobar is king of the north of Ireland during the whole floruit of his nephew Cuculain. Fergus, however, a hero of a large tolerant nature, still dwells amongst the Red Branch, one of their greatest champions. In one bardic scene we perceive him and his cousin, the youthful Concobar, seated under the trees of the lawn at Emain Macha, playing a game of chess, while, hard by, the boys of the military school of Ulster are exercising themselves at goal.

It was at this time that Cuculain came to the school, and Fergus took upon himself the martial tuition of the boy.[1]

Finally, Fergus rose in rebellion against Concobar, impelled to that step by a great personal wrong. Concobar loved a beautiful girl named Deirdre*, to whom, according to some, he was married. She,

1. Cuculain, a little boy, stole away from his mother at Dundalk, to Emain Macha, and suddenly joined the young princes in their sports. They endeavoured to drive him away, but Cuculain dispersed them all with this hurle.

however, eloped to Scotland with Naysi*, the eldest of three great champions of the age, sons of Usna*. This Naysi is described as having a skin white as snow, hair like the plumage of the raven, and a voice resonant as the surge of deep waters; while Deirdré was the most beautiful of all the women of ancient Ireland—golden-haired, her voice sweeter than the harp.

Finally, the brothers, with Deirdré, returned into Erin under a deceitful promise from the king and under the pledged protection of Fergus mac Roy. Concobar, however, broke through the protection of Fergus, and his warriors slew the sons of Usna. Deirdré herself died of grief and shame at being made the subject of a ribald jest. There is a poem attributed to her with these lines:—

> "O man, who diggest the grave, make it deep and wide,
> I too shall sleep on the bosom of my love."

Cuculain seems to have been then a boy; but he is represented as meeting Deirdre and comforting her. He, however, never faltered in his allegiance to his uncle, Concobar mac Nessa.

Fergus now rebels; is joined by Cormac Conlíngas*, the king's son, half-a-dozen conspicuous champions, and by a great portion of Ulster. After this, a terrible war, in which Emain Macha is burned; but finally, Fergus mac Roy and his faction are driven out of the north, chiefly by the great prowess of Conaill Carna*. He and his friends fly into Connaught, where they enter military service with Queen Meave* and her husband, Aileel Mōr*, king of Connaught. At the commencement of the great epical war between Queen Meave and the Ultonians, Fergus was her chief warrior and the captain of her host.

Queen Meave now takes up the quarrel of the great exile, and forms a coalition of the whole of Ireland against Ulster; though the pretext of the war was, that the Ultonians refused to lend her the Black Bull of Cooalney—a legendary druidic beast having a human soul in the body of a quadruped, and a voice filling the territory with a delicious music, of terrible size and strength, the "black jewel" of the Ultonians.

At the date of this invasion which has been chronicled in the year 2 A.D., the great champions of the Ultonians were afflicted with a magic stupor, so that they were without sense or strength. Thus, a field is made clear for Cuculain on which to exert his terrible prowess.

As the host of Queen Meave go on towards Ulster, they find their stragglers and marauding parties cut off as though some mysterious malign influence preceded them. Near the Boyne, the chariots and horses of two of their greatest champions gallop madly into the camp with the headless trunks of the champions and their charioteers strapped into their places. The same day, reaching the Boyne, they find a tree planted in the midst of the river bearing a ghastly trophy—the four heads of the slain men fixed upon the pointed prongs.

"I know not who can be doing these things," said Fergus, "if it be not my little pupil Setanta*, the son of Sualtam*."

But doubts are set at rest. A twig-hoop, fresh cut, is brought to Fergus with the name of Cuculain written upon it in Ogham, fastened round a pillar-stone by the young hero himself.

Now, Cuculain attacks the invaders by night with his magic sling, slaying hundreds. Himself, the swiftest of Meave's warriors cannot overtake.

Finally, through the influence of Fergus whom he loves, Cuculain makes a formal compact with Meave that he will cease from slinging and from his irregular and nocturnal slaughter, if she will undertake not to cross the river Dee invading Ulster, until he shall be subdued in single combat.

The compact is made; and, at what is now called Ardee,[2] in the County of Louth, day by day, Cuculain met and slaughtered the bravest and most renowned warriors of all that age; but no help arrives, and the hero grows every day more exhausted.

His father, Sualtam, has been despatched to arouse the Red Branch, but in vain; and the hero not knowing the cause, is dejected

2. The remains of giant tumuli still exist at this spot. Indeed, all the tumuli in this portion of Ireland and which belonged to personages more ancient than Cuculain, were believed to have been raised over heroes slain by him.

and deems himself forsaken. Nevertheless, he fights on without yielding. At last, the most potent warrior of the south of Ireland, Lōk [Mac Favash]*, comes out against him, assisted by the Mōr Reega*, the war-goddess; but after a terrible struggle, Cuculain slays Lōk and wounds the goddess. In this combat he was himself sore wounded, and his two blackbirds[3] slain; and that night he lifted up his voice in the forest, lamenting his desertion and the conspiracy of all men against him.

The next hero brought out against Cuculain was an ancient friend and ally, Fardia*, son of Daman, of Firbolg race, who had been his schoolfellow in the isle of Skye. Indeed, Cuculain at that school seems to have been Fardia's "fag," polishing his armour and tying up his spears. Fardia, by great bribes and through a promise given in intoxication, and perhaps, too, from his believing that Cuculain would retreat at his command, is induced to come out against the northern champion; so, Cuculain, with difficulty enduring his wounds and his deserted and forsaken condition, is now suddenly confronted by his old and dearest friend.

After a passionate colloquy, ensues a tremendous strife, during which the water of the Avon Dia holds back for fear. The war-steeds of the host of Meave fly terrified, and the women and camp-followers break forth south-westward. The invincible Cuculain slays Fardia; but afterwards weeps and mourns over the dead body of his friend.

All this time, too, Cuculain seems to have been subject to the wizard charms of a weird being called Cailitin,[4] a druid of Queen Meave; therefore, fights with only half his strength.[5]

3. There is some weird druidic idea contained here, the clue to which has been lost.

4. It was not until Cuculain slew Cailitin that he became invincible. After that nothing could stop him. His death, however, was eventually brought about by the sons and daughters of Cailitin.

5. *Editors' note*: See W. B. Yeats's version of these events in *On Baile's Strand* (1904).

After the last duel, Cuculain does not come forth again. Queen Meave and the great host of the Four Provinces* invade Ulster and plunder the whole province. Retiring, however, they are overtaken on the plain of Gaura in Westmeath, by the quick-journeying champions of the Red Branch—now aroused from their fatal stupor. Concealed in a weird mist filled with fires and lights, the flashing of chariots and swords, amid which, too, is seen the Red Hand of Ulster*, the banner of the north, descend the Clanna Rury*, Concobar mac Nessa and his knights upon the retreating host of Meave.

In the ensuing battle the Red Branch are beaten and all but exterminated, when Cuculain reappears, at first weak and bound with bandages; but ere long, apparently by the aid of the god, Lu* [Lu Lamfáda*], his father, he recovers his strength and goes out to battle in his war-chariot with Læg* by his side, surrounded by tutelary gods and demons of slaughter, his form exaggerated through mists of terror—not now as Cuculain militant, but invulnerable and invincible like a god. Before him he sweeps the whole Meavian host westward to the Shannon, and at Athlone set up trophy-stones, smitten with his sword from adjoining hills.

Be it remarked, however, that true to his nature, when Meave's host is thoroughly beaten, Cuculain himself protects her retreat and saves her flying warriors from the vengeance of the pursuers.

This great termagant of the west, Queen Meave, has a counterpart in the same or immediately succeeding ages in the east, in Leinster, called Meave the Half-Red, who suffered no king to reign in Tara who did not make her his bride.

The western or Connaught Meave, however, was by far the most renowned. She is described as having yellow hair and a pale face. She went out to battle like a man-of-war, bearing spear and shield. A wounded knight in the presence of Cuculain describes how a tall woman with golden hair and a pale face came through the battle and discharged her spear against him. "I know that woman well," replied Cuculain, "it was Meave of Cruhane; and I myself would have fallen at her hands had I not fled." There is no account preserved anywhere, even in the tale from which this passage is taken, of the flight of Cuculain before Meave. On the contrary, Meave is always represented as being in the direst fear of the northern champion. In one place, at sight of him, she cowers beneath her shield; in another, springs down from her chariot and flies; and in a third, collapses, utterly panic-stricken and overwhelmed with abject terror.

Cuculain, Son of Sualtam

The student of Irish history, arrived at this point, may not be inaptly compared to one who, after journeying through some sombre and intricate forest, whose gloom is not wholly unrelieved by small moonlit glades and the cheerful tinkle of living streams, amid whose shadows are seen passing shapes weird and unearthly, now, suddenly emerging, finds around him the night, indeed, but such a night! flashing, as with stars and northern lights. Now, all over and on every side the bardic firmament glitters with bright-burning fires, heroic names and deeds innumerable, amongst whom, stars of the first magnitude, shine out the Champions of the North, the Red Branch Knights, Children of Rury.

Heretofore the student, toiling along a path considerably shortened in this rapid narrative, has beheld Ireland producing her great names sparingly, but now, approaching the age of the Incarnation, he beholds how the island starting, as if from some magic slumber, all the deep fountains of life suddenly unsealed, teems as with some vast parturition. Out of the ground start forth the armies of her demigods and champions an age bright with beautiful heroic forms, loud with the trampling of armies and war-steeds, with the roar of chariot-wheels and the shoutings of warriors—in the North the Red Branch, in the South the Ernai* or Clan Dēga*, in the West Queen Meave and her Champions, and in the South-east that mysterious Half-Ked Meave and her martial grooms. From what dragon's teeth and when sown sprang forth this warlike crop?[1] An Irish bias may possibly affect

1. My own explanation is, that the ethnic history has been tampered with; that these heroes and heroines are the immediate posterity of the gods.

my judgment in this matter, though I should be sorry, indeed, that truth should, in any way and for any object, suffer through this cause, but I cannot help regarding this age and the great personages moving therein as incomparably higher in intrinsic worth than the corresponding ages of Greece. In Homer, Hesiod, and the Attic poets, there is a polish and artistic form, absent in the existing monuments of Irish heroic thought, but the gold, the ore itself, is here massier and more pure, the sentiment deeper and more tender, the audacity and freedom more exhilarating, the reach of imagination more sublime, the depth and power of the human soul more fully exhibit themselves.

To understand and test the force of my words the literature itself must be studied, if not in the original, then, in exact translations, for, neither here in this superficial sketch, nor in the more full and minute narrations of my epic series, in which the literature has been toned and condensed into the uniformity and homogeneity of a single integral composition, as I am well aware, is full justice done to the subject.

Here, in this age which surrounds the Incarnation, start forth the pre-historic or semi-historic demi-gods and champions of the Irish race.

Now, to Sualtam and Dectera* is born Setanta, surnamed Cuculain, whose glory fills the whole bardic records of the age. During his career he bears the weight of the vast epos into which the history of the times has resolved itself. Wild and improbable as is the whole narrative, weird with incursions from the supernatural world, with wizardry and enchantments, spurning the laws of nature, of space, and time, dazzling with the wild light of incredible heroisms, loud and agitated with the rush and noise of gigantic shapes writhing in superhuman battles, recalling the fabled wars of gods and Titans, or the Miltonic strife of celestial and infernal powers, the profound and vital humanity with which the whole is instinct, touches and stirs the spirit with the strangest and most unapprehended emotions. Like the moon, when through some wild obscure sky, ploughing her path amid the driving scud, a moment seen and then deep buried in the entombing clouds, but only to emerge undimmed, flooding the night with her glory; so through the spaces of that bardic sky, so through the shifting chaos of obscure epic tale, and the broken fragments of antique ruined[2] verse, ever flashes on the eye the wonderful glory of this extraordinary hero, till on the plains of Murthemney* it sets for ever in enduring night.

Yet, once again, in the unsubduable imagination, which ever accompanies the course of Irish history till the extinction of Irish independence, four centuries later a vision of the hero strikes upon the eye. St. Patrick, preaching at Tara to the assembled kings, declares that the hero and his comrades of the Red Branch, though types of all that is great and admirable to his hearers, now suffer the torments of hell, shut in for ever with the damned. Lægairey*, son of Nial*, refuses to believe, and challenges the apostle to the proof. Straightway an icy blast sweeps over the plain of Tara, cutting to the marrow of the bones with its keen fierce breath. "What means this icy blast?" cried the shuddering King. "It is a blast out of hell," answered the Saint. "Her broad gates are opened." "I see far away, eastward, a vast and snow-like mist that covers the face of the whole land. What is this, O Talkend?" "It is the Red Branch loosed from hell. The mist is the breath of their mighty men and war-steeds, and the steam of their sweat suspended above their host, and they are concealed in its folds." "Through the mist I see dark flying flakes, resembling the flight of dark birds innumerable." "They are the clods cast upward from the swift hoofs of their war-steeds," answered St. Patrick. Then, through the mist, emerge the champions of the Red Branch, and, conspicuous above all, the form of the immense hero,

2. The history and character of Cuculain and the great Champion of the age, cannot be determined from any single tale or poem. They traverse the whole literature as it treats of this age. Therefore, not one or ten tales would adequately suggest to the modern student the bardic conception of these Heroes. To the ancients each tale was imaginatively complete, being but a part of a great whole, with which they were, more or less, fully acquainted. Hence, one of the chief principles which has determined my own epic treatment of the history of Cuculain to its existing form. In telling one story I have drawn materials from many.

Cuculain, borne in his magic war-chariot, guided by Læg, armed as the bards ever described him, and drawn by the Liath Macha* and black Shanglan*, sweeping over the plain like a shadow along the slopes of some mountain range. In the ensuing interview Cuculain utters these words: "I am he who was called the Hound of Ulla*. I was not a Hound for the guarding of cattle, but a Hound for the protection of territories and the defence of nations."

I have said it is the profound and vital humanity of his career, even more than his greatness, which touches and stirs the reader. We see him as a little boy,[3] with his sword of lath* and toy shield, escaping by night from his mother's palace, eager to commence his warlike education under his uncle at Emain Macha; not creeping like [a] snail unwillingly to school, but with his little brazen hurle* driving hockey-balls before him, casting forward his toy javelin and running to catch it ere it fell, overflowing with eagerness and hope. We see him downcast and gloomy at the thought of leaving his comrades and his games, though invited by the High King and the great Knights of Ulla to feast along with them.[4] We see him knighted, the wild wayward boy, exerting his terrible strength before the hosts

3. His mother refused to allow him to go, but the boy hearing that Slieve Fuad, now the Fews mountain, near Newtown-Hamilton, Co. Armagh, lay between Dûn Dalgan* (Dundalk) and Emain Macha, escaped by night, making this mountain his sign-post. Slieve Fuad was a sacred mountain and steeped in mythical traditions. The bare fact that it is mentioned at all, in connection with Cuculain, is proof to me, recognizing the genius of the literature, that it was believed to be one of the haunted mountains in his post-mortal career. When he reached Emain Macha, Concobar and Fergus mac Roy were playing chess under the trees of the lawn.

4. Concobar and the Knights proceeding to a feast given by Culain the Smith invite the boy to join them. Setanta refuses till the game of hockey is finished. Arriving after dark at the house of the Smith, he is attacked by a huge dog, which he slays with his hurle. The Smith laments over the faithful dog, but Setanta promises to perform the duties of the dog until another equally good is procured; hence his surname Cu-Culain, the Hound of Culain.

of Ulla*, smashing the offered war-chariots and breaking the best weapons into fragments. We mark how he confounded[5] the great champion Conaill Carna, and laughed back at him discomfited, going southwards alone to wet his weapons in the blood of southern enemies, his chivalrous modesty[6] and innocence when the naked queens bar his mad path against Emain Macha, his defeat and contumely when Curoi[7] Mac Dary* cut off his long war-like tresses, after which, with boyish vanity and shame, he retired into lonely places in

5. Having procured his first war-chariot and weapons, Cuculain compelled his charioteer to drive south into Mid-Erin, that he might signalize his taking of arms by slaying some of the enemies of his country. On the frontier he is pursued by Conaill Carna, who is guarding the border, and who desires to turn him back. Cuculain, with a stone, breaks the chariot-pole of Conaill. The hero is rolled out in the dust, and the boy looks back, laughing, and taunts him with his rotten chariot gear, and so goes forward into the enemies' country. At the point where the Mattok meets the Boyne, was the Dûn of three wizard champions, sons of Nectan*. These he slays in single combat, and returns to Emain Macha with their heads. At this point, upon the Boyne, there still stands the ancient tumulus of the sons of Nectan, a beautiful grassy mound, sloping downwards to the Boyne. Knowing the genius of the literature, I confidently expected to find a mound at this place and was not disappointed.

6. A madness descends on him when he sees Emain Macha, and he designs its destruction. By the advice of Cathvah* the Druid, naked women are set before him, seeing whom, he is confused and distressed, so that the warriors capture and disarm him. Cuculain was liable to the Berserkar rage.

7. He accompanies Curoi mac Dary to the conquest of the Isle of Man. There he loves Blana, daughter of the king, also loved by Curoi. The maiden returns the love of Cuculain. Curoi mac Dary defeats and overpowers Cuculain, who was then but a stripling, and carries off Blana to his fortress in the west of Kerry—Cathair Conroi—still in existence. Cuculain, when his hair was grown, slays Curoi mac Dary, and brings away Blana to the North. The bard of Curoi follows them, and, seizing Blana, springs with her over a lofty cliff into the sea. It was the son of this Curoi mac Dary, Lewy mac Conroi, who, along with Erc, and assisted by the supernatural aid of the sons of Cailitin, afterwards slew the hero.

In another tale, this Curoi mac Dary is represented as rising out of the sea, like some elemental genius.

the North. His love for Emer[8], and the hope long deferred, his education in the isle of Skye[9] under northern warrioresses, and the strong friendship there formed with Fardia the great Fir-bolgic champion, his wars against Queen Meave, when deserted and alone, wetting nightly his sylvan couch with his tears; in single combats, ceaseless, ever renewed, he barred the gates of the North against the Four Provinces of Erin; his strife with Fardia, the most profoundly tragic scene in all literature, and his lamentations over his slain friend; his reappearance, as if from death, at the battle of Gaura, bound with bandages and sick with wounds, when he led the beaten Red Branch to victory, sweeping the armies of Queen Meave across the Shannon; his battles over all Erin, labour and suffering unceasing in the cause of his nation, the thick coming omens of approaching doom, the broken *geise** the singing of the weird god of death,[10] the weeping of all the queens of Ulla for his impending fall, the return of the Clan Cailitin[11] armed with all the powers of hell and darkness to effect his overthrow, the departure of the Red Branch, and Cuculain once

8. This was his wife. Emer's father refused leave for the marriage, stating that Cuculain had not completed his education. It was after this that he went to Scotland. Hence his appearance in the Scotch traditions, and in the Ossian of Macpherson. After his return the father was still inexorable. Cuculain bore her away from Lusk, Co. Dublin, her native place, to Dûn Dalgan (Dundalk), defeating all who attempted to bar his progress. When Cuculain first saw Emer, she was sitting on the lawn of her father's Dûn, teaching embroidery to young girls, her pupils.

9. The Amazonian Queen of the island was Scathach*, pronounced Skyah, whence Skye. When Dr. Johnson and Boswell visited the island, they were shown a well of clear delicious water, called Cucullin's well. In Macpherson the name is always so spelled. In their tour, a Highland lady repeated for them a poem descriptive of Cuculain's two war-steeds [Liath Macha and black Shanglan], which shows, that there were, even then, in Scotland, genuine traditions of the heroic age of the Gael.

10. Æd of the Golden Harp. It was foretold that he should hear him.

11. Cuculain had slain the enchanter, Cailitin. By the direction of Cailitin, Queen Meave maimed his six children, lest they should depart from the study of magic arts and become warriors. They spent their lives learning enchantments, and, returning to Erin, induced Queen Meave to invade Ulster once more. It was

more on the plains of Murthemney resisting the Four Provinces, and through that last red battle his pupil and protégé advancing against him already overwhelmed with numbers, and then the end—Cuculain dying, having made himself fast to a tall pillar-stone, "that he might not die in his sitting or lying, but that he might die in his standing" while his blood ran down to the lake,[12] where the unconscious otter lapped up the noblest blood in all the land. Through his whole career, in war and peace, in the world and out of it, in spite of all the cold dictates of reason and logic, the heart of the reader is stirred and his imagination inflamed by the contemplation of all that terrible and superhuman heroism, and the knowledge of those deep wells of pity, tenderness, and love, whence sprang those gentle deeds and words which, even more than his heroism, go to the formation of the noblest character ever presented in literature.[13]

The foregoing on Cuculain appears in O'Grady's *History of Ireland: Critical and Philosophical.*

O'Grady begins History of Ireland *with an account of Irish time that goes well beyond the Ice Age (or the "Glacialis Ierne," as O'Grady calls it). He explains the ancient system of kings, describes the ancient seat of the Ard-Rie* (high king) of Ireland as well as the coming of the Milesians from Spain and their conquest of the*

---

with enchanted weapons, furnished by them, that Erc and Lewy mac Curoi* slew the hero.

12. Lochan an Tanaigté, about five miles southwest of Dundalk. I believe the Lake and stone still exist.

13. So extraordinary is the gentle and chivalrous side of Cuculain's character that Crowe, an eminent Irish scholar, was led to suggest that the whole Cuculainian epos was recast in the post-Patrician centuries, with the object of investing the hero with the most remarkable attributes of our Lord himself. It is, however, certain that the gentler side of the heroic age issues from the pre-Christian ages side by side with the strong.

Tuátha De Danan, the predominant indigenous people of Ireland at the time. The Tuátha De Danan were driven underground, where they continued their existence as the immortals, the sídhe *or fairies. The coming of the Milesians may have actually happened, but the details of their arrival in Ireland are enshrouded in myth. Just before O'Grady introduces Cuculain, he explains the political tensions between the Red Branch Ultonians under Concobar (inhabitants of present-day Ulster) and the Olnemacta under Queen Meave (inhabitants of present-day Connaght).*

Boyhood of Cuculain

And wears upon his baby brow the round
And top of sovereignty.
—Shakespeare[1]

Cuculain filius Sualtam, fortissimus heros Scotorum.
—Tierna[2]

Ferrogane* calls Konal Karna* the bravest of the Red Branch. Perhaps he was at the time; but his preeminence was soon to be taken away. A sun was rising before which his star was to grow pale.

Dectera, one of the sisters of Concobar Mac Nessa, married a prince whose patrimony lay along the shores of the Muirnict, and whose capital was Dûn Dalgan. They had one child, a boy, whom they named Setanta.

As soon as Setanta was able to understand the stories and conversation of those around him, he evinced a passion for arms and the martial life, which was so premature and violent as to surprise all who knew him. His thought for ever ran on the wars and achievements of the Red Branch. He knew all the knights by name, the appearance and bearing of each, and what deeds of valour they had

1. *Editors' note*: William Shakespeare, *Macbeth*, ed. Barbara A. Mowat and Paul Werstine (New York: Simon & Schuster, 2013), 4.1.87–88.

2. *Editors' note*: "Cuculain, son of Sualtam, greatest of Scottish heroes." Attributed to Tierna, Abbot of Conmacnois, eleventh century. Aside from in O'Grady's *History of Ireland*, this quotation is also given in *The Irish Fairy Book* (London: Fisher Unwin, 1909), 56.

severally performed. Emain Macha, the capital of the Clanna Rury, was never out of his mind. He saw for ever before his mind its moats and ramparts, its gates and bridges, its streets filled with martial men, its high-raised Dûns* and Baths, its branching roads, over which came the tributes of wide Ulla to the High King. He had seen his father's tribute driven thither, and had even longed to be one of the four-footed beasts that he beheld wending their way to the wondrous city. But above all, he delighted to be told of the great school where the young nobles of Ulster were taught martial exercises and the military art, under the superintendence of chosen knights, and of the High King himself. Of the several knights he had his own opinion, and had already resolved to accept no one as his instructor save Fergus Mac Roy, tanist* of Ulster.

Of his father he saw little. His mind had become impaired, and he was confined in a secluded part of the Dûn. But whenever he spoke to Dectera of what was nearest his heart, and his desire to enter the military school at Emain Macha, she laughed, and said that he was not yet old enough to endure that rough life. But secretly she was alarmed, and formed plans to detain him at home altogether. Then Setanta concealed his desire, but inquired narrowly concerning the partings of the roads on the way to Emania*.

At last, when he was ten years old, selecting a favourable night, Setanta stole away from his father's Dûn, and before morning had crossed the frontier of the tuath*. He then lay down to rest and sleep in a wood. After this he set out again, travelling quickly lest he should be met by any of his father's people. On his back was strapped his little wooden shield, and by his side hung a sword of lath. He had brought his ball and hurle of red-bronze with him, and ran swiftly along the road, driving the ball before him, or throwing up his javelin into the air, and running to meet it ere it fell.

In the afternoon of that day Fergus Mac Roy and the king sat together in the park that surrounded the king's palace. A chess-board was between them, and their attention was fixed on the game. At a distance the young nobles were at their sports, and the shouts of the boys and the clash of the metal hurles resounded in evening air.

Suddenly the noise ceased, and Fergus and the king looked up. They saw a strange boy rushing backwards and forwards through the crowds of the young nobles, urging the ball in any direction that he pleased, as if in mockery, till none but the very best players attempted to stop him, while the rest stood about the ground in groups. Fergus and the king looked at each other for a moment in silence.

After this, the boys came together into a group, and held a council. Then commenced what seemed to be an attempt to force him out of the ground, followed by a furious fight. The strange boy seemed to be a very demon of war; with his little hurle grasped, like a war-mace, in both hands, he laid about him on every side, and the boys were tumbling fast. He sprang at tall youths like a hound at a stag's throat. He rushed through crowds of his enemies like a hawk through a flock of birds. The boys, seized with a panic, cried out that it was one of the Tuátha from the Fairy Hills of the Boyne, and fled right and left to gain the shelter of the trees. Some of them, pursued by the stranger, ran round Concobar Mac Nessa and his knight. The boy, however, running straight, sprang over the chess-table; but Concobar deftly seized him by the wrist, and brought him to a stand, but with dilated eyes, and panting.

"Why are you so enraged, my boy?" said the king, "and why do you so maltreat my nobles?"

"Because they have not treated me with the respect due to a stranger," replied the boy.

"Who are you yourself?" said Concobar.

"I am Setanta, the son of Sualtam, and Dectera, your own sister, is my mother; and it is not before my uncle's palace that I should be insulted and dishonoured."

This was the debut and first martial exploit of the great Cuculain, type of Irish chivalry and courage, in the bardic firmament a bright particular star of strength, daring, and glory, that will not set or suffer aught but transient obscuration till the extinction of the Irish race; Cuculain, bravest of the brave, whose glory affected even the temperate-minded Tierna, so that his sober pen has inscribed, in the annals of ancient Erin, this testimony: "Cuculain filius Sualtam fortissimus heros Scotorum."

After this, Setanta was regularly received into the military school, where, ere long, he became a favourite both with old and young. He placed himself under the tuition of Fergus Mac Roy, who, each day, grew more and more proud of his pupil, for, while still a boy, his fame was extending over Ulla.

It was not long after this that Setanta received the name by which he is more generally known. Culain was chief of the black country of Ulla, and of a people altogether given up to the making of weapons and armour, where the sound of the hammer and the husky noise of the bellows were for ever heard. One day, Concobar and some of his knights, passing through the park to partake of an entertainment at the house of the armourer, paused awhile, looking at the boys at play. Then, as all were praising his little nephew, Concobar called to him, and the boy came up, flushed and shy, for there were with the king the chief warriors of the Red Branch: Leairey Bewda, with his heavy brow and deep-set, observing eyes, Fergus Mac Lēda*, King of Rathlin, Conn Mac Morna, and his friend Felim, son of Kelkar*, Cormac Conlíngas, the High King's son, and Fergus Mac Roy, besides others. But Concobar bade him come with them to the feast, and the knights around him laughed, and enumerated the good things which Culain had prepared for them. But, when Setanta's brow fell, Concobar bade him finish his game, and after that proceed to Culain's house, which was to the west of Emain Macha, and more than a mile distant from the city. Then the king and his knights went on to the feast, and Setanta returned joyfully to his game.

Now, when they were seen afar upon the plain, the smith left his workshop and put by his implements, and having washed from him the sweat and smoke, made himself ready to receive his guests; but the evening fell as they were coming into the liss*, and all his people came in also and sat at the lower table, and the bridge was drawn up, and the door was shut for the night, and the candles were lit in the high chamber.

Then said Culain, "Have all thy retinue come in, O Concobar?" And when the King said that they were all there, Culain bade one of his apprentices go out and let loose the great mastiff that guarded the house. Now this dog was as large as a calf, and exceedingly fierce, and he guarded all the smith's property outside the house, and if anyone approached the house without beating on the gong which was outside the foss*, and in front of the draw-bridge, he was accustomed to rend him. Then the mastiff, having been let loose, careered three times round the liss, baying dreadfully, and after that remained quiet outside his kennel, guarding his master's property. But inside they devoted themselves to feasting and merriment, and there were many jests made concerning Culain, for he was wont to cause laughter to Concobar Mac Nessa and his knights, yet was he good to his own people and faithful to the Crave Rue*, and very ardent and skilful in the practice of his art. But as they were amusing themselves in this manner, eating and drinking, a deep growl came from without, as it were a note of warning, and after that one yet more savage; but where he sat in the champion's seat, Fergus Mac Roy struck the table with his hand, and rose straightway, crying out, "It is Setanta"; but ere the door could be opened they heard the boy's voice raised in anger, and the fierce yelling of the dog, and a scuffling in the bawn of the liss. Then they rushed to the door in great fear, for they said that the boy was torn in pieces; but when the bolts were drawn back, and they sprang forth eager to save the boy's life, they found the dog dead and Setanta standing over him with his hurle, for he had sprung over the foss, not fearing the dog. Forthwith, then, his tutor, Fergus Mac Roy snatched him up on his shoulder, and returned with great joy into the banquet hall, where all were well pleased at the preservation of the boy, except Culain himself, who began to lament over the death of his dog, and to enumerate all the services which he rendered to him.

"Do not grieve for thy dog, O Culain," cried Setanta, from the shoulder of Fergus, "for I will perform those services for you myself until a dog equally good is procured to take the place of him I slew."

Then one, jesting, said, "Cu-Culain," and thenceforward he went by this name.

It was about this time that he was presented with a companion and attendant, Læg, son of the King of Gowra, for Rury Mōr* had brought his father a captive to the north, and his son Læg, born to him in old age, in the north, was given to Cuculain when he returned to Dûn Dalgan for the first time from Emain Macha, and he was four years older than Cuculain.

Upon Concobar Mac Nessa's ascension to the Ard-Rieship of Ulla, a great banquet is held at Emain Macha. A shrill cry rings through the city that night followed by the sounds of battle. The feast is disbanded, the king calls his counsel, and Cathvah, the druid seer, prophesies that the bride of Fedlimid, the chief bard of Ulla, will give birth to a child who will cause dissension among the Red Branch. Rather than kill this child, called Deirdré, Concobar has her secluded in a tower. With the memory of the portents fading away, Concobar loosens his control over Deirdré once she has grown to be a woman. She falls in love with Naysi (Naoise), one of the three sons of Usna, a prominent Red Branch knight. Naysi fears that the king will reprove him, for Concobar regards her as his rightful bride. Then the Clanna Usna desert Concobar and decamp to Alba, and Concobar passes a sentence of perpetual banishment. Fergus Mac Roy is disconsolate because of the absence of the sons of Usna and manages to persuade the king to reverse his sentence. Deirdré, however, fears betrayal. Despite Fergus's attempt to protect the sons of Usna, they are slain, along with Fergus's son. This leads Fergus to rebel against Concobar, taking with him two-thirds of the Red Branch knights. Though he is subdued in the civil war that follows, he ultimately flees to Olnemacta (Connaght) and joins forces with Queen Meave just as the wars of the Tan-bo-Cooalney are breaking out.*

Cuculain Is Knighted

Then felt I like some watcher of the skies
When a new planet swims into his ken.
—Keats[1]

One night in the month of the fires of Bel, Cathvah, the druid and star-gazer, was observing the heavens through his astrological instruments. Beside him was Cuculain, just then completing his sixteenth year. Since the exile of Fergus Mac Roy, Cuculain had attached himself most to the Ard-Druid*, and delighted to be along with him in his studies and observations. Suddenly the old man put aside his instruments, and meditated a long time in silence.

"Setanta," said he at length, "art thou yet sixteen years of age?"

"No, father," replied the boy.

"It will then be difficult to persuade the king to knight thee and enroll thee among his knights," said Cathvah. "Yet this must be done to-morrow, for it has been revealed to me that he whom Concobar Mac Nessa shall present with arms to-morrow, will be renowned to the most distant ages, and to the ends of the earth. Thou shalt be presented with arms to-morrow, and after that thou mayest retire again for a season amongst thy comrades, nor go out amongst the warriors until thy strength is mature."

1. *Editors' note*: John Keats, "On First Looking into Chapman's Homer," in *John Keats: Complete Poems*, ed. Jack Stillinger (Cambridge, MA: Belknap Press of Harvard Univ. Press, 1982), 34, ll. 9–10.

The next day Cathvah procured the king's consent to the knighting of Cuculain. Now, on the same morning, one of his grooms came to Concobar Mac Nessa, and said, "O Chief of the Red Branch, thou knowest how no horse has eaten barley, or ever occupied the stall where stood the divine steed which, with another of mortal breed, in the days of Kimbay Mac Fiontann, was accustomed to bear forth to the battle the great war-queen, Macha Monga-Rue*; but ever since that stall has been empty, and no mortal steed hath profaned the stall in which the deathless Lia Macha was wont to stand. Yet, O Concobar, as I passed into the great stable on the east side of the court-yard, wherein are the steeds of thy own ambus, and in which is that spot since held sacred, I saw in the empty stall a mare, grey almost to whiteness, and of a size and beauty such as I have never before seen, who turned to look upon me as I entered the stable, having very gentle eyes, but such as terrified me, so that I let fall the vessel in which I was bearing curds for the steed of Konaul Clareena, and she approached me, and laid her head upon my shoulder, making a strange noise."

Now, as the groom was thus speaking, Cowshra Mend Macha*, a younger son of Concobar, came before the king and said—"Thou knowest, O my father, that house in which is preserved the chariot of Kimbay Mac Fiontann, wherein he and she, whose name I bear, the great queen that protects our nation, rode forth to the wars in the ancient days, and how it has been preserved ever since, and that it is under my care to keep bright and clean. Now, this day at sunrise, I approached the house, as is my custom, and approaching, I heard dire voices, clamorous and terrible, that came from within, and noises like the noise of battle, and shouts as of warriors in the agony of the conflict, that raise their voice with short intense cries as they ply their weapons, avoiding or inflicting death. Then I went back terrified, but there met me Minrowar, son of Gerkin, for he came but last night from Moharne, in the east, and he went to look at his own steeds; but together we opened the gate of the chariot-house, and the bronze of the chariot burned like glowing fire, and the voices cried out in acclaim, when we stood in the doorway, and the light streamed into the dark chamber. Doubtless, a great warrior will appear amongst the Red Branch, for men say that not for a hundred years have these voices been heard, and I know not for whom Macha sends these portents, if it be not for the son of Sualtam, though he is not yet of an age to bear arms."

Thus was Concobar prepared for the knighting of Cuculain.

Then in the presence of his court, and his warriors, and the youths who were the comrades and companions of Cuculain, Concobar presented the young hero with his weapons of war, after he had taken the vows of the Red Branch, and having also bound himself by certain gæsa. But Cuculain looked narrowly upon the weapons, and he struck the spears together, and clashed the sword upon the shield, and he brake the spears in pieces, and the sword, and made chasms in the shield.

"These are not good weapons, my King," said the boy.

Then the king presented him with others that were larger and stronger, and these, too, the boy brake into little pieces.

"These are still worse, O son of Nessa," said the boy, "and it is not seemly, O Chief of the Red Branch, that on the day that I am to receive my arms I should be made a laughing-stock before the Clanna Rury, being yet but a boy."

But Concobar Mac Nessa exulted exceedingly when he beheld the amazing strength and the waywardness of the boy, and beneath delicate brows his eyes glittered like glittering swords as he glanced rapidly round on the crowd of martial men that surrounded him; but amongst them all he seemed himself a bright torch of valour and war, more pure and clear than polished steel. But he beckoned to one of his knights, who hastened away and returned, bringing Concobar's own shield and spears and sword out of the Tayta Brac*, where they were kept, an equipment in reserve. And Cuculain shook them and bent them, and clashed them together, but they held firm.

"These are good arms, O son of Nessa," said Cuculain.

Then there were laid forward a pair of noble steeds and a war-car, and the king conferred them on Cuculain. Then Cuculain sprang into the chariot, and standing with legs apart, he stamped from side to side and shook and shook, and jolted the car until the axle brake, and the car itself was broken to pieces.

"This is not a good chariot, O my King," said the boy.

Then there were led forward three chariots, and all these he brake in succession.

"These are not good chariots, O Chief of the Red Branch," said Cuculain. "No brave warrior would enter the battle or fight from such rotten foot-hold."

Then the king called to his son Cowshra Mend Macha and bade him take Læg, and harness to the war-chariot, of which he had the care, the wondrous grey steed, and that one which had been given him by Kelkar, the son of Uther, and to give Læg a charioteering equipment to be charioteer of Cuculain. For now it was apparent to all the nobles and to the king that a lion of war had appeared amongst them, and that it was for him that Macha had sent these omens.

Then Cuculain's heart leaped in his breast when he heard the thunder of the great war-car and the mad whinnying of the horses that smelt the battle afar. Soon he beheld them with his eyes, and the charioteer with the golden fillet of his office, erect in the car, struggling to subdue their fury. A grey long-maned steed, whale-bellied, broad-chested, behind one yoke, a black, tufty-maned steed behind the other.

Like a hawk swooping along the face of a cliff when the wind is high, or like the rush of the March wind over the smooth plain, or like the fleetness of the stag roused from his lair by the hounds, and covering his first field, was the rush of those steeds when they had broken through the restraint of the charioteer, as though they galloped over fiery flags, so that the earth shook and trembled with the velocity of their motion, and all the time the great car brayed and shrieked as the wheels of solid and glittering bronze went round, for there were demons that had their abode in that car.

The charioteer restrained the steeds before the assembly, but nay-the-less a deep purr, like the purr of a tiger, proceeded from the axle. Then the whole assembly lifted up their voices and shouted for

Cuculain, and he himself, Cuculain, the son of Sualtam, sprang into his chariot, all armed, with a cry as of a warrior springing into his chariot in the battle, and he stood erect and brandished his spears, and the war-sprites of the Gæil* shouted along with him, for the Bocanahs and Bananahs and the Geniti Glindi, the wild people of the glens, and the demons of the air, roared around him, when first the great warrior of the Gæil, his battle-arms in his hands, stood equipped for war in his chariot before all the warriors of his tribe, the kings of the Clanna Rury and the people of Emain Macha. Then Cuculain bid Læg let the steeds go, and they flew away rapidly, and three times they encircled Emain Macha. Then said Cuculain—

"Where leads the great road yonder?"

"To Ath-na-Forarey and the border of the Crave Rue," said Læg.

"And wherefore is it called 'the Ford of the Watchings'?" said Cuculain.

"Because," said Læg, "there is always one of the king's knights there keeping ward and watch over the gate of the province."

"Guide thither my horses," said Cuculain, "for I have sworn not to lay aside my arms to-day until I have wetted them in the blood of one of the enemies of my tribe; and who is it who is over the garrison this day?"

"It is Konal Karna who commands there this day," said Læg.

Now, as they were drawing near to the ford, the watchman heard the rolling of the chariot and the trampling of the horses, and they sent word to Konal that a war-chariot was approaching from Emain Macha, but Konal came out of the Dûn with his people, and when he saw Cuculain in the war-car of the king, and his glittering weapons around him, he began to laugh, and said,

"Is it arms the boy has taken?"

And Cuculain said, "Indeed it is, and I have sworn not let them back into the Tayta Brac until I have wetted them in the blood of one of the enemies of Ulla."

Then Konal ceased laughing and said, "You shall not do this, Setanta, for you shall not be permitted," and he held back the horses, but Cuculain forced the horses onwards, and Konal fell back.

Then cried Konal to his charioteer, "Harness my horses, for if this mad boy ventures into the territory of the enemy and meets with hurt I shall never be forgiven by the Ultonians." Now the territories of Mid-Erin were hostile to Concobar through the expatriation and defeat of Fergus.

But the horses were quickly yoked, and Konal Karna dashed through the ford, and straightway he came up to Cuculain and drave for awhile abreast of the boy, urging him to return. Then Cuculain stood up on both feet with his legs far apart in the car, and raising high above his head in his hands a large stone which Læg had picked from the highway, he dashed it with all his force on the pole of Konal Karna's chariot, and the pole was broken in twain, and the chariot fell down, and the chief of the Red Branch, Konal Karna, the beauty of the Ultonians, was rolled out of the chariot upon the road, and was defiled with dust.

"Do you think that I can throw straight?" cried Cuculain; "and now that you remind me, it is one of the vows of our order never to go out with insecure trappings, rotten chariot-poles, or the like."

Then Konal got up out of the dust, and swore that if a step would save Cuculain's head from the men of Meath* he would not take it.

But Cuculain laughed again, and Læg urged on the steeds. Now as they drew near the Boyne and the point where it receives the waters of the Mattok, there was a great Dûn. In this Dûn lived three brothers, the three sons of Nectan, renowned amongst the tribes of Meath for valour and strength. Then as they drew nigh the Dûn, Cuculain shouted insults and challenges with a loud voice, for the brothers had seen the war-car of Concobar Mac Nessa far away, and their own chariots were prepared, and they had despatched messengers on every side to cut off the retreat of the men of Ulla. Then Læg checked the horses, and Cuculain descended upon the ground, and fitted an iron bullet to his sling, and he slung and killed the first of the warriors, and slung again and killed the second, and he slung the third time with all his might against the warrior, who was almost upon them, his strong shield held before him, while he crouched down in the chariot, and the iron bullet passed through the bronze shield and through his forehead, and went out behind. Then Cuculain drew his sword, and ran and cut off the heads of the slain, and sprang into the chariot, and Læg flogged the steeds, who flew northwards again, swifter than the wind, for already they saw signals and fires, and horsemen galloping across the country to intercept their passage to the north. But they escaped out of the jaws of the enemy, and reached Ath-na-Forarey, and when Konal saw the heads of the men of Meath, and recognized who were those warriors, he was filled with wonder, and he sent men-of-war to conduct him back to Emain Macha, and the whole city came out to welcome the young knight. Then his arms were hung up in the Tayta Brac, but Cuculain himself went back to his comrades, and he slept with them, and did not go out with the Red Branch.

The Donn Cooalney

I met a lady in the meads,
Full beautiful, a fairy's child.
—Keats[1]

Like a bright star, when the wind is high, revealing and concealing itself, a moment seen, and then again deep-buried in the driving clouds, Cuculain is revealed and hidden, crossing the spaces of the bardic sky, ere attaining the region where he blazes out with surpassing splendour, dimming all the lesser lights in that heroic age. We see him still a boy helping to subdue Mananan's* isle in the Muirnict, or sacking the Dûn of Curoi Mac Dary, or learning subtle feats of arms under Skaáh*,the Amazon of the northern seas, or, in spite of obstacles, bearing away with his swift steeds the beautiful daughter of the Brugh-Fir* of Lusk*, or, like another Samson, thinking it a little thing to raise the wall-pillars of Bricrind's* Dûn, that his wife Emer might come in when the warriors of Concobar shut to the doors of the great Dûn, fearing a strife amongst the Red Branch, year after year, his fame waxing greater, if not throughout Eiré, at least amongst his own people, though as yet but a stripling.

Now, all this time, the sovereignty of Aileel and Meave was growing stronger over the regions west of the Shannon, and after the expatriation of Fergus, when he entered into the service of Queen

1. *Editors' note*: John Keats, "La Belle Dame sans Merci," in *John Keats*, 270, ll. 12–14.

Meave, the borders of their realm extended further into the heart of Erin, so that many foreign chieftains in the uttermost parts of the island entered under her protection, and her name and power were felt from the borders of the Crave Rue to the southern sea. For the queen, she ever went out to war beside her lord, hurling the javelin like a man-of-war, and evermore were martial works a delight to her, the hosting and the battle, the subjugation of foreign kings, the driving away of booty and lines of weeping captives, and her authority extended over the Four Provinces of Erin. For age came slowly upon her lord, and his strength was relaxed, but the flush of a divine origin made full her veins, and her eyes waxed not dim for years, nor was her authority diminished, and ever she marshalled her warriors, and went out to battle in their midst, and Fergus, the exile, was the captain of her battalions under her. But the Clans of Ulla alone refused to give her honour, for the Red Branch held the province firm under the authority of their mighty king; and as when the founder casts many pieces of rusty metal into the furnace, and they come forth one strong and shining bar, so was the province of Ulla beneath its king.

Now, Meave had many herds of cattle and flocks of sheep, nor neglected she the arts of peace, and amongst her herds was a snow-white bull of a pure and noble breed, brought from overseas in her ships, and many an ounce of red gold, and many finely-woven garments, and hard swords, had she given in barter for the Fionbannah. But the Ultonians also imported from overseas a bull of the purest and noblest breed that ever came into Erin, and he was the marvel of all who beheld him, for his exceeding size, strength, and beauty. And not without a divine discernment was the Donn Cooalney, for it was his pleasure each day to see armed youths play at arms before him, and to hear harpers harping, and the recitation of noble tales; but at night in his keep he loved music sweeter than the harp, and it filled the whole cantred*, and some say that he had the gift of speech. Like a god was he honoured by all the Gæil, and Dary, King of Southern Cooalney, was he who had the custody of the bull. Blacker than the cock-chaffer was the Donn Cooalney, there was no white spot upon his body.

When Meave saw the honour in which he was held, and how her vassals and tributary kings went often to Ulla, and how her authority was imperilled, she resolved to possess herself of the bull; therefore, she sent Fergus Mac Roy as an ambassador, beseeching the King of Cooalney that he would permit the bull to be brought to her to Rath Cruhane*, that his blood might be mingled with the herds of the Olnemacta*, and that he would be received with all honour, and restored back straightway with an armed escort. Nevertheless, she concealed another mind, and revealed it not to Fergus, for she feared him. Then Fergus took horses and horsemen, and fared eastward, and on the third day he reached the Dûn of the King of Cooalney. It was night, and the bridge of the loss had been drawn up, filling the gateway at the other side, so they beat upon the brazen gong, and at the noise, the three sons of Dary—Ros and Fiechna and Iomna—came down, and received Fergus and his people hospitably.

Then was the old king glad when he knew who it was that was come unto him, even the mighty Fergus Mac Roy, and how the great queen in the west had sent him an ambassador to himself, and he arose from the place where he was crouched before the fire with alacrity, and shrilly ordered a feast to be prepared, and the great candles to be lit, the bards and jugglers to be summoned, and the chess-tables set in order, and ever he bustled to and fro with many words, and oftentimes approached Fergus with assiduous hospitality; and though his sons would gladly have conversed with the renowned warrior, and he with them, he would not suffer them, but ever despatched them to and fro; and many times he declared that though Concobar Mac Nessa might make him an exiled king, yet would he send the Donn Cooalney westward to the great queen, and the brows of the young princes darkened when they heard it.

After that, supper was set before Fergus and his knights, and the old king sat beside Fergus, and related to him how he, above all the Ultonians, had been elected to the custody of the Donn Cooalney, and how the chieftains of Erin came humbly to him beseeching him that they might be permitted to see the bull; and he brought to Fergus a bard who chanted the pedigree of the bull, and he related minutely all the habits of the Donn Cooalney, even to such as by themselves were not agreeable to hear. Then at last Fergus, for the ruddy ale was circling in his veins, and his mind was hot and choleric, laughed aloud, and uttered words in which the scoff was thinly veiled. This, when the king perceived, he was enraged; but dissembled, and presently he rose up and left the hall, striding wrathfully amongst the hounds and servants. Also there came one to him and said, "The horsemen who have come with Fergus Mac Roy are openly boasting that it was through fear that you consented to send away the bull." But this was a device of the king's sons [i.e., the sons of Dary], for they feared the wrath of the High King, and they themselves were knights of the Crave Rue. Then the king would have hastened back to let loose upon Fergus the flood of anger which had gathered in his breast, but the young men suffered him not.

There, then, Fergus and his people slept in the Dûn, unconscious of the change; but in the morning, when the strangers were outside the foss and rampart, the people of the Dûn suddenly drew up the bridge, and bade them return back empty to the queen, for that he should not bring away the bull. Then was Fergus mightily enraged, but nay-the-less, he departed, and fared rapidly westward, and on the third day arrived at Rath Cruhane; and when he related all to the queen, she wept tears of bitterness and anger, and reviled Fergus Mac Roy.

Then Meave sent messengers, through the Four Provinces, to all who were confederate with her, or feared her, and from Eyrus to Cahirmán, and from the borders of the Crave Rue to Oilean Arda Nemed, and the utmost limits of Borda Lu, there was a stirring and commotion, as when the summer wind shakes the forest with its leaves. For out of every rath, green-sided and fossed, and out of every strong cathair came forth the warlike children of Milith, with their weapons and their bravery, their horsemen, and scythed* chariots. Fiacha Mac Fireaba and Eiderkool*, headstrong and silly, Nathcrandal, with his salves and incantations, and lying druids, and strong Bras Mac Firb, Lord of the Osree. From the pleasant harbour in the south-west, where the Isle of Bera raises its lofty head out of the sea, came the two sons of Neara*. Young were they and brave, and eager for the war, but they escaped not the red hands of Cuculain when he met them in the forest advancing in front of the host. Out of the east came Bron and Breena, ruthless warriors, joint kings of Ben Edar, and they took tribute from the timid merchants of Bal-a-Clia. With a fierce crew came they, thirsting for the destruction of the Clanna Rury. Not so warlike came Lon, and Uala, and Dill, the three sons of Gara, with their bards; from the wooded Lake of Derryvara, they came, and they were dear to the Shee, for that their people had cherished the unhappy children of Lear*, when they abode swan-like in the lake, lurking in the coverts along the shore, and Lehâne, of the children of Ith*, whose white Dûn glittered amid its trees above the waters of the Bandon. Lewy Mac Neesh*, the true friend of Cuculain, and Fir-Mac-Be*, the false friend, and Fireaba Larna, with arrows by his side, and songs in his mouth, light as a gossamer, from the sources of the Lua; Lok Mac Favash, King of the Shiel Heber, o'er whom fluttered unseen the daughter of Ernemine, a spectre terrible and foul; but she did not escape the spear of Cuculain, though she vexed him. Dûn Coffey was his palace and capital, and strongly he governed his territories; the sons of Kior from the Berba, and of Cumeyrga from that sweet vale among the Galtees*, down which rolls the Aherlow.

But out of Olnemacia, out of the ancestral territories of Aileel and his kindred clans, came the six strong sons of Magach, the son of the Horse, Ket, and Mohcorb, and Awlin, Endee and Skanal, and Atga; and there came Cormac Conlíngas, he that escaped out of the massacre in which Conairey Mor was slain, the ally he, and dear friend of Fergus. Also there came bands of the Fianna*, fair, pure warriors, for out of every mountain, dell, and river, and sacred forest, and out of their haunts upon the sea shore, congregated the lesser Fianna, putting on vulnerable flesh to assist the great queen. But the greater Fianna cared not for the children of Milith, but disregarded them altogether.

Then all these came together with their battalions to Magh Ai*, and the four plains of Ai, Moa and Markeen, Sleshin and Keeltān, were filled with the uproar of the warriors, the whinnying of horses, and the creaking of the innumerable chariots.

But Meave was troubled in her mind as she thought of the great prowess of the Red Branch, and how the province was bound together, firm and strong, beneath its king. Therefore, while the kings of Olnemacia and the foreign confederates were gathering themselves together to the four plains of Magh Ai, Queen Meave set forth to go to Moy Tura, to consult with the prophet that dwelt there, and she left Aileel sitting in the door of the Dûn, looking forth with dim eyes, and his heart was warmed when he heard the martial din around him, and she left Fergus moving about among the battalions upon the plain, distinguishable from afar, and Cormac Conlíngas directing the evolutions of a squadron of swift chariots.

But this time the vision of the prophet was darkened, and he said no intelligible word, save that the brains of Mesgœra* alone would slay Concobar, but of the result of the war he spake not, but unmeaning noises came out of his mouth. Then the High Queen was troubled and disturbed, for a great fear came upon her, and she bade the charioteer urge the steeds back again to Magh Ai, but in spite of shame she bowed her lofty head, gold-crowned, into the chariot and wept. But anon, weeping, she was aware that a maiden of divine aspect sat at her feet in the chariot, weaving a strange-hued web, and, as she wove, she sang. Fair and sweet was the maiden, with smooth, gold hair, the ruddy blood glowing in her tender nails.

"Who art thou?" said the queen.

"I am Faythleen the prophetess, I am the guardian of thy race; from sacred Tara have I now come, and I am weaving good for thee, my queen." "How look my hosts southwards in Magh Ai?"

"Bloodied all, and crimson."

"And how look the Clanna Rury, in the north?"

"Bloodied all, and crimson. I see the young hero of Murthemney—Culain's swift hound—his war-mace in his hand, beating down the Four Provinces. Beware of him, my queen. Beware of the youth with the deadly sling. Make no bargain with him, for that bargain thou shalt rue. Hence must I speed away quickly, to spread amazement in the hosts of Ulla. They shall not return to their right mind for a season. And do thou hasten forward the expedition, for thou shalt conquer the province ere they be aware."

So saying, she passed away quickly, like a shadow that flees across the plain when the March wind blows, and Meave returned to Magh Ai. And when they saw the royal squadron, and the queen's chariot in the midst, the whole host shouted. Then they drew back the covering of the chariot, and the great queen stood erect in her chariot, her spear in her right hand, and the golden cath-barr* upon her head, and before her great bosom a round shield, and, on high above the glittering shield, her countenance, serene and pure.

Now Fergus Mac Roy was moving through the whole host, marshalling and directing, conspicuous among the warriors as an antlered stag that stalks amid the herd, and his voice resounded above the din and clamour of Magh Ai. But when the royal cavalcade appeared from the north, and the whole host was confused, and shouted, he bore it with difficulty, and turning half round, and leaning on his spear, looked askance and slightly to where the great queen stood erect armed in her chariot; but when she saw Fergus, her pale, pure countenance was disturbed, and she sat down quickly, and bid them draw to the covering of the chariot, and urge the steeds onward to the royal Dûn. Now Aileel sat in the doorway, and Orloff, their youngest son, sat by his side, preparing a scourge for his steeds. With a shrill voice Aileel chid his wife; but she answered softly, and led him into the Dûn, for it was evening.

In the chapter "The Donn Cooalney," Queen Meave consolidates her forces, and the prophetess Faythleen tells her that she foresees her hosts all bloodied and crimson, with Cuculain reigning triumphant. At the same time, Concobar is at Emain Macha brooding on the war to come. An "insane" mist has found its way into the dûns *of the great Red Branch chiefs and all are feeling glazed and uncertain, fighting each other or engaged in "unreal fights," while their real enemy, Meave's host, is on the move. Leairey Bewda, unaffected* *by the mist, is able to begin countering it. He and his men, following an ancient Fomorian* custom, build a fire to consume the "druidic cheat" and seal the ashes in an urn, which they intern in an underground chamber, surrounded by a great cromlech. The damage has been done, however, for the druid spells have thrown all the great chiefs—even those around the lake of the sacred cow, Donn Cooalney—into states of confusion and disarray. Meanwhile, the hosts of Queen Meave advance toward Murthemney.*

Only a Name

Have ye seen his face?
Have ye beheld his chariot?
—Keats[1]

On the next day the whole host of Queen Meave was put in motion, and the sons of Neara, riding in one chariot, went on in front, and they came that evening to Delvin and camped there, and after that they went on continuously, and they crossed the Shannon and the Inny, and went past the great lakes of Meath, and thence past the rath of Odba, wife of Herēmon*, and they were within two days' march of the frontier, and yet saw no sign of the Red Branch. But on the morrow after that, the sons of Neara met the tracks of two chariots, faring southwards in the direction of Tara, and they followed the tracks and came to a glade in the forest, and they saw that those whose were the chariots had slept there that night, and the glade was partly rough and stony, and partly good pasture, and they saw that two horses had been tethered in one part, and two in the other. Moreover, they saw that one of the chariots had departed thence towards Emain Macha, and the other in the direction of Tara. Then they returned to their route, going on always to Cooalney. But the host was very great, and the place woody, and they spent that day hewing down trees and tearing away brushwood, and the passage that they made through that wood was called ever after, the

1. *Editors' note:* John Keats, *Hyperion*, in *John Keats*, 262, ll. 233–34.

Track of the Chariots. Now the next day the sons of Neara advancing again, came upon the wheel-tracks of a chariot going on before them to Cooalney, and they said: "It is the same chariot that went southwards yesterday to Tara." Then they pursued the track till they came to an ancient pillar-stone, the grave of some warrior slain long since in the glades of that forest, and upon the pillar was a hoop of fresh-cut osier, and upon it Ogham characters, newly inscribed, and in the evening they came to the council of the kings, having the hoop in their hand. Now Aileel sat at the end of the pavilion nodding, and the silver wand trembled in his hand, and the queen sat upon his right hand, and Fergus stood upon his left hand, wrangling with the assembled kings; but the queen was incensed at the authority with which he spake. Then when she saw the sons of Neara, she smiled and beckoned them to herself, for they had been brought up with her own sons, and she took the hoop from their hands and gave it to the Ard-druid to read, but he could not. Then it was handed to Fergus, and with difficulty did they persuade him to look into the Ogham, for the kings desired one thing, and Meave supported them, and he was enraged with her and them. But when he read the Ogham, he started as one starts when stung by an ant, and inquired of the sons of Neara how they came by the hoop, and they told him.

"It is an Ogham taught by Cathvah to the youths of the Ultonians," said Fergus. "Cuculain is the name inscribed on the hoop. He is the youngest of the Knights of the Bed Branch."

"Then, have we not much to fear?" said Meave.

To return to Cuculain. In his paternal territory, when not at Emain Macha, or in the service of Concobar, he ruled his father's clan, having been elected to the kingship of Cooalney by the chiefs, and inaugurated by Concobar. Very gradually he withdrew from the control of Dectera, the battalion of the territory, and the governance of the port and shipping, and the imposition of the tributes. He released his father from his confinement, and always Sualtam moved around the territory along with his son, but avoided Dectara his wife.

Now, at the time that the host of Meave had commenced their march eastward, Cuculain rose early one day, for he had made an appointment with Faythleen, the deceitful prophetess of Tara, and in the grey of the morning he set forth from Dûn Dalgan alone; but in the chariot Emer had put many things, as for a long journey. Presently Cuculain, hearing wheels, looked round, and he saw his father in his chariot following behind. Then was Cuculain displeased, nevertheless he did not send his father back. Thus they rode on together, and crossed the frontier of the province, which was the Oun Dia, and Cuculain looked back and saw the druidic mist covering the province like a great fleece, and he marvelled what it meant, and so they rode on, and when it was evening they came to a glade in the forest, and Cuculain let down his father's chariot and arranged the rugs for him to sleep, and he tethered his father's horses in the northern grassy part of the glade, and his own among the moss and stones and coarse grass. Now, very early the next day, in the still morning, he awoke, and heard, as it were, the clamour of a mighty host, and he climbed up into the branches of a lofty elm-tree, and, far away, he saw the standard of Queen Meave, and the banners of the sons of Heber* and Ith, and the standard of Tara, and of the children of Leairy Lore, and the whole host preparing to set out north-eastward to Cooalney, to the borders of the Crave Rue. Then Cuculain made haste and came down, swinging rapidly from branch to branch like a wood cat, and he awoke his father, and he bid him urge his steeds swiftly northward to Ath-na-Forarey, and to Emain Macha, and to arouse the Red Branch far and wide, for that the Four Provinces of Erin were gathered together for the devastation of Ulla. Then Sualtam made haste and scourged his steeds, and they flew northward swiftly, but Cuculain held on upon his course southward. Nevertheless he found not the deceitful prophetess where she had appointed, and he was enraged, for it was to gratify Emer he had gone thither, and the same night he travelled northwards again, and skirted the sea, and went round the forest, and preceded the Four Provinces, moving on before them to Cooalney. Then he cut down a twig with his sword, and notched his name upon the twig, and made a hoop of it, which hoop was found by the sons of Neara and brought unto Fergus. For he said, "I shall give them warning, and not fall upon them unawares."

Now Cuculain was not quite alone upon that expedition, for there were with him two companions, yielding, indeed, no great succour in war, but whose clear voices and comradeship he did not despise when loneliness and sorrow encompassed him after each fierce combat at the Oun Dia, when alone he held the gates of the province against the men of Meave. For at Dûn Dalgan, while he was yet a boy, there was an old man, a worker in leather, who wrought sandals and shoes for the household of Dectara. He had no children, and his wife was long since dead, and he had lived alone in his house by the wayside, on the road leading out of Dûn Dalgan, eastward to Drum Rury, to the patrimony of Bricrind the satirist. But both himself and his father before him had been accustomed to rear singing birds, nor did they confine them in prisons of wicker-work or twisted findruiney*, and the birds sung in and around the house enlivening the mind of the old man. Now, Cuculain was accustomed to sit with him, and the old man taught him the mysteries of his art, so that, while yet a child, he became skilful in that craft, and he wrought at the old man's side. Moreover, Æd Enver boasted to him that he was of the race of Luprachān*, a descendant of Dana, who, in ancient days, occupied Tara, and he told how the Clanna Luprachān ruled widely over Erin, teaching noble arts to the Gæil, and how they dwelt now immortal in fairyland. So spake the old man, and he taught the boy also much concerning birds, and the birds came to Cuculain equally with the old man. Now when Cuculain was raised to the Rie-ship of the tuath, and all men brought him presents, Æd Enver, who was now very aged, and received from his clan the maintenance which was the old man's right according to the law, came to the palace and presented Cuculain with two young blackbirds of the purest breed, and these attached themselves closely to Cuculain. Vale Darig and Ceolān were their names, and they accompanied him on this journey. But after the fight with Lōk Mac Favash they were no more seen, whether that they were washed away in the spray of that fierce conflict, or, fluttering round were smit by the weapons, or, being terrified, had flown afar, but Cuculain was sorrowful that night, being alone in the hollow forest.

Then the next day the host of Meave moved onward once more, and the sons of Neara advancing not far from the camp, and following the track of the chariot that preceded them, came to where was a spear fixed deep in the ground; and it seemed as if two-thirds of the spear was sunk into the hard ground, and one third only remained above. Now, that morning Fergus had gone round to the out-posts, and had given strict injunctions not to slay the man whose chariot track they had seen, but that he should be taken alive; and as the sons of Neara were wondering at the cause why the spear had been fixed there in the ground, Fergus and his people came up to them. But Fergus uttered a cry of joy when he beheld the spear where it stood erect between the two wheel-tracks, and he saw that it was cast from the hand of the warrior turning round in his chariot, as he rode, to be a challenge and attestation of his prowess to the host of Meave; but the sons of Neara, light-chattering, were curious to know why Cuculain should have delayed to drive that spear into the ground, for they said it was driven in with blows. Yet it was plain that the chariot had not stopped, and there was no foot-mark, nor was the extremity of the spear marred at all as with blows. Then the sons of Neara urged on their horses; nevertheless, their haviour was not so gallant as before, for their minds misgave them, and they were astonished at the great size of the spear-tree.

Then Fergus Mac Roy found Orloff among the van in his gilded chariot, while he danced along the chariot-pole, brandishing his light spears, and Fergus bade him return, and he would not; wherefore he drave him back to the host with blows, and he returned weeping to the queen, where she rode with chariots before her, and behind, and on each side of her, and she was incensed. Then a vast rumour diffused itself through the host concerning Cuculain, and that night in the council there was dissension, and the voice of Fergus might be heard through the camp contending with the kings of the Four Provinces. For Fergus desired that the great warriors of the host should form the van, and the kings derided him. But when the council was dismissed, Fergus returned, and he found the queen alone in the pavilion, and he addressed her and said:—

"Fitter were it for thee, O queen, to have remained in thy own Dûn and seen to the government of thy household, than to march upon this foray with thy lord, silly from age, and thy son, Orloff, silly from youth. At home in thy own palace thou shouldst have remained with these, for here thou art a disturbing influence, and partest from me the authority over the loose array of this great host. For thou art not thyself fit to govern men, and make provision to secure victory, or to give the necessary commands in battle, and against me, who am, thou dost countenance the headstrong and mutinous kings. And this thou too thyself well knowest, but it is a delight to thee to appear before all the people with thy weapons and martial bravery, and to hear them shout when they see thee shield-bearing in thy great war-chariot, and thy head gold-crowned above the host. For it is because of this, and not for thy knowledge of war and government, that the clans of Aileel have not long since put him aside, and raised the Tanist to the Ard-Rieship of the province; for with thy fair face and thy stature beyond women, and thy shining shield, thou hast bewitched them, and also the far coming kings of the south. For if thou hast sometimes in the edge of battle cast thy spear into the hostile ranks, well knowedst thou that thy chariot was thick-ringed with warriors, the mightiest in the land, and not one of those that would not die a thousand deaths rather than that one tress of thy yellow hair should receive any hurt. And no such great accomplishment is this of thine, for many a time in warlike forays have I seen women contend with spear and shield against opposing warriors with more cunning and ferocity than have been granted to thee. And this I tell thee, for thy greater behoof. Like an eagle that hovers above the moor-fowl on the mountain side, there hovers one above this host who delays his stroke, but will quickly deal out death. Far-shooting Cuculain, the son of Sualtam, goes before us, his sling is in his hand, and no stronger than the leaf of the sycamore will thy shield be against his bullets, and well I know he will not err if against thee he bends the Crave

Tawl*. For verily in Emain Macha have I seen him smite far aloft the wheeling swallow. Therefore, now be persuaded by me, queen, and return with thy lord and with the boy. For greatly I fear for thee when I see thee amid the host with the gold cath-barr upon thy head, thy shield far seen, and thy god-like stature, and with difficulty do I draw away my mind to the care of this great host."

Now, ere Fergus had uttered many words, the queen arose from where she sat, her fair, pure countenance marred with great anger, and with trembling hands she seized a javelin, and cast it at Fergus, but he watched, and stepped aside, and the javelin hissed through the wattled* walls, and passed out into the camp; but ere she could seize another, he ran to her, and seized her with his strong hands and forced her back into her throne, and held her still, and she spat at him. But he took up his speech where he had stopped, and went on to the end, and when he had made an end he gathered together the weapons that were at her side, and went out of the pavilion, stalking moodily to his own booth.

Now, outside the Royal Pavilion there was a throng of men, and amongst them a warrior slain, for a javelin had pierced him behind the ear; Yeoha Glûnduff was his name, and he was a Rie-damna* of the Province of Lahan*.

The Crown Tawl

Then the next day they began to draw nigh to the frontiers of the territory of Concobar Mac Nessa, and that day the best warriors in the host went together, in bodies of ten, in advance of the main army, and they sustained no hurt. In the evening they encamped, and the sun set, and not long after the moon rose and the stars began to shine, and the blue hills all round, and the wide horizon were bathed in the moony glare. Then, when the host was preparing the booths of the chieftains and their sedgy beds, cooking suppers, and cleaning chariots and horses, and a vast din arose out of the camp, suddenly there was a cry as of a warrior smitten to his death, and the whole host became silent, like the sea beneath frosty stars when its waves fall down and are still, and in that stillness was heard a faint, clear, far-off twang, mingled with hissing, followed by another cry, as of a man smitten. Then one uttered the word, "Cuculain," and the whole host was in an uproar, and numerous battalions sallied forth, scouring the forest and the hill-sides the whole night. But now in front and now behind, from the south and from the north, sounded the clear twang of the Crave Tawl, and ever some warrior cried out, smitten by the deadly bolt. Then there was held a council of the kings, and Meave was not there, but Fergus Mac Roy occupied her place on the right hand of Aileel, and the authority of Fergus was great over the kings, for Meave had sent messengers to each of them that they should obey Fergus. But when men inquired of Fergus concerning Cuculain, Fergus related the first coming of Cuculain to Emain Macha, and the dispersion of the young nobles before the king's palace, and Cormac Conlíngas took up the tale, and told how he had slaughtered the huge mastiff of Culain the smith, and acquired his surname, and how he had attached himself to Fergus above all the other knights, and other Ultonian exiles told many surprising things concerning Cuculain. Then the kings proposed that Fergus should go to him and offer a great bribe, so that he might pass over to the host of Meave, and forsake the Red Branch.

And Fergus said, "Ye will not persuade him, for when I rebelled against Concobar Mac Nessa, one, not sent by me, urged him to leave the school at Emain Macha, and come out and join our hosting, but he wept bitterly, and would not come out. Neither will you persuade him now, when he is the sworn knight of the King of Ulla."

Nevertheless, the project was pleasing to the assembled kings, and Fergus consented to bear the conditions to Cuculain. Then the next morning, ere the sun rose, Fergus mounted his chariot and drove far out in front, and he bid the charioteer guard the horses till he returned, and advanced by himself, and clomb an eminence, and lifted up his voice on high, and shouted, calling Cuculain by his old name, Setanta; and Cuculain heard him in his secret place, and he cast aside his arms, and ran through the forest, and he threw himself upon Fergus and kissed him, and wept.

Then Fergus told him the conditions which he had come bearing, and Cuculain answered resolutely that he would not forsake the Red Branch, nor the king. Then Cuculain led Fergus along with him, and brought him to his secret place, and there were his horses feeding, and his chariot, and no wheel-tracks leading thither. Then he arranged skins for Fergus, and went down to the stream below and speared two salmon, and with his sling he slew two wild geese in the marshes of the river, and he returned to Fergus and cooked them, and he took mead and ale out of his chariot, and they caroused and conversed until the evening star arose. Then Fergus went away to where was his chariot, and returned to the camp.

But amongst the assembled kings that night he told them how Cuculain had scorned their bribe, and even as he spoke, the Crave Tawl sounded from the distant hills, and the people died. But the kings said that the bribe was not sufficient, and they urged Meave to offer her daughter Fionavar in marriage, and Meave answered hotly and proudly; but after a space, she smiled an evil smile, and consented to the arrangement, and that Cuculain should be governor of Olnemacta under her, to the exclusion of her own sons, and that, if he preferred it, she would make him Monarch of Ulla, in the room of Concobar Mac Nessa.

Then Fergus arose in great wrath, and dashed his spear upon the ground, but his eyes burned like coals of fire, and his voice rattled in his throat.

"Full well I know thy meaning, and in vain wouldst thou conceal from me the thing that is in thy mind, crafty and perverse woman. Yet Cuculain thou shalt not this time ensnare to his destruction with lies. Nevertheless I am willing to go to Cuculain with these conditions if the assembled kings will guarantee their performance, and take the young hero Cuculain under their protection."

But the High Queen trembled before the wrath of Fergus, and the assembled kings, Ket the son of Magáh, Lewy Mac Neesh, and Nathcrandal, and Lok Mac Favash guaranteed the performance of the conditions, and extended their protection to Cuculain.

Then in the morning Fergus Mac Roy went forth to Cuculain's secret place, and he found Cuculain lying on the ground upon his back, with a red-billed blackbird on his finger, and he and the blackbird whistled to one another alternately, and when he saw Fergus he started to his feet, and received him hospitably as the day before. But when Fergus told him the conditions which he had come bearing, Cuculain looked down upon the ground, and traced with the point of his spear upon the ground. Then Fergus said no more, and after that they feasted and caroused till the evening star arose. Then said Fergus, "Is there any condition on which thou wilt cease slaying the people?" and Cuculain said, "There is, but it would not be seemly for me to put it forward."

After that Fergus departed, and returned to the camp, and Cuculain took his sling, and clomb to the brow of the hill, and looked northwards, and saw no sign of life throughout broad Ulla, and he was astonished at the coming not of Concobar and his knights.

But before the assembled kings, that night in Meave's camp, Fergus Mac Roy related how Cuculain had despised their conditions, and Meave said, "There are a hundred of our people slain every night, and my trackers and scouts cannot surround him; but when seen, he ever evades them with his light feet, and if my people so perish night by night, I think not many of us will cross the Shannon returning to Olnemacta, nor of our allies to their own homes. Are there any conditions which this bloody youth will accept, and so cease from his slinging and slaying?"

And Fergus said, "There is such a condition, but he refused to make it known to me, but said that we ourselves should propose it."

Then they all debated what this should be, and when they came to no result, they appealed again to Fergus, and Fergus said:

"Brave, and not bloody-minded, is Cuculain, and he loves not this nocturnal slaughter which he inflicts upon us, nightly guarding the borders of the Crave Rue. Let us make a treaty with Cuculain after this manner: That the host of Meave shall not cross the Oun Dia invading the lands of Ulla until Cuculain be subdued in single combat, and that he engage to meet a warrior each day."

Now the kings were surprised if Cuculain would accept such conditions, but nay-the-less, they and Meave ratified the proposal.

Now when it was morning, and Fergus was ascending into his chariot, he saw a youth of the camp entering his chariot also, making as though he would follow him. Then said Fergus:

"Who art thou, O youth?"

And he said, "Eiderkool, am I, a flaut* of the Clan Farna, and I desire to give my horses exercise."

"Beware that thou followest not me," said Fergus, "for I shall slay thee."

Then Fergus and his charioteer rode away northwards, and after a space Eiderkool and his charioteer went after; but in his silly heart he threatened great things, and deemed that huge renown would be his before the setting of the sun. From the shores of Inver Scena had he come, where his Dûn looked across the great mere, and chieftains not many were around him in that barren region, and he was great in his own eyes, loquacious and empty, and he buzzed around the camp like a bee. But his mother sent him forth boasting that no braver warrior followed in the Tân*, and she lamented that she had permitted him to follow arms, for that in science and poetry his excellence was as great, and that he might be Ard-Druid or Ard-Ollav* of all Erin, had he chosen to excel in those arts; and much she boasted amongst her women, and the wives of her vassals. And she trusted to a prophecy of Fiontànn, for he was Ard-Druid of the nation of Kasàr, and when all that people perished, he was preserved, and he dwelt in the dells of Carn Tuhall, leading a divine life, like the Tuátha, teaching those who resorted to him, for he conversed equally with the Shee, and with the sons of Milith, and he had eaten of the nuts of the sacred tree. Now when she wearied him, he uttered a doubtful prophecy—"that no one would go into danger so lightly as her son"; but the father of Eiderkool was a noted ollav*, and his wife was a weariness to him.

Now Fergus went forward to where Cuculain was, and Cuculain hastened to meet him. Then Fergus unfolded the terms to Cuculain, and Cuculain rejoiced when he heard. After that, Fergus returned to the camp, but ere long he observed the double track, and he feared treachery, and bade the charioteer return at full speed.

Eiderkool, on his side, had followed till the chariot of Fergus stopped, and after that he drew aside into the forest, and descending, followed Fergus Mac Roy, treading the intricacies of the labyrinth; but he went cautiously, for great was his fear of Fergus Mac Roy. Now when Fergus had departed from Cuculain, he returned to his charioteer exulting, and they gallopped up to the dell, and Cuculain looked out and saw a warrior advancing towards him, and Cuculain came out to meet him hospitably, and he inquired the cause of his coming.

"I am come to see thee," said Eiderkool, "to know whether thy fame is equal to thy deserts."

And Cuculain laughed and said, "And now having seen me, how do I appear unto you?"

And Eiderkool answered, "Thou art comely, indeed, and not unwarlike to look upon, but amongst great warriors thou wouldst not be noticed at all, nor even amongst forward striplings wouldst thou attract any considerable attention, and I believe that I myself could easily subdue thee."

And Cuculain said, "Return now, youth, unharmed to the camp, for under the protection of Fergus, my friend and tutor, hast thou come here. Therefore, I would not harm thee. Return again to the camp."

Then Eiderkool began to be very brave, and he reviled Cuculain, and stepped forward to slay him. Therefore Cuculain made haste back to where were his weapons, and facing Eiderkool, he executed a dexterous sword-stroke at the feet of Eiderkool, by which he jerked a clod of the green turf into his breast, cone-shaped, cut neatly with a rapid turn of the wrist. "Return back to the camp, now, for I would not slay thee," cried Cuculain; but he would not [return]; and after that Cuculain made a rapid stroke behind the shield of the other, and shore clean away the apple of gold into which his hair between his shoulders was fastened—for Eiderkool delighted in adorning himself. But when he still pressed on, Cuculain's anger rose, and he smote him so that he died, and his charioteer took away the body and bore it back to the camp, and Fergus met him, and turned back likewise to the camp.

Now, that night among the assembled kings, Fergus related how Cuculain had accepted the terms proposed by the Four Provinces.

Then said Meave, "I greatly desire to behold this youth, and I prythee, O Fergus, bring him down with thee into the camp, that we may see him"; and Fergus looked narrowly upon the queen, but she said:

"I meditate no guile against the youth, though my dear son, Orloff, was slain by his hands; for well I know that if he accepts those conditions, not many hours longer will he behold the sun, but these kings and myself extend to him our protection, and guarantee to him a safe departure out of the camp."

Then the next morning, ere the sun rose, Fergus set forth for the last time with chariots and warriors, and he returned with Cuculain, and Cuculain's friends who were in the camp ran forward to meet him—warriors who had been fostered at the court of Concobar Mac Nessa, ere enmity had arisen between the Red Branch and the remainder of the children of Milith, through the expatriation of Fergus, and the supremacy of the great queen—Lewy Mac Neesh, and Fir-Mac-Be, and many others, for Cuculain had many friends; but there came not Fardia, the son of Daman*, the son of Dary, chief of the western Fir-bolgs. He had learned feats of arms along with Cuculain, at the hands of Skaáh, the warrior queen of the ragged Isle, far away in the northern seas, and they had together sacked the City of Cahirmán, sailing thither in their ships, for Cuculain's territory bordered on the sea, and he had a naval station, and much shipping.

But the kings of Erin were astonished when they beheld Cuculain, for smooth and pleasant was his countenance, and his stature not great, and that day he played at goal with the men of Erin, and they gave him changes of raiment and keeves* of water in his wattled house, and he dressed himself and came in to the feast. And the great queen had pity upon him when she saw him, and knew that ere long he would be slain, guarding the frontiers of his nation, and she relented from her wrath for the slaying [of] Orloff and the sons of Neara, and she placed him between herself and Aileel at the banquet, and Cuculain hearkened to Aileel when he spake, and the old king forgot his churlishness, and conversed pleasantly with Cuculain. And on the morrow, when the time came that he should depart, the great queen kissed him before the whole host, for very gentle was the aspect of Cuculain, and all the women grieved when they saw Fergus lead away the youth to the other side of the ford.

After astonishing the kings of Erin, Cuculain enters into battle at the ford, taking on his opponents one at a time. The best warriors, even with druidic assistance, cannot beat him. On the seventh day he meets his father, Sualtam, and they drink ale and mead while Sualtam tells of his adventures. He tells of a great clamour in the king's Dûn at Emain Macha and how he rode south to raise the other chiefs to march on Cooalney. Concobar has fallen, and Leairey, by tanistry, must assume the Ard-Rieship. Meanwhile, Queen Meave and the kings of the Four Provinces hold counsel. Fergus Mac Roy shames

those who would retreat in fear from Cuculain, the "bard-loving captain of the Red Branch." Lewy Mac Neesh, chief of Clan Falva, rises up and claims he will not lift his spear against Cuculain, whom he believes Queen Meave has misjudged. Though Meave becomes enraged, Lewy does not let the charge of cowardice provoke him and stubbornly refuses to fight, even as she praises him. Meave then persuades Fireaba Larna—a man that Lewy was bound by gæsa *(in a "bond of bardic brotherhood") to avenge—to enter into combat with Cuculain. But Lewy becomes aware of the plot and launches a counterplot. He knows an old friend, a poet, Angus Lamderg, who has just killed a man in a fight at a fair, and takes the homicide into sanctuary, and Lamderg becomes one of the household. Lamderg meets Cuculain to tell him not to slay Fireaba.*

The next to face him is Lōk Mac Favash ("king of a mixed people to the south"). The battle is fierce, and the foes almost evenly matched, and though Cuculain is being tormented by a spectre ("the horrid ghoul that had accompanied him unseen from the south") and a great eel that attempts to pull him into the ford, he fends off spears and clubs. Lōk Mac Favash holds his own and enters into close combat with Cuculain, who strikes him down with a great stone, then "crushe[s] him down under the water." Meave is not happy. She arranges for Farba, the Fir-bolg, to go next, but he declines, being too proud. Then she calls for Fardia, another Fir-bolg, a people that Meave holds in contempt (they do not descend from Milith). Much effort is made to tempt him to enter into combat. But his gæsa *forbade him from dining with children of Milith. Cormac Conlíngas is sent as an envoy. But no temptation will lead him to "look in anger upon Cuculain." Fionavar finally convinces Fardia to see the Queen. After much feasting, Meave unfolds the resolution of the Saba* of her kings: Fardia shall fight Cuculain. He consents to fight in the morning, not because he fears "the druids and their hilltop satires" but because he fears he might lose his resolve. Fardia "array[s] himself in his battle dress" and goes out to meet Cuculain.*

The Affliction of Cuculain

And shapeless sights come wandering by,
The ghastly people of the realm of dream
Mocking me.
—Shelley[1]

Now, it was evening and chilly with frost, when Cuculain awoke out of the swoon, and his limbs were stiff, so that he could not walk, and he lay down again and wept, not for the pain, but for loneliness and sorrow. But after that, he essayed to move once more, and as he arose, lo, an aged woman [was] milking a very lean cow, and she sat with her back to Cuculain, and a garment drawn over her head, and Cuculain marvelled when he saw her, for he deemed that all had fled out of that land. Then he approached her, and begged that she would give him of the milk to drink, for he was very faint. But she answered that she would not give him to drink unless he blessed her. Then Cuculain smiled in spite of his faintness, and did what she desired. Thereupon she turned round and looked upon Cuculain, and Cuculain uttered a cry, for there was the face of a ghoul within the hood, and he recognised the thing that had plagued him at the ford. But with a foul noise of victory and success the spectre vanished from his sight, and the hero leaned trembling against one of the trees in the forest.

1. *Editors' note*: Percy Bysshe Shelley, *Prometheus Unbound*, in *The Complete Poetry of Percy Bysshe Shelley*, ed. Donal H. Reiman, Neil Fraista, and Nora Crook (Baltimore: Johns Hopkins Univ. Press, 2012), I.36–38.

Then he hurried through the forest fear-stricken, and he came to his place, and the horses whinnied when they heard him.

But, all that night, Cuculain's mind was clouded and disturbed, and he said that his clan had conspired against him, seeing that he was abandoned and alone, warring now for many days against the whole host of Meave, keeping ward over the gates of the province. And now too, he knew that he should die, for the thought of flight, and of the surrender of Murthemney to the waster came not at all into his noble mind. But he called upon all the Red Branch by name, lamenting loud Leairey the Victorious, and Kelkar the son of Uther, Fergus Mac Lēda, Factna Mac Mahoon, and his foster-brethren, sons of the High King, and Konal Karna, dearest of all, and his voice penetrated the starry night, for he cried out as a woman cries when him she loves has forsaken her; so in his agony Cuculain, the son of Sualtam, lifted up his voice, and the men of Meave heard him, for he said that he was forsaken, and all men leagued against him. Moreover, as the moon set, he saw faces that moved amongst the trees mocking him, and horrid things, formless and cold, estrays out of the fold of hell, wandering blots of the everlasting darkness, and there was laughter in the hollow chambers of the forest, and again the Ban-Shee* of Lōk Mac Favash smiled at him and beckoned, and the cold water-serpent clung around his feet, and all the sweet chords of his mind were torn or unstrung, and the Shee delivered him over to great affliction. For, like an army of devastators that waste and burn and drive away, leaving behind them blackened homes and streams made thick with blood, so wasted they all the pleasant tracts of his noble spirit. Now, the horses affrighted pulled madly at their tethers, but anon when he sank down like a stone they approached him wondering, and he felt their warm breath upon his face. Then the demons that affrighted him gave back, and he arose and put an arm around the neck of either steed, and stood between them trembling. With their fleet limbs, swifter than the naked winds of March, had he borne away the daughter of Manach out of Bregia*, Munfada and Rayleen Gall were their names; they were pale yellow in hue, save on the breast of one, where the wind-pipe enters the lungs, a spot of purest white. For two hundred cumals* he had purchased them, and he gave them to Emer. But with her own hands each day she fed them with barley and white curds and sweet whey; very gentle were they, and they knew the thoughts of those that loved them.

Then a milder mood came over the mind of Cuculain, and he remembered his friends who were with Meave, and how they had received him coming, and he recalled the firm friendship of Lewy Mac Neesh, and especially he thought of Fardia, the son of Daman, now warring among the Clanna Gædil* in Espân*, and, as he thought on these things, lo, the dawn trembling through the forest, and the hoar-frost glittering on the grass.

Then started forth Cuculain, and he drew from the chariot the venison which he had cooked, and ate thereof, and drank his last draught of ale, making a gurgle in his strong bare throat, and his strength revived in him. Nevertheless his countenance was hollow and wan, dull were his splendid eyes, and there was a wound in his hand and in his leg and in his left side, and his noble breast was mangled, and all his body black with dried gore.

Then he tore away the iron-work from his chariot, and filled the broken centre and upper rim of his shield, strapping it tightly with the leathern reins, and with the colg* that was by his side he hewed down a young fir-tree, and shore away the crackling branches, and cut off the top. After this he brake off the steel peak of the chariot, and sunk it into the rough spear-tree, and bound it firmly to the wood. Then arose Cuculain, the unconquerable, striding through the forest, and he wondered which of the great champions of Meave should be brought against him that day and when he came out into the open, he beheld the whole south country filled with a vast multitude, as it had been the Ænech of Taylteen or the great Feis* of Tara when the authority of the Ard-Rie is supreme, and all the tribes of Erin gather together with their kings. But he saw not at first who was the champion that had come out against him, and he advanced through the willows, and came to the edge of the ford, and looked across, and he saw Fardia, son of Daman, of the Fir-bolgs, and Fardia looked upon Cuculain, and Cuculain looked upon Fardia.

Fardia and Cuculain enter into close combat. Neither will back down. Fardia refuses to slay his foe, who refuses to retire. Cuculain sends his spear, Gæ-Bolg, plunging into Fardia. Meanwhile, Læg, Cuculain's charioteer (and slave "according to the laws of Ulla"), leaves Emain Macha and crosses the frontier as chariots and men advance in the other direction en route to defend the seat of the Red Branch. Læg carries on south toward Dûn Dalgan and Cuculain. He tarries at the tuath of King Fiontann and meets with "the miserable Croothnean," a guild chief, and asks for help. Læg refuses to give armour as a pledge for that help and chastises the chief fiercely. Before moving on, he calls on a bard to "chant tales of ancient heroes," including Cuculain. Læg eventually reaches the ford and washes the blood from Cuculain and weeps over him. The host of Meave erupts all around them, and the Donn Cooalney is captured and taken westward. The northern clans are aroused at this point, and the great wars of the Tan-bo-Cooalney commence. Volume 1 of History of Ireland *ends with Meave's host laying waste to Murthemney and Cuculain meeting with the Tuátha De Danan as he plans his next attack.*

Cuculain and Emer

Love out of his cradle leaped,
And clove dun chaos with his wings of gold.
—Shelley[1]

It was at this time [after the defeat of Murthemney] that Fergus Mac Roy rose from the champion's throne, like some vast rock left bare by the down-sinking billow, when after a tempest the great waters along the western shore rise and fall. So seemed the mighty captain of the Tân as he arose, and the assembly was silent until he left the pavilion, and after that many of the younger knights demanded that Bailey Mac Buan should sing. An Ultonian, captive he, and doomed ere long to a sorrowful death. Dear was he to the women of Ulla, but he loved a maiden not of his own province, and thus sang the son of Buan to the accompaniment of his small tympan:—

CUCULAIN: "Come down, O daughter of Forgal Mánah*,
Sweet Emer, come down without fear,
The moon has arisen to light us on our way,
Come down from thy greenan* without fear."

EMER: "Who is this that beneath my chamber window
Sends up to me his words through the dim night?

1. Percy Bysshe Shelley, *The Witch of Atlas*, in *The Complete Poetical Works of Percy Bysshe Shelley*, ed. Thomas Hutchinson (London: Oxford Univ. Press, 1921), 373, ll. 298–99. ("Leaped" should be "leapt" and "chaos" should be "Chaos.")

Who art thou standing in the beechen shadows,
White-browed, and tall, with thy golden hair?"

CUCULAIN: "It is I, Setanta, O gentle Emer!
I, thy lover, come to seek thee from the north;
It is I who stand in the beechen shadows,
Sending up my heart in words through the dim night."

EMER: "I fear my proud father, O Setanta,
My brothers, and my kinsmen, and the guards,
Ere I come unto thy hands, O my lover!
Through their well-lit feasting chamber I must pass."

CUCULAIN: "Fear not the guards, O noble Emer!
Fear not thy brothers, or thy sire,
Dull with ale are they all, and pressed with slumber,
And the lights extinguished in the hall."

EMER: "I fear the fierce watch-dogs, O Setanta
The deep water of the moat how shall I cross?
Not alone for myself, I fear, Setanta,
They will rend thee without ruth*, Cuculain."

CUCULAIN: "The dogs are my comrades and my namesakes;
Like my Luath, they are friendly unto me,
O'er the foss I will bear thee in my arms—
I will leap across the foss, my love, with thee."

EMER: "Far and wide all the tribes and the nations
Over Bregia, northwards to Dûn-Lir,
They are kin to my father and his subjects—
For thy life I fear, O noble Cuculain.

CUCULAIN: "On the lawn within the beechen shadows
Is my chariot light and strong, bright with gold;

And steeds like the March-wind in their swiftness
Will bear thee to Dûndalgan ere the dawn."

EMER: "I grieve to leave my father, O Setanta,
Mild to me, though his nature be not mild;
I grieve to leave my native land, Setanta,
Lusk with its streams and fairy glades.

"I grieve to leave my Dûn, O Setanta,
And this lawn, and the trees I know so well,
And this, my tiny chamber looking eastward,
Where love found me unknowing of his power.

"Well I know the great wrong I do my father,
But thus, even thus I fly with thee;
As the sea draws down the little Tolka,
So thou, O Cuculain, drawest me.

"Like a god descending from the mountains,
So hast thou descended upon me.
I would die to save thy life, O Setanta,
I would die if thou caredst not for me."

Then was Meave grievously enraged, hearing a second time chaunted the praises of the son of Sualtam; but she dissembled her wrath, and thus addressed the noble wife of Aileel Finn* with crafty words:—

"O noble Fleeas, surely this is an impious thing and not seemly, that the bards should thus hymn perpetually the name of that beardless youth, who perished but as it were to-day, and leave unsung the mighty heroes of old time—the children of Partholān and Dēla, or the sons of Milith of Espân. This indeed I would much prefer; but if we must needs sing the prowess of our foes, I myself would desire to hear, fitly chaunted, the brave deeds of Cethern Mac Fiontānn*, who singly assaulted the host of the Tân. But truly thy bards alone can adequately sing the praises of heroic men."

Now Meave had herself contended with the great northern warrior, and had wounded him in the battle, whom indeed she had first insulted, for the dazed hero had come naked, hastening to the relief of Cuculain, and the great Queen, unqueenly, had diverted herself with his state, uttering jests among her captains. But in her crafty mind she deemed now that much praise would be given to her by that bard who should chaunt the brave deeds of the heroic champion of Dûn Cin-Eich.

The Contest for the Championship

O thou who plumed with strong desire
Wouldst float above the world, beware,
A shadow tracks thy flight of fire—
Night is coming.
—Shelley[1]

Then Fleeas desired the chief bard of her territory to chaunt upon this theme, for he sat one place removed upon the right-hand side of Aileel Finn; but he, perceiving the wiles of Meave, and being, moreover, self-willed and ungovernable—for in the days of Meave the bards with difficulty brooked the commands of kings—made as though he heard only her desire that he should sing, and recurred again to the theme, detested indeed by Meave, but grateful to many of the knights, and most so to the bardic class, and he sung the contest of Cuculain for the championship of Ulla.

Cuculain Raised to the Championship

"What thunder of the hoofs of horses is this?
What rolling of the wheels of chariots?
Who are these mighty men that come through the defile
To thy still, gleaming lake, O son of Imomain?

1. Percy Bysshe Shelley, "The Two Spirits," in *The Complete Poetical Works of Percy Bysshe Shelley*, 609, ll. 1–4. (Should read: "O thou, who plumed with strong desire / Wouldst float above the earth, beware! / A Shadow tracks thy flight of fire— / Night is coming!")

"What magic rites of these, what songs of druids
Rending thy Fæd-Fia,* Mananān?
Who are these that fear not the face of Uath*,
Thy terrible face, O Uath of the Lake?

"Lægairé [Buada]*, son of Conud, son of Iliach,
And Conaill, the triumphant, and the third,
Cuculain Mac Sualtam in his boyhood,
Like a star, pure and lustrous in the dawn.

"They strive for the champion's seat of Ulla,
And thither to the lake they have come
To abide by the word of the wise Uath,
Dividing to each warrior his due."

UATH: "Why from my face have ye torn
Mananān's veil, whereby we live unseen?
From my magic labours here by Loch Uath
Ye have roused me now in an evil hour."

CUCULAIN: "Give us pardon for our fault, O mighty Uath,
But these claim the first right against me,
Saying theirs is the Champion's Throne of Ulla,
But do thou decide between us three."

UATH: "Go back, foolish boy, to thy tutors,
Strive not with thy betters, Cuculain;
But do thou, Conaill, the victorious,
And Lægairé, of the triumphs, contend.

"Lay here upon this flag thy head, Lægairé,
With my adze* I will cut thy neck in twain.
Do this and the glory I will give you,
And the Champion's Throne of Ulla shall be thine."

"Then fell thy noble countenance, Lægairé,
And thus sad-browed didst thou reply

'In the battle-shock contending I will perish,
But not thus, not thus, O son of Imomain."

UATH: "Thou hast won, O son of proud Amargin,
O golden-tresséd champion of Emain,
Fearless, bow thee down, Conaill, the mighty,
The glory and the championship are thine.

"Back he shrank, Conaill, the Victorious,
His heavy-tressed locks shook with rage—
'I care not for glory if thou slay me—
What avails me my glory if I die.'

"Then glowed thy bright face, O Setanta,
And thou layedst thy bright head upon the flag,
Crying, 'Give me the great honour, mighty Uath,
To be Champion of Ulla though I die.

"'Be my name renowned among the nations,
Be my glory sung through all time,
I shall live in the list of Ulla's champions,
I fear not thy adze, just and wise Mac Imomain.'

"Then the god leaned down over Setanta,
Drawing back the yellow hair from his white neck,
And beside Cuculain upon the flag-stone
His tears rained down for the boy.

"Three times upon thy neck, O Setanta,
He loweréd the cold shining brass,
Then he cried, 'Arise, O Setanta!
Rise Champion of Ulla, O fearless Cuculain.'"[2]

2. It will be remarked that this eagerness for personal distinction does not mark the manhood of Cuculain.

The singing of the bards greatly angers Queen Meave, who chastises them for their perceived insolence. Confident of her victory, the queen announces to the gathered kings and captains of the Tân that tomorrow they may divide their booty and disperse. Fergus warns that the dispersion of the host will surely mean the destruction of the Olnemacta and should thus be delayed until they can confront the Red Branch, who are just then awakening from their stupor. Cailitin, the enchanter, offers further warnings of the "raging wolf whom men call Mac Beg and Mac Sultam," speaking with such ire of Cuculain that he arouses the hatred of the Tân against his memory. The proud queen becomes increasingly anxious, until she is troubled by visions that foretell of giant heroes and bloody battles. As Fergus attempts to calm her, the huge forms of armed men, the host of Concobar mac Nessa, appear on the wide plain to the north. Meanwhile, deep in the forest, Læg is nursing Cuculain back to health, though the hero remains in a severely weakened condition. As his stupor begins to lift, the hero and his footman travel to join the Red Branch, who greet them with loud shouts of acclimation. Still recovering, Cuculain soon falls into a deep sleep, even as the great battle of the Tan-bo-Cooalney commences. During the battle, warriors clash mightily across the wide plain and, after a fierce struggle, the vengeful Fergus sends Concobar reeling. At this very moment, Cuculain's battle cry can be heard ringing from the distance.

Lu Lam-fada Mac Æthleen

But a blast met them, or it was Cuculain.
—Ancient Bard[1]

Now meantime Læg, indignant, but with an impotent wrath, hastened from the tent-door of Cuculain to the rampart, and as hastily returned, or to the stable where were the war-steeds, and who, neighing, kept stamping, and pulled madly at their halters, or to the chariot-house, where the brass and gold of the chariot glowed like burning fire, instinct with a war-spirit, longing for the battle. Then, again, he hastened downwards, and stood upon the rampart hard by the gateway of the Clans of Murthemney, his soul confused with a blind rage, and past him, perpetually, there went ox-waggons laden with the wounded of the Clanna Rury, who groaned lying upon the blood-soaked rushes, and Læg stamped upon the rampart, and tore his auburn hair, and hastened again to the pavilion of his master, where Cuculain still slept. But Læg wondered when he saw him, for his countenance was fresh and fair, and nobler to look upon, and greater seemed the son of Sualtam than at any time since he had attained to manhood, and taken his place amongst the warriors of the Red Branch, and longed to awake him, nevertheless he feared to break the geis. But as he stood at the door, he deemed that he heard voices speaking and conversing in low tones. Yet was there no one in the tent. Then Læg trembled, and a cold fear crept about the roots of his hair, and he hastened back again to the rampart.

1. *Editors' note*: No source can be found outside of O'Grady.

But now Læg could no longer contain himself, and fiercely he inveighed against the wounded knights returning from that field of slaughter. For seeing the husband of Acaill*, he cried:—

"Make haste, now, Glan, son of Carbad. Charioteer, yon passage third from the east will lead thee soonest into the north. He desires to see again his dear wife, Acaill. Heed not his wounds. They come opportunely to one hastening to his wife."

And again—

"Is it thou, Cumascra Mend Macha, thou of the stammering tongue and hesitating hand? Brave son of Concobar, I welcome thee returning victorious from the battle."

And to Yeoha Ec-beul, father-in-law of Conaill Carna—

"Neigh, horse-mouth. Much provender awaits thee in Ultonian stables. Stained is thy green bratta*, but within thy skin is clean. Fear not, valiant hare, how nobly dost thou fly before the clogs of the Olnemacta!"

So roared Læg, mad with shame and wrath; but meantime, the great host of the Four Provinces was submerging the Clanna Rury. For as of those who all night long contend with the powers of wind and sea, and they hope that the day may bring some relief; but in the grey tempestuous dawn, the sea breaks through their riven timbers, and the light of life goes down into darkness and the grave; such then was the anguish of the Clanna Rury; but no coward hearts were theirs, bard-nourished champions, devoid of fear. For amid the deafening din of the brazen deluge immersing fought on in silence the scattered fragments of the Red Branch—branch now stripped by the wild winds of war—the Clanna Rury, breathing fierce breath, terrible in that dread moment.

Like the arms of some great bay or harbour, there stretched forth into the plain, piercing the multitude of the Tân, the battalions of two matchless champions, of Conaill, son of Amargin, on the south, and of Lægairé Buada on the north. But far other than a peaceful haven was the wild expanse which they enclosed, rolled over by the waves of war, bright with the stress of battle, loud with the crash of meeting hosts, the clang and reverberation of smitten brass. And now all hope was taken away, for the battalions of the Red Branch were isolated in the midst of the plain, and between them many a rapid cohort of the spearmen of the Queen, and many a swift squadron of her chivalry had rushed, running straight or aslant, according as they had opportunity, and they were seizing the gates all along the right centre and the left centre, while in the centre the Ard-Ries fought, and the King of Ulla, being overpowered, kept retreating to the rampart.

At every gateway there was a bridge that crossed the trench, for the stems of trees were extended from bank to bank, and upon them lay others, lying transverse and close together, across which the chariots and the men-of-war went forth to battle. At each of these gates was stationed a company of warriors, whose duty it was to remove the bridge what time the last of the Clanna Rury should be received within the rampart, in case of disaster, and to cast into the gateway trees, with all their branches, the leafy tops having been removed, an effectual defence by reason of the crooked pointed limbs. Also, they purposed to run the smooth stems of fir-trees through the forks on the inside of the ramparts, so that none from without might remove them, strong though the assailing warriors might be and daring. This at some of the gateways those within did, when the men of Meave had destroyed the bridges; but at others, the Clanna Rury issuing forth, fought in defence of the bridges.

All this time the star of Emain Macha grew pale. One by one, like lights in a king's banqueting-hall, after the guests have departed, when the slaves go about and extinguish them, so one by one went down the battle-standards of the Clanna Bury over the plain.

Still hard by the great central gate, and on the right of where the Ard-Ries fought, floated the Red Hand of Emain Macha, and around it silent, terrible, fought the bravest of the Clanna Rury, and thither collected the remnants of every shattered battalion, if by any means they could escape thither, when their cohorts were broken and dissipated by the mighty men of Meave.

And now, too, there were strange shapes[2] seen, and dim discerned abominable forms, and shrieks, and horrid laughter, as of those who laughing yell in the insane house, for out of darkness infernal and the caves of death, where Destruction, wandering, cries amid the darkness to his children, and summons round him the hosts of hell, they arose, passing through the maddened souls of men, and were seen visibly in the light of day—withered, blasted faces, unclean doleful shapes, as of men and women, and where the slaughter was greatest they danced, and raised in their accursed hands the hot blood of heroes with horrid yells. The bauves* were there, and the wives of Ned* reeled amid the carnage; but far thence fled bright Angus* before that ghastly brood, fair god of the silver-winding Boyne, to thee dearer the music of thy own sweet stream, where beneath Slane it chimes over its pebbly bed, and thy green palace[3] over against Rosna-Ree*, and sweeter than all strife the melody of thy stricken lute, or lovers' talk beneath the evening star.

It was about this time that to Cuculain, sleeping, there appeared a vision. Before him stood the form of a mighty warrior equipped as if for battle. A bratta of green silk he wore, fastened by a golden brooch, and from his countenance a light shone. With deep marvellous eyes he gazed upon the hero.

And Cuculain, trembling, said:—

"I know thee who thou art, Ioldāna*. Signifying what hast thou come up out of the realms of the unseen."

But that other answered, and his voice was low and grave, musical as the deep strings of the harp, and deep and terrible like the voice of the great sea:—

2. These shapes, according to the ancient Irish bards, appeared visibly after all great battles. Of the Tuatha De Danan there were two divisions corresponding to the angels and devils of mediæval times. Thus the step-mother of the Children of Lir, who transformed them into swans, was expelled by the gods from their company, and converted into a demon of the air.

3. This is the great Rath of New Grange, sacred to the Dagda (Zeus) and also to Angus.

"Awake now, Setanta, and go forth to war, for thy people summon thee to deliver them. Fear not the powers of earth and hell, for I am ever around thee. I have relaxed upon thee the oppression of the Clan Cailitin,[4] and healed thy many wounds, and restored thee to thy ancient prowess, therefore, thou shalt go boldly against hundreds, and battalions shall not put thee to flight. Moreover, I have poured a magic mist around thee, so that thou shalt seem greater than human, with Panic in front of thee, and Terror issuing out of thy countenance. The Clan Cailitin will come against thee, and the Mor Reega will for the last time embattle herself against thee. Fear not them nor her, for those thou shalt destroy, and after that no magic arts shall be powerful to hurt thee, and her thou shalt conquer, so that henceforward she will be thy lover and thy protectress. Nevertheless, few indeed shall thy years be, but while time lasts thy glory shall endure, and thy name shall be known unto the earth's ends. Nor shall thy death come suddenly or without warning. Thou shalt hear Mac Manar* and see Rod*,[5] and it is the remnant of the Clan Cailitin who will destroy thee."[6]

Then the divine voice ceased, and Cuculain, awaking, beheld Læg in the doorway, and heard the roar of the magic amulet, and the moaning of the sea and the triumphant shouts of the Four Provinces. Thereat, a fierce wrath filled all his veins, and he sprang swiftly from his couch and put on his battle harness. First, a soft, linen lēna*, of twenty-seven folds, next his skin, that his armour might not abrade it, and over that his battle-shirt. Seven-fold was that shirt, of seasoned leather, cut from the hide of wild-bulls. It descended upon his thighs, but from the hips downwards it was slashed, in order that it might not inconvenience him in running, and Læg fastened the clasps of glittering findruine. Then, around his waist Læg clasped the waistpiece, also seven-fold, where more

4. It was not until Cuculain destroyed this clan that he became invincible.

5. These were gods who announced death to heroes.

6. Vide supra, the six children of Cailitin who came not to the war.

than elsewhere the warrior needs protection. After that, Cuculain put on his outer lēna of very fine linen, bordered at the collar and at the extremities with golden thread, and upon which Emer had wrought many fair embroidered forms, and it descended to his white strong knees; also, Læg strapped on his sandals, winding over ankle and instep the pliant strap, and, though in haste, turned down the ends under the loop, after which he despatched Læg to yoke the war-horses, but he himself fastened his hair with a golden clasp that it might not be spread around his face in the battle. Over his right shoulder he cast his sword-belt, the belt that sustained Cruaideen*, and round his waist his girdle, and therein he slung his mace and his brazen colg, and fitted thereto the leathern satchel filled with balls of iron. Over his shoulders, too, he cast his bratta of crimson silk, and in front it was firm and close to his figure, but loose behind his back, and he fastened it upon his breast with a wheel-brooch of shining gold. Then upon his head he set his brazen helmet lined with soft doeskin; but while he armed himself might be heard distinctly the beating of his heart, and with difficulty might a man distinguish his motions, so swiftly did he move his nimble hands. Last of all he took his shield, passing his left arm through the loop, and took hold of the strong handle, and in his left hand seized the Gæ-Bolg*, which none else in Erin might wield, and in his right the Crann-tawl*; of red yew was that sling, thicker than a man's wrist, and the string thereof was of twisted wires of findruiney. It was a geis[7] to him that he should miss any cast with that sling.

Then sprang forth from the tent the son of Sualtam; and when he saw the plain, and the Red Branch routed, a fell rage grew to madness within him, and a cry from unseen mouths arose around him as he ran. Moreover, the son of Lir*, the mighty genius[8] of the

7. The first intimation to Cuculain of his approaching death was his failure with the sling.

8. This was Mananān, the most potent as well as the most spiritual and remote of the gods.

storm-swept promontories of the sea, waved above him his magic wand, and transformed him as he ran past Læg and his horses, and sprang to the summit of the rampart. There he shouted the battle cry of the clans of Ulla. Terribly then rang the voice of Cuculain across the battle.

‘Αριστεία* Conculain

"Is this the undefiléd hound
Whom thou callest the life of the Ultonians."[1]

"I foretold last year
That there would come an heroic Hound—
The Hound of Emain Macha*."[2]

"He had not a boasting word,
Nor vaunted he at all,
Though marvellous were his deeds."[3]

"They called for his thunder-feats."[4]

It was then that Fer-lōga* announced his coming to Aileel, and Aileel prophesied from him the defeat of the mighty host which Queen Meave had gathered out of the Four Provinces.

But he, Cuculain, the son of Sualtam, stood afar upon the rampart of the Clanna Rury, a portent of war clear seen like flame against the dark western clouds, terrible in his beauty, and his voice rang across the battle like the shout of a battalion, or the sound of some mighty trumpet explored by the blasting of the breath of a giant. As

1. T.B.C., p. 110. *Editors' note*: O'Grady's note early in the text identifies T.B.C. as the "Tân-bo-Cooalney, O'Daly's MS. Translation, Royal Irish Academy."

2. National MSS, Vol. II., p. 32.

3. T.B.C., p. 18.

4. T.B.C.

when mariners in the western main plying southwards past Dûn-na-m-arc "and the House of Donn, whose ship the tempest shakes, and the wild billows buffet; and they, in the darkness and the storm, hear around them the thunder of the waves upon iron coasts, who, being impotent, anticipate certain death; and as when, to them rounding suddenly and unawares some concealing promontory, there shines far away the ship-protecting light which crowns that black rock that was the grave of Iar*, and afar over the tossing waters there streams the glorious ray. So welcome and so glorious, to the beaten Red Branch, whom death and despair now encompassed, over whom rolled the wild waves of war, and the brazen billows of the Tân, appeared far away, westwards, the coming of the son of Sualtam, and the pealing of his war-shout afar on the edge of the battle. Silent then as the grave, and still while one might count five, became the whole of that war-swept plain, and straightway, with a heaven-ascending shout, the Clanna Rury sprang triumphant upon their foes.

Then shouted Cuculain, looking southwards:—

"Go back, thou son of Rossa Roe*. I, too, once fled from thee, though swordless. Go back! contend no more against the Clanna Rury, for surely if I meet thee in the battle I shall slay thee."

For Fergus had gone nigh unto slaying the Ard-Rie of all Ulla; but when he heard the voice of Cuculain he stood a moment in amazement, holding his bloody sword in his hand. Then slowly he retreated into the ranks of the Olnemacta. Him too Cormac Conlíngas withdrew, having hastened thither from the north to save his father's life.

But Cuculain, planting his great spear in the ground, drew his sling and fitted thereto an iron bolt, where thong and timber joined. Into the loop he passed his thumb, and bent the crann-tawl upon his right knee, gazing, as he bent, upon where the remnant of the nations of Cooalney and Murthemney were overborne by the sons of Lon-Cras. Of them two were in front of the others, Finn, the fourth son of Lon-Cras, and Caibdeen the sixth. Lords were they of Teffia, ruling over many tribes, and at that moment Finn had his mace raised in the act of striking one of the vassals of Cuculain. But ere the blow descended, Cuculain slang. Like the sound of a gong was the back-springing sling, and like a fierce blast so hissed the twisted thong of the crann-tawl, and the deadly bolt sped afar. There fell Finn, who had that day slain many of the people of Cuculain, smitten through shield and breast by the unerring missile. Further north, his brother Caibdeen, in his chariot, galloped past a battalion of Cuculain's people, who, having been thrown into confusion, were pressed close together, and unable to wield their weapons. Along the edge of the disordered mass the scythe of that warrior's chariot share the helpless warriors, guided deftly by the charioteer, but Caibdeen himself stood erect in the chariot, protecting the charioteer with his shield, when once more the crann-tawl sounded. The second bolt smote the left-hand steed in the forehead, who, plunging forward, fell, and the chariot was over-turned, and those within it rolled forth upon the plain; but as Caibdeen was rising from the ground, Cuculain struck him, and the iron missile passed quite through his head, from the left temple to the right. Then retreated the sons of Lon-Cras and their nation, and Cuculain's people, with a shout, went forward.

Swifter than words can tell was the slinging of Cuculain, nor might man discern the rapid movements of his hands, but ever flashed afar the sweep of that bright sling, and ever hissed the sling-thong through the air.

Then, too, was it that seeing Dûvac Dæl Ulla*, who had gotten to the rear of Lægairé Buada, and was bursting the left flank of his battalion, seeking to break through to hold the rampart and the gates, Cuculain cried:—

"O Dûvac, thou reptile that rendest in the rear of the host, desist now straightway, or it will be thy death."

Now Cuculain and Dûvac had been schoolfellows; and he, fearing, hastened back to where was his chariot, dreading the wrath of the far-casting son of Sualtam.

Northwards then slang Cuculain where the Maineys* of the Seaboard were routing the nations of Fergus Mac Lēda, and of these he slew three in succession, giving relief to the Ultonians; and there, too, Fergus Mac Lēda again dashed forward against the men of Meave. Also, on the extreme edge of the battle, northward, he slew three men of great stature, whose names are not recorded. He confused, too, the Clan Tomalta, conspicuous with their blood-red armour and accoutrements, and the Clan Guairé, who fought with great spears ending in a triple prong, and a nation whose name is not recorded, but whose warriors were all armed with battle maces of bright brass. Also he confused and routed the Clan Sibna, and the Clan Murdoc, and the sons of Talc, and he slew three dark-browed nobles of the children of Sealan.

So Cuculain kept perpetually slinging; and wherever he saw the Ultonians overpowered, at that point he continually slang, shooting over the heads of the Clanna Rury, and the men of Meave kept falling, and the distress of the Ultonians was relieved, and the severe pressure of the foe was relaxed. Moreover, at the appearance of Cuculain, all who fought about the gateways in the left centre of the embankment had themselves retreated; nevertheless, many of them were intercepted by the Clanna Rury and slain, who, now released from stress of battle on the front, faced round against those who had gotten in their rear.

But meantime Læg had harnessed the horses and yoked the chariot, and he sprang thereinto, and guided the steeds straight to the entrance in front of where they were, beside which entrance, upon the right, Cuculain stood slinging. Loud then shouted Læg to those at the entrance, who were preparing to reconstruct the bridge over the foss, and they opened to the right hand and the left. For Læg had leaped into his place in the chariot, and with difficulty did he keep his footing, so wild and unmanageable were the steeds, swifter than the swiftest horses in the chariot race contending for the victory, so eager were they to enter into the battle.

Now Cuculain heard the mighty roar of the revolving wheels, and the thunder of the trampling of the steeds, nevertheless, once again he slang, and struck the foremost champion of the Clan Yeoha of Loch Erne, for they were of the army of Meave, though they meared with the western Ultonians, and he snatched his spear from the ground, preparing to spring into the chariot. Straightforward then rushed the steeds, raging for the battle, and with the chariot they cleared the deep wide foss, twenty feet was it in breadth from bank to bank; but hardly had they alighted with a mighty crash on the further bank, when Cuculain stood by the side of Læg, having bounded from the lofty rampart, and once more he shouted, and once more the host of Meave was confused, and the Red Branch dashed upon them dealing death.

Then, indeed, few were the champions of the world who would have faced the son of Sualtam, whom merely to behold, men trembled, for there was Panic in front of him, and Terror issued out of his countenance; and he ran out upon the chariot-pole of the chariot, and stood with one foot on the pole and one on the back of the Liath Macha, and laughed in the fierceness of his wrath, for not like a mortal fighter was the hero that day, but like a genius of war. Long had they laid the hero under spells, fairy-stricken and enfeebled, by the force of druidic arts. But now, as out of the caves of death, he arose again in his invincible might, shaking off that magic sorrow and the oppression of the enchanters. Then flapped his warlike tresses, even as a sail flaps, sharp-sounding in the blast, and he quaked in his anger like a bulrush in the river, when swollen by spring rain the brown torrent rushes headlong to the sea. Out of his countenance there went as it were lightnings, and showers of deadly stars rained forth from the dark western clouds above his head, and there was a sound as of thunder around him, and cries not his own coming from unseen mouths, and dreadful faces came and went upon the wind, and visages not seen in Erin for a thousand years were present around the hero that day, and there was a clamour as of a multitude following behind, when the son of Sualtam went forth into the great battle.

Loud then pealed the voice of the Hound, for with his the Ioldāna mingled his voice of power, as then, when at Moy Tura, he brake the ranks of the Fomorian giants. Then sprang Queen Meave from her chariot, and fled away upon her feet; then were the Maineys confused, and Cet, with the chivalry of Moyrisk, swerved southwards; then were the war-horses of the Tân terrified, and the familiar spirits of Queen Meave put to flight.

Moreover, as they went, Læg ran out in front the great chariot-spear, through its loops beneath the pole, and made it fast at his feet with the brazen clasp; and with a lever on the right hand and the left, he unfolded the battalion-rending scythes, to see if they would work freely, so that like some vast bird of war, with out-stretched glittering wings, that chariot seemed to skim the ground.

Now was it that, from their lethargic rest, awaked the earth-demons, even the nether gods, through whose dark chambers subterrene echoed the thunder of the war-steeds' hoofs, and the roof of whose dûn profound was shaken with a mighty oscillation. Loud then through the realms of gloom reverberated the voice of Orchil, the sorceress, summoning Fovart and her sisterhood of the deep, a dim consistory, and the earth-fiends arose against the son of Sualtam. Like the billows of the sea, the firm plain uplifted itself against Cuculain, so that the chariot-wheels sank into the ground, and the hoofs of the horses were impeded and their progress was retarded, and their draught distressing. Which seeing, Cuculain addressed his steed, and he said:—

"O Liath Macha, it was not thus that thou didst bear into battle thy divine mistress what time she went out against the Fōmoroh, but swiftly through wet places and dry, thou didst urge thy course; and, O Liath Macha, the eyes of all Erin are upon thee and me this day."

Thereat the noble spirit of the Liath Macha was grieved, and against the yoke mightily he bent his broad chest with the strength of twenty horses, and out of the earth by main force he drew black Shanglan and the war-car, and then those peerless horses exerted their terrible strength, and through marble and whinstone crashed the revolving wheels of the war-car as the great steeds went on. Behind them the track of the chariot-wheels was like the mearing of a territory. Then saddened and astonished, the earth-demons sank into their deep abode, and again Læg urged on the steeds of Cuculain straightforward into the thickest throng of the battle.

Far out in front of the chariot then sprang Cuculain, holding the Gæ-Bolg in his right hand, and before him the Clanna Rury divided to the right and to the left, for here they were again retreating before the men of Meave. First, then, Cuculain slew a mighty champion of the Dergtheena, a prince among the nation of Curoi Mac Dary, who from their great Dûn in the hills of Slieve Mish ruled a wide territory. Him holding the battle-plough* of the Roscathals Cuculain smote through the shield and the left breast, for on his arm the shield still lay, while with mighty hands he grasped the ironwork of that warlike instrument. Then it was that Cuculain saw Lewy Mac Conroi*, who was hesitating in his heroic mind whether he would advance against Cuculain, in protection of his people, and meet at his hands a hero's death, and test that dim southern prophecy which said that by his hands should fall the Hound of Emain Macha.

But as he deliberated, Cuculain, seeing him, said:—

"O Lewy Mac Conroi, submit thyself now to me and I will not hurt thee. I have slain thy father, and will not slay thee."

Loud then in reply rang the spear of the southern hero on Fabâne*. Nevertheless, though mighty was the strength of the great son of Curoi Mac Dary, harmless with bent point and splintered tree rebounded the spear of the warrior.

Then ran forward Cuculain, and disarmed him with his irresistible hands, and the companions of Cuculain took him captive.

After that Cuculain slew two other of the champions of that nation, and before him dispersed the Clans of Slieve Mish. Also he routed the descendants of the ancient Lúhara, who dwelt by the hill-enfolden lakes of Locha Lein, and thence southwards to Inver Scēna and were surnamed the Flaming; also, a strong battalion from Assaroe, where their territory meared with the Ultonians, and the children of Lægairey, of the Bloody Altars. So Cuculain routed all the left centre of the host of Meave, and, standing, beckoned Læg to approach. Bright then with the light of valour was the countenance of Cuculain, as he sprang into the chariot beside Læg, and sent forth his taunts against the Olnemacta, exulting in his invincible prowess, for not yet was his manhood confirmed, but such was his age, as when youth and manhood join, and still untouched by the razor were his lips, and, for all his heroic greatness, the unbridled wantonness of youth was strong within him. Moreover, now he had saved the life of his king, and repelled Dûvac Dæl Ulla on the north, and had routed the battalions of Meave over all the left centre of the Clanna Rury, and there gathered round him, and after him his ancient comrades, and schoolfellows, and dear friends, and the remnant of the Clans of Cooalney and Murthemney, who were subject unto him, and loved him, and a warlike glee and wanton exhilaration filled his spirit. Therefore, when he stood beside Læg in the chariot, he said:—

"Guide now the steeds to the right centre of the battle. And this shall be as it were a race of chariots at Tailteen; so shall I mock and deride the host of the Four Provinces. Therefore, give to me my balls of jugglery."

And Læg said:—

"Thou art a witless idiot, O Setanta. Is this a time to indulge thy mad freaks, when the Olnemacta are routing the Ultonians over all the right centre? If thou carest not for thyself have at least a care for thy charioteer, who, shieldless, has no protection save what lies in thy skill and warlike prudence, of which right little dost thou possess. Verily, if I return to Emain Macha in safety, never more will I be charioteer of thine. Truly my brothers[5] made a wiser choice."

And Cuculain answered:—

"When I took thee to be my charioteer, O Læg, I then said—'Not beside me or over me shalt thou be smitten by a hostile weapon, but through me'; and in our many battles, hast thou ever yet received any wound?"

Then was the mind of Læg troubled when he remembered the never-failing care with which his master watched over him in danger, and he gave Cuculain the balls of glittering brass, and urged on the steeds. Across the plain then they flew, between the Clanna Rury and the Olnemacta, and where they went the men of Meave shrank away. Through a field of slaughter dashed then the war-car, and over the mangled bodies of heroes, and the blood bespattered the war-car, and reddened the tires of the wheels and the spokes. But above the

5. Id, charioteer of Conaill Carna, and Sheeling of Lægairé Buada.

head of Cuculain there was as it were a bright circle, so did he with a single hand cause those eight balls to revolve, watching warily, nevertheless, lest a spear or a bolt from the men of Meave should smite his charioteer or himself, and the Clanna Rury laughed when they beheld him; and afar off Concobar Mac Nessa, wounded, but vigilant, watched his career and antic feats—but the men of Meave were the more terrified.

Nevertheless there came out a great champion of the Olnemacta, and he said that now surely would the Hound fall at his hands, and that he would acquire great renown. Therefore, when Cuculain was looking southwards and upwards, he ran forward from the Olnemacian ranks to slay Cuculain as he passed. But Cuculain, not turning his head aside, but looking straight before him, darted one of the eight balls through his brain, and continued his juggler's wheel with seven.

"I swear the oath of my territories, O Setanta," cried Læg, "that a prettier feat of war thou hast never yet performed."

Now the name of the slain man was Cuir, the son of Dalot.

Then Cuculain cast the balls high aloft, and as they fell, dropped them one by one into their place, and he changed the Gæ-Bolg from the left hand to the right and again sprang forth upon the chariot-pole. It was then that Cuculain heard sobbing voices and a sound of the muffled lamentation of women, and he said:—

"O Fathâne and Colla, why do you weep? My end is not yet. I shall this day advance the Red Hand of my nation over all the nations of Eiré, and I shall cause to flourish the fair fields of Ulla. Why do you weep?"

And there answered him voices out of the air:—

"Like a child playing on a tide-surrounded isle art thou this day, O Setanta, upon whom night descends, and the great sea arises irreversible with mutterings and noises, and hungry eyes glare around him from the deep. Against thee now the mighty Cailitin and his wizard sons embattle themselves. Nations they have ruined, and kingdoms made desolate. Yea, against them the high gods wage vain war. As the bright wave, foam-crested, glittering, which the hollow cavern, loud with fearsome echoes, and peopled with abominable shapes, draws within its depths, so shalt thou descend into their pit. Go not southwards, Cuculain. Stay now thy destroying hand, and let the Clanna Rury work their own salvation."

And Cuculain answered:—

"Surely I shall go southwards, O fairy queens. Not to husband ignobly for my own pleasure have I this great strength which lives within me to-day. Now am I not my own, but I am sent forth by unseen kings, and whither they guide me I will go."

Swifter than hawks then southward flew the steeds of Cuculain, and before him the men of Meave fled to the camp. Clear seen from afar stood the son of Sualtam, the destroying hawk of the Tân, speeding southwards to where, in the right centre, still raged the hottest battle, and there, like clashing tides, the Olnemacta and the Red Branch contended. Then was it that the Clan Cailitin embattled themselves against Cuculain.

Meantime the son of Sualtam had sprung out in front of the chariot, advancing against the men of Meave, but there withstood him Fræch, the son of Fiach, advancing through the ranks of the Olnemacta.

Glorious indeed was the appearance of that hero. With a tinkling he ran through the host, for on his spear there were rings that rang forth a sweet faint melody as he ran. He it was who had come to Rath Cruhane as a suitor of Fionavar, leading in his train those weird harpers of whom men often spake, but never before saw. Vain then and since had been his suit, though he boasted that his mother was the goddess Bē-bind. Musically now over the shoulder of Cuculain rushed the spear of the western champion, but in return Cuculain pierced him through the very boss of the shield, and through the middle of his breast where the breast bones join.

After that there came against him Lon, and Uala, and Dil, and along with them three warrioresses. All these practised druidic arts, but their arts availed not against Cuculain, and he slew them all with the Gæ-Bolg and with Cruaideen. Then it was that the dear son of delicate Uala ran forward to avenge his father, but his courage fell when he saw the giant spear of Cuculain dropping blood, and beside it the face of the hero, haggard, terrible, raging in his destructive wrath, and quickly he shrank back amongst the ranks of the Olnemacta.

There Cuculain routed the host of Meave on the right centre of the Ultonians, and kept moving southwards to meet Conaill. From him Cet and the sons of Maga retreated. Bravest he in all Erin after the son of Sualtam, nevertheless he and his brethren went back before Cuculain, which to him was the most renowned of his achievements. Nevertheless, there came against him two warrior druids, Imræn and Imroe, trusting in their magic power, but they were slain by the son of Sualtam and by Lu Mac Æthleen.

Meantime Læg kept moving after him, not silently, for while Cuculain was routing the foe, Læg perpetually shouted. Then returned the warrior to his chariot; around his lips there was a foam, and from his forehead down upon his neck the great veins had swollen out like ropes. Thereafter Læg unfolded the left scythe and charged southwards, and where he went the battalions of Meave were confused, and chariots and fighting men were cast in heaps, and rolled over one another inextricable.

Which seeing a brave southern hero, Liathān, said to his charioteer:—

"O Mulcha, let us stay now this destroying hawk. The hero does not live who can meet him in single combat; but come now, charge against his chariot, and haply in the confusion I may find an opportunity to slay him."

Then the charioteer gave reins to his steeds; and, on the other side, Læg, being very wary and vigilant, and looking all round under the borders of Fabâne, saw him, and calling to Cuculain, gave rein to the steeds. Like thunder was the roar of the wheels on both sides, and the trampling of the galloping steeds as they closed, and elsewhere the battle was still while the chariots drew nigh. But Læg kept perpetually guiding the chariot-spear, so that it might pierce the breasts of one of the steeds; and Mulcha, on the other side, guided so as to avoid it, for of glittering brass it extended in front of the chariot-pole. But as they closed, the horses of Cuculain rose against the others, and trampled them into the ground, and passed over them, and the great war-car crushed like rotten timber the chariot of Liathān, and that warrior was slain by his own chariot, and by the trampling of Cuculain's steeds. Then Cuculain made much of his horses, and said:—

"O Liath Macha, thou hast not done a more gallant deed since the day that thou slewest the steed of Ercoill, on that day when we went to be judged by him, and all others fled before him and his terrible fire-breathing steed."

So they went southwards, and Cuculain lifted up his voice, and Conaill answered, for he was much exhausted fighting all day against the great southern nations under Cathir, son of Eterskel*, and Cairbré* the fair and great. Seeing Cuculain, the great son of Conairy Mōr leaped from his chariot, and his brother, Oblinni, whose foot was yet unhealed, guarded the steeds. Him Cuculain missed, and the spear stuck trembling in the ground behind; but ere the Southern could cast, Cuculain sprang upon him with his battle-mace. With the first blow he stunned his arm within the shield, and with the second he slew him. He also slew Oball his brother, who endeavoured to draw the spear from the ground. For he and Oblinni struggled with it, endeavouring to withdraw it and retreat amongst the ranks of the Clan Dēga. Them Cuculain slew—a cause of great grief in the south of Erin. Here with his battle-mace he routed the nations of the Ernai, also the men of Hirna, whose footmen were swifter than their chivalry, and the nations of Boirné, until fair-visaged Corc gave hostages to the Clanna Rury, for the conquered appealed not in vain to Cuculain for mercy. There, too, against Cuculain came an ancient comrade, Fir-bē, a prince of the Olnemacta. With 505 warriors he had come to the hosting, and Cuculain, enraged, cast his spear lengthwise at him and slew him, for the mighty beam struck him in the mouth and brake all his jaws.

Then sounded in the ear of Cuculain a voice which he knew, and it said:—

"Now, O Setanta, strengthen thyself, for against thee the powers of hell embattle themselves. Hid in dark clouds Cailitin and his mighty brood are upon thee."

But Cuculain looked up, and he saw a darkness moving towards him from the camp of Meave, and a deadly chill transfixed his heart as he looked, and a wild horror over-spread his face. And again the Ioldāna spake:—

"Not alone for the Red Branch shalt thou now fight, but for all the nations of Eiré, who, thee beaten, will no longer yield men and heroes, and fair peaceful fields, but her fens shall be enlarged, and dragons shall dwell there, and slimy unnameable monsters, and all manner of foul creeping things, and few and base shall her people be."

Then by his magic art Lu spread a vision before the hero, and Cuculain saw his native land, sea-girt, like a picture, with all her tuaths and mōr-tuaths*, and, like silver threads, he saw her everlasting streams; south-westward the mighty Shannon running from its source at Connla's Well*, where glistened the sacred hazel, and the fairy queens who guarded it, and he saw the Three[6] Waters starting from Slieve Blahma* glittering through mid-Erin as they ran; the noble Slaney, too, he saw, and the Liffey returning to its source; the lordly Boyne crowned with woods, and the palaces of the immortal gods; the Bann with its sacred estuary; the Drowis, and the Lee silver-flowing, untroubled, like a dream, and the sacred mountains of Eiré, and her plains and many woods, her sea-piercing promontories and storm-repelling bays. And Cuculain saw her warlike tribes dwelling afar, and heroic forms in all the territories, and over Eiré all the peoples raising to him high memorials, and hymning his name in songs. Also, the god caused him to see strange lands with mightier streams and fiercer suns, and the race of the ancient Gædil there dwelling, and his name there renowned.

Then the vision faded, and Cuculain saw before him a sword,[7] the haft towards him. Like glittering diamond it shone, and the handle was inlaid with wondrous pearls, and on its starry sides were there graved verses in such an Ogham as Cathvah never taught to

6. Suir, Nore, and Barrow.

7. This was the Fraygarta, the sword of Mananān, with which Lu had destroyed the Fomorians.

Ultonian youths. True was that sword and pure, and the hero seized it and went on against the Clan Cailitin. On the edge of the moving darkness strode Glas Mac Dalga, and Cuculain cried with a voice warning—"Son of Dalga, thou art not of their race, come forth from amongst them." And three times Cuculain called to him, and three times he refused. Then went on that mighty hero against the weird brood, fearless, alone, and a silence, and a terror fell on all the hosts of Erin. Alone went the hero, him nor god nor tutelar spirit, nor any of his class of power accompanied, repelled afar by the might of the Clan Cailitin. From their hills and grassy thrones remote, the gods of Erin watched him: Bove Derg from his cloudy turrets above the waters of the Aherlow; the great Dagda from his fairy palace by the Boyne, over against Ros-na-ree. Alone went the hero, while around him nations trembled; but into his heart the Ioldāna breathed his own lavish soul, and that fierce wrath, begotten of solitary thought, and outrage, and sacred pity, with which in the ancient days he led the arisen gods against the Fōmoroh, laying waste at Moy Tura their accursed ranks. Far flashed around him a starry radiance; he went swiftly, moaning as he went, and his voice was like the low brool of distant thunder heard behind hills, when the storm-spirit murmurs in his wrath; from the depths of his soul, shaken with a mighty rage, arose the blackbird of his valour, and floated in a visible shape above his head; gigantic waxed thy stature, Riastarra*! Alone he went down against the Clan Cailitin, as one who goes down into hell, the darkness gathered him in.

Within as from far distance there arose reverberations and horrid echoes as from deep caverns, and voice calling to voice, as of troop encouraging troop, and a noise of a crash, as of giants falling, a clangour of brass, and the thunder-pealing cry of the son of Sualtam amid the deafening uproar. Through rolling clouds there gleamed lurid lightnings, revealing things nameless, not to be described. From their tombs brake forth the ancient dead at the noise of that strife like the shock of worlds, for the earth stirred herself, and the dead arose out of their sleep of ages. Then time gave up her secrets and births to be, and her veiled nations and generations arose rank behind rank.

Like a torrent's fall their voices sounded from afar, summoning him to their deliverance, their thin voices unheard in the crash and roar of that awful strife.

Then were the hosts of Erin disordered, and the battalions clashed together; then sprang champions forth out of their chariots, and the steeds were panic-stricken, and flew through the plain with the war-cars. Now, too, was heard the voice of Cuculain, and he cried:—

"I know thee, O Mōr Reega. Four-footed thou dost not deceive me. What doest thou here in the shades of hell, thou queen of the mountain-dwelling gods? When wilt thou cease to persecute me, for I fear thee not?"

Thereafter arose the sound of a boy's voice, shrieking, being pursued, and then silence. Slowly then, like a mist, that magic darkness melted into the air, till that last inky blot had vanished, and on the reddened sward lay the enchanter, and his twenty-seven sons together, and further west, by himself, towards the camp of Meave, lay Glas Mac Dalga, and the hero stood alone, swordless, but with Fabâne still on his left arm. Amongst the dead was found the body of Fiecha Mac Fir Phœbé, the exiled Ultonian.

Then ran forward the hosts of the Clanna Rury, and the men of Meave brake and fled, some to Tara, and others following the course of the Three Waters, and there fled southwards the Ernai and the Clan Dēga, the Dergtheena and the Dairfeena, the Fir-morca and the people of Lōk Mac Favash, the Corca Lewy and the southern Fir-bolgs; but Queen Meave and the Olnemacta fled to the Shannon, pursued by the Clanna Rury and Cuculain. Nay-the-less, Cuculain himself checked the pursuit, and in the rear of their host he raised up his shield and guarded the retreat of Queen Meave, until they crossed the Shannon at Ath-a-Luan* Mic-Lewy. Then, on the eastern bank of the river, Cuculain set up a trophy and memorial, three great pillar-stones, hard by the stream. Queen Meave, on her part, sent back the Donn Cooalney to the Ultonians, and Cuculain led back the Red Branch into the north, with the captives and the plunder.

In the City of Ath-a-Cliah

Wrapped in thy scarlet bratta I see thee stalk through the city's
Narrow and populous streets.
—Longfellow[1]

For six years Cuculain rode triumphant over the nations of Eiré, and extended far and wide the authority of the Red Branch, and installed Lewy Rievenerg* as King in Termair; but at last the year drew on in which Cuculain should die.

In that year there was peace throughout all Eiré, and a suspension of war upon all sides, and the authority of Concobar Mac Nessa was very great. For Meave had made terms with him, and the kings of Munster and Leinster were submissive, and the four columns of Tara held Meath subject to the young king of Temair*. Then Concobar Mac Nessa resolved to send forth an expedition against the isles of Alba* and the marine districts, where he had colonies and subjects, but where his authority was lessened by reason of the great wars in Erin. Now before that, there came tributes to him even from the isles of Ore, where Cuculain Mac Sualtam had broken the power of the native races, and established the authority of the king of Ulla.

Then there was a great hosting of the Red Branch, and of volunteers from the rest of Eiré, and this expedition went forth out of Ath-a-cliah, which the foreign merchants called Eblana [Dublin],

1. *Editors' note*: Henry Wadsworth Longfellow, "To the Driving Cloud," in *The Complete Poetical Works* (Boston: Houghton Mifflin, 1910), 64, ll. 3–4. (In the original, Longfellow has "blanket" not "bratta.")

and it was subject to Lewy Rievenerg. But Concobar and his council determined that Cuculain should not go upon that expedition, for they said, "As long as Cuculain is in Erin so long will all those who would gladly rebel remain peaceful, but Ulla, being denuded of her warriors, will thus be safe on account of the great fear in which men hold Cuculain." Now Cuculain was not pleased at that resolution, nevertheless he submitted, but he came down to Ath-a-cliah and witnessed the departure of the Red Branch, and crossed the Tolka, and entered the walled city of Ath-a-cliah, and he and the great knights of the Clanna Rury were entertained publicly that night; but in the morning, ere it was day, the embarkation began, and perpetually until noon oared galleys were going down the Liffey to the sea, laden with warriors and stores, and the warriors shouted as each galley went off, and the unwarlike citizens clamoured along the shore; but lower down where the river broadens, between Ben Edar [Howth] and the opposite shore, they formed into lines before they went out into the open sea. All the great captains and princes of the Red Branch approached Cuculain, saluting him affectionately and sadly ere they departed, for a dark rumour went abroad that day through the host; but Cuculain and Læg, Lewy Rievenerg and his queen, Devorgilla*, were upon a raised place beside the wharf on the north side of the river. Along with them was Conaill, surnamed the Victorious, and Lendabar his wife, who had accompanied her great lord southwards to the sea; also his son, Euryal Glun-mar, for the other son [Leix Land-Mōr] went off early in the morning, leading volunteers from the districts east of Slieve Blâma. But Conaill Carna was disturbed in his mind, and his noble countenance was marred, nor exulted he in the martial display, nor in the brilliant warriors before him, and he, with a sad countenance, said to Cuculain:—

"O Cu, there are evil rumours abroad concerning thee this day; and I think that there is not wisdom in the Saba of the High King, though one of them is my own father, that they should send forth all the flower and strength of the Red Branch for the conquest of that barren coast and those naked isles, leaving thee only to be a mainstay of the realm. And this, too, thou well knowest, Lewy, for between friends it may be mentioned, that without the Red Branch thy sovereignty is lost. For thou wast elected partly out of reverence for an omen, but principally on account of thy foster-father, Cuculain, and the great power and authority which he, and he only, though I displease him by saying it, has procured for the Clanna Rury. For beyond the Four Pillars of Tara, who unsupported are powerless, thou hast no force to quell anywhere an insurrection, and thy enemies are like the sands of yonder shore. For all Leinster is in the hands of tribes hostile to thee, obedient to the sons of Finn, the son of Ross Roe, and the son of Cairbré Nia-far*, Erc*, the fair-haired, a subtle-minded and ambitious youth, himself a son of the king of Tara; and in the south are the children of Cathīr, son of Eterskél, king of the Ernai, and the descendants of that mighty monarch slain hard by where we now sit, and all the west is subject to that great Queen, whom fear alone causes to obey thee. And thou art king of Erin, and entitled to hold the great assembly at Temair only because of Cuculain and the Red Branch, though, too, thy birth is right royal.

"But thinking upon these things, O Cu, my mind misgives me this day, when I think of Ulla emptied of the Clanna Rury, and of thee, with old men and boys, and a feeble battalion of trained warriors against a sudden hosting of our enemies. For I think, O my dear foster-brother, that though thy countenance is mild, and though thou art dear to the women of Ulla, and though the Red Branch honour thee like a god, that elsewhere throughout Eiré there is not a household in which thy name is not like a curse, for there are not many tribes in Fohla out of which thou hast not at some time slain a son, or a father, or a brother, and there is a tide of vengeance which is growing against thee, and which thou hast incurred fighting for our king, being always the first to enter a battle, and the last to leave it, for the Clan Humōr in the west abhor thee since that great battle in which thou didst conquer them at Rath Cruhane; and now the power of that Province has passed altogether into their hands,[2] and

2. The authority of the sons of Aileel was, however, subsequently restored. After the death of Aileel there was a war between Senbus, supported by the Clan

Queen Meave leans upon them, and Erc, the son of Cairbré Niafar, nurses against thee a vengeful heart, since that great battle at Ros-na-ree, where thou slewest his father, and brake the power of the nobles of Meath and Bregia; and at Finn Cora thou slewest Finn his brother, the son of Rossa Roe, king of Lahan; and his sons are now powerful; and at Gabra, hard by towards the west, thou didst slay Liath Maina and the kings of Munster; and at Letter Lee thou didst conquer and slay Curoi Mac Dary, and his sons yet live and are powerful; and at Moy Femen thou didst overthrow the Clan Dēga, and Temair Luhara thou didst sack, and Garmān; and there is no part of Eiré in which thou hast not sown some bitter seed. Also, there is that prophecy about the Clan Cailitin[3] who, they say, have even gone down to hell searching for means by which to destroy thee; and now, O my dear foster-brother, thus shalt thou do. If the men of Erin invade Ulla, thou shalt retreat before them, passing into remote fastnesses, or to Emain Macha, which is fortified; but go not out into the open against them, and when I return with the Red Branch we will take vengeance and exact a four-fold eric*. And this I say, being much thy elder, and loving thee above all others, for since that feast[4] at Dûn Rury no jealous spirit ever touched me, though before that thou wast knighted I was chiefest in renown, and Legairé Buada next to me."

And Lewy Rievenerg said:—

Humōr, and Mainey Ahrimail. The latter was victorious, and died grandævus in the reign of Tuhal Tectmar, king of Erin. See O'Flaherty's "Ogygia."

3. By the advice of Cailitin, Queen Meave returning, brake the right hands and the right feet of the six surviving children of Cailitin, that they might devote their lives to druidism and enchantments.

4. This was the palace of Bricrind, the satirist; and it was at this feast, owing to the wiles of Bricrind, that then commenced the celebrated dispute between Cuculain, Conaill Carna, and Lægairé Buada, concerning the right to the Champion's Throne of Ulla. After the expulsion of Fergus Mac Roy, the military chief of the Red Branch, some such dissensions must have arisen. This dispute forms the subject of a historic tale, called "The Feast of Bricrind."

"To thee, O dear foster-father, it is due that I hold in Tara the silvern wand of Yeoha Feidleea [his grandfather]; and though slender my power, yet no foe shall approach Murthemney unless my warriors be overthrown, and myself slain."

But Cuculain smiled upon Lewy Rievenerg, and answered Conaill thus:—

"O foster-brother, thou art sad because thou art departing and I am left behind, and I, too, am sad for the same cause. I also shall one day die like those who were better than me, who perished in Moy Tura the Upper and the Lower, where perished of yore the heroic Firbolgs, and the Fōmoroh; and the sons of Milith perished who were greater and nobler than we, and who fought against the gods, and drave them to the hills and the protection of the Fæd Fia; and I think at times of my own ancestor, the heroic Iar, who died in the night and in the storm, overwhelmed by the waves, when his ship brake in the darkness against the black rock most treacherous, and they say his tomb is on the summit, where four great stones support a huge flag; but I, when I die, shall be slain in battle, breathing forth warlike breath, defending the Red Branch, and my people who elected me to be their king, and of whom many have already perished fighting beside me. But death shall not surprise me, for I shall see certain portents. I shall hear the music of Orphid, the son of Manar, and see Rod the son of Lir. These things the gods of Erin have promised me, and they made me strong who was weak, and great who was little, and when they indicate to me that I must die, then shall I die. Thou, Conaill, and others may avoid death, but I am in the hand of the gods, and aught that they indicate I must do."

But Cuculain turned to Furbey*, the Cæsarian, who was near him and said: "I think, Furbey, that thy slinging will soon render mine obscure, though I, too, could shoot very straight, but I practised industriously that I might excel."

Then Furbey blushed and laughed, for he was a boy, and many an hour had he spent at this exercise in solitary places, and deemed that it was not known.

But after that there came a lewd fellow out of the street saying:—

"Which among you is Cuculain, the great warrior, concerning whom the poets everlastingly sing, saying, 'That he is, by far, the best man in all Erin'?"

And Cuculain looked upon the man, smiling pleasantly, and said:—

"O, gracious citizen, I am he."

But the other answered, with an oath such as men used then, "That Cuculain was not fit to buckle his armour on Angus, the son of Humor, for he had seen the Clan Humōr while they lived under the protection of Cairbré Nia-far;" and he also said, "That the youth with red hair [Læg], and the gold band round his forehead, was the greatest warrior in that presence."

Whereat amongst the princes there arose much laughter, therefore Conaill was unable to repeat his suit to Cuculain, and he parted with a very sad heart. Then the last of the flooring that ran from the wharf to that galley in which Conaill, son of Amargin, sailed, was taken away, and the white oars began to move where, unseen, the oarsmen plied their manly labour.

The ship went down the stream, but Conaill stood upon the deck, turning round from time to time, as the ship went on. Yet in his heart there was a feeling as if an ice-cold hand were touching the springs of life, and with difficulty he repressed the rising tear, and already he plotted in his deep heart that terrible vengeance which he exacted afterwards on the slayers of Cuculain.

But Cuculain and Læg wandered through the city of Ath-a-Cliah,[5] wondering at the many strange things there, for there was much traffic, and many persons passing to and fro, and a roar of wheels and of hurrying feet. Moreover, along the streets, behind windows of bright glass, were exposed many curious goods of the merchants, and tempting wares of all kinds, both those which were native to the land, and

5. The trade of Dublin with the Continent must have been considerable at this time. In the second century the division of the dues of this port caused a great war. See "Battle of Moy Leana." See Tacitus on the commercial greatness of Ireland in his own time. Dublin was at this time a city of timber.

what was brought beyond the seas by the merchant; and Cuculain and Læg wandered on from window to gay window, for in some were choice swords, and spear-heads, and body-armour, and in others were chariots, some strong and low-wheeled and scythéd for war, but others also for pleasure, and vehicles for the transfer of goods, and for the service of those that tilled the soil. And they passed by windows in which were exposed mantles and lēnas of wool, linen, and silk, decorated with gold thread or silver, and with the labours of the embroidering woman, and others in which were rolls and leaves of parchment in which men's thoughts were inscribed; and Cuculain wondered at this, for timber and stone only were used amongst his people for that purpose, and the form of the letters too was different; and they came to another house, in which there were small images of horses cut in timber, and of warriors' chariots and horses set upon a flooring of deal, and beneath the flooring, wheels, so that the whole might move forward together, and warriors sat in the chariot, of whom one drove while the other, as it were, fought, and the head of the fighting man nodded as the wheels went round. This Læg purchased, remembering a small fair head at Dûn Dalgan, taking from his belt a small silver weight, for uncoined gold and silver were then used instead of money, and of this the rechtairé* of Cuculain received much in return for the wool which his estates produced abundantly.

So through the city of Ath-a-Cliah walked the heroes; and Cuculain was dejected when he looked upon the people, so small were they, and so pale and ignoble, both in appearance and behaviour; and also when he saw the extreme poverty of the poor, and the hurrying eager crowds seeking what he knew not. But they, on the other hand, were astonished at the heroes, the greatness of their stature, the majesty of their bearing, and their tranquillity; also, at the richness and brightness of their apparel, the whiteness of their skin, and their long hair, parted in the middle and rolling over their shoulders. For, amongst the citizens of Ath-a-Cliah, they seemed like scions of some mighty and divine race long since passed away.

But after this they visited that place in which justice was dispensed amongst the citizens of Ath-a-Cliah; and it so happened that when Cuculain entered there was a great trial proceeding, concerning the assassination of a princess [Dove*, in Irish Dûbh], who was slain beside the river, by the servant of Enna, whose father's palace was upon the hill called Forcarthen, and the court was crowded. Nevertheless they gave way before the princes, and a murmur passed through the assembly as they entered, for their fair countenances seemed to lighten that dim place, and far above the crowd appeared their mighty shoulders and lofty heads, and the business of the court was suspended. So, for a space, stood Cuculain and Læg, and they listened to the administration of the laws of the city. On a raised seat sat the presiding ollav. Fat was he, and uncomely to look upon, but a bright and nimble spirit illuminated his unheroic visage; and Cuculain and Læg laughed at his swift mirth-moving comments and interrogations as the case proceeded; also, Cuculain wondered at his marvellous sagacity, and reasonableness, and minute acquaintance with the ancient laws of Ollam Fodla*, for he himself being a king, was president of the Cûlairechta* of his nation, although in Ath-a-Cliah, being a city of merchants, many alterations and innovations had been made; then between two ollavs, one defending and the other prosecuting the charge against the man-slayer, there arose an unseemly dispute and much bickering and clamour, amid which the warriors retired and went forth, but there followed them many of the people.

But after that they set forth with the retinue, and a great multitude had assembled at the place from which they should start, and where the retinue were already in readiness, and when Cuculain entered the chariot, they shouted; and though many of them were very meagre to look upon and thinly clad, yet they cried out lustily in honour of the renowned Prince, for his fame had gone abroad over the whole land, and warmed many cold, and lit many dark souls. But amongst them, also, were dark and angry faces of warriors who had fought at Rosnaree, under Cairbré Nia-far, and at Gabra, under Finn Mac Rossa, and of dispossessed lords of territory, whom Cuculain and the Red Branch had driven out, and who, now in poverty and disgrace, nursed a sad life in Ath-a-Cliah. But Cuculain and Læg set forth to travel northward, and they passed the Tolka, and drave by the sea-side, with a retinue of eighty men, according to the law, and they came to Lusk, and were entertained that night by Forgal Mánah, who conversed loftily with Cuculain, advising him in many things, for he was a judge and a man in authority, nor remembered he now that slaughter which Cuculain had made amongst his people when he fled with Emer, and at every ford and narrow pass between Lusk and Dûn Dalgan was forced to fight with the people of Forgal, bearing away his wife, beautiful Emer, who was surnamed the eloquent and the proud.

But in the morning Cuculain and his people set off again, and it was evening when they reached Dûn Dalgan, and the hounds recognised him afar off, baying lustily, and in all the windows of the Dûn there was a ruddy light, illumining the lime-trees and elms upon the lawn, and the bright stream[6] that traversed it, starting from the well-head beneath the Dûn, and in which Cuculain, as a child, had been wont to play, building there dams and mimic bridges, and in which Connla* now did the same, after the manner of children delighting in such things.

Then the draw-bridge was let down, creaking on brazen hinges; and in the gateway of the rampart stood Emer, having on her breast Fionscōta*, and Connla stood beside her, holding her right hand. Happy that night was Emer, knowing that her lord was not needed for that foreign service of the Red Branch, remembering not at all [the] prophecies, and omens, and the dim predictions of the soothsayers of Ulla; therefore, she stood radiant in the gateway, having the appearance of a beautiful and happy maiden, though six years had passed since she was the bride of Cuculain; and when he saw her, Cuculain sprang forth from the chariot; but Læg took the boy into the chariot, setting him on his knee, and entrusted the reins to his tiny hands, and so they drave round to where were the stables and

6. This stream is said to flow still from the neighbourhood of what is believed to be the remains of Cuculain's palace.

chariot-houses in the rear of the dûn; and soon the wide court was filled with an immense noise, the washing of steeds and chariots, and the cries of horseboys, and the loud voice of Læg controlling them and directing.

But within the dûn, in the great central chamber, supper was prepared; and when those who travelled had removed from themselves the stains of travel, they all came into the lofty and bright chamber, set around with tall waxen candles that glittered upon polished shields and spear-heads all around. A long table extended from the north southwards, and at one end sat Cuculain, and Læg, and Emer, and the Ard-Druid and Ard-Ollav of that small realm, and the hostages and young princes in fosterage. There then they feasted joyfully, while the music of the harp and reed was heard, and Cuculain talked and laughed much that night, for he was by no means of a morose disposition, nor accustomed to wear a severe countenance at a feast; and Connla, at the lower table with the ruder warriors and swine-herds, whose society he most affected, displayed the toy-chariot, rolling it upon the table; but when it was exhibited at the lower table there was a loud laughter, when the rough warriors saw how the head nodded in the chariot as the wheels went round; and thus they amused themselves till there arose the shanachie* of the realm, and he sang of the history of Lewy Rievenerg, the high king of all Erin, and how Yeoha Faydleea ruled over Erin, and begat the three Finns of Emain, and how they and their sister Clohra brought up Lewy, and how the brothers rebelled; and of that great battle at Ath Comhar, and the ghastly present made to the high king, and of Lewy solitary grieving he sang, and of his residence at Dûn Dalgan, and the parental care of Cuculain; also of that Convention at Temair, and of the soothsayer starting forth from slumber and crying:—

"I have seen a youth weeping beside a couch at Emain Macha, and on the couch lay a hero, dying of a wasting and nameless sickness, being stricken by the divine people. That youth weeping shall be your king."

Then they all drank a pledge in honour of the High King, and Devorgilla his queen, for Lewy had been often in that hall, a young unknown prince, ere that election, and he was faithful and affectionate beyond all others to Cuculain.

But after that Cuculain and Emer, Læg, and certain others withdrew to the greenan of Emer, and conversed in a more private fashion, and Cuculain described all that he had heard and seen in Ath-a-Cliah; and of the warriors some played at chess, but others, and these the best, conversed with the queen. For pure and good was the wife of Cuculain; her mind eager concerning the noble and the true, and those who conversed with her were happy for many days.

Thus were they employed in that bright chamber; but out on the waves of the Muirnict there was a sound of singing voices, and the music of the harp and reed, mingled with the wash of waters, and the noise of a thousand oars in the row-locks, and in every ship the bards' song was concerning Cuculain, and dark prophecies were chanted, and many rough warriors wept that night.

On the eve of Samhane, Concobar and his people gather at Emain Macha to feast, though none of his great warriors is present. During the feasting, the high king gives a speech in celebration of the three mighty champions of the Ultonian realm, Cuculain being the greatest. But the celebration is cut short by the entrance of the ban-ecla*, who reports that "there is a great hosting of all the Four Provinces of Rath Cruhane," which results in rebellion across much of Eiré and the destruction of the Red Branch.*

The Last Hosting against Cuculain

The hoarse note of rebellion, tumultuous and swelling.
—Ancient Bard[1]

It was in the dusk of the evening as [Queen Meave] returned alone from the pasture-ground and the quarter of her herdsmen hard by the palace, and as she passed through the lawn of her dûn, beneath the trees, that the Clan Cailitin appeared unto Queen Meave, and the great Queen screamed when she saw them. Nevertheless, the old vindictive spirit returned into her mind when she knew that they had come back into Erin, all-powerful, having acquired magic attributes, before which even those who dwelt invisible in the mountains were impotent, and she said that now at last would the Red Branch be rooted out, and Cuculain, son of Sualtam, overborne and slain. Wherefore, she sent a far summons to her allies and friends, and all who held rebellious thoughts against the Ultonians, and against the king [Lewy Rievenerg] whom they had set up in Tara.

It was fourteen days ere all these came together to Rath Cruhâne, and selecting the chiefs, she harangued them in a secret assembly, having first dismissed Fergus upon distant service to the extreme west of the province. There she enumerated all that the nations of Eiré had suffered at the hands of the Red Branch, and how now an opportunity of gold was within their reach, seeing that Cuculain only remained in Erin out of all the might of the Clanna Rury, and

1. *Editors' note*: No source for this epigraph is found outside of O'Grady.

that no power could restrain him from entering the battle against them, even alone, should they invade his realm or any part of Ulla, and that now the withered and blasted brood had returned to Erin, and how all the soothsayers had prophesied that their return would be fatal to Cuculain, and she said:—

"O Lewy Mac Conroi, hast thou the heart to go upon this hosting?"

Then Lewy Mac Conroi answered fiercely, relating the slaughter of his father at the hands of Cuculain, and at his hands the destruction of his palace and the subjugation of his nation, and there before the assembled kings he renounced his allegiance to the Clanna Rury, and all love and gratitude to the son of Sualtam.[2]

Then was Queen Meave glad, and she turned to Erc and said:—

"At least thou, O Erc, wilt cleave to the Clanna Rury, so dextrously have they used thee for their own good."

And Erc answered:—

"The Clanna Rury have ever been most gracious to me, and most so Cuculain, son of Sualtam, who with Emer, his beautiful wife, have oftentimes hospitably entertained me in their palace at Dûn Dalgan."

But Queen Meave smiled, and said:—

"Surely, wise and prudent is the Sāba of the King of Ulla, and very crafty and politic is the Prince of Murthemney. Kind words, and a welcome, and banquets they give thee, and thou for them holdest Mid-Erin in subjection. Thou art still young, O son of the King of Erin, and therefore very confiding and simple."

Then Erc blushed with shame, and said:—

"My sister, Acaill, who was as a mother unto me when I was a child, and tenderly reared me until she went northwards into Ulla as the bride of Glan, son of Carbad, strictly enjoined me that I should

2. Cuculain was the foster-father and upholder of Lewy [Mac Conroi]. Early in his career he had sacked Cathair Conroi, the palace of Curoi Mac Dary, in the mountains west of Tralce, and there slain the father of Lewy, and broken down the Clan Conroi.

be faithful to the Red Branch." But Queen Meave, laughing scornfully, said:—

"Who is Acaill that she should govern the thoughts of men? It is not right that a woman should take upon herself authority and rule. Thou didst well to obey her when thou wast a child; but a king governs himself, and is guided by his own counsel. Knowest thou who slew thy father, thou gentle and forgiving?"

And Erc answered:—

"O mighty Queen, I will go out upon this hosting. Again in my mind hast thou awaked visions of vengeance, and wrath at last appeased, and disgrace outworn, and humiliation set aside. For the princes of Meath and Bregia say to me, taunting, 'O Erc, son of Cairbré, how long shall remain unavenged the bloody grave of thy heroic sire, whilst thou, in sleek, ignoble ease, livest vilely, confederate with those who slew him, and who expelled all the nobles loyal to thy line, and set up against thee in Tara this lily-hearted youth. But thou art traitor to thy race, for thy father was Cairbré Nia-far, King of all Erin, and his father Rossa Roe, a stock of Royal Branches, and his father Fergus of the Rings, King of Erin, and his father Nuada the Snow-white, who drave the Clan Dēga out of Tara and ruled in their stead, being a descendant of that Crimthann who, with Rury Mōr, contended for the Ard-Rieship of all Erin, his race even then kingly, when the Red Branch was yet ignoble and unknown. But thou art a rank weed, misusing the soil that nourished thy royal-hearted sires.' So they speak to me in secret, casting taunts. And when I go down to Ath-a-Cliah I see there stern countenances full of wrath and scorn, and limbs of heroic mould in mean raiment, and maimed warriors who perilled all for my father, and they gather together in groups, and look side-long at me as I pass, holding silence. Yea, and in my hall when the poets sing I feel the veiled satire, the half-discovered appeal, and the half-revealed contempt, and my life is a burthen to me, and without joy this permitted sovereignty. Well I know who slew him, for it was Cuculain, the son of Sualtam, on that fatal day at Ros-na-Ree, when the Boyne flowed red with the blood of my nation. I too fling aside my allegiance, and if in battle I meet the son of Sualtam, I shall slay him, or he will slay me."

Also, Concobar and Mac Nia disclaimed their allegiance, whose father the son of Sualtam had slain, and whose nation he had reduced, so that they acknowledged the sovereignty of the Clanna Rury.

Then was there a swift hosting of the allies of Meath, and, for the last time, Murthemney was invaded by the great Queen of the Olnemacta.

Flight to Emain Macha

Boom, storm-bell.
—Edmund Strong[1]

On the morrow, after the feast of Samhane, Cuculain and Læg arose early, for they intended that day to hunt in the forests eastward in Cooalney. Around the dûn there was a noise of preparation, for the hounds bayed in their osiered* cars, and the slaves were bringing forth the nets and boar-spears. Below, the Muirnict glittered, sharp smitten by the bright frosty ray. On a stone seat, hard by the door-way on the left, sat Cuculain; on his right was Luath, the favourite hound, and between his knees Connla, listening with wondering eyes, while Cuculain related to him, in simple child-like fashion, how in the ancient days Fuad and Murthemney had conquered that country, and he described their battles and sufferings, and how they cleared the ancient forests, and built dûns, and made pasture-land for their cattle.

Then Cuculain, raising his eyes, saw Lavarcam emerging from a beech grove, and moving slowly across the lawn. To her Cuculain hastened gladly, indicating to Læg that he should put back the preparations, and he received the ban-ecla, pouring forth a torrent of friendly welcome and affection, and he led her into the palace into

1. *Editors' note*: Edmund J. Armstrong, "The Prisoner of Mount Saint Michael," in *The Poetical Works of Edmund J. Armstrong*, ed. George Francis Armstrong (London: Longmans, Green, 1877), 182.

the greenan of Emer, but the beautiful ban-ecla sighed as she went, and the bright tears shone in her eyes.

Thereafter entered Emer, and she likewise received the ban-ecla joyfully, and said:—

"O dear Lavarcam, it is long since you have been at Dûn Dalgan, and now shall you remain here for many days."

But while she yet spake, there entered a slave bearing a tray of polished findruiney, and she spread upon the table a cloth of fine linen, and laid thereon such viands* as were customary in those days; brown thin cakes of fine flour, prepared with cream and honey; small rolls of fresh butter, and water-cresses from the stream, also glistening glass and mead in a silver jug with a lip of ruddy gold; but Lavarcam, though she drank the ruddy mead, and affected to eat, nevertheless ate not, and she stammered in her speech, though before very eloquent. Then said Cuculain:—

"Thou art pale, O Lavarcam, and all thy limbs tremble. Thou comest, I think, bearing tidings of some great woe. Is it concerning my uncle, the High King of all Ulla, that thou hast now come? Much do I fear concerning him since that fatal battle at Derry Da Væh."

Him the ban-ecla answered:—

"Cuculain, I have a message unto thee from the High King and the Sāba of the Ultonian nation, who strictly enjoin thee to come straightway to Emain Macha, there thou mayest be under the protection of Cathvah, and the druids and wizards of the Clanna Rury. For the children of Cailitin have returned to Ireland, having great power, who have travelled the round world seeking means to destroy thee, and to dispel thy magic attributes and the favour of the Shee, and they say that they have even gone down to hell seeking means to destroy thee. Therefore, not without reason, O dear Setanta, is my face pale, and all my limbs tremble."

So spake the ban-ecla, and the flood of her sorrow overflowed, and she lifted up her voice and wept, lamenting for the hero.

But when she heard that word the daughter of Forgal Mánah stood up from her place, concealing her face with her hands, and uttered a loud and piercing cry, for now the old weird prophecy was accomplished, and the end of all things was at hand, and the light of life went down into darkness and the grave, and the women of the dûn heard it and ran in, even her dear friends, and the daughters of the chieftains and nobles of all that territory who were in fosterage with Emer, and who daily grew more to resemble her in noble thoughts and gracious lofty mien, and when they heard of the return of the Clan Cailitin, they too lifted up their voices and fell each upon her knees, and they raised the cry of the dead, such as mourners raise over a king slain; and the grinding women and the slaves around the dûn heard it, and they raised up their voices weeping for the untimely end of the hero; but Cuculain supported Emer, and laid her white and motionless upon a couch, and gave her in charge to Lavarcam, and he met Læg at the door, and the men of the household, and he said:—

"These are bad tidings, O Læg; nevertheless I have not received those monitions which have been foretold to me, and till they arise I fear not that wandering clan. But go now and make preparations for our departure, for I must go on straightway to Emain Macha, obeying the command of the High King and his Saba, who desire that I shall henceforward, at Emain Macha, remain under the protection of the Cathvah and the druids and wizards of the Ultonians."

Then departed the warriors, pale and silent, smitten with a speechless sorrow, and the youths who were in fosterage came round Cuculain weeping, and to them Cuculain spake pleasant comfortable words, repeating what he had said to Læg, and their sorrow and terror were allayed.

All round the dûn moved the servants and men-of-war, hastening on the departure, and fierce and low were their words when any slackened or blundered in his task, eager that Cuculain should reach Emain Macha, and be under the protection of Cathvah and the druids of Ulla; nor did they or Cuculain know of the hosting, for this the ban-ecla concealed, knowing that thereafter it would not be in their power to bring away Cuculain out of Murthemney.

Then came the tanist of the realm, and to him Cuculain gave the kingdom in charge, in words few and low, but of great authority, advising and dissuading; and ere noon they went forth from Dûn Dalgan, along the road which led to Emain Macha, with attending warriors and chariots. In one chariot travelled Emer with Fionscōta, pale and silent, with large woe-stricken eyes, and in another Cuculain, and Læg, and Connla. At nightfall they were met by Genānn Gruag-Sulus, the son of Cathvah, with a company of the standing battalion of Emain Macha, and certain of the Ultonian druids, and they passed that night with the bru-fir* of the territory, and on the next evening they approached Emain Macha, and Cuculain was glad when he saw the lights of the city, and the princely homes of the Red Branch; but Læg uttered bitter words, and recalled their return thither in old times how triumphant, having conquered the enemies of the Ultonians.

Then came forth from the city the standing battalion of Emain Macha, heavy-armed troops marching in strict order, and they enclosed the chariot of Cuculain, and kept back the shouting concourse, who joyfully beheld the coming of Cuculain, for the warriors feared lest Cuculain should learn [of] the impending invasion, and a strict charge concerning this had gone out from the Sāba, with speedy death as the penalty of its infringement.

So they approached the royal dûn, and Concobar Mac Nessa, and Mugain*, the High Queen of the province, received Cuculain and Emer joyfully at the threshold of the dûn, and the young knights took charge of Cuculain, and Mugain and her women took charge of Emer and the two children.

That night they feasted as at other times in the Tec Mid-cuarta*, and Cuculain sat in his place in the Champion's Throne, and Emer in her place beyond all the queens and princesses of Ulla, for she ranked next to the High Queen herself amongst the women of the Ultonians. Bright shone the vessels of glass and bronze, silver and gold, and bright glittered the bronze capitals of the great pillars, and the canopy above the High King's couch, and the joinings of the rafters of the lofty hall were apparent. But the feasting and merriment were alien to their thoughts, and an ice-cold hand touched the life-springs of every heart that night.

There was Cathvah the Ard-druid of the Ultonian nation, surnamed Iarn-glunah*, the mighty wizard, but his face was troubled, for all the omens pointed to sorrow, and his magic arts were confused, and some strange new power overshadowed him. There too was Genānn "of the lightsome countenance," very dear he to Cuculain, and he sat next to the champion, and there too Nieve* the druidess, the daughter of Kelkar, who, above all the women, loved and honoured the hero, and it was upon them that the Ultonians placed their chief reliance, for the power of Cathvah was broken by the enchantments of the children of Cailitin.

After the feast Cuculain and Læg went into the women's apartment, and Cuculain conversed that night after his wont, and he played at chess with Sencha Mac Aileel, the orator, and won from him three games, and Cuculain said:—

"O son of Aileel, I have beaten thee three times; yet never before have I won against thee even one game in three."

But the thoughts of the orator were elsewhere, and his mind confused.

In the great banqueting-hall the High King dismissed the warriors, and held a close council of the druids. One by one the candles went out through the vast chamber; but the druids gathering close together conversed long in low grave voices, for very real and terrible to them was that prophecy and the power of the Clan Cailitin.

At this council it was determined that Cuculain should, that night, be under the protection of Genānn, and should sleep in his chamber where were his idol-gods, and his instruments of magic, and they thought that Genānn, before all others, would be able to shield him against the might of the wandering clan.

Cuculain Hears the Singing of Mac Manar

"Whirl away, whirl away,
Eddying gust whirl the leaves
And the dust; lash the bay
Till it whitens;
Never spare it till it brightens,
Till it darkens, till it lightens
White and grey, white and grey.

"Bow the branches, conqueror!
Twirl the foam as it wreathes,
Twist the fern upon the scaur,
Toss the tarn until it seethes;
Sweep the world, overwhelm
Bending oak and tottering elm,
Scourge the forest and the sea,
Let the scudding rack be curl'd,
And the foamy flakes be whirl'd,
Sound a trumpet in the rocks—Victory!

"Eddying gust, whirl the leaf
With the dust to the bay-
Whirl away! . . .
One I trembled to the sighing
Of a maiden who is dying
Far away.

"And the merry sunshine thrilled me,
And the rapture of the May
Stirred within me, and it filled me
Full of life, and I was gay,

As I flickered on the spray,
Till a hoar-frost came and killed me,
Whirl away, whirl away!"
—Edmund Armstrong[1]

That night Cuculain and Genānn Gruag-Sulus slept together in the same chamber, and Genānn brought into bed with him his idol-gods and his instruments of magic, hoping to shield his dear friend and schoolfellow from the weird powers which were now abroad.

Without, a tempest raged with wind and heavy rain; but after a space Cuculain reached across his hand to the bed in which Genānn slept to awake him, but the other was not at all asleep, and Cuculain said:—

"O Genānn, there is a martial preparation forward in Emain Macha, for I hear the rumbling of wheels and the voices of captains giving commands, and more than once I heard the door of the Tayta Brac opened. There is a hosting forward, and I have not been made aware of it or consulted as before. Wherefore is this?" And Cuculain started up in his bed as he spake.

Then Gruag-Sulus trembled, and his heart refused to beat; but Cuculain went on.

"There is an invasion somewhere, and they have concealed it from me, fearing that wandering clan, but if the gods permit the Clan Cailitin to slay me, they will slay me here in Emain Macha as well as on the frontier. Once before there went a host southwards to protect the marches, and they were all boys, and Beta Mac Bœn of the Olnemacta, with his people, slew them, and along the Avon Dia, between that stream and Dûndalgan, their blood was shed over the land. And now, too, there are few mature warriors left in Ulla, and

1. *Editors' note*: Edmund J. Armstrong, "September Equinox," in *Poetical Works*, 454–55.

if there is a war, and I not at hand, there will again be a renewal of that piteous slaughter."

But meantime Cuculain had fastened on his sandals and thrown a bratta over his shoulders, and was going to the door when Genānn sprang forward and cast his two arms around his waist, and said:—

"Thou shalt not go forth to-night, Cuculain, or thou shalt go forth having slain me. There are evil powers abroad against thee. This expedition is doubtless to ward off a border foray, or to pursue some vile band of cattle plunderers from the west of the Shannon. Go not abroad, O dear Setanta."

Then Cuculain laughed, and said:—

"Thou art right, O dear schoolfellow; it is not fit that I should rush forward wherever there is a sound of battle like some hardened fighters, who then only seem to live."

Cuculain lay down again and, deeming that he slept, he heard a voice[2] singing, and it said:—

"O Prince of Murthemney, O flame of the Heroes of Eiré!
What ails thee that thou art so slothful?
Arise! put on thy might as of yore.
Son of Lu, hound unconquerable, scatter thy enemies,
Scatter thy enemies, O Cu,
Cuculain Mac Sualtam."

Then Cuculain told the dream to Genānn, but Genānn knew that it was no dream, for he too had heard the voice singing.

But in the morning, those who were permitted to approach Cuculain made light of the expedition, as had Genānn Gruag-Sulus, saying that it was to repel some border foray; and they laid plans to appease Cuculain's curiosity, and prevent him from going out and learning tidings of the great invasion by Meave and the son of Cairbré Nia-far, and the strain put upon the whole Province to collect some resisting force.

2. This voice came from the weird children.

But it seemed to them best that he should be entertained with tales of ancient heroes, to which at all times Cuculain listened gladly. Cuculain was pleased when he heard it. Moreover, the council had laid injunctions upon him, that he should not go abroad into the city and the surrounding country; and this, too, approved itself to his own judgment, for he too believed in wizardry and incantations, and the power of intercession and prayer; and he believed that Cathvah, and Genānn, and Nieve were able to draw over him some weird spiritual shield against the spiritual foe.

That day the great central chamber was set in order, and Cuculain and Emer, the queens, and the great warriors who had not yet gone away southwards, sat there, and were entertained by Heim* the royal bard, who for them related the history of Lu Lamfáda and the mighty eric, which he had put upon the three sons of Turānn, and the sufferings of the brothers, and the implacable wrath of the mighty Ioldāna; but not of Lu Lamfáda were the thoughts of the assembly that day. To the bard Cuculain attended, carefully explaining all to Connla as the tale went on.

But when the tale was ended, then Cuculain, and Læg, and the attending knights went down to the place, in which were the young princes of Ulla, who were in fosterage with the High King; and Cuculain and Læg looked around them with great affection upon that noble park, where they knew well every nook and tree, and much they conversed with the knights who surrounded them, recalling old adventures and pleasant incidents of that happy life, for as yet books had not imposed their tyranny over youthful minds; but the boys were there taught the management of steeds and chariots, and how to guide the scythed-chariot, and to close or let out the deadly shining blade, and to run forward upon the chariot-pole, also to fight from the chariot, to hurl the spear when the steeds galloped, and to protect the charioteer against a rain of blunt javelins, and how to leap swiftly and surely from the rapid chariot, and to leap thereinto again, and all that pertained to such warfare. There noble knights taught them these warlike arts, and also to charge in lines with firmly-held spears, and to move quickly and skilfully the shield, and to cast with unerring aim and immense force the battle-stone of the combatant, and all the noble exercise of that warlike age; also to swim, and to ride, and to play at chess, beside their boyish pastimes, which too were encouraged, for there were those who professed the knowledge of the laws relating to such games, and who decided disputes and awarded small erics as in weightier matters, so that they might love law and hate lawlessness.

Nor did the wise Cathvah suffer their minds to lie unused while in other things they were made skilful and bold, for there they were taught to reverence the unseen people—the mountain-dwelling immortal children of Mōr-Reega, and the descendants of Nemeth, and they learned also the history of their people, and the great deeds of their ancestors, adorned with all that the love and reverence of the bards might suggest, and each boy knew the history of the founder of his tribe, and where inurned lay his ashes beneath the green rath, or in its house within the walled cathair, nor deemed they then that one day that earth would be removed for the cultivation of the soil, and that the stones which their pious ancestors had set up would be ravished from their place, to build fences and pave roads by a more ignoble race; and beneath many a small tunic there were nourished noble thoughts, nor deemed they that they were nobler than their sires, though they were; nor flourished then the vile teachings of Cailitin, and those who reviled the things of old; and many a bad verse was there made by heroic youths, and many an ill-constructed tale by noble boys.

But Cuculain and the knights moved onward, and he marvelled that no games or exercises were exhibited that day, for the boys went about in small groups forgetful of their daily pastimes, for there was a cloud over all Emain Macha. But when they saw Cuculain, they all ran together to him out of the remote parts of the lawn, and from amongst the trees where they listened to their elders relating the deeds of Cuculain, which he had performed and forgotten in that small theatre of his fame, and which they had themselves received from their elders, who were then his comrades and co-evals.

Around him the boys crowded, and many of them seized his hands and kissed them, and they kissed the bratta that hung from his shoulders; but after that, like a stream that bursts through some restraining barrier, their young hearts were dissolved in tears, and there was a sound of sobbing voices around the son of Sualtam, and they said:—

"O Cuculain, they say that it is the end of thy career, and that thy victorious attributes are over, and that they who will destroy thee are returned to Erin, and as dear art thou to us as to those who went southwards to the plain of the Fardia to fight for thee when the great warriors of Ulla refused to go: and we, too, would give our lives for thee if we could preserve thee from that accursed clan."

But Cuculain smiled, and said that though he should perish there would come greater warriors than himself out of that place, which was, indeed, not true, and he said that it was a false rumour, for that he should hear Mac Manar and see Rod.

The boys after that followed him to the borders of the permitted ground, and there stood looking after him as he went up to the King's palace.

But that night Cuculain's quiet spirit was troubled, and he said to Genānn:—

"I do not feel this night as I was wont to feel, O dear schoolfellow, for there is a blankness and desolation in my mind, such as one experiences when alone in a strange country, nor do I recognise in my spirit that strength and happiness which those unseen princes used to supply always before; for I was ever aware of a spirit, not my own, with my own spirit, and this horror comes over me, that the gods themselves have forsaken me, and I think that, unwittingly, I have done some great wrong against them or against men."

And Genānn said:—

"It is the enchantment of the Clan Cailitin that is around thee, and though our power is weak to protect thee, thou must not leave us."

And Cuculain said:—

"What is the form of Mac Manar, according to the traditions of the soothsayers of Erin?"

And Gruag-Sulus said:—

"To thee and those like thee, he is young and very beautiful, and like a tender girl in feature and in limb, and of a most gentle aspect. But they say that to others he appears like a demon, more frightful and horrible than aught, which the eye of man awake or in dream hath ever seen. He carries a harp of pure gold; and against the melody of that harp they say that not even the gods themselves are secure; and it is said, too, that he is the strongest of the gods, and in the end will slay them all, for he alone is really immortal, nor was he made so by eating of the herd of Mananān, but he is immortal in his own right, and while things endure he will endure. And there is no singing so sweet as his, and no music like the music of his harp, suggesting things never seen or heard, beauty beyond all beauty, and nobleness to which the knighthood of earth may not be compared, and visions of love and bliss, and of worlds fair and good. Such virtues the soothsayers of Erin say reside in the strings of that harp."

And Cuculain said:—

"That is well, O Genānn, he shall not find me unprepared."

But again that night Cuculain heard the tramp of armed men, and the hoarse voices of those who gave command, and the rolling of wheels, and the distant noise of martial preparation; for from the ends of the Province, from Assaroe, in the west, Dûn Sobharcy in the north-east, and Aula Neid, beside the Foyle, were arriving continually—cohorts of warriors, the residue of the Clanna Rury, moving southwards to resist the great invasion, and they were ordered to enter Emain Macha by night, and thence, being armed and instructed, they went southwards to the frontier.

Then a fiery wrath possessed Cuculain, and a fierce tide of angry blood raced through his veins, and he started forth with a cry, and said:—

"Ye are deceiving me, and I am surrounded with traitors and liars; there is a great invasion from the south, and ere this my realm is overrun, and my people are slain and made captive, and the territory which I have sworn to defend is made desolate."

But Genānn cried out, too, but in terror, and he said:—

"What is this, O Cu, that has come over thee, that thou standest thus aghast and pallid, and thy eyes are like burning fires beneath thy brow?"

But Cuculain answered him not.

And Genānn said again:—

"Rouse thyself, O Cu, it is the Clan Cailitin enchanting thee."

And Cuculain said:—

"Didst thou not see them, O Genānn?

And Genānn said, "Whom?"

"Lu himself in that form in which he came to me before, but now more distinct, and that awful Queen who they say rules over the gods. They stood before me and said:—

"'O Cuculain, thy people are slain and made captive, and thy dûn is dismantled and thy territory eaten up, for Erc, with all the nobles and warriors of Meath and Mac Nia, and Lewy Mac Conroy with the Ernai and the Clan Dēga, and that bitter and relentless Queen with the might of the Firbolgs and the Clan Humōr, have invaded Murthemney, and why dost thou delay to go out against them as of yore, for we are still with thee?'"

But while he still spake, Cuculain moved his head round slowly and said:—

"What music and singing is this that I hear in the dim mysterious night? I have not heard such at any time"; and so he stood listening, while he still held Genānn, and the voice sang, heard indeed by Cuculain, but unheard by Genānn:—

"Day ends in night, and the sun in the breast of Lir,
The might of the warrior will not save him when his end comes.
Hearken, O Hound, to the strains of Mac Manar!
It is for thee I sing, O Cu,
Cuculain Mac Sualtam."

Then Cuculain approached the window, and he saw Mac Manar in the moon-light—him who would slay even the gods—and that harp in his slender hands, all golden.

And Cuculain said:—

"It is enough, O schoolfellow, my end is come. I shall perish in this battle, but the high gods of Erin are around me, and I shall die, as I have lived, under their hands."

So spake Cuculain in his ignorance, trusting in phantoms, for they, the Tuátha of Erin, were far from him that night, watching with sad eyes as the shadows closed around the hero. So speaking, he burst back the door with its bolts and bars, rending them in sunder with his great irresistible hands; but outside were innumerable faces, the faces of strong resolute men close round the door, for they watched there nightly, and Cu was amazed when he saw them; but Genānn took him by the hand and said:—

"O Cuculain, it is already morn; wait now till the day is fully come, and then thou shalt go southwards against the enemy. But these warriors will be slain ere they suffer thee to pass."

Cuculain lay down again till the day was fully come, and Cathvah came into the chamber, and they told him what had happened during the night, and Cathvah and Genānn both said that it was by the enchantment of the Clan Cailitin that he had seen the divine appearances; but Cuculain was silent, for he believed them not, making preparations, and he went into Læg's chamber, and cried out to Læg to arise, but Læg was still sleeping, and he demanded from Fion-Cu* the key of the Tayta Brac, where were his arms; but Fion-Cu had put away the key, and Cuculain said:—

"It boots not, Fion-Cu. Thou shalt but gain employment in the afternoon for the King's kerd* to repair the injury."

Fion-Cu opened the door of the resounding chamber, and the shield of Cuculain had fallen from its rack in the night. Then Cuculain returned to Læg, who was still asleep, and Cuculain looked upon him sleeping, and said:—

"I alone have heard Mac Manar, and to me only has the warning come. Yet thou, O dear comrade and charioteer, wouldst answer with clamour and insult were I to announce that I will go alone upon this expedition, or take with me another than thee. Very elate and insolent wert thou on that day when thou wast made my charioteer, and thou didst vex the souls of thy brothers, Sheeling, the charioteer of Legairé, and Id, the charioteer of Conaill, saying, that to thee was entrusted the care of the bravest of the Red Branch, exasperating the minds of thy elders, and thou hast done and said many vain-glorious things therefore; but now thou shalt perish in Murthemney before them, guiding my steeds through the battle: but I thought not our death should be so soon, but that thou wouldst grow old with me at Dûn-Dalgan, and I marvelled how years would change thy mood, but now we shall die together on the southern marches, holding the gates of Ulla against the South, which has been our task always and appointed duty. Sleep on awhile now, for bitter will be thy waking, O dear comrade."

So spake Cuculain above the sleeping warrior; but Læg turned his face to the wooden partition, and composed himself again to slumber.

Then Cuculain went forth again; but in the court, between the Crave Rue and the Tayta Brac, there met him the queens of the Ultonian kings, who had come to Emain Macha, both those whose husbands had gone abroad with Conaill Carna, and those whose warriors fought now on the southern frontier against the great host of Erc and Queen Meave, and the High Queen of all Ulla was with them, and Nieve, the prophetess, and Einey Inûva, a very dear friend, and one of those who sat weeping beside his couch when the Red Branch brought him back out of Mid-luhara*, where he wandered naked, stricken by the Shee. There Nieve the beautiful prophetess, approached him, and took him by the hand, and said:—

"O Cuculain, we have heard of the vision, and of thy determined resolve which we cannot gainsay, but we have this one request to make of thee, namely, that thou shalt postpone thy departure till the morrow, and that thou shalt go this day to Glan-na-mōhar* where Cathvah has his druidic abode, and I shall consult the auguries of the soothsayers of Ulla this night, and in the morning I shall announce to thee their purport. For here there is an enchantment around thee, and thy spirit is confused by the Clan Cailitin; but there the power of Cathvah will be greater to defend thee, and I shall give thee a true answer from the auguries, and this request I urge on behalf of the women of Ulla, for, though to the rest of Eiré thy name is a terror, and though the warlike tribes of Ulla worship thee like a god, yet none have been so faithful to thee as we, and we have guarded thy renown, and rebuked every slander, for thou hast been like a dear brother to those of us who are young, and like a child to those of us who are old, and our love towards thee may not be told, O dear Setanta. For of those who clave to Concobar Mac Nessa in the great rebellion thou alone wert gentle[3] to the unhappy daughter of Felim; and as was the commencement of thy career so has it been up to this, and now, O Cuculain, be persuaded, and grant this last favour to us."

But Cuculain saw, behind the rest, where stood the daughter of Forgal Mánah, pale and tearful, and he yielded to that petition.

But after that they passed northwards to Glan-na-mōhar, Cathvah and Ferceirtney, Genānn Gruag-sulus and Nieve the daughter of Kelkar, and Cuculain, and Læg; and Nieve was joyful that day, for she said that the Clan Cailitin would be overpowered in that glen.

But that night Cuculain saw no visions, and Cathvah shed a veil over the glen, an emanation of the Faydfia of Goibneen*; but the eyes of Genānn Gruag-sulus were opened that night, and he saw in spirit the Clan Cailitin traversing all Ulla, and like hounds on the track searching every valley and hill-side, and every dark wood seeking Cuculain, and alone upon his bed he trembled excessively like one sick of an ague, overcome with great fear, and he prayed earnestly to the immortal people that night, and practised his wizard arts; but Cathvah and Nieve sat together sleepless all the night, deeming in their fond minds that they could shield the son of Sualtam.

In the grey of the morning then came a woman to Nieve, and desired her to leave the Dûn with her, for that she had tidings of great moment to communicate; and Nieve went out with the woman, for

3. Cuculain is mentioned as meeting Deirdré after the death of the sons of Usna, and endeavouring to comfort her.

she deemed that she was the daughter of Finntann Mac Niel who had come with her to Glan-na-mōhar, but ere long she found herself wandering alone in the glen, and a dense mist all around.

For the veil of invisibility covered not the paddock in which the steeds were, and the Clan Cailitin shrieked on the mountain-tops, when they saw beneath them in the glen the two great steeds of Cuculain, and by their enchantments they withdrew the prophetess from the dûn.

But about the same time Cuculain awoke, and he dressed himself and went out, and there met him at the door, as he deemed, the daughter of Kelkar the son of Uther, even Nieve the fair-haired prophetess, and she said:—

"Gird on thy armour now, O son of Sualtam, for the high gods of Erin are around thee. Go forth as of yore, for thou shalt pursue the host of Meave southwards beyond the Boyne, and shalt slay Erc and Mac Nia, and Lewy Mac Conroi, and work deliverance for us as heretofore."

Then was Cuculain glad, and hastened forward the departure, and Læg ran to the paddock and cried to the horses as was his wont, throwing back the barred gate; but the steeds at the other end of the field stood stock still like sulky mules, and they stood facing one another hard by the fence.

Then was Læg angry and ran forward to where they were, and black Shanglan went behind the Liath Macha, and as Læg tried to seize the Liath Macha he presented to him his side, and so moved round refusing to be taken, and Læg was astonished at this and said:—

"What is this, O Liath Macha, that has come upon thee? Never hast thou been thus with me before, for high-spirited, and docile, and light of foot wert thou ever yet when I summoned thee, but now thou art mulish and sulky, and like a farmer's rough garran."

And Læg again sprang at him to hold him, and he became fierce and intractable, and after that he fled before him keeping along the fence; and also the Dûvyeelan fled with him, keeping by the fence inside the Liath Macha. And Læg said:—

"This is an evil foreboding."

Then he returned to the Dûn, and Cuculain himself came down to the field, and he stood in the gateway, and lifted up his clear-toned voice, but the steeds stirred not, and the Liath Macha held down his head, and all his foam-white mane drooped down to the ground, and Cuculain approached and caressed him, and there fell from the eyes of the steed, blood-stained tears, while he caressed him, and after that Læg led in the steeds, but they went slowly and reluctantly.

Now when Læg entered the chariot-house, he found the great chariot-pole broken in twain; for the Mōr Reega had passed that way in the night and snapped it with her mighty hands, a warning to the heroes. But Læg fastened the parts roughly together until he should reach Emain Macha.

Læg harnessed the steeds, and so they drave on to Emain Macha, and the sun was just rising as they left Glan-na-mōhar. But as they travelled Cuculain said to Læg:—

"I marvel much, O Læg, remembering the appearance and face of Nieve, the prophetess, as she spake with me this day."

And Læg said:—

"That is true, O Setanta; for though I honour her above all the women of Ulla, save thy own wife, I felt towards her this day a strange repulsion. Yet glad was I when she gave thee the word to go southwards."

And Cuculain said:—

"Her form was indeed the same, but I missed the strangely sweet smile with which she is accustomed to converse, and the glory that is shed from her pale, pure countenance; also, in her voice, that strange trembling, as though she ever repressed inward tears, and in her haviour that swift brightness as of one who, at a word, might pass forth from the world and mingle with those children of the mountains who are invisible and immortal."

After that they drave rapidly onward, and it was noon when they reached the King's Dûn, and there their hearts were again fretted by the mourning and the tearful faces. But Cuculain took Emer aside that no one might witness their separation, and he said:—

"O Emer, not so soon did I deem that a darkness should overwhelm thy bright life, or that thou wouldst be left a widow in thy youth. Not such I deemed would be thy lot when I tempted thee to fly from thy father's dûn, and when thou gavest up all for my sake. But much already hast thou suffered being the wife of a warrior, though thou wert not by nature formed to suffer but to be glad."

But Emer, speechless, clung to him still weeping, and he charged her that she should send Connla to Alba to be instructed by Eefa*, who had also instructed himself, and after that he disengaged himself from her, and kissed her, and also Connla and Fionscōta, but the boy asked him, "Whether he would not return again soon?" and Cuculain said that until he returned Connla should be a protector to his mother, and Connla said that he would, and so went forth Cuculain; and he sprang into his chariot, and Læg let the steeds go, and the loud wheels brayed through the city, which was lined with children, and women, and unwarlike people, and there was a vast and confused clamour and mourning along the streets as they went, instead of the shouts which had so often greeted him there. And as they emerged from the city towards the east Cuculain looked back upon the city, and he said:—

"O city of my heart, O nurse of heroes, Emain of the Red Branch, how often have I come unto thee bearing victory and spoils, and now I leave thee with a heavy heart, and depressed. It is our last journey, O Læg. We shall not go back again to this dear city, O Læg. We shall not return to Emain Macha any more."

After that they went to the palace of Dethcœn, Cuculain's nurse, for he was accustomed to visit her ere he went abroad to war.

As they crossed a tributary of the Oun Callân, they saw two beautiful maidens in the stream washing, and one of them held up a lēna in both her hands which was pierced and torn, and where the holes were there were bloody stains, and the stains would not come out for all their washing, and Cuculain said:—

"No other omens are needed now; I have heard Mac Manar, and Rod too I shall see in his own time."

As they passed Rath Fohla it is said that they saw a vision of the angels of God singing.[4]

After that they drave on again, and they arrived at Slieve Few; and it was upon that mountain that Cuculain had first seized the Liath Macha, for he found him there grazing beside the lake on the hill side, and he sprang upon him and seized him by the long white mane, and that was said to have been the most desperate struggle in which he was ever engaged, for the divine steed, having been seized, fought with him and fled; but he could not release himself from his grasp; and Cuculain subdued him to his hand, and tamed his mighty soul; but the country all around there was uncultivated and woody, and it was evening when they reached it, and the gloaming of the day.

And Læg said:—

"This is a hill of which the poets sing many things."

And Cuculain said:—

"We can well believe them looking upon it, for it is nobler and more lovely than the mountains of Eiré. It was my road-post when first I sought Emain Macha, escaping by night without the knowledge of my mother. Therefore has it been always dear and venerable to me from a boy, and it is the home of happy and benignant spirits. The summit is sacred to Lir, and is called the Shee Fionaháh, and they say that Lir has there his fairy palace which no man may see; and it was from thence his children set forth with their step-mother to visit Bove Derg at his fairy palace upon the Galtees, on that journey in which, at Derryvara, they were so cruelly transformed. I myself have heard them singing in the northern seas, and I then thought I never heard music so sweet or so sad."

And he also said:—

4. This is an addition of some Christian bard. It was on Rath Fohla that St. Patrick's Monastery was situated in the modern city of Armagh. The legend says that the heroes' hearts went forth in sympathy with that singing, so that God showed his mercy upon them.

"I never saw Slieve Few so beautiful as this night, for all its sacred dells and heathery promontories are lit up with the gold-red rays of the setting sun."

So conversed the warriors, for the sun was then setting, and shed a golden glow over that noble hill where dwelt Lir and his people unseen in its fair mysterious folds.

But as they travelled they saw a smoke on the edge of the wood that ascended not into the still air, but lay low, hovering around the leafless trees, and soon they saw where a party of wandering outcasts had made their encampment beside the wood, and they sat around the fire cooking, for a brazen pot was suspended from a branch between forked supporters, and they were cooking their evening meal.

And Læg said:—

"Methinks I never saw such miserable wanderers as these. There are three men and three women all very old, and wretched, and meanly clad."

But when the outcasts saw Cuculain, they lifted up their voices in a harsh and dissonant chorus, and said:—

"Right well have we chosen our encampment, O mighty Prince, for we said that this way thou wouldst go down to the battle, and we knew that no arts or persuasions would restrain thee that thou shouldst not come out, as of yore, to the assistance of thy people. Hail to thee, O Cuculain, O flame of the heroes of Eiré, and to thee, O illustrious son of Riangowra*."

But as they spake they all stood up, and they were very hideous to look upon, marred, as Cuculain and Læg thought, by some evil destiny. They were clad in the skins of black he-goats, and on the breast of each, instead of pin or brooch, was the shank-bone of a heron, or a swan, or such like bird; their arms and legs were lean and bony, but their hands and feet large, and they were all maimed in the right hand and the right foot.

But Cuculain answered them as was his wont, for many such a greeting had he received from unwarlike people and outcasts, for such especially cherished his glory. Then, as Læg was urging on the steeds, one limped forward and stood before the steeds and said:—

"O Cuculain, partake with us of our poor repast, not meet for princes, but such as we outcasts can procure trapping wild animals; and we ourselves are like wild animals hunted to and fro. They say indeed that in many a poor man's cot thou hast eaten food, and sat beside many a humble fire, not knowing thy own greatness."

And Cuculain said:—

"The night is already upon us, O Læg, and we cannot travel further, let us not insult these unhappy people, maimed and outcast, by refusing what they offer."

Læg reluctantly consented, and unharnessed the steeds from the great war-car, having first brought it beside a stream that ran down from that sacred lake upon the mountain, and he washed the chariot-wheels carefully, and dried them, and spread a covering over the chariot to protect it from the dew, and he returned to Cuculain, who sat beside the fire amongst the outlaws, for it was cold, and he was chill from sitting all day in the war-car. Nevertheless he was not warmed by the fire.

But Cuculain was glad when the charioteer drew nigh, for he was distressed at the conversation of those homeless people, and their countenances, and their forms, for their wretchedness sat lightly upon them, and they were very gay, and mirthful, as they sat holding the flesh on skewers of the rowan tree over the embers, and they made obscene jests, and answered in a language which he could not comprehend, and it seemed to him that the women were worse than the men. Moreover, the sun set, and the darkness came down, and mysterious sounds came from the sacred hill, the noise of the trees, and of the falling water, and he saw nought but these unlovely faces around.

When the flesh was cooked they gave a portion to Cuculain, and he ate thereof, but Læg refused with an oath. Then these outcasts laughed and sprang to their feet, and they joined hands around them twain, and danced upon their misshapen feet, and sang:—

"Sisters and brothers, join hands, he is ours;
Let the charm work, he is ours.

A rath in Murthemney holds twenty-eight sculls—
Work on, little charm, he is ours!"

"Hast thou heard, Cuculain, of Clan Cailitin?"

But Cuculain drew his sword, crying:—

"O brood of hell, see now if your charms are proof against keen bronze."

But they bounded away nimbly like goats, and still encircled him, singing. Then one plunged into the wood, and all followed; and there was cracked obscene laughter in the forest, and then silence; only the noise of the wind in the trees, and the gentle murmur of the stream, lit now with the beam of the rising moon. Cuculain stood panting, and very pallid, with wide eyes; but Læg crouched upon the ground.

And Cuculain said:—

"They are gone, O Læg. It was some horrible vision. Here was the fire where the grass is yet unburned, and there is no trace of the rowan-tree spits, or of the flesh."

But Læg with difficulty recovered himself, and spake with a stammering tongue, and they found there no trace of the encampment of the outcasts save the skin of a wolf lately slain.

And Cuculain said:—

"I marvel, O Læg, how the mighty and righteous Lir, to whom this mountain is sacred, can suffer within his precincts that horrid brood. O mountain-dwelling, unseen king, shield us at least within thy own borders against these powers of darkness."

The End

Down where the broad Zambesi river
Glides away into some shadowy lagoon
Lies the antelope, and hears the leaflets quiver,
Tân shaken by the sultry breath of noon,
Hears the sluggish water ripple in its flowing,
Feels the atmosphere with fragrance all opprest,
Dreams his dreams, and the sweetest is the knowing
That above him, and around him, there is rest.
—Percy Somers Payne[1]

Cuculain and Læg slept not that night; and as they spake concerning those withered people, Læg said that such a brood could never have been the children of Cailitin whom he had known; but Cuculain said, "Nay, O Læg, these devils are his true children"; and again he said, "But, lo! now the Mourne hills eastward are grey with the growing dawn, let us proceed straightway, for now there is sufficient light to avoid the chasms and wet places until we reach the road that leads into Dûn-dalgan."

Then Læg harnessed the steeds and yoked the chariot, and they went forward, and Læg was perpetually restoring the weapons to their places, for they were disarranged, and this he did secretly, that

1. The author of these beautiful lines was the son of Somers H. Payne, rector of Upton, County of Cork. His early death has been, I believe, a serious loss to Anglo-Irish literature. *Editors' note*: Percy Somers Payne, "Rest," in *A Treasury of Irish Poetry in the English Tongue*, ed. Stopford Augustus Brooke and T. W. Rolleston (New York: Macmillan, 1905), 568, ll. 9–16.

he might not increase the sadness of Cuculain, for it was an evil omen; but Cuculain observing it, said:—

"It matters not, O Læg, I have heard the music of Mac Manar, and ere long I shall see that son of Lir. We go down now to die upon the plains of Murthemney, but Lu Lamfáda and the great goddess, the Mōr Reega, go with us, and from our death thenceforward we shall be under their protection."

As it grew light, and as the war-car and the heroes were seen, there was a great change in all the territories through which they passed. For before them the land was desolate and forsaken, and neither cattle nor men might be seen, only empty fields and deserted homesteads; but behind them there were cattle and sheep in all the fields, and the craftsman wrought, and the tillers of the soil and pastoral tribes attended to their labours, the hamlets received back their inhabitants, and children sported in their accustomed play-grounds. For a many-voiced rumour went abroad, and the forests and mountain fastnesses and the strongholds of the lakes yielded up their fugitives, when men heard that the great champion had gone southwards against the host of Meave.

It was about noon when Cuculain and Læg beheld the first signs of the invasion, and saw afar the lurid smoke of conflagrations, and heard the distant noise of battle. Then the old heroic rage burned in their hearts, and Læg unfolded and closed the glittering scythes, to see if they would work freely, urging on the steeds, and Cuculain stood erect in the chariot, looking southwards, and he cried:—

"O Dûn-dalgan, Dûn-dalgan, thou city of my sires, my own city, how red now are thy consuming flames; but on the other march there shall be a red eric for thy destruction, when the Boyne shall receive the hosts of that bitter and relentless queen, and their horses shall trample down their footmen, and mariners out in the Murinet will wonder at the ruddy tide which those sacred waters will roll down to the sea. O Erc the Fair-haired, and thou Lewy Mac Conroi, returning now into Mid-Erin, ye will pray that your horses may be swifter than hawks. On, on, O royal-hearted Læg, the Tuátha of Erin are around us this day, Lu Lamfáda on the right, and on the left that mighty queen who rules over the gods, and above us that strong god[2] who showed his mercy upon me when I fell in the wilderness of Mid-Lúhara, O Liath Macha, my precious one, on the heaven-kissing mountain I took thee.[3] The forests crashed around us contending, the spirits of Lough Liath arose at the noise of our strife, and the daughter of Cuilin roared, but I clung to thee and held thee, and subdued thee, O fairy steed."

And Læg answered:—

"What is this that has come upon thee, O Cu? I have not heard thee thus vaunting at any time."

So Cuculain vaunted, for his mind was disturbed by the enchantments; but suddenly he ceased, and, stooping, seized Læg by the shoulder with his left hand, so that he cried out for the pain, and Cuculain said:—

2. There is a strange story, pregnant with psychological and historical meaning, of how the gods of Inver Amargin, i.e., the mouth of the Ovoca, summoned Cuculain into fairyland to protect them from an invasion of northern demoniac powers, and how Cuculain, having routed these, was seized with oblivion of his previous life, and dwelt in the invisible world, having a goddess for his bride, but that, eventually, he was cast out from heaven, and fell in the wilderness of Mid-Lúhara, in Murthemney. "It was then," says the legend, "that Cuculain gave the three high leaps, and the three south leaps of Murthemney," slew those sent to take him, and abode naked in the wilderness. After this he was brought to Emain Macha, and lay there twelve months with wandering thoughts. Eventually Mananān, son of Lir, the god of the sea, waved over him his magic mantle and restored him.

We see here an attempt, which failed, to transfer the hero into the rank of the gods. The immediate origin of the legend was probably a fit of melancholia, oppressing Cuculain with its consequent fancies and imaginations, and which was attributed to the gods.

3. The seizure of the Liath Macha by Cuculain is described in the Feast of Bricrind. Cuculain and the Liath Macha, sang the bards, encircled Erin in that strife. There is a vastness and greatness in the bardic treatment of heroes to which I have not found myself able to ascend. The tomb or temple of the Liath Macha was on the Boyne, but it was on Slieve Fuad that Cuculain seized him.

"They have departed, O Læg; but now I said that beside our galloping steeds they went with us to the battle; but they have deceived us and deserted us. Dost thou hear that laughter? We are forsaken."[4]

Then Cuculain turned round in the chariot all flaming, and roared against the high gods of Fail, and the peal of that cry resounded across Erin; but there was no answer, only echoes in the hollow folds of the mountain, and once again, made mad with sorrow and rage, Cuculain roared a challenge against the immortal gods, but again his voice fell to a hoarse whisper, and leaning past Læg in the war-car, he said:—

"Who art thou? I like not thy sleepy eyes and dusky tresses. Thou art not a pleasant or profitable companion for one who enters into the battle."

But there answered him a voice, saying:—

"I am Rod, son of the boundless Lir. It was foretold that thou shouldst see me, and I alone of the Tuátha Dē Danā will go with thee into this battle, and I shall be with thee to the end."

Then Cuculain bowed his head in the chariot and wept, and said:—

"O Læg, the end of all is come, and this supreme horror, that even the gods themselves should have deserted us."

Then there approached the flying scattered battalions of the Red Branch, driven out of Murthemney by the great host of Meave, and Cuculain stayed them, and re-formed their broken bands in the mountains of Cooalney, breathing into them his own unconquerable soul.

Ere dawn the next day he climbed into the Eagle's Nest; and it was there that the men of Meave first saw him revealed in the light of the rising sun, and their host was confused at the sight, when they beheld him afar, and they retired into Conaill Murthemney. It was

4. The Clan Cailitin took upon themselves the forms of Cuculain's patron deities, that they might seduce him to Murthemney. They also held perpetually before his mind a vision of his territory ravaged by the men of Meave.

with difficulty, after they saw Cuculain, that their captains prevailed upon them to risk a battle against him.

After this Cuculain defeated the host of Meave in seven great battles on the plains of Murthemney, and the tombs of those he slew are scattered over all that land. Many times he drave them southwards to the Boyne, but they were reinforced from mid-Erin, and the Ultonians who fell were not replaced. But on the eighth day, Cuculain looking round, saw the remnant of the Red Branch overwhelmed, and it was about five miles south and west of Dûn-dalgan.

More terrible than at any other time was the son of Sualtam in those battles which he entered in the naked majesty of his irresistible strength, shorn of his glory, and having lost his magic attributes, for this time he went to war like one who has devoted himself to death. Around him the shadows thickened, but like a light in darkness, his valour shone the brighter as before his fast-lessening warriors he charged the armies of the great Queen. Over the plains of Murthemney, between Dûn-dalgan and the Boyne, pealed the voice of the son of Sualtam, shouting amid his warriors, and ever the southern host gave way before him, and their battalions were confused.

Then northward in the hills collected the people of Ulla, the unwarlike tribes, seeing afar that one hero, and the fast-lessening ranks of the Ultonians, where the great champion of the north fought on against the immense overflowing host of the Four Provinces.

But as the Ultonians grew less in the dread conflict, the southern warriors precipitated themselves upon Cuculain, and like a great rock over which rolls some mighty billow of the western sea, so was Cuculain often submerged in their overflowing tide; and as with the down-sinking billow the same rock reappears in its invincible greatness, and the white brine runs down its stubborn ribs, so the son of Sualtam perpetually reappeared scattering and destroying his foes. Then crashed his battle mace through opposing shields; then flew the foam-flakes from his lips over his reddened garments; baleful shone his eyes beneath his brows, and his voice died away in his throat till it became a hoarse whisper. Often too Læg charged with the war-car, and extricated him surrounded, and the mighty steeds tramped down opposing squadrons, and many a southern hero was transfixed with the chariot-spear, or divided by the brazen scythes.

It was on the eighth day, two hours after noon, that Cuculain raising his eyes beheld where the last of the Red Branch were overwhelmed, and he and Læg were abandoned and alone, and he heard Læg shouting, for he was surrounded by a battalion, and Cuculain hastened back to defend him, and sprang into the chariot, bounding over the rim, and extended Fabâne above him on the left. There he intercepted three javelins cast against the charioteer by a Lagenian band; but Erc, son of Cairbré Nia-far, pursued him, and at the same time cast his spear from the right. Through Cuculain it passed, breaking through the battle-shirt and the waist-piece, and it pierced his left side between the hip-bone and the lowest rib, and transfixed Læg in the stomach above the naval. Then fell the reins from the hands of Læg.

"How is it with thee, O Læg?" said then Cuculain.

And Læg answered:—

"I have had enough this time, O my dear master. Truly thou hast fulfilled thy vow, for it was through thee that I have been slain."

Then Cuculain cut through the spear-tree with his colg, and tore forth the tree out of himself; but meantime, Lewy Mac Conroi stabbed black Shanglan with his red hands, driving the spear through his left side, behind the shoulder, and Shanglan fell, overturning the war-car, and Cuculain sprang forth, but as he sprang, Lewy Mac Conroi pierced him through the bowels. Then fell the great hero of the Gael*.

Thereat the sun darkened, and the earth trembled, and a wail of agony from immortal mouths shrilled across the land, and a pale panic smote the vast host of Meave when, with a crash, fell that pillar of heroism, and that flame of the warlike valour of Erin was extinguished. Then too from his slain comrade brake forth the Liath Macha, for, like a housewife's thread, the divine steed brake the traces, and the brazen chains, and the yoke, and bounded forth neighing, and three times he encircled the heroes, trampling down the host of Meave. Afar then retreated the host, and the Liath Macha, wearing still the broken collar, went back into the realms of the unseen, and entered his house upon the Boyne, where, since the ancient days, was his mysterious dwelling-place.

But Cuculain kissed Læg, and Læg, dying, said:—

"Farewell, O dear master, and schoolfellow. Till the end of the world no servant will ever have a better master than thou hast been to me."

And Cuculain said:—

"Farewell, O dear Læg. The gods of Erin have deserted us, and the Clan Cailitin are now abroad, and what will happen to us henceforward I know not. But true and faithful thou hast ever been to me, and it is now seventeen years since we plighted friendship, and no angry word has ever passed between us since then."

Then the spirit went out of Læg, and he died, and Cuculain, raising his eyes, saw thence northwestward, about two hundred yards, a small lake called Loch-an-Tanaigté*, and he tore forth from himself the bloody spear, and went staggering, and at times he fell, nevertheless he reached the lake, and stooped down and drank a deep draught of the pure cold water, keen with frost, and the burning fever in his veins was allayed. After that he arose, and saw northwards from the lake a tall pillar-stone, the grave of a warrior slain there in some ancient war, and its name was Carrig-an-Compan. When Cuculain first saw it there was standing upon it a grey-necked crow, which retired as he approached. With difficulty he reached it, and he leaned awhile against the pillar, for his mind wandered, and he knew nothing for a space.

After that he took off his brooch, and, removing the torn bratta, he passed it round the top of the pillar, where there was an indentation in the stone, and passed the ends under his arms and around his breast, tying with languid hands a loose knot, which soon was made fast by the weight of the dying hero. But the host of Meave, when they beheld him, retired again, for they said that he was immortal, and that Lu Lamfáda would once more come down out of fairyland to his aid, and that they would wreak a terrible vengeance. So afar they retreated, when they beheld him standing with the drawn sword in his hand, and the rays of the setting sun bright on his panic-striking helmet. So stood Cuculain, even in death-pangs, a terror to his enemies, and the bulwark of his nation.

Now, as Cuculain stood dying, a stream of blood trickled from his wounds, and ran in devious ways down to the lake, and poured its tiny red current into the pure water; and as Cuculain looked upon it, thinking many things in his deep mind, there came forth an otter out of the reeds of the lake and approached the pebbly strand, where the blood flowed into the water, having been attracted thither by the smell, and at the point where the blood flowed into the lake, he lapped up the life-blood of the hero, looking up from time to time, after the manner of a dog feeding. Which seeing, Cuculain gazed upon the otter, and he smiled for the last time, and said:—

"O thou greedy water-dog, often in my boyhood have I pursued thy race in the rivers and lakes of Murthemney; but now thou hast a full eric, who drinkest the blood of me dying. Nor do I grudge thee this thy bloody meal. Drink on, thou happy beast. To thee, too, doubtless, there will some time be an hour of woe."

Then to Cuculain appeared a vision, and he deemed that he saw Læg approaching, riding alone on black Shanglan, and he was glad therefore, and he deemed that Læg applied healing salves to his wounds. And Cuculain said:—

"Go now straightway to Emain Macha, O Læg, and say to Concobar that I here in Murthemney will contend till I perish against the invaders of Ulla, and give my benediction to my uncle, the great King of the Ultonians, and to all the Red Branch; and go to Emer and tell her not to weep for me, but to let her grief be of short duration, and that I will remember her while life endures."

Then to Cuculain it seemed that Læg, frowning, said:—

"Surely, O Cu, thy peerless and noble wife, beautiful Emer, thou wouldst never forget."

After that Cuculain deemed that Læg went off to Emain Macha, and that he heard the sound of the hoofs afar, going northwards, and a terrible loneliness and desolation came over his mind, and again he

2. Patrick Tuohy, *So Stood Cuculain*, woodcut. Frontispiece to Standish O'Grady, *The Triumph and Passing of Cuchulain* (Dublin: Stokes, 1919).

saw the faces of that wandering clan, and they laughed around him, and taunted him, and said:—

"Thus shalt thou perish, O Hound, and thus shall all like thee be forsaken and deserted, and they shall perish in loneliness and sorrow. An early death and desolation shall be their lot, for we are powerful over men and over gods, and the kingdom that is seen, and the kingdom that is unseen belong to us," and they ringed him round, and chaunted obscene songs, and triumphed.

Nevertheless they terrified him not, for a deep spring of stern valour was opened in his soul, and the might of his unfathomable spirit sustained him.

Then was Cuculain aware that the Clan Cailitin had retired, as though in fear, and there stood beside him a child, having a strange aspect, and he took Cuculain by the hand, and said:—

"Regard not these children of evil, my brother, their dominion is but for a time."

And Cuculain said:—

"What god art thou who hast conquered the Clan Cailitin?"

Thus perished Cuculain—"mild, handsome, invincible," "cœv, aulin, cinláca."[5]

5. "Gælicé, caom, alainn, coingleacac."

PART TWO

Essays

1

Fleshing Dry Bones

O'Grady's Sensory Revivalism

Renée Fox

The translation, collection, and dissemination of old Irish stories—folk tales, historical chronicles, bardic sagas such as the Ulster Cycle[1]—that began in earnest in Ireland in the 1860s occasioned countless reflections from their purveyors on the relationship between Irish literary sensibility and the facts of the Irish past as well as on the role of the chronicler (ancient *or* contemporary) in synthesizing the two into useable history. Whether in academic translations such as Eugene O'Curry's *Lectures on Manuscript Materials of Ancient Irish History* (1861), bardic histories such as Standish O'Grady's *History of Ireland* (1878–80), popular histories such as Emily Lawless's *Story of Ireland* (1887), or sagas such as Lady Augusta Gregory's *Cuchulain of Muirthemne* (1902), the Irish past could rarely be transmitted unaccompanied by self-conscious considerations of how, why, and to what ends Irish history was being dragged out of its cromlechs and into the purview of the late-nineteenth- and early-twentieth-century Irish intelligentsia. W. B. Yeats makes this point clear when he devotes much more of the introduction he wrote

1. The Ulster Cycle is the set of Irish legends from which O'Grady takes his stories of Cuculain; this set of tales, preserved primarily in manuscripts from the twelfth to the fifteenth centuries, contains the famous "Donn Cooalney" story that we find in volume 1, chapter 7, of *History of Ireland*.

for Lady Gregory's *Cuchulain* to how she tells her stories than to the stories themselves, waxing ecstatically about the life force of the "Kiltartanese" idiom Lady Gregory uses for her translation.[2] In a note appended in 1902 to his essay "The Celtic Element in Literature" (1897), in which he argues that the modern Irish poet can reach divine heights only by imagining history as a synchronicity of all time rather than a chronological procession of moments, Yeats insists that he "could have written this essay with much more precision and have much better illustrated [his] meaning if [he] had waited until Lady Gregory had finished her book of legends, *Cuchulain of Muirthemne*,"[3] because to Yeats her idiom itself aesthetically expressed this historical synchronicity.

Whether presenting Irish legends and histories in deliberately nonliterary ways or raising them into the realms of poetry, modern nineteenth-century writers of the Irish past could not help but consider Irish legend and the modern Irish imagination inhabiting the same visionary spectrum and ponder how their historiographical methodologies might aid or interfere with the dissolving of temporal boundaries between the Irish past, present, and future. This essay argues that Standish O'Grady's historical musing in *History of Ireland*, in particular, marks a turning point in nineteenth-century stories of Ireland, one where Irish history becomes a living, experiential phenomenon rather than a contained body of knowledge to be acquired. Cobbling together models of historical transmission from

2. As Yeats writes, describing the Gaelicized dialect Lady Gregory invents for her "translation," "Some years ago I wrote some stories of medieval Irish life, and as I wrote I was sometimes made wretched by the thought that I knew of no kind of English that fitted them . . . but now Lady Gregory has discovered a speech as beautiful as that of Morris, and a living speech into the bargain" (introduction to Lady Augusta Gregory, *Cuchulain of Muirthemne* [1902; reprint, Gerrards Cross, UK: Colin Smythe, 1973], viii).

3. W. B. Yeats, "The Celtic Element in Literature," in *The Collected Works of W. B. Yeats*, vol. 4: *Early Essays*, ed. Richard J. Finneran and George Bornstein (New York: Scribner's, 2007), 138.

Victorian historiographers, romantic poets, and his fellow Irish historians, O'Grady develops an explicitly embodied resuscitative sensibility—an affective historical aesthetic in which the meaning of the past emerges in the historian's ability to make it a felt, living entity in the present moment—that later, in the hands of Yeats, Lady Gregory, and others, came to underlie the Irish Literary Revival. O'Grady was neither the first nineteenth-century Irish writer to suggest that Irish history was unfinished nor the first to lionize poetry itself as the potential savior of Irish culture,[4] but he was the first to suggest that Irish history's open-endedness was itself a kind of sensory poetic and was thus rife with revitalizing potential.

One of O'Grady's most important exhumatory precursors was Eugene O'Curry, the first professor of Irish history and archaeology at the Catholic University of Ireland, from whose work *Lectures on the Manuscript Materials of Ancient Irish History* (1861) O'Grady borrowed much of the raw material for *History of Ireland*.[5] The archaeological language of excavation O'Curry uses in his prefatory remarks to describe his collection and translation of the manuscripts

4. Samuel Ferguson's ballad version of the *Táin Bó Cuailnge* (Cattle Raid of Cooley), called "The Tain-Quest," though prefaced by a summary of the story as a whole, focuses entirely on the legend of how the story was lost, recovered, and lost again several centuries after it supposedly took place. "The Tain-Quest" ultimately transforms the poet into the hero of Celtic mythology and renders the unappreciative Irish audience its villains.

5. Although one of O'Grady's school friends wrote vaguely after O'Grady's death that he "was under the impression that . . . [O'Grady] had some colloquial knowledge of Irish," it has been fairly well established that O'Grady's knowledge of the Irish language was minimal at best (Alfred Perceval Graves, "Foreword," in *Standish James O'Grady, the Man and the Writer: A Memoir by His Son* [Dublin: Talbot Press, 1929], 12). As Yeats writes in *The Trembling of the Veil*, "I think he knew no Gaelic" but took many of his legends "from the dry pages of O'Curry and his school, and condens[ed] and arrang[ed]" them "as he thought Homer would have arranged and condensed" (*The Autobiography of William Butler Yeats: Consisting of* Reveries over Childhood and Youth, The Trembling of the Veil, *and* Dramatis Personae [New York: Collier Books, 1965], 148).

quickly becomes a language of exhumation: that "yet unwritten story" of Ireland is a "great body of which, the flesh and blood of all the true History of Ireland, remains to this day unexamined and unknown to the world." Not quite capable of resuscitating the Irish past through aesthetic means, O'Curry instead sets himself the task of digging the bodies out of the ground to be revived by others and feels that in disentombing the fleshy corpses he has done his "duty to [his] country so far as it lies in [his] power to do at all."[6] This act of patriotic disinterment became O'Grady's "first introduction to the wonder world of Irish heroic and romantic literature," and he felt he "owe[d] directly to [O'Curry]" the whole of the first volume of *History of Ireland*, titled *The Heroic Period*.[7]

Although O'Curry offered up the "great body" of Irish history to others' poetic sensibilities, he expressly resisted being any sort of bardic figure in his own right. "I almost begin to fear you will set me down as a story-teller, and not a lecturer upon the grave subject of the Materials of our Ancient History," he begins the eighth of his lectures,[8] offering perhaps an inadvertent pun on his exhumatory practice as he tries to bracket off storytelling from the pedagogical presentation of the "grave subject" of Irish manuscripts. O'Curry's aims are explicitly academic: he wants to expose people to the materials of Irish history with which they are unfamiliar so that they can become acquainted with ancient Irish customs, "many of which, to this day, [still] characterise the native Irish people."[9] The fates of ancient Ireland and modern Ireland are thus intimately intertwined in O'Curry's project. He insists at the beginning of his first lecture that although "the history of ancient Erinn, as of modern Ireland, is yet unwritten," the manuscripts he will be presenting furnish ample

6. Eugene O'Curry, *Lectures on the Manuscript Materials of Ancient Irish History*, delivered at the Catholic University of Ireland during the sessions of 1855 and 1856 (Dublin: Hinch, 1878), vii.

7. Quoted in H. O'Grady, *Standish James O'Grady*, 13–14.

8. O'Curry, *Lectures*, 273.

9. Ibid., 282.

material "from which that history may be constructed."[10] The grammar of this sentence makes it impossible to determine whether he envisions these materials as fodder for the to-be-written history of ancient Ireland or the to-be-written history of modern Ireland, and in collapsing the two—in imagining that access to ancient Celtic history is an essential part of writing modern Irish history—O'Curry lays the foundation for O'Grady's *History* and the later nineteenth-century Revival efforts that his project of literary exhumation will make possible.

Critics have argued that nineteenth-century Irish writers and historians coped with their sense of Irish history as a still-unfinished story by adopting narrative strategies that implied desired ideological endings on the near horizon,[11] but for many nineteenth-century writers of Irish history the still-to-be-written quality of the Irish "story" encouraged a self-reflexive focus on the nature of historical narratives and on their own methodological approaches. O'Grady echoes O'Curry in calling Irish history "yet unwritten" but uses this unfinishedness as an opportunity to promote a mode of history writing that makes no attempt to be "an exact and scientific treatment of the facts supplied by our native authorities" (*HI* 2:16; p. 48). Although he writes that such an undertaking would be "the only true and valuable method of presenting the history of Ireland to the notice of *the world*" (*HI* 2:16, italics mine; p. 48), he suggests immediately thereafter that this method is not the most valuable method for presenting the history of Ireland to *Ireland*. For the "existing state of the Irish mind," he writes, "mere history, and treated in the method in which history is generally written at the present day" (*HI*

10. Ibid., 3.

11. See, for example, R. F. Foster, *The Irish Story: Telling Tales and Making It Up in Ireland* (Oxford: Oxford Univ. Press, 2002): "The point of the Story of Ireland as retailed in classic form was, in fact, that though all the elements were there (villains, heroes, helpers, donors), it had not yet reached its ending. But through omission of elements that did not suit the fairy tale, and adherence to standard narrative forms, the right ending could be inferred" (6).

2:17; p. 48), would be of little interest. Instead, Ireland needs a history that will inspire the imagination, and O'Grady promotes his own imaginative historiography as the only way of penetrating the "frozen zone" of the Irish mind (*HI* 2:18; p. 49). He imagines his ideal student of Irish history fully immersed in a landscape of the past, treading a path through a "sombre and intricate forest," full of "shapes weird and unearthly," until, "suddenly emerging, [he] finds around him the night, indeed, but such a night! flashing, as with stars and northern lights" (*CP* 200; p. 63). This metaphor of historical apprehension as all-encompassing space foregrounds bodily experience and sensory overload: the "tinkle of living streams," the "dazzling" light of heroes, the "loud and agitated . . . rush and noise" of battle, the spirit "touche[d] and stir[red]" by "vital" humanity (*CP* 200; pp. 63–64)—all of these compose a living environment rife with physical sensation, intense enough to penetrate a "frozen mind." O'Grady's version of unfinished history is no tourist path from which the past can be viewed in a detached and leisurely way, but an affective bombardment that demands ongoing, present-tense, embodied engagement.

In *The Story of Ireland* (1887), Emily Lawless borrows O'Grady's image of Irish history as a twisting, affectively demanding path; but whereas O'Grady's student ultimately finds himself in glittering, dazzling, shining heroic clearings, Lawless's traveler along the dangerous and unaccountably crooked road of history comes upon only more twists and more uncertainty. O'Grady, in other words, imagines his readers following a path of history that leads to full sensory apprehension, but the path Lawless's readers follow leads only to ever more inapprehensible paths. *Story of Ireland* begins by describing Irish history as a gothic landscape, "a long, dark road, with many blind alleys, many sudden turnings, many unaccountably crooked portions; a road which . . . bristles with threatening notices, now upon the one side and now upon the other, the very ground underfoot being often full of unsuspected perils threatening to hurt the unwary." Lawless then suggests that trying to be a guide on such a perilous road is frightening and must be approached in the "gravest" fashion possible because of the bearing this gothic landscape has "upon that portion of history which has still to be born."[12] The language here—"crooked" road, "gravest" fashion, and a history "still to be born"—hints that in Lawless's imagination the next phase of the Irish story might be in danger of being stillborn. She not only emphasizes a very different kind of affective experience of history than does O'Grady—one with fear, uncertainty, and obscurity rather than dazzling pleasure at its center—but also insinuates that the writing of this history will rarely offer the kind of culmination that truly reinforces social or ideological cohesion.[13]

Lawless's metaphor of a dark and gothic path implies that *writing* Irish history does not resolve or complete it but instead opens the Revivalist possibility that following any sort of pathway (dark or otherwise) backward from the present into the Irish past will materially shape how the modern Irish consciousness develops. Writing history, in other words, is not an effort in moving from past to present, but an endlessly recursive and transformative process that affects multiple temporalities simultaneously. Lawless ends her book by warning writers of Irish history to beware the methods of their chronicling lest future generations repay them in kind; her closing cautions readers against "forgetting that our place in the same panorama waits for another audience, and that the turn of this generation has still to come."[14] She underscores, in other words, not

12. Emily Lawless, *The Story of Ireland* (New York: Putnam, 1887), ix, x.

13. Heidi Hansson makes a slightly different, twofold argument about the open-ended nature of Lawless's history. She contends that Lawless wrote in an unauthoritative tone in order to tiptoe around a field dominated by authoritative male historians, but she also argues that Lawless's unwillingness to present a single, infallible narrative of Irish history allows her to indicate through her writing style as well as her editorial choices that any totalizing, univocal story of Irish history overlooks "the fundamental uncertainty—or plurality—of Ireland's past" ("History in/of the Borderlands: Emily Lawless and the Story of Ireland," in *Liminal Borderlands in Irish Literature and Culture*, ed. Irene Gilsenan Nordin and Elin Homsten [Bern: Peter Lang, 2009], 63).

14. Lawless, *Story of Ireland*, 418–19.

only the yet-to-be-writtenness of Irish history and the accountability of present-day history writers to those who will follow but also the ways in which historiography creates temporal uncertainty, necessarily entangling past, present, and future. Although both Lawless and O'Grady metaphorize Irish history as living experience, they nonetheless come to very different conclusions about how much revivifying power and cultural authority an Irish historiography could or should have. The writing of Irish history leaves Lawless's Ireland in danger of being stillborn, even as it simultaneously points to the sensory breakdown of temporal divisions essential to the Revivalist imagination. O'Grady, in contrast, imagines his heroic history awakening the Irish imagination and revealing an island that "teems as with some vast parturition" (*CP* 201; p. 63). It is no wonder that Yeats found Lawless "in imperfect sympathy with the Celtic character" but saw O'Grady as "all passion."[15]

O'Grady's passionate belief in the possibility of a Celtic revival emerges in the extensive methodological introductions, asides, and even epigraphs that he includes in the two-volume *History of Ireland*. These elements are among the most detailed and the most manic of the theoretical scaffoldings with which Irish writers buttressed their versions of Irish legend and demonstrate how clearly O'Grady's understanding of his project foregrounds the subjective, sensory imagination as the primary conduit of historiographical experience. Several critics, including Geraldine Higgins, Gregory Castle, and Roy Foster, have argued that imagination and poetic form are central to O'Grady's notion of historiography. I do not want to reiterate their claims for O'Grady's imaginative desires or idiosyncratic poetic style so much as to analyze how the paratext around his "poetic" history (his introductions, his asides, his epigraphs) theorizes the relationship *between* poetry and history as one of experiential resuscitation.

15. Quoted in Margaret Kelleher, "'Wanted an Irish Novelist': The Critical Decline of the Nineteenth-Century Novel," in *The Irish Novel in the Nineteenth Century: Facts and Fictions*, ed. Jacqueline Belanger (Dublin: Four Courts Press, 2005), 197.

In the introductions to both volumes of the *History*, O'Grady draws a distinction between factual histories and imaginative histories, a distinction that many critics have traced back to his fascination with the Victorian historian, philosopher, and satirist Thomas Carlyle.[16] In insistently dismissing "every work which one takes up affecting to treat of the past in a rigid and conscientious spirit" as "merely archæological" and thus "fertile only in things the reverse of exhilarating" (*HI* 1:iii; *HI* 2:3; pp. 42, 36), O'Grady reiterates Carlyle's repeated denigration in *Past and Present* (1843) of what he calls "[d]ryasdust" scientific historiography—history that does nothing but collect and order the "old osseus fragment[s]" of the past visible to the naked eye, history that, like O'Curry's, exhumes without reviving.[17] In his essay "On History" (1830), Carlyle laments the vast gap between the "passion" and "mystery" of action, on the one hand, and the "chains" of linear narrative, on the other—between the deep time of all that has been and the single-dimensionality of the historical chronicle that attempts to make sense of it. He insists that the "writer fitted to compose History" in its most boundless, atemporal sense "is hitherto an unknown man."[18] By substituting for a detached, linear narrative the impressionistic and atemporal bardic sensibility viewed as both the origin point and the desired aim of the Irish historical imagination, O'Grady positions *History of Ireland* as precisely the kind of spiritual historical composition that Carlyle felt to be impossible.

Modeling his own work on what he sees as the bards' "unceasing" transformation of history "into the realm of artistic representation"

16. For detailed analyses of the relationship between O'Grady's and Carlyle's theories of history, see Geraldine Higgins, *Heroic Revivals from Carlyle to Yeats* (New York: Palgrave Macmillan, 2012), and Michael McAteer, *Standish O'Grady, Æ, and Yeats: History, Politics, Culture* (Dublin: Irish Academic Press, 2002). But many critics, including Yeats (*Autobiography*, 264) and Roy Foster (*Irish Story*, 11), have identified Carlyle's stylistic influence on O'Grady in more cursory ways.

17. Thomas Carlyle, *Past and Present* (1843; reprint, London: Dent, 1960), 48.

18. Thomas Carlyle, "On History," in *Thomas Carlyle: Historical Essays*, ed. Chris R. Vanden Bossche (Berkeley: Univ. of California Press, 2002), 8.

(*HI* 2:6; p. 38), O'Grady, in the introduction to volume 1 of the *History*, emphasizes the value of the aesthetic makeup of a historical document over its lists of names and places. If some "certainty of misrepresentation" (*HI* 1:vi; p. 44) inheres in imaginative history, it is "misrepresentation" only in the most superficial and factual sense. In whatever way bardic literature distorts historical actuality, it equally offers insight into the nature of bardic culture itself and thus represents a far more authentic and meaningful collection of historical knowledge. O'Grady goes so far as to suggest that "history" contained in bardic literature cannot actually be misrepresented because the "huge bright mirror" (*CP* 202; p. 64) of this literature reflects the bards themselves and the imaginative culture in which they lived. That is, the history that matters is the history of how heroes have been represented, not the history of the heroes themselves.

O'Grady's introduction of Cuculain insists upon this point, emphasizing Cuculain's titanic representational value even more than his superhuman deeds. "Now . . . is born Setanta, surnamed Cuculain, whose glory fills the whole bardic records of the age. During his career he bears the weight of the vast epos into which the history of the times has resolved itself" (*CP* 203; p. 65), O'Grady writes, keeping his readers' attention focused on Cuculain as an aesthetic construction, a glorious record, a historical symbol. Cuculain's heroism is indistinguishable from his literary presence, and his literary presence makes him apprehensible to the senses by "touch[ing] and stir[ring] the spirit": the "wonderful glory of this extraordinary hero" only "*flashes on the eye*" "through the shifting chaos of obscure epic tale, and the broken fragments of antique ruined verse" (*CP* 203, my emphasis; p. 65). O'Grady's footnote to these lines underscores the irrevocably literary nature of Cuculain's "history and character" by reminding us that they "traverse the whole literature as it treats of this age" and that his own "epic treatment" of Cuculain in *History of Ireland* has been determined by the multiplicity of ways the story of Cuculain has been told. For O'Grady, Cuculain represents not just an Irish heroic ideal but also an Irish literary ideal, an aesthetic construct whose perpetual reproduction across the annals of history reveals the energetic capacity of the Irish mind. In O'Grady's understanding of history, aesthetics trumps accuracy at every turn, and bardic literature itself—its multiplicity of versions, its tendency to idealize the heroic, its desire to "inflame" the mind as much as to inform it—provides historical insight into "the enormous fecundity and force of the imagination of a people" (*HI* 1:vii; p. 44) who had the capacity to produce and to take pleasure in such representations.

By the time O'Grady writes his introduction to volume 2 of *History of Ireland*, published two years after the first volume, he has begun to draw an essential distinction between history and bardic poetry: he now describes the latter as "the stumbling-block . . . [and] also the glory, of early Irish history" (*HI* 2:13; p. 45). In contrast to volume 1, in which he begins to denigrate bardic poetry even as he makes an impassioned argument for the essential historical meaning that inheres in the poetry of a historical text, volume 2 argues that the bardic literature of ancient Ireland presents a conundrum for anyone trying to access the truth of Irish history. This poetry "cannot be rejected, because it contains historical matter which is consonant with and illuminates the dry lists of the chronologist, and it cannot be retained, *for popular poetry is not history*," he writes (*HI* 2:13; my emphasis; p. 45). He proceeds to dismisses the need for—and his claims to—historical truth altogether and defines his project in terms of its creatively generative potential instead: rather than rediscovering the past, he wants "to make this heroic period once again a portion of the imagination of the country" (*HI* 2:17; p. 48), implying that making the past imaginatively live again is an endeavor wholly separate from reproducing its realities and will produce an alternative form of historical truth. Although other nineteenth-century European historians also conceived their projects in explicitly resuscitative terms—especially the French historian Jules Michelet, who famously described his work as an act of resurrection, writing that history "gives life to these dead men, resuscitates them"[19]—

19. Quoted in Roland Barthes, *Michelet*, trans. Richard Howard (New York: Farrar, Straus and Giroux, 1987), 102.

O'Grady is unique in that resuscitation for him is a metaphor for neither objectivity nor accuracy. For Michelet, historical resuscitation is a form of historicist responsibility, implying an unmediated historiographical mode in which historians shepherd dead men back to life but do not transform them by doing so. For O'Grady, in contrast, making the past live again in the contemporary imagination has become antithetical to unmediated historical veracity, and rather than continuing to argue that scientific history falls short because it fails to understand that the aesthetics of imaginative history provides access to essential and incontrovertible historical accuracies, he pitches his poetic project explicitly in opposition to any kind of history.[20]

As early as the first volume, O'Grady begins to conceive "history" as an aesthetic experience instead of as a compendium of factual truths. In a lengthy aside about the importance of imagination, in which he writes that the events and deeds of a nation "are no more history than a skeleton is a man" (*HI* 1:22),[21] he describes the dawn of history in the language of visual art, substituting the emergence of aesthetic legibility—the visible materialization of shapes, lines, and colors—for the development of knowledge across time: "flakes

20. Later, in the introduction to volume 2, O'Grady retreats from this distinction between history and bardic literature, but when he renews his claim from volume 1 that ancient poetry has a fundamentally historical character, the nature of this character no longer resides in its aesthetics, as it does in volume 1. Rather, he claims that a "more matured reflection" allows him to now see the "distinctly historical character of the age around which that literature revolves," to which he was blinded before by "the blaze of bardic light . . . [that] so dazzled the eye and disturbed the judgment, that I saw only the literature, only the epic and dramatic interest" (*HI* 2:32).

21. Higgins quotes this line as well as O'Grady's preceding claim that "legends represent the imagination of the country; they are that kind of history which a nation desires to possess," as part of her argument that O'Grady made imagination rather than actuality the center of his historical project (*HI* 1:22, quoted in *Heroic Revivals*, 20). She does not, however, discuss the rest of this passage or its increasing turn to aesthetic and sensory language.

of fleeting and uncertain light wander and vanish; vague shapes of floating mist reveal themselves, gradually assuming form and colour; faint hues of crimson, silver, and gold strike here and there" (*HI* 1:21). The legends themselves are a "concealing veil," a "weird strange light," for in this aesthetic dawn "the intellect of man, tired by contact with the vulgarity of actual things, goes back for rest and recuperation, and there sleeping, projects its dreams against the waning light and before the rising of the sun" (*HI* 1:22). Despite their gossamer nature, however, these legends "have their own reality. They fill the mind with an adequate and satisfying pleasure. They present a rhythmic completeness and a beauty not to be found in the fragmentary and ragged succession of events in time" (*HI* 1:22–23). The legends may lack for sunlit clarity, but they possess "the glory of changing and empurpled mist" (*HI* 1:22), and their protean nature allows them to transcend temporal boundaries. O'Grady writes this entire description of the development of the old legends in the present tense, suggesting by his grammar that the aesthetic dawn is outside of historical time (or at least outside of ongoing time). Even more importantly, the aesthetic collapsing of history into a timeless ethnographic present also dissolves any division between maker and audience. Despite the initial suggestion that legends are a form of aesthetic recuperation from day-to-day vulgarity for those who made them, it is entirely unclear from the present tense of these passages whose mind gets filled with the "satisfying pleasure" of these legends or who feels their "rhythmic completeness and . . . beauty."

This confusion is, of course, O'Grady's point, and upon closer reflection it is never clear whether the aesthetic process he describes is that of the ancient bards, that of his experience in reading ancient bardic poetry, or that of his own creation of modern poetry. When he asks, "But what of these concealing glories, these cloudy warriors, and air-built palaces? Why not pass on at once to credible history?" (*HI* 1:22), he addresses at once his source materials and his own methodology, both writing himself into a poetic tradition and defending the value of this tradition on highly sensual grounds: history may be credible, but legend is satisfying, pleasurable, rhythmic, beautiful. If actual events are nothing more than a dry skeleton (the kind that "[d]ryasdust" archaeologists undoubtedly exhume with relish), then bardic poetry fleshes the past into a living, feeling body that can experience and be experienced, across multiple sensory planes, times, and spaces. Emphasizing the sensory nature of art allows O'Grady to create a mode of apprehending history that is an alternative to the chronological march of time, one in which he can privilege how one *feels* the past over what one *knows* about the past.

In this privileging of affect over epistemology—as the multiple epigraphs from John Keats and Percy Bysshe Shelley in the *History* suggest[22]—O'Grady takes many of his aesthetic cues from the nineteenth-century romantic poets. A significant number of these epigraphs come from poems in which the poets take up mythologies as their subject matter, further intimating that O'Grady sees his transmission of Irish legend as a form of romantic poetry: in the selections included in this edition alone, O'Grady quotes from Shelley's *Prometheus Unbound* and *The Witch of Atlas* as well as from Keats's "La Belle Dame sans Merci," *Hyperion*, and "On First Looking into Chapman's Homer." These epigraphs come from poems that are preoccupied with the transformation of ancient myth into new imaginative forms that could, in Shelley's words, "awaken . . . the sympathy of their contemporaries." As Shelley writes in his preface to *Prometheus Unbound*, the verse drama from which O'Grady takes his epigraph to the chapter entitled "The Affliction of Cuculain" (*HI* 1:228; p. 107), "Poetical abstractions are beautiful and new, not because the portions of which they are composed had no previous existence in the mind of man or in nature, but because the whole produced by

22. Although not all of O'Grady's epigraphs are from Keats and Shelley—others are from Shakespeare and Milton, Homer himself, the "ancient bards," and some of O'Grady's Anglo-Irish contemporaries, such as Edward Dowden—his choice to group canonical English writers and the most famous Western bardic poet with Irish bardic poets and contemporary Irish writers emphasizes his vision of his history eliding chronological distinctions and elevating Irish legend into the realms not just of high mythology but also of high poetry.

their combination has some intelligible and beautiful analogy with those sources of emotion and thought, and with the contemporary condition of them." In other words, Shelley sees the poet as both mimetic and creative, borrowing from what is external and extant in the world but inspired to find in it a "new life . . . which drenches the spirits even to intoxication."[23] His verse drama is explicitly *not* an attempt to simply re-create the lost drama of Aeschylus from which he takes his plot, but rather an effort in transforming ancient mythology to impress the modern imagination with "beautiful idealisms of moral excellence," to show how "the mind can love, and admire, and trust, and hope, and endure."[24]

The lines that O'Grady uses to preface "The Affliction of Cuculain" are from the first act of *Prometheus Unbound*, in which the punished Titan Prometheus describes the torments he has suffered chained on a mountain for stealing fire from the gods:

> And shapeless sights come wandering by,
> The ghastly people of the realm of dream,
> Mocking me.[25]

O'Grady unabashedly models on Shelley's lines the language of Cuculain's suffering in this chapter, writing that Cuculain "saw faces that moved amongst the trees mocking him, and horrid things, formless and cold, estrays out of the fold of hell, wandering blots of the everlasting darkness, and there was laughter in the hollow chambers of the forest" (*HI* 1:229; p. 108). Including Shelley's lines in an epigraph mere paragraphs before borrowing so closely from them emphasizes the likeness O'Grady imagines between Cuculain and Prometheus as romantic heroic emblems as well as O'Grady's own self-conscious desire to push romantic affect even further than its

23. Percy Bysshe Shelley, *Prometheus Unbound*, in *The Major Works*, ed. Zachary Leader and Michael O'Neill (Oxford: Oxford Univ. Press, 2003), 230–31.

24. Ibid., 232.

25. Ibid., 234.

early-nineteenth-century extremes. Both Prometheus and Cuculain might be tortured by the shapelessness of mocking specters—by what can be felt, sensed, and experienced rather than by what can be rationally discerned—but O'Grady takes Cuculain's mocking specters to a new level of sensory excess when he makes them "cold," "horrid" "blots of everlasting darkness" in addition to just "formless." He associates these shapeless specters with Cuculain's feverish anxiety that he has been forsaken by all the men he has loved, an anxiety of historical disavowal that threatens to strip him of his entire sense of self: "so wasted they all the pleasant tracts of his noble spirit" (*HI* 1:230; p. 108). But Cuculain's reawakening as he "remember[s] his friends," figured as the coming of the "dawn trembling through the forest," is presaged in O'Grady's performance of literary interrelations at the beginning of this chapter—his conspicuous revision of Shelley suggests that remembering one's formative interlocutors is as profound a path to literary revival as it is to Cuculain's spiritual revival. In deliberately juxtaposing Shelley's lines with his own amendment of these lines, O'Grady not only immerses Cuculain in a tradition of romantic heroic sensibility but also foregrounds the essential role that literary inheritance—the self-conscious adaptation and transformation of older literary forms to new ends—plays in his revivalist historiographical aesthetic.

O'Grady's use of lines from Keats's sonnet "On First Looking into Chapman's Homer" as an epigraph to the chapter "Cuculain Is Knighted" (*HI* 1:122; p. 77) stresses the importance of affect to this revivalist aesthetic, offering Keats's poem as a model for how he envisions the ancient stories of *History* reviving in the sensual imagination of contemporary readers. Keats's sonnet was inspired in 1816 by his first experience reading the seventeenth-century poet George Chapman's translations of Homer. Keats already knew Homer's work through Alexander Pope's famous eighteenth-century translations; in the early nineteenth century, the latter were the most widely read translations of Homer's Greek epics. According to the sonnet, reading Pope's translations prevents immersion in Homer's texts, and Keats describes this prior experience with Homer in the language of detached tourism: "Much have I travell'd," "many goodly states and kingdoms seen," "Oft of one wide expanse had I been told / That deep-brow'd Homer ruled."[26] Augustan translations have allowed no imaginative access to Homer's text itself; they have only mediated it in measured and alienating ways, permitting it to be seen but not actively engaged or experienced.

The poem shifts dramatically when Keats turns to his experience of Chapman's translations, moving from the language of observation to the language of embodiment: "Yet did I never breathe its pure serene / Till I heard Chapman speak out loud and bold."[27] In this *volta*, Keats not only makes his first direct reference to the texts he is reading (as opposed to the metaphors of travel he has used to describe Pope's texts) and explicitly describes his experience of another poet's voice but also puts his own senses at the center of his encounter with Chapman. He "hears" Chapman's voice rather than simply reads his words, and this sensory interaction allows him to "breathe" Homer, to physically bring the text into his body. Chapman's translation is thus less a form of mediation than it is the opening of a direct conduit between Keats and Homer, one that Keats imagines manifesting in intimate bodily experience—the same kind of experience O'Grady hopes for when he imagines his bardic legends "fill[ing] the mind with . . . satisfying pleasure."

O'Grady's use of the first two lines of Keats's sestet to introduce the chapter "Cuculain Is Knighted" underscores his sense of how the "right" translation of ancient texts can generate feeling that blurs the temporal boundary between old and new. The lines—"Then *felt* I like some watcher of the skies / When a new planet swims into his ken" (my emphasis)—explicitly allude to Sir William Herschel's discovery of Uranus in 1781, although they also prefigure Cuculain as the renowned knight that the druid and "star-gazer" Cathvah foresees in the heavens (*HI* 1:122; p. 77). Uranus, of course, was not a

26. John Keats, "On First Looking into Chapman's Homer," in *Keats's Poetry and Prose*, ed. Jeffrey N. Cox (New York: W. W. Norton, 2009), 54–55.

27. Ibid.

"new" planet when Herschel discovered it, nor was Cuculain a new hero when O'Grady wrote *History of Ireland*. Uranus was instead a very, very old planet that had been concealed from view until Herschel saw it, just as Homer's ancient poetry had been inaccessible for Keats until he read Chapman's translations and just as, in O'Grady's mind, the heroes of ancient Irish history have been trapped in "dumb remnants" (*HI* 2:1; p. 35) until *History of Ireland* makes them speak. In describing the planet as "new," and by extension describing Chapman's Homer as "new," Keats emphasizes (and O'Grady reemphasizes) the aesthetic power of translation not just to find a lost past but also to revitalize it, to transform it from something that is dead and distant into something different, something living, active, "swimming" in the present moment. By using these lines as an epigraph in volume 1 of his *History*, O'Grady anticipates the explicitly revitalizing desire he expresses in the introduction to volume 2: "to make this heroic period once again a portion of the imagination of the country."

Yet in borrowing from this particular poem by Keats, O'Grady does more than simply find language to appropriately convey his wish to make his ancient hero new and alive for modern Irish readers. He also enmeshes himself in the canonical romantic literary tradition that, as Yeats would later ecstatically reiterate in an essay on Shelley's poetry, "seek[s] to awaken in all things that are, a community with what we experience within ourselves"—a tradition that, for the young Yeats, offered a model for how sensory experience could create symbols that "transcend particular time and place . . . and bec[ome] living souls."[28] In using this epigraph, O'Grady presents himself both as a Chapman figure, offering an authentic and "bold" version of ancient bardic poetry that revives it and allows it to be embodied in a way that the translations preceding him have not been able to, and as a Keats figure, a romantic poet who frees

28. W. B. Yeats, "The Philosophy of Shelley's Poetry," in *Collected Works*, 4:55, 62.

mythological image from the bounds of rigid classicism to make it a part of the symbolic, sensory present. O'Grady envisages *History of Ireland* transforming the Irish mythic past into an Irish poetic future, one in which the past itself, whatever it may be, matters far less than the ecstatic aesthetic process it catalyzes. His ideal romantic historiography, in other words, would not simply find compelling poetic language to describe a mythical past but also find in that past an aesthetic experience for and in the present moment, an experience that fundamentally changes *now* through its refleshing of *then.* Just as "On First Looking into Chapman's Homer" derives its lyrical power not from Homer's tales themselves, to which Keats never even alludes, but from the new sensory phenomena and poetic possibility that emerge from ancient poetry rewritten "as truly an original poem,"[29] so too does O'Grady's epigraph from the sonnet emphasize the bidirectionality of the lyrical resuscitation in *History of Ireland*: that is, it emphasizes not only the way poetic language allows "the charred relics of the hero . . . [to start] forth to run a new career of glory in the imagination of his people" (*HI* 1:xviii–xix; p. 56) but also the way these newly revivified relics might themselves, as they later do for Yeats, create new lyrical life for modern Irish readers and writers.

29. Samuel Taylor Coleridge to Sara Hutchinson, Feb. 12, 1808, in Samuel Taylor Coleridge, *Collected Letters of Samuel Taylor Coleridge*, ed. Earl Leslie Griggs, 6 vols. (Oxford: Clarendon Press, 1956–71), 3:68.

2

Lost (and Found) in Translation

The Masculinity of O'Grady's Cuculain

Joseph Valente

In *Irish Classics*, Declan Kiberd observes that turn-of-the-century Ireland inherited in Cuculain a heroic paragon of manly virtue, already "famous for chivalry," whose peculiar blend of exemplary attributes perfectly suited the task of forging Irish national identity as a manly identity, though his profile might uncannily smack, for this very reason, of the "public school boy in [Irish] drag"—that is, "a disguised version of the British Imperial present." He argues that "Cuculain was noted for combining a propensity to pagan violence against enemies with a Christlike sensitivity: but this was exactly the commendation much praised in the muscular Christians of Eton and Rugby."[1] But scholars who focus primarily on the source materials themselves rather than on their modern revival offer a notably different and more persuasive analysis of those materials' late-colonial adaptation. Far from locating something like a British-flavored manliness anachronistically lodged in the Red Branch Cycle, the popular translators of the cycle undertook, for strategic reasons, to retrofit the bardic heritage to the canons of late-Victorian respectability, to bowdlerize and embellish the heroic narratives so as to infuse them

1. Declan Kiberd, *Irish Classics* (Cambridge, MA: Harvard Univ. Press, 2001), 403.

with the aesthetic and ethical decorum the translators would like, and would claim, to have discovered. Their *true* inheritance was precisely this project of transvaluation, and their greatest debt in this respect was to one fabulist-translator in particular, Standish James O'Grady.

The strategic reasons behind the revivalist rewriting of the Ulster Cycle are not far to seek. As Maria Tymoczko observes, the *Táin Bó Cuailnge* (Cattle Raid of Cooley)—the very heart of the heroic cycle—could have only proven "an embarrassment" to Irish cultural nationalism if "translated fully and accurately." For instead of "establishing the greatness of Ireland's cultural heritage" and, with it, the innate ethnic virtue and dignity of the people themselves, the ancient warrior feats and the manner of their undertaking would serve "to confirm the stereotypes of the Irish as wild, uncivilized and in need of conversion,"[2] everything that the British press's image of the Irish as porcine, simian, and otherwise bestial had impressed upon the popular imagination. To avoid this self-arraignment, the Revivalist translators found it prudent to suppress certain parts of the Red Branch Cycle, to sanitize others, and to embellish, if not misrepresent, still others. O'Grady supplied the conceptual template for this practice by distinguishing between an idealized pole or essence of the Red Branch tales and their baser but adventitious elements or parts. In this way, the falsification of the Gaelic materials, so that "the nobler conception of any character, is . . . to be preferred to the ignoble" (*HI* 1:xiii; pp. 50–51), might be justified by reference to the higher, more comprehensive (if contradictory) truth of their spirit:

> I have endeavoured to trace the mental and physical personality of the heroes and heroines in their essential elements, and to discover that order of events which best harmonises with the records and traditions of the poets, and the characters of their heroic personages. Hence it follows, that in order to be faithful to the generic

2. Maria Tymoczko, *Translation in a Postcolonial Context* (Manchester, UK: St. Jerome, 1999), 66, 68, 82.

> conception, one must disregard often the literal statement of the bard. That the whole should be fairly represented, one must do violence to the parts upon which, indeed, no more violence can be wrought than they inflict upon one another, perpetually diverging in detail, though in unison generally as to the main idea of characters and events. (*HI* 1:x–xi; p. 51)

In order "to make this heroic period once again a portion of the imagination of the country" (*HI* 2:17; p. 48), O'Grady had to suit his adaptation to the country's increasingly respectable imagination of itself.

The main focus of this concerted gentrification of the mythic Gaelic past was the figure of Cuculain himself. Contrary to popular academic opinion, advanced Irish nationalism and its cultural proponents in the Literary Revival could never simply embrace a posture of so-called colonial hypermasculinity, for whatever such an ensemble of phallic ferocity, truculence, and self-aggrandizement might promise as a vehicle of martial resistance to British rule, it would also be hostage to the prevalent imperialist notion that the Irish were unworthy of or unready for the fruits of such resistance, the prerogative of self-determination. That is to say, the tendency to unbridled and aggressive self-will endemic to hypermasculinity augured ill for collective self-government. And yet if there ever existed an authoritative Irish exemplar of such hypermasculinity, it is surely the Cuculain of the *Book of Leinster* or the *Dun Cow*. From his scheming to find illicit advantage to his defiance of tribal superiors, from his cruelty in combat to his easy participation in the misogyny of his culture, the Hound of Ulster personifies the Gael as "an essentially [or excessively] masculine race."[3] So while the Revivalist adaption of the legendary strong man sought to render him the indigenous personification of advanced Irish nationalism, it simultaneously aimed to

3. Here I modify the phrase "an essentially feminine race" given in David Cairns and Shaun Richards, *Writing Ireland: Colonialism, Nationalism, and Culture* (Manchester, UK: Manchester Univ. Press, 1988), 42.

cleanse him of his indigenous turbulence in favor of a more controlled Anglo-style manliness, which had become synonymous, in both popular and elite discourse, with fitness for freedom. To glorify his ethnic progeny, then, Cuculain had to be seen as channeling the ferocity expected of the elite warrior into a strenuous discipline and dutifulness beneficial to the tribe and as embodying an animal vigor self-sublimated into something like moral rigor.

Standish O'Grady set the tone and provided the discursive means for effecting this ideological "translation" of Cuculain the hypermasculine specimen into Cuculain the paragon of manliness. Written in the midst of a medieval revival across the British Isles and before the Irish Revival proper, O'Grady's free rendition of the Red Branch tales introduced the masculine ideals and institutions associated with the former into the latter. In so doing, his practice split the difference between cultural assimilationism and cultural reappropriation—a sterling, if aristocratically inflected, instance of what Homi Bhabha has dubbed "colonial mimicry."[4] On the one hand, O'Grady relocates codes of Arthurian-style chivalry among the Ultonians, centuries earlier, thereby claiming authorship of this civilizing, Anglo-identified discourse for the aboriginal Irish. It was precisely O'Grady's historical metalepsis in this regard that paved the way for Lady Gregory to use the *Morte D'Arthur*, in good conscience, as a model for *Cuculain of Muirthemne*, published two decades after *History of Ireland*.[5] On the other hand, O'Grady's specific representation of these courtly ideals come unmistakably filtered through the defining literary and social institutions of Great Britain at its imperial apex, whether it be the romances of Thomas Carlyle (which O'Grady quite affected) or the game ethics of the British public school. In thus representing Cuculain as a progenitor of English-style manliness after the fact or its imitator *avant la lettre*,

4. Homi Bhabha, *The Location of Culture* (New York: Routledge, 1994), 85–92.

5. Lady Augusta Gregory, *Seventy Years* (New York: Macmillan, 1974), 391.

O'Grady looked to controvert the invidious gender stereotypes of the Irish by reference to the very standard used to impose them.

In this essay, I consider four leading areas of O'Grady's trans-lingual makeover of Cuculain, from his early training to his mature triumph.

EMAIN MACHA

As Tymoczko has observed, O'Grady transposed the Irish heroic narrative onto the generic frame of the Victorian boys' adventure tale, a preferred cultural site for conflating chivalric ideals with the public-school ethos.[6] This synthesis in turn dominates O'Grady's historical novel *The Coming of Cuculain* (1894). To take one example, O'Grady grossly sentimentalizes Cuculain's initial rejection and ultimate acceptance by the Boy Corps so that his moral sensitivity and social club ability receive equal billing with his precocious might. As a result, Cuculain's introduction to Emain Macha, mediated by an invitation to join in team sports, resonates unmistakably with Tom Brown's introduction to rugby, albeit in a key elevated by O'Grady's fulsomely romantic diction: "Truly he was the pure burning torch of the chivalry of the Ultonians in his time."[7] O'Grady seems to have envisioned the Boy Corps as a public school for medieval Knights of the Cross, and Cuculain's graduation in fact comes with a knighting ceremony at wide variance, ideologically and institutionally, from his "taking up of arms" in the other translations. This formal investiture of knighthood marks the young hero's inculcation not just in the skills of battle ("to hurl spears . . . to train war-horses and guide war-chariots; to lay on with the sword and defend themselves with sword and shield"[8]) but also, and almost comically, in the high-minded

6. Tymoczko, *Translation*, 171. Tymoczko also remarks that O'Grady's Irish tales form "an analogue to medieval romance" (171).

7. Standish James O'Grady, *The Coming of Cuculain* (London: Methuen, 1894), 44.

8. Ibid., 49.

menu of self-restraining virtues, the amalgamation of which went by the single name "manliness":

> to speak appropriately with equals and superiors and inferiors and to exhibit the beautiful practices of hospitality according to the rank of guests[;] . . . to drink and be merry in the hall, but always without intoxication[;] . . . to respect their plighted word and be ever loyal to their captains; to reverence women, remembering always those who bore them[;] . . . to be kind to the feeble and unwarlike; and all that it became brave men to feel and think and do in war and in peace.[9]

Rewriting the Red Branch as the Round Table, in an adolescent pastiche of courtly style ("plighted troth," "ever-loyal"), the catalog forecasts Cuculain's espousal, in upcoming adventures, of ethical values that either were conspicuously eschewed by him in the original text (e.g., respect for rank) or were anachronistic for Red Branch society at large (e.g., a medieval "reverence [for] women").

O'Grady's mighty efforts to establish Cuculain's behavior as a type of public-school chivalry bore a double influence. On one side, his work modeled all subsequent popular translations of the heroic cycle. Eleanor Hull prefaced her own popular compendium *Cuculain: The Hound of Ulster*, published in 1909, with the assurance that these tales of ancient Ireland breathe a chivalric nobility of a most authentic kind, where "authentic" may be taken as a cognate of "O'Gradyesque":

> [A]s the Arthurian legend all through the Middle Ages set before men's minds an ideal of high purpose, purity of life, and chivalrous behaviour . . . so these old Irish romances, so late rescued from oblivion, come to recall the minds of men in our own day some noble ideals. . . . For rude as are the social conditions depicted in these tales and exaggerated and barbaric as is the flavour of some

9. Ibid.

of them, they nevertheless present to us a high and often romantic code of natural chivalry.[10]

Hull thus follows O'Grady in crafting a complex historical metalepsis wherein the Red Branch Order, having been re-created in the image of an Arthurian virtue contoured by still more current notions of Victorian manliness, is designated the earlier and unsurpassed repository of such virtue under the vaguely oxymoronic label *ideal chivalry.*

Hull's reference to "some of them" speaks to the strategy of editorial selectivity—introduced once again by O'Grady himself—that proved necessary to sustain the impression of an ancient Irish chivalry. O'Grady and his epigones modified the composition or proportions of the manuscript narratives to enable incidents with a courtly tenor to anchor the cycle as a whole. Betty Hutton goes the farthest down this road. In her rendition of the *Táin*, as Tymoczko points out, she replaces all the less-respectable parts of the epic "with noble, heroic or tragic stories from other parts of the cycle."[11]

For this reason, perhaps, Hutton's *Táin* became a favorite at St. Enda's School, which is to say it became the chief mediation of Standish O'Grady's impact on Pádraic Pearse and his young charges. Pearse's curricular aims at St. Enda's, to instill "struggle, self-discipline, self-sacrifice," whereby "the soul rises to perfection,"[12] resonate less of the heroic ethos found in the Red Branch Cycle than of the ideal of manliness inculcated in the British public school as replicated in O'Grady's translation—the Emain of Macha as the rugby of Thomas Arnold. Not surprisingly, the Cuculain that Headmaster Pearse erected as the focus of identification—"part of the mental life of the teachers and the taught"—mirrored O'Grady's manicured

10. Eleanor Hull, *Cuculain: The Hound of Ulster* (London: Harrap, 1909), 13–14.

11. Tymoczko, *Translation*, 74.

12. Pádraic Pearse, *The Story of a Success* (Dublin: Maunsel, 1917), 35–36. For background on Pearse, see Patrick Bixby's essay in this volume.

construction. "We were anxious," Pearse writes, "to send our boys home with the knightly image of Cuculain in their hearts, and his knightly words ringing in their ears."[13] And this revisionist effort culminated in Pearse's own children's pageant *The Boy Deeds of Cuculain*, a centerpiece of his school's yearly theatrical calendar. As Elaine Sisson, historian of St. Enda, remarks, Pearse's composition "omits certain incidents which are unflattering to [Cuculain]."[14] Philip O'Leary more specifically notes that Pearse rejects "episodes which present Cuculain in a negative, especially an excessively violent light"[15]—in sum, those incidents that violate the code of chivalry retroactively assigned to Cuculain in O'Grady's histories and then in the Revival at large.

WAR(P) SPASM

The ultimate *parade virile* in the entire Ulster Cycle is Cuculain's patented *riastrad*, or "warp spasm," and the exorbitancy of this state of upheaval crystallizes the ideological problems Cuculain's seemingly inestimable hypermasculinity posed for his nationalist boosters. In the heat of battle and the grip of rage, the Hound convulsively morphs into a towering, distorted, preternaturally violent figure, much like the Incredible Hulk, only in far more graphic bodily detail. A scholarly translation of Cuculain's metamorphosis after the death of the Boy Corps captures the horrific effect:

> [T]hen his first distortion came upon Cú Chulainn so that he became horrible, many-shaped, strange and unrecognisable. His haunches shook about him like a tree in a current . . . every limb and every joint, every end and every member of him from head to

13. Pearse, *The Story of a Success*, 21.

14. Elaine Sisson, *Pearse's Patriots* (Dublin: Cork Univ. Press, 2004), 95.

15. Philip O'Leary, *The Prose Literature of the Gaelic Revival, 1881–1921: Ideology and Innovation* (University Park: Pennsylvania State Univ. Press, 1994), 257.

> foot. He performed a wild feat of contortion with his body inside his skin. His feet and his shins and his knees came to the back; his heels and his calves and his hams came to the front. The sinews of his calves came on the front of his shins and each huge, round knot of them was as big as a warrior's fist. The sinews of his head were stretched to the nape of his neck and every huge, immeasurable, vast, incalculable round ball of them was as big as the head of a month-old child.
>
> Then his face became a red hollow. He sucked one of his eyes into his head so that a wild crane could hardly have reached it to pluck it out from the back of his skull on to the middle of his cheek. The other eye sprang out onto his cheek. His mouth was twisted back fearsomely. He drew the cheek back from the jawbone until the inner gullet was seen. His lungs and his liver fluttered in his mouth and his throat. He struck a lion's blow with the upper pallet . . . so that every stream of fiery lakes within came into his mouth from his throat was as large as the skin of a three-year-old sheep. The loud beating of his heart . . . was heard like the baying of a bloodhound . . . or like a lion attacking bears. . . . [T]he hero's light rose from his forehead so that it was as long and thick as a hero's whetstone. As high, as thick, as strong, as powerful and as long as the mast of a great ship was the straight stream of dark blood which rose up from the very top of his head and became a dark magical mist.[16]

If size matters, not to mention gargantuan might and invincible mettle, then the transformed Cuculain must be seen to represent the zenith of heroic masculinity in the warrior mode. But at the same time and for the same reason, Cuculain also falls below the spectrum of humanity altogether and becomes a pure monstrosity, one reminiscent of the images of feral, bestialized natives promulgated in imperialist popular culture. Nor does Cuculain's lapse in properly human subjectivity derive merely from the sudden hideousness of his

16. Cecile O'Rahilly, ed. and trans., *Táin Bó Cúalnge from the Book of Leinster* (Dublin: Dublin Institute for Advanced Studies, 1967), 201–2.

lineaments or the savagery of his presence. As Jeremy Lowe notes, the terms *riastrad* and its alternate *siabrad* "are both used as impersonal passives," which indicates that the warp spasm, though emerging from within the champion's body, occurs outside his volition or capacity for self-control.[17] At moments of warp spasm, Cuculain is entirely prey to "bodily excitation," or what the Victorians would call the anarchy of animal spirits, which at once overwhelms and dissolves his very identity, gender and otherwise.

O'Grady's translations could do little to soften the barbarous impression left by the *riastrad* other than simply to abridge or bowdlerize the textual interludes given over to this organic emblem of hypermasculinity. At one point, O'Grady converts the hyperembodied phenomenon of *riastrad* into its abstract, affective correlative, "There was Panic in front of him, and Terror issued out of his countenance" (*HI* 2:266; p. 123), a rendition that suggests incontinence on the part of his adversaries rather than himself. Further along in the same passage, O'Grady gives the *riastrad* a meteorological figuration: "Out of his countenance there went as it were lightening, and showers of deadly stars rained forth from the dark western clouds above his head" (*HI* 2:267; p. 123). Instead of depicting a full-frame agitation that takes physical possession of Cuculain, the warp spasm of the manuscripts, O'Grady lifts the event from the material-bodily stratum to the facial region, the very seat of subjectivity, which is pitched against the more tumultuous heavens. Cuculain retains possession not only of himself and his own ferocity, as it were, but also of the natural violence of the storm as well. Instead of a heroism nearly allied with bestiality, Cuculain exhibits, on Grady's account, a manliness close to godliness. On multiple occasions, finally, O'Grady all but excises the *riastrad* and leaves in its place its rarefied opposite, a halolike configuration, thereby portraying Cuculain's defining experience of somatic engrossment

17. Jeremy Lowe, "Kicking Over the Traces: The Instability Cuculainn," *Studia Celtica* 34 (2000): 124.

and distortion as spiritual transcendence: "Bright then with the light of valour was the countenance of Cuculain," and "above the head of Cuculain there was as it were a bright circle" (*HI* 2:270, 272; pp. 132, 133–34). Where the *riastrad* had threatened to reduce Cuculain to a brute, O'Grady effects a transfiguration (in every sense) that elevates him to a divinity. Lady Gregory's borrowing of this radiant, rarefied trope of the *riastrad* in her wildly popular work *Cuchulain of Muirthemne* (the most direct influence the trope exerted) came with a gloss to precisely this effect: "And it is then Cuculain's anger came on him, and the flames of his herolight began to shine about his head . . . and he lost the appearance of a man, and what was on him was the appearance of a god," and, again, "[H]is anger came on him, so it was not his own appearance he had on him but the appearance of a god."[18] In either case, the godliness signified by the circle of light is more Christian than pagan, which is to say it works to sanctify in contemporary Irish terms the otherwise brutish and bloodthirsty exploits that bring Cuculain his fame.

FIR FER

Of the sanguinary exploits on Cuculain's ledger, none looms more savage than his use of the legendary spearlike weapon, the Gæ-Bolg. Piercing the anus and irradiating throughout the body, the Gæ-Bolg does not just kill; it debases and even dehumanizes its victims, exceeding in its felt consequence all of the ancient engines of war. It has been said to produce "the greatest abasement of the male gendered heroic person."[19] One might translate this sentiment and say that the Gæ-Bolg is in its combination of lethal destruction and eroticized abjection a singularly unchivalric instrument of battle or, more

18. Lady Augusta Gregory, *Cuchulain of Muirthemne* (1902; reprint, London: Murray, 1911), 239, 217.

19. Ann Dooley, "The Invention of Women in the *Tain*," in *Ulidia*, ed. Jim P. Mallory and Gerard Stockman (Belfast: December, 1994), 127.

precisely, a singular battlefield violation of the chivalric code. Therefore, it was inevitable that O'Grady, the writer most obviously responsible for ascribing that code to Cuculain, should downplay almost to the point of erasure Cuculain's signature device of mayhem. As the excerpts from *History of Ireland* in this volume attest, O'Grady occasionally mentions death by the Gæ-Bolg in passing, but he never elaborates on its operation or its effects. Still more importantly, he quietly minimizes its appearance in favor of a "magic sling," which he (mis)represents as Cuculain's weapon of choice.

But O'Grady had further reason to downplay, so far as possible, Cuculain's use of the Gæ-Bolg. Although the chivalric code would in fact have been unknown to a historical Cuculain and his compatriots, there did exist one dominant ethical principle in Gaelic warrior culture, the law of Fir Fer, loosely rendered as "fair play" and etymologically as "the truth of (a) man." Fir Fer applied mainly to one-on-one combat and held the participants to rules of conduct that adhered to reliably demarcated notions of even-handedness. Such combat, of course, provides the narrative spine of the *Táin Bó Cuailnge*, a series of set pieces in which Cuculain defeats in slow but sure succession the great champions enlisted under the banner of Queen Meave. In almost every instance, Cuculain finishes off these fights and his opponents by deploying the Gæ-Bolg. Because the uniquely ravaging capacity of this weapon can be accessed by Cuculain alone, it is on its face a clear violation of the "fair fight" principle of Fir Fer and, as Gaelicists have noted, "is repeatedly condemned by [Cuculain's] foes on these grounds."[20] "Fir Fer" translates as "the truth of (a) man" because it enjoins a certain gendered respect that each combatant is to accord the other. Beneath the boastful trash talk these champions all spew—and the Revivalists all subsequently censored—they are held to recognize the manhood of the other by engaging him on

20. Philip O'Leary, "Fir Fer: An Internalized Ethical Concept in Early Irish Literature," Éigse 22 (1987): 2.

equal terms and to prove (both test and manifest) their own manhood thereby. In this light, the bodily unmanning of Cuculain's foes by the disintegrative force of the Gæ-Bolg serves as an objectification of his refusal of this elementary form of soldierly recognition and thus as the purchase of (hyper)masculine power at the expense of his own "man's truth" or, in modern terms, his manliness, of which chivalry was O'Grady's extended metaphor.

By Revivalist consensus, the acme of combat-zone chivalry in the *Táin* comes with the Fardiad, the protracted contest between Cuculain and Fardia. Enamored of this episode as a monument to the "true spirit of chivalry" among the native Irish, certain Revivalist translators rendered it emblematic of the *Táin* in toto. After a series of bouts interspersed with conversation lasting days, Cuculain ultimately slays Fardia and then mournfully bewails him, giving the encounter its famously touching quality. O'Grady plays up the chivalric spirit of this face-off by setting it against the background of a relationship forged within a youthful warrior academy and modeled on public-school forms of affiliation: "The next hero brought out against Cuculain was an ancient friend and ally, Fardia, son of Daman, of Firbolg race, who had been his schoolfellow in the Isle of Skye. Indeed, Cuculain at that school seems to have been Fardia's 'fag,' polishing his armour and tying up his spears . . . so, Cuculain . . . is now suddenly confronted by his oldest and dearest friend" (*CP* 213; p. 60). To preserve this chivalric impression, O'Grady expurgates not only the venomous insults in which both fighters engage but also what is arguably the climax of the entire episode, the moment of Fardia's passing. In Cecile O'Rahilly's translation, Fardia tells Cuculain that "[y]ours is the guilt for my blood" rather than the laurels of victory and speaks of himself as one of the "heroes destroyed in the gap of betrayal,"[21] strongly suggesting that Cuculain's coup de grace constitutes a dishonorable piece of warcraft. In Thomas Kinsella's translation, which specifically looks

21. O'Rahilly, *Táin Bó Cúalnge*, 229.

to restore material purged in the Revival, Fardia offers a still more overt indictment of Cuculain:

> You have killed me unfairly
> Your guilt clings to me
> As my blood sticks to you.

He proceeds, inconveniently, to charge Cuculain with "deceit" in his plying of the Gæ-Bolg, which "passed . . . into [Fardia], so that every crevasse and every cavity of his body was filled with its barbs."[22] By excising such testimony to the shady viciousness of Cuculain's methods and moving directly to his far more anomalous indulgence in grief and regret after he slays Fardia, O'Grady sets the stage for the Revivalist enshrinement of this episode, transforming the tenor of the original scene into its very opposite. Cuculain's violation of the basic native code of Fir Fer becomes instead his exemplification of the far more elaborate and exacting standards of Arthurian courtliness.

BATTLE FURY

To be sure, Cuculain's infringement was not atypical of the warriors of ancient Ireland. Philip O'Leary notes that although Fir Fer comprised a rigorous code of personal honor, it was nonetheless systematically transgressed on all sides in the pursuit of public glory.[23] It is one of those laws, usefully unpacked by Slavoj Žižek, that carries within itself an unofficial but approved underside devoted to its own infraction.[24] As such, Fir Fer emerges over the course of the tales as the site of a momentous ideological contradiction: the highest ethical

22. Thomas Kinsella, *The Tain* (Oxford: Oxford Univ. Press, 1969), 197. For O'Grady's version, see Standish Hayes O'Grady, *The Tain bo Cuailgne*, in *The Cuchulinn Saga in Irish Literature*, ed. Eleanor Hull (London: Nutt, 1898), 195.

23. O'Leary, "Fir Fer," 13.

24. Slavoj Žižek, *The Metastases of Enjoyment* (New York: Verso, 1994), 54–55.

concept of Gaelic warrior culture admits of the most treacherous violation of its terms as "an acceptable means to the all important end of fame."[25] In thus exposing this contradiction, the manuscripts of the Ulster Cycle cast a skeptical glance at the masculinist ideology of the warrior culture represented and solicit a skeptical glance from their audience as well. The precept of Fir Fer provides the narrative with an alternative to the philosophy of martial success at all costs, and because this alternative standard is internal to Red Branch society, its structural breach cannot but register as a flaw or deficiency in that society, a failing on the society's own terms.

The contradictions surrounding Fir Fer represent only one slice of the critical perspective that the Ulster Cycle brings to bear on its subject. As noted Gaelicist Jeremy Lowe has shown, there is massive textual evidence that Cuculain's avid pursuit of nonpareil heroic stature had a destabilizing effect not just on native codes of honor, such as Fir Fer, and on the coherence and stability of his own embodied being in the world but also most importantly on the existing social order he was called upon to defend.[26] Indeed, on the consensus of today's old Irish scholars, *the* Táin *and surrounding documents were far more concerned with critiquing than with celebrating warrior culture and its violent standards of heroism.* As Joan Radner puts it, "Ireland's noble warriors, however admirable, were tragically self-destructive and ineffective,"[27] a sentiment she finds Cuculain himself confirming in his famous pronouncement, "Conscar bara bith" (Battle fury destroys the world). Daniel F. Melia seconds Radner's thesis as a kind of foundational paradox: "The more successfully [the warrior class] is able to fulfill its function, the more dangerous it is

25. O'Leary, "Fir Fer," 1.

26. Jeremy Lowe, "Contagious Violence and the Spectacle of Death in *Tain Bo Cuailange*," in *Language and Tradition*, ed. Mary Tymoczko and Colin Ireland (Amherst: Univ. of Massachusetts Press, 2003), 84–85. See also Lowe, "Kicking Over the Traces," 121–24.

27. Joan Radner, "'Battle Fury Destroys the World': Historical Strategy in Ireland's Ulster Epic," *Mankind Quarterly* 23 (1982): 55.

to the society which it serves."[28] Cuculain is not just centrally implicated in this indictment; he is, in Lowe's words, "perfectly placed to challenge the very core of the heroic ethos."[29]

It is this "challenge" that O'Grady and his followers not only elided but reversed. In encouraging a profoundly celebratory view of Cuculain's actions, they lionized him as the avatar of an "heroic ethos" elevated to the status of an uncomplicated communal ideal. Cuculain's individual valor and rapacity are revived as simply conducing to rather than *also* menacing the Ultonian social regime. In this respect, we might say that the minting of a national hero, purified of any residual ethical dross, required the misrecognition of the "national" history under construction and a misreading of its founding scriptures. At the same time, the supplanting of ancient legend with modern mythos posing as "history"—the past, misrecognized, *passing* as current—just might be O'Grady's greatest achievement. As Ernst Renan famously opines, "Forgetting, I would even go so far to say historical error, is a crucial factor in the creation of a nation."[30] For a cultural revival, this sort of forgetting or enabling historical error is necessary to turn the mere recovery of the past into its effective repurposing for the present. As O'Grady divined, the rampant hypermasculinity of Cuculain past must be refashioned into the manliness of Cuculain present if he were to be as effective a *symbolic* force in the cause of nationalist self-assertion as he was a material force in the quest for personal self-aggrandizement.

28. Daniel F. Melia, "Parallel Versions of 'The Boyhood Deeds of Cuchulainn,'" *Forum for Modern Language Studies* 10 (1974): 220.

29. Lowe, "Contagious Violence," 95.

30. Ernst Renan, "What Is a Nation?" in *Nations and Nationalism*, ed. Homi Bhabha (New York: Routledge, 1990), 11.

3

Honor, Individuality, and Nationhood in O'Grady's Cuculain Narrative

Michael McAteer

Among the many writers during the Literary Revival in Ireland to be influenced by the work of Standish O'Grady, perhaps the most significant, and the most underestimated, was none other than James Joyce. Although O'Grady's two-volume work *History of Ireland* is not mentioned in the famous discussion between Stephen Dedalus, Æ, John Eglinton, and others concerning Shakespeare's relation to Hamlet in the "Scylla and Charybdis" episode of *Ulysses*, his paternal ghost is present in two aspects at least: the twin ideas of authority and paternal lineage with which Stephen is concerned in his esoteric theory of an ancestral connection between Shakespeare and the ghost of Hamlet's father; and the allusion, during the course of local literary gossip among those present (that Stephen listens to with disdain), to Dr. George Sigerson's bold claim that Ireland's "national epic remains to be written."[1] The ghost of O'Grady in Joyce's great work hovers within this phrase.

History of Ireland, first published at the author's expense because no publishing company at the time saw any prospect for its impact, is preoccupied with paternal kinship and is presented by the author

1. James Joyce, *Ulysses* (London: Penguin, 1992), 246.

as an epic narrative of ancient Irish history.[2] Even if *History of Ireland* never achieved the epic stature to which it aspired, and even as we acknowledge how removed *Ulysses* is in style and content from O'Grady's work, it remains the case that O'Grady was the first classics graduate from Trinity College to engage the ancient Irish sagas in a literary-historical mode and the first to attempt to write a modern epic of ancient Ireland along the lines of the Greek epics of Homer. O'Grady even went so far as to claim that in the *Odyssey* itself Homer refers to Ireland. Observing that the Roman writer Plutarch refers to the island of Ogygia mentioned in the *Odyssey*, home to the goddess Kalypso, as "lying on the west of Britain," O'Grady suggests that Homer did have Ireland in mind, judging by the "tone of mingled awe and interest with which the more ancient classical writers refer to this dimly known island" (*HI* 1:22–23). Given the importance of the *Odyssey* to Joyce's *Ulysses*, O'Grady's assertion is significant when evaluating the relations that Joyce draws between ancient Greece and modern Ireland in *Ulysses* and not just the "Calypso" episode in which we first encounter Mr. Leopold Bloom.

The story of Cuculain in O'Grady's version of the *Táin Bó Cuailnge* (Cattle Raid of Cooley) in *History of Ireland* is undoubtedly his most enduring achievement, but its political and cultural significance is open to further exploration not just in relation to the Irish Literary Revival but also in relation to the broader social values that characterized life in Ireland in the decades following Irish independence. This is so because of the two audiences to which O'Grady

2. In an open letter to Lady Gregory in his newspaper, the *All-Ireland Review*, following the publication of her work *Cuchulain of Muirthemne* in 1902, O'Grady tries to correct the record and overcome the perception that Gregory got there first. Reminding her (and his readers) that he had first written down the Cuculain tale a long time earlier, he reveals that he could not get a publisher for it and had to have it printed and published at this own expense: "But I am glad to find that a great many people—you amongst the number—have followed on my track, and that, though I went out into the wilderness alone, as a sort of pioneer, a good many are going out after me" ("Letter to Lady Gregory," *All-Ireland Review* 3, no. 23 [Aug. 9, 1902]: 3–4).

directed his writings: the first, educated gentlemen primarily of Anglo-Irish stock; the second, Irish male adolescents from the broad spectrum of Irish society. The object in the first instance was to alert the Irish gentry to the "Greek" virtues that O'Grady observed in Cuculain and the Ulster Cycle. This knowledge would then form a basis upon which the Anglo-Irish gentry could orient their culture toward Irish life, acquire a deeper understanding of the traditions native to the island, and rescue themselves from their isolation in Irish society. This isolation, which O'Grady endeavored to break, arose in part from the success and the radicalization of Irish nationalism in the 1870s under the stewardship of Charles Stewart Parnell and Joseph Biggar at Westminster; it also owed much to the popularity of Michael Davitt's antieviction campaign in the West of Ireland during this same decade. O'Grady knew, however, that this isolation was also self-imposed, a consequence of absenteeism and an Anglo-Irish habit of looking constantly to Westminster for the protection of its interests in Ireland. He understood that most of the Anglo-Irish gentry had made little attempt to engage the customs and the culture predating their acquisition of Irish territory during the Elizabethan and Cromwellian plantations of the seventeenth century. In his address to this landowning gentry of Ireland in *Toryism and the Tory Democracy* in 1886, he is explicit on the point: "They [the Irish tenant farmers] are hostile because you and your class would not become frankly and loyally Irish on these your Irish estates, and in the midst of Irish people."[3]

More significantly in the long run, O'Grady's story of Cuculain exercised a significant influence on the minds of young boys coming into adulthood during the 1900s and 1910s. Published in 1894, *The Coming of Cuculain* was aimed directly at this reading group and later became a staple in the diet for the boys of Pádraic Pearse's school at Rathfarnham, St. Enda's School (Scoil Éanna), when it

3. Standish James O'Grady, *Toryism and the Tory Democracy* (London: Chapman and Hall, 1886), 247.

opened its doors in 1908. After Irish independence was gained in 1921, O'Grady's tales of Cuculain became part of the curriculum in the Irish Free State primary schools. To this extent at least, O'Grady succeeded in fulfilling the desire he wrote about in the second volume of *History of Ireland* in 1880: to "make this heroic period once again a portion of the imagination of the country, and its chief characters as familiar in the minds of our people as they once were" (*HI* 2:17; p. 48).

Seamus Deane has been the foremost scholar of Irish literature to call into question the heroic mode that came to prominence in the Irish Literary Revival. He considers it to have exercised a debilitating influence in Irish social and political life ever since the foundation of the Irish Free State and Northern Ireland in 1921. Deane evaluates the habit of ennobling Irish tradition and antiquity within the Revival as a symptom of Ireland's historical experience of colonial subjugation rather than as an effective means of resisting English political and cultural control of Ireland.[4] In *History of Ireland*, O'Grady was undoubtedly engaged in mythmaking, and his tales of Cuculain in particular would become significant for later Irish writers in fashioning cultural values for an emerging independent Irish state. It is equally true that Ireland acquired an exotic allure in O'Grady's treatment of these tales. In volume 1 of *History of Ireland* (1878), O'Grady is adamant about the liveliness of the national record of Ireland from earliest times: "Clear, noble shapes of kings and queens, chieftains, brehons, and bards gleam in the large rich light shed abroad over the triumphant progress of the legendary tale" (21). Whatever he might claim about the real historical origins for this record, his narrative can be regarded as an example of the type of heroic fantasy that Deane identifies in the literature of the Irish Revival. Yet we should observe that O'Grady himself anticipated, by almost a century, the skepticism within late-twentieth-century

4. Seamus Deane, "Heroic Styles: The Tradition of an Idea," in *Theorizing Ireland*, ed. Claire Connolly (Houndsmills, UK: Palgrave Macmillan, 2003), 25.

postcolonial analysis of Irish culture toward the packaging of Irishness for tourist consumption.[5] In February 1900, as the work of the Irish Literary Theatre was gaining attention in Dublin and London, he commented skeptically in his newspaper the *All-Ireland Review*, "In fact I feel towards the whole Irish literary movement, except the Language movement, something of the same feeling, though, of course, on a very different plane, that I feel to the tourist movement."[6] In drawing on manuscript sources—collected, translated, and published earlier by Eugene O'Curry—to shape a narrative of Cuculain, O'Grady had in mind certain ideas of a nation, the role of culture in its sustainment, and the values imparted through it. Although these ideas certainly granted prominence, allure, and mystique to Ireland through its body of ancient stories, the forms of Irish nationhood that they entertained ought not to be thought of as a colonial symptom.

In assessing the cultural politics of the Cuculain narrative according to O'Grady's idea of nationhood, we should first observe a distinction and a relation that he draws in volume 1 of *History of Ireland*: "A nation's history is made for it by circumstances, and the irresistible progress of events; but their legends, they make for themselves" (22). By this account, history is a matter of determinism, whereas legend is one of creative freedom. The distinction is important, but so too is the relation. Following Thomas Carlyle in particular, O'Grady was convinced that ancient legends arose out of historical circumstances and that the past could be read through

5. Seamus Deane writes that "as a country for tourists—internal and external—Ireland is in many respects unreal, really unreal, in the sense that the construction of its 'real' status and that of its consumer fantasy are inseparable activities" (*Strange Country: Modernity and Nationhood in Irish Writing since 1790* [Oxford: Clarendon Press, 1998], 149). For further discussion of Irish tourism as fantasy and kitsch, see David Lloyd, *Ireland after History* (Cork: Cork Univ. Press, 1999), 89–100, and Colin Graham, *Deconstructing Ireland: Identity, Theory, Culture* (Edinburgh: Edinburgh Univ. Press, 2001), 132–52.

6. Standish O'Grady, "The Bending of the Bough," *All-Ireland Review* 1, no. 8 (Feb. 24, 1900): 5.

the narratives of ancient civilizations. Cuculain, therefore, is granted supernatural power, and the stories of his battle with the armies of Queen Meave over the Bull of Cooley are full of invention, sometimes wildly so. This drama of creative freedom always relates back, however, to traditions of ancestral inheritance, ancient customs, and the Irish landscape that Cuculain inhabits. In the first volume of *History of Ireland*, Cuculain kills Lōk Mac Favash when he "raise[s] on high above his head the mighty pebble, standing with legs apart in the ford, and dashe[s] it on the centre of the huge shield of Lōk Mac Favash" (209). Just before this violent display of warrior strength, Cuculain notices in the world around him the traces of history that mark the immediate landscape: "Then [he] looked a moment to the wide heaven and the sun, for it was blazing noon, and his lips moved, and, swerving swiftly to the right, he stooped. Now a row of great pebbles crossed the ford, the work of some ancient king" (208–9). Cuculain distinguishes himself here through an act of violent strength. The freedom it grants him is shown in that wide expanse of sky and the heat of the sun that he apprehends immediately. It is a freedom of the type that Yeats describes in the preliminary verse to his collection *Responsibilities* (1914): "Only the wasteful virtues earn the sun."[7] The stone with which Cuculain kills Mac Favash belongs in substance to these same stones placed in ancient times to make a crossing over the ford. These stones convert Cuculain's action into historical myth and grant honor to his violent act, for that act is not simply a random use of force: it is revealed as a manifestation of historical destiny.

In O'Grady's narrative of Cuculain, honor is most certainly the expression of that type of chivalric code that we encounter in such Victorian works as *Idylls of the King* (1859–85) by Alfred, Lord Tennyson. Colin Graham highlights the importance of *Idylls of the King* in spreading the idea of chivalry in Victorian England, with

7. W. B. Yeats, "Closing Rhyme," in *The Collected Works of W. B. Yeats*, vol. 1: *The Poems*, ed. Richard J. Finneran, 2nd ed. (New York: Macmillan, 1997), 101.

chivalry acting as "the ethical and behavioural code of the Arthurian myth."[8] Drawing on the work of Mark Girouard, Graham notes the impact that Tennyson's work had on Prince Albert, prompting him to have Queen Victoria's Robing Room in the Palace of Westminster decorated with paintings on the subject of the Arthurian legend.[9] Although the works of Tennyson and other Victorian authors, such as William Morris, approximated to ideas of British Celticism to varying degrees, they lack one aspect present in O'Grady's writing that lends his idea of Cuculain's honor a different inflection—the connection to a living landscape. The ancient raths and cairns to be found throughout Ireland were all-important to O'Grady because they functioned as marks of ancient historical episodes that survive in the fragments of stories that make up Irish mythology, fragments that he attempted to work into "epic proportion and reasonableness" (*HI* 1:48). Not only did O'Grady write a version of the Cuculain legend, but he also wrote stories that were based on the actual recorded events and personalities of the Elizabethan period in Ireland and reprinted a fact-based account of them in 1896.[10] By connecting the places that feature in these stories of Elizabethan Ireland to the incidents and characters of the Cuculain legend, O'Grady introduced the idea that early-modern Irish history could be traced back to the ancient mythology. Thus, he found it important to identify the stories of Cuculain and the Ulster Cycle with actual places in Ireland.

The Flight of the Eagle (1908) is O'Grady's fictional account of Red Hugh O'Donnell, one of the last Ulster Gaelic chieftains to

8. Graham, *Deconstructing Ireland*, 54–55.

9. Ibid., 57. See also Mark Girouard, *The Return to Camelot: Chivalry and the English Gentleman* (New Haven, CT: Yale Univ. Press, 1981).

10. These works include *Red Hugh's Captivity: A Picture of Ireland, Social and Political, in the Reign of Queen Elizabeth* (London: Ward & Downey, 1889) and *The Bog of Stars, and Other Stories and Sketches of Elizabethan Ireland* (London: T. Fisher Unwin, 1893). For the fact-based account, see Thomas Stafford, *Pacata Hibernia, or A History of the Wars in Ireland during the Reign of Queen Elizabeth* (1633; reprint, London: Downey, 1896).

fight against the army of Queen Elizabeth I before departing to the European continent in "the flight of the Earls." Cuculain's spirit is seen to live on in that part of Ulster where the wars of the Bull of Cooley were believed to have taken place. O'Grady's version of the story describes O'Donnell traveling through this area. Noting that Gaelic bards of yore had compared O'Donnell to Cuculain, O'Grady depicts O'Donnell passing spots associated with Cuculain's exploits: "Ardee, the Ford of Far-dia, where Cuculain had stood in the gap of Ulster, and held the gates against Queen Maeve's armies . . . past many a dolmen and mound marking the graves of champions whom he [Cuculain] had slain."[11] O'Grady emphasizes O'Donnell's stature as an Irish warrior in the sixteenth century by tracing this journey through those places in Ulster associated with the heroic deeds of Cuculain in Irish mythology. Bearing this relation in mind, we should acknowledge that the type of honor celebrated in *History of Ireland* belongs indeed to the courtly tradition of knights, nobles, and monarchs that we encounter in Tennyson. It is distinctive within this tradition, however, owing to the particular places in the Irish landscape by which O'Grady connects ancient Irish mythology to early-modern Irish history. It is a form of honor associated as much with Irish places as with ancient customs.

The past is marked upon the landscape, as when Cuculain actively expresses the nobility of Ireland as a historical nation. In *History of Ireland*, then, nobility serves two purposes that are not quite in line with one another: the grandeur of Irish mythological history and the distinctiveness of a single individual. O'Grady's Cuculain might well be said to betray a particularly High Church Protestant virtue of freely choosing to sacrifice himself in defense of customary institutions. The strongest moments of pathos derive from the solitude that this sacrifice entails, for Cuculain appears not to embody the collective spirit of Irish nationhood, but rather an individuality that

11. Standish O'Grady, *The Flight of the Eagle* (Dublin: Sealy, Bryers and Walker, 1908), 244.

testifies to an internal rupture within the Irish community itself even as it is distinguishes Cuculain as the greatest warrior of antiquity. In O'Grady's account of the *Táin Bó Cuailnge*, for example, Cuculain is obliged to defend the fortress of Ulster alone against the army of Connaught because the wizard Cailitin has paralyzed the Red Branch army with an enchantment. At first, individuality sits easily with codes of honor after Fergus reaches an agreement between the kings of Connaught and Cuculain that Queen Meave's army will not be permitted to invade Ulster territory until Cuculain is defeated in single combat (*HI* 1:164; p. 104). As the narrative unfolds, however, the honorable aspect of individuality is tested severely as Cuculain is subject to a trial that is spiritual as much as physical, trying his status as the foremost representative of Irish nationhood. This test is first evident through the ways in which the old folk customs of rural Ireland work not to strengthen but to weaken the warrior during his trial of strength. At a point of exhaustion from combat in defense of Ulster, Cuculain is approached by the figure of an old woman who leads a lean cow and requests a blessing in exchange for a drink of milk. After he agrees, the figure turns around, and Cuculain cries out, "for there was the face of a ghoul within the hood," and he "recognised the thing that had plagued him at the ford" (*HI* 1:228; p. 107). Sixteen years after the publication of the first volume of *History of Ireland*, W. B. Yeats adapted this exchange of milk with an old woman to the stage in his play *The Land of Heart's Desire* (1894). In Yeats's play, it serves as a pretext for the visitation of a fairy being, who steals a young married woman from the world of the living.[12] In the opening episode of *Ulysses*, Joyce also takes up this old Irish superstition of the milk giver or the milk collector as a witch. In the morning at Martello Tower, when Stephen sits down to breakfast tea with Buck Mulligan and Haines, an old woman enters with a keg of

12. W. B. Yeats, *The Land of Heart's Desire*, in *The Collected Plays of W. B. Yeats*, 2nd ed. (London: Macmillan, 1952), 58–59.

milk. This woman becomes an emblem of the fairy world depicted in *Land of Heart's Desire*, "a witch on her toadstool."[13]

When Cuculain's boyhood companion Fardia is brought before him to fight, the conflict is amplified between individual bravery and loyalty to a traditional code of honor, a code that represents the communal bonds of nationhood. In advance of their combat, Cuculain moves Fardia to tears when he laments how his loyalty to the king of Ulster has separated him from the Irish people: "My people have indeed abandoned me and conspired for my destruction; but there is no power in Erin to dissolve my knightship to the son of Nessa and my kinship with the Crave Rue. Though they hate me, yet I cannot eject this love out of my heart" (*HI* 1:235). At this point, Cuculain is obliged to kill a man whom he regards as a brother in order to protect the citadel of Ulster and uphold the chivalric code of the Red Branch Knights. His trial is no longer just a test of his unexcelled prowess as a warrior; it is now a test of the comradeship from which his brave deeds take their motivation. It is a trial that heightens the tension within the symbolic meaning of Cuculain for the Irish nation as a whole. He is a warrior whose complete loyalty to ancient customs symbolizes the communal bond of nationhood. Yet he is equally the warrior who stands alone.

This tension in the symbolic meaning of Cuculain's heroism becomes most glaring in his battle with Fardia. Cuculain's honor derives from his fidelity to the traditions in which he was raised, but in this hour of supreme courage in defense of Ulster he is obliged to commit an act that is essentially dishonorable: kill a friend. In this way, loyalty produces dishonor, curiously anticipating the bitter divisions of brother against brother in the civil war that followed Ireland's independence in 1921. Cuculain might well sustain the heroic code to which nationhood makes its ultimate appeal in volume 1 of *History of Ireland*; in so doing, however, he is separated from

13. Joyce, *Ulysses*, 15.

everyone around him. He becomes completely representative of an ancient ideal of Irish nationhood—an ideal that expresses the value of communal belonging—only when he is completely separated from the brotherhood to which he belongs because of the spell that has been placed upon them. At the end of volume 1, his servant Læg discovers him seriously wounded. It is only at this point that the Red Branch Knights awaken from the enchantment that was put upon them and the war of the Bull of Cooley between the army of Ulster and the army of Connaught begins in earnest. Not before Cuculain reaches his weakest point is the Red Branch capable of shaking off the spell and going to battle. So it is only in the solitude, perhaps even the defeat, of the noble warrior that the collective spirit of Irish nationhood rises again. It is telling in this respect that in his hour of advanced suffering Cuculain is visited by a long litany of divine and historical spirits as he lies beside Læg (*HI* 1:236–37). These spirits testify to his place in the pantheon of Irish gods and warriors, but they also appear to him as phantasms, removing him from the world of action and heroic deeds. In this sense, the appearances amount to a rather Joycean paradox: they destabilize the very ancestral inheritances that they manifest by being presented to the reader in a ghostly, impressionistic way.

Although the second volume of *History of Ireland* restores to Cuculain the honor of his actions, it does not resolve this tension between individuality and nationhood. Keen to stress ancient Greek qualities of heroism and elevation, O'Grady names Ioldāna (Lu Lamfáda) the patron god of Cuculain—a god who is the source of the sciences and who corresponds to the Greek god Apollo (*HI* 2:72). Accentuating the valor of the Ulster warrior, Queen Meave's aged husband, Aileel Mōr, asserts that all the forces in the world would not be capable of defeating him (*HI* 2:218). Furthermore, Cuculain's ability to resist the magical spells that were put on the Red Branch of Ulster by the enchanter Cailitin not only emphasizes a spiritual as well as a physical power but also demonstrates a certain suspicion on O'Grady's part that druidism is a kind of "priestcraft." Cuculain becomes more clearly representative of the nobility of the Irish nation as a whole in the second volume when Ioldāna tells him that he will henceforth fight not only for the Red Branch of Ulster but also for "all the nations of Eiré" (*HI* 2:278; p. 138). He adds, however, that should Cuculain ever be killed, the Irish land will no longer yield heroes, but "dragons," "slimy unnameable monsters and all manner of foul creeping things," and its people will be "few and base" (*HI* 2:278; p. 138). In the end, Lewy Mac Conroi kills Cuculain, a death that O'Grady describes in the biblical terms of Christ's death on the cross, with the sun darkening, the earth trembling, a "wail of agony from immortal mouths" waving across the land, and "a pale panic" running through the vast army of Queen Meave when "that pillar of heroism" falls with a crash and "that flame of the warlike valour of Erin was extinguished" (*HI* 2:342; p. 184). Cuculain stands out, in O'Grady's rendering of the *Táin Bó Cuailnge*, as the greatest warrior of the ancient Irish world. In the magnificence of this complete giving of himself to the cause of his comrades as well as in the physical and spiritual strength that he shows in overcoming his opponents, O'Grady's Cuculain presents a troubling matter for readers who were expected to take inspiration from the grandeur of the Ireland's mythological inheritance. Cuculain is in the end not an archetype because his valor gives expression not to the unity of a nation but rather to his own terrible isolation, separated from his Red Branch comrades under the spell of Meave's wizard and standing in the face of her army. Although the *honor* of Cuculain's character as presented by O'Grady rests on his fidelity to the customs, traditions, and filial bonds of the tribal Gaelic Irish way of life, that honor reveals itself fully only when these things have been all but overturned through treachery and dark magic.

For all the verve and enthusiasm of *History of Ireland*, then, there is a pathos to the story of Cuculain that verges on despair. This attitude would show itself subsequently in O'Grady's own uncertainties about the direction that Irish life was taking in its social and cultural forms as his earlier narratives began to exert their influence on the Irish Literary Revival. One example is an incident that O'Grady records in a June 1900 issue of the *All-Ireland Review*.

During the course of a conversation with a man on a train, he wondered if Ireland would ever amount to anything as a country. The man was doubtful, expressing the view that the Irish were probably good for nothing but soldiering or something with an element of excitement about it. Instead of taking this conversation as a cause for pessimism, O'Grady got the idea into his head of drilling young boys in Kilkenny in a quasi-military fashion and duly embarked on this endeavor.[14] Here we find not just a throwback to an ancient martial code followed by Cuculain and the Red Branch Knights but also a forerunner of the Volunteer movements founded by Unionists and Nationalists in 1912 and 1913 during the period of the Home Rule crisis before the outbreak of the First World War. The political and economic motivations of O'Grady's local project typify his political ambiguities. Later in that same year, 1900, he cites "the rudimentaries of military drill and discipline" taught to pupils by the Christian brothers as a positive training that should be required of all Irish boys. The purpose, however, would not, in his view, be to build up an Irish separatist military resistance force (the objective of the Irish Volunteers later). On the contrary, it would be to create a huge militia capable of defending "this western flank of the Empire," drawing money into the Irish economy through army wages and the demand for military equipment.[15]

O'Grady's account of Cuculain in *History of Ireland*, therefore, could serve as an inspiration for militant Irish nationalism but also for a militant Irish wing of British imperialism. This apparent contradiction came through in the different ways that O'Grady's writing was taken up in Ireland in the 1900s and the 1910s. Clearly taken with O'Grady's work, Pádraic Pearse had the boys of St. Enda's perform a pageant of O'Grady's play *The Masque of Finn*. Elaine Sisson claims

14. Standish O'Grady, "The Great Enchantment," *All-Ireland Review* 1, no. 25 (June 23, 1900): 3.

15. Standish O'Grady, "Our Boys," *All-Ireland Review* 1, no. 41 (Oct. 13, 1900): 7.

that this play was first performed in Kilkenny sometime between 1898 and 1901.[16] This dating is possible because the play was based on excerpts from *Finn and His Companions*, which O'Grady first published in 1892. *The Masque of Finn* was certainly performed in Kilkenny in 1907. It was published that year with a notice that it had been performed in Kilkenny on July 5, 1907.[17] Based on the first episode of *The Masque of Finn*, dealing with Fionn McCumhaill, the hero of the Ossianic Cycle of ancient Irish tales, *The Coming of Fionn* was performed by the Pearse's students at St. Enda's in Rathfarnham in March 1909. This performance was part of a double bill with Douglas Hyde's play *The Lost Saint*.[18] Four years later, in May 1913, with the Ulster Volunteer Force already well organized and armed, Pearse advertised a performance of another pageant, Cuculain's defense of Ulster at the ford against his one-time companion Fardia, a direct reference back to O'Grady's original account in *History of Ireland*. Judging by Sean O'Casey's advertisement of the pageant in a letter to the *Irish Worker* in June 1913, the scale envisaged was to be impressively large: the pageant would express the epical qualities of the Ulster tale that O'Grady sought to convey in his original narrative: "Two hundred performers will take part in this pageant. Here will be shown the Boy Corps of Ulster hurling on the field. The news of Cuchulainn's wounding; the march of the boys to defend the frontiers till the Hero recovers; the scene of the men of Ireland around their Camp Fires; the attack by the Boy Corps of

16. Elaine Sisson, *Pearse's Patriots: St Enda's and the Cult of Boyhood* (Cork: Cork Univ. Press, 2004), 106.

17. Standish O'Grady, *The Masque of Finn* (Dublin: Sealy, Bryers and Walker, 1907), 2.

18. Sisson draws our attention to a review of this performance published in the *Irish Nation (and Peasant)* on March 27, 1909 (*Pearse's Patriots*, 106, 218). Philip O'Leary also notes a review of the performance by Seán MacGiolla an Átha that was published on the same day in *An Claidheamh Soluis* (*The Prose Literature of the Gaelic Revival, 1881–1921: Ideology and Innovation* [University Park: Pennsylvania State Univ. Press, 1994], 255).

Ulster; and, finally, in the last act, the 'Battle of the Ford' between the two Heroes, Cuchulainn and Feardiadh."[19]

By contrast, we have the isolated, remote, and poignant figure of Cuculain in Yeats's cycle of Cuculain plays, starting with *On Baile's Strand*, the first performance of which inaugurated the Abbey Theatre in December 1904, along with Lady Gregory's play *Spreading the News*.[20] As Yeats's plays emerged over the course of thirty-five years, the sense of isolation in Cuculain's solitary defense of Ulster, which O'Grady brought to the fore in *History of Ireland*, would grow to become an emblem of Yeats's own sense of isolation and the isolation of the Protestant Anglo-Irish community as Ireland moved toward political independence. Beyond this, there is a sense of Ireland itself as a nation defying the course of modern society in attempting to hold on to customs and religious values that were coming to appear outdated in developed societies as the influence of technology on daily life grew ever more widespread. Two very different legacies—Pearse's military cult of the hero and Yeats's nostalgia for the solitary man of ancient ways—testify to the power and ambivalence of O'Grady's narrative of Cuculain.

19. Sean O'Casey, "Letter to *The Irish Worker*," quoted in Patrick Pearse, *The Battle of the Ford*, in *Patrick Pearse: Collected Plays/Drámaí an Phiarsaigh*, ed. Róisín Ní Ghairbhí and Eugene McNulty (Dublin: Irish Academic Press, 2013), 295; for Pearse's advertisement of *The Battle of the Ford*, see 293–94.

20. Robert Hogan and Michael J. O'Neill, eds., *Joseph Holloway's Abbey Theatre: A Selection from His Unpublished Journal "Impressions of a Dublin Playgoer"* (Carbondale: Southern Illinois Univ. Press, 2009), 46.

4

Cuc(h)ulain in Bronze

The Afterlife of a Republican Icon

Patrick Bixby

When Pearse summoned Cuchulain to his side.
What stalked through the post Office? What intellect,
What calculation, number, measurement, replied?
We Irish, born into that ancient sect
But thrown upon this filthy modern tide
And by its formless spawning fury wrecked,
Climb to our proper dark, that we may trace
The lineaments of a plummet-measured face.
—W. B. Yeats[1]

Written in the final year of the poet's life, "The Statues" finds W. B. Yeats returning again to the figure of Cuculain, who had featured in his poems and plays throughout his long career. Yet here the poet's attention to the greatest of the Knights of the Red Branch is twice mediated: first, through the private mythology of Pádraic Pearse, who called on the warrior as a model for heroic resistance when he led the Irish Volunteers in taking the Dublin General Post Office in the spring of 1916, commencing a valiant but failed rebellion against British rule; second, through the public sculpture by Oliver Sheppard, who cast Cuculain in bronze as an emblem of heroic

1. W. B. Yeats, "The Statues," in *The Collected Works of W. B. Yeats*, vol. 1: *The Poems*, rev. 2nd ed., ed. Richard J. Finneran (New York: Simon & Schuster, 2010), 345. Reprinted with permission.

self-sacrifice, an emblem that was adopted to commemorate the Easter Rising in 1935, marking a continuity between the deeds of Irish legend and the events of the recent past. And behind both of these evocations stand the influential mythohistorical accounts of Cuculain and his contemporaries fashioned by Standish O'Grady. Yeats had drawn inspiration from these writings for a series of plays produced in the years leading up to the Rising, plays that had conjured Cuculain in the hope that he might rouse the Irish to overcome what Yeats perceived as their present degradation. In "The Statues," with a series of pressing questions, Yeats provokes his readers to consider the figure rendered in bronze and its relationship to the tradition of Western art, especially the time-honored concern with form, proportion, and precision, as well as its relationship with the character of the Irish people after the events of 1916. He incites us to consider, moreover, the place that the Irish people occupy within the modern world, albeit a place, as Michael McAteer points out in this volume, that links them with the customs and values of an earlier age. The answers that Yeats suggests in the poem's final lines identify the figure of Cuculain as a potent symbol of that linkage, which binds the poet and his contemporaries to "that ancient sect" of Irishmen who are defined by their noble, resolute, and yet entirely unfettered ideals.

The Irish people, according to one of Yeats's most resonant phrases, have been "thrown upon this filthy modern tide" and find themselves living in an age of increasing chaos brought on not just by revolution and world war but also, according to the poet's disturbing conjecture, by the "formless spawning fury" of democratic governance, crass commercialism, and racial degeneration. Yet they might still be saved by the reemergence of some mysterious order. That order can be found in the shadowy premodern epoch of Ireland's history, defined by individual heroism, aristocratic hierarchy, and dynastic continuity, all embodied in the figure of Cuculain; it can be found, too, in the precise configurations of classical aesthetics, exemplified by the sculptural practice of determining a true vertical with a plummet hung from a string. In "The Statues," Yeats traces this artistic sensibility from ancient Greece as it passes from epoch to epoch and culture to culture until it finally arrives in twentieth-century Ireland. The bronze statue of Cuculain gives material form to the abstract beauty of Pythagorean numbers and establishes a continuity, running through the Western tradition, between the harmonious forms of Greco-Roman sculpture and the heroic art and literature that have sustained the Irish people, including Pearse himself, in the face of racial and cultural deterioration. For Yeats, Cuculain thus becomes emblematic not just of the Irish struggle against an invading British culture but also of a heroic ideal that stands against the corruptions of the entire modern world. That this emblem is so closely identified with Ireland, in turn, suggests the special role of the Irish people among modern nations in combating the vulgar, debased, and anarchic forces of contemporary history—forces that, as it happens, found their expression in the English institutions that were synonymous with the British Empire. What is more, this identification suggests that the Irish people are essentially aristocratic in nature and that this nature must be reawakened so that they may ascend, through a kind of artistic aspiration, to their appropriate place in the order of things. Aesthetic striving, in other words, gives rise to cultural, spiritual, *and* political transformation. The "terrible beauty" of Pearse's actions, which Yeats had famously evoked in his poem "Easter 1916,"[2] contributes to this transformation precisely insofar as it engenders an assault on the formless, degenerate, and unheroic state of the modern world.

Until the end of his life, Yeats continued to seek an antidote to this condition in the cultural traditions of the Irish people, revisiting the theme for one of the final times in the stark conclusion of "The Statues." With these densely packed lines, the poet suggests what is for him the resounding significance of Cuculain for modern Ireland: Cuculain's is "the proper dark" of premodern or pre-Enlightenment

2. W. B. Yeats, "Easter 1916," in *The Collected Works of W. B. Yeats*, vol. 1: *The Poems*, 2nd ed., ed. Richard J. Finneran (New York: Macmillan, 1997), 182–84.

consciousness that reigned before the current positivistic consciousness of industrialization, commercialization, and democratization, which have stifled the contemporary imagination and tore down social hierarchies. But it bears reiterating that this significance is also bound up with the meaning that Yeats attributes to a particular work of art, which commemorates the spirit of Pearse's actions against all manner of modern ugliness, especially empire, while expressing the harmony of classical aesthetics and Pythagorean numbers—"calculation, number, measurement"—in its own lines and contours. To be sure, Yeats intimates that the statue of Cuculain elevates the artistic achievements of the Irish Literary Revival, including his own poetry and plays, to a level that surmounts even the events of the Easter Rising as forces shaping the contemporary character of the Irish people. The significance of the Cuculain bronze, which Yeats indicates with this sweeping argument for the power of art, becomes even more striking, if also more uncertain, when we look at the various influences that gave rise to it and the many ideological functions that it served. All of these influences and functions bear out the conflict between past and present, antiquity and contemporaneity, tradition and transformation, and exemplify the ambivalent force of myth in the modern world. But, more to the point, the history of this remarkable aesthetic object, seen as the manifestation of an ancient cultural legacy that had survived into a new age, encompasses a variety of competing ideas about what postcolonial Ireland should be or might become.

This survival depended in no small part on O'Grady's histories of ancient Ireland, which provided both Yeats and Pearse with heroes that they believed might serve as role models for their contemporaries. Trained in modern languages (English, French, and Irish) at the Royal University of Ireland and then in law at the Honorable Society of King's Inn, Pearse spent much of his career as a schoolmaster. He founded an experimental academy called St. Enda's School (Sciol Éanna) in 1908 to promote the revival of the Irish language and to further the cause of Irish nationalism. Drawing inspiration from the distant past, the young schoolmaster intended for the academy to harken back to the educational system prevailing in ancient Ireland, a system that was, according to his well-known essay "The Murder Machine," "the best and noblest that had ever been known among men."[3] In pagan times, this system had produced Cuculain and the Boy Corps of Emain Macha, and in Christian times it had produced Enda and his companions in Aran. Pearse believed that a "heroic tale" of the sort offered in O'Grady's histories was "more essentially a factor in education than a proposition from Euclid" and that the tale of Cuculain in particular offered an important example for his students because it furthered his aim of fostering the knightly traditions of "courage and strength and truth." This ambition was opposed to the "soulless thing" that was the English educational system in Ireland, which was designed to develop in young men "the peculiar type of efficiency demanded by the English Civil Service."[4] An important element of Pearse's pedagogy was the re-creation of knightly traditions through plays and pageants based on the heroic past of Ireland. To celebrate the Feast of St. Enda in the spring of 1909, for instance, the boys performed plays by Douglas Hyde and O'Grady, who attended rehearsals and addressed the students regarding the significance of his drama. Over the next few years, as both Joseph Valente and Michael McAteer remind us in their essays in this volume, the school produced several pageants based on the stories of Cuculain, including an elaborate show in 1913 that focused on his connection with the Boy Corps of Emain Macha. From the outset, Cuculain was recognized as the school's unofficial mascot, a symbol of its attempt to redeem Ireland from the taint of a corrupt age and especially from the modern, materialistic values associated with England.

More than anything, Cuculain came to stand for an ideal of heroic self-sacrifice, which Pearse saw as essential to the struggle for Irish independence from the United Kingdom. Near the entrance to the school, he placed a painting by Edwin Morrow depicting Cuculain in

3. Patrick Pearse, "The Murder Machine," in *The Murder Machine and other Essays* (Dublin: Mercier, 1976), 15.

4. Ibid., 21.

a scene from the *Táin Bó Cuailnge* (Cattle Raid of Cooley), when the young warrior-in-training learns "that the man who took up arms on that day would earn great fame, but would also die young."[5] Around the painting were inscribed the words of Cuculain's response, which Pearse had adopted as the school's motto: "I care not though I were to live but one day and one night provided my fame and deeds live after me."[6] The proclamation neatly encapsulates the ideal of heroism that Pearse came to espouse, an ideal centered on the image of a steadfast individual who faces overwhelming odds in the name of a sacrificial glory. That this glory might not just immortalize the name of an individual but also redeem his people is a consequence emphasized by Pearse's attempt to draw a parallel between Cuculain and Christ: both lose a battle with their enemies on earth that their sacrifice might sanctify their followers. The Christian parallel, which casts the hero as a redeemer, perhaps undercuts Cuculain's desire for personal glory but substantiates Pearse's call for a kind of patriotic religion founded on the old Gaelic order *and* the Irish Catholic faith. As a leader of the Easter Rising, Pearse put these ideals into action in spectacular fashion, directing a ragtag group of Irish Volunteers against an occupying British military that far outnumbered and outgunned them. Despite the overwhelming odds, and despite the fact that the larger effort to capture police barracks and governmental buildings across the island had been countermanded, Pearse proceeded with his plan to take the General Post Office in the center of Dublin and to read the Proclamation of the Irish Republic from its steps. Only by doing so, he believed, could the rebels redeem their contemporaries.

This overriding concern with sacrifice, redemption, and immortality, so often associated with nationalist imagining, is nicely captured in material form by Sheppard's statue, which still stands in the General Post Office today. Sheppard was a longtime friend of Pearse, which may account for the choice of Cuculain as a subject for his art,

5. From the *Táin*, quoted in Robert Tracy, "'A Statue's There to Mark the Place': Cú Chulainn in the GPO," *Field Day Review* 4 (2008): 206.

6. Pearse, "Murder Machine," 22.

though Sheppard himself acknowledged having read Lady Augusta Gregory's book *Cuchulain of Muirthemne* (1902) in the years leading up to his work on the statue. Sheppard had also been acquainted with Yeats and his work for many years, having made frequent visits to the Abbey Theatre during its first decade, so he would have been very familiar with the poet and playwright's treatment of the figure. Whatever his inspiration for *The Death of Cuchulain*, Sheppard selected the subject for his statue in 1911 and entered the plaster cast in the Royal Hibernian Academy Annual Exhibition of 1914 rather than submitting a work on a more customary subject from Greek mythology.[7] Considered Sheppard's masterpiece, the statue depicts Cuculain at the moment of his death as the fallen warrior slumps against the pillar to which he has tied himself in order to face his enemies until the very end. Dressed in nothing more than a loincloth, the heroic figure still holds his sword in his right hand, his arm draped over the pillar, while his head reclines so far to the left that it is nearly horizontal, the closed eyes directed toward his limp left arm below. The posture recalls the Christian pietà, especially Michelangelo's famous late-sixteenth-century example, although Sheppard's creation is tipped so that the figure retains a vertical orientation even in death.[8] On Cuculain's shoulder rests a raven, traditionally the symbol of death, which in this case is an indication to his enemies that the warrior has finally succumbed to his wounds. The whole, which stands something less than life size, is rendered in a style that recalls not only Italian quattrocento sculpture but also late-nineteenth-century French and British bronzes on classical themes, with hints of Rodin's modernist innovations. The statue thus exhibits a striking admixture of pagan and Christian elements, which suggest the redemptive power of an individual whose self-sacrifice promises

7. Judith Hill, *Irish Public Sculpture: A History* (Dublin: Four Courts Press, 1998), 157.

8. Many commentators have noted this connection. See, for instance, ibid., 156; John Turpin, *Oliver Sheppard, 1865–1941* (Dublin: Four Courts Press, 2000), 138; and "Poetic Portrayal of a Fighting Hero," *Sunday Business Post*, Nov. 4, 2007.

to transform fatality into immortality. Perhaps more than any other example in the Irish tradition, Sheppard's sculpture embodies the heroic ideals explored in the poems and plays by Irish Literary Revivalists and in the educational rhetoric of the Gaelic Revivalists such as Pearse, all of whom sought to restore a lost cultural vitality that might, in turn, transform present social and political conditions.

When Éamon de Valera—president of the Executive Council (prime minister) of the Irish Free State, founder of the Fianna Fáil party, and veteran of the Easter Rising—dedicated the statue at the General Post Office in April 1935, he was also evoking a kind of redemptive and regenerative power, albeit one that would serve less-lofty political ends. On the recommendation of John L. Burke, de Valera selected the statue as an official monument for the Easter Rising and in May 1934 convinced the Executive Council to have the statue cast in bronze and placed in the General Post Office, marking the site where Pearse had read the Proclamation of the Irish Republic and made his stand against British forces. Sheppard's statue was considered to be well suited to the purpose not only because it graphically displayed the ideal of self-sacrifice that had motivated Pearse and his followers nineteen years earlier but also because it linked their actions with a deep national past, which could be traced into an ancient Gaelic order of heroic values and communal bonds. In selecting the statue, of course, de Valera also suggested a strong continuity between those ancient heroic ideals, the deeds of 1916, and his own postcolonial regime. If the postcolonial nation-state had to be acknowledged as something new, something contingent on recent historical events, then the Irish nation that it represents was seen nonetheless to have a profound past and, even more important, a promising future under the new regime.[9] To highlight this continuity, de Valera had the pedestal of the statue engraved with the proclamation and the names of its signatories, all of whom had been executed by the British government for their role

9. For more on this aspect of the national imaginary, see Benedict Anderson, *Imagined Communities* (London: Verso, 2006), 11–12.

in the Rising. Placed on this pedestal, the Cuculain bronze became a national memorial that connected the present to a glorious history of struggle, sacrifice, and heroism that might redeem contemporary Ireland with its spiritual power.

The dedication ceremony for the statue served as the occasion for de Valera to dramatically reaffirm the connection between his postcolonial regime and this heroic version of the past. To celebrate the anniversary of the Rising and the installation of the monument, he staged a grand military parade through the streets of Dublin, which ran down its main thoroughfare, O'Connell Street, and past the General Post Office. Large crowds came out in a drizzling rain to watch as uniformed veterans of 1916 marched proudly through the streets, trailed by army bands playing the national anthem. To signal the beginning of the unveiling ceremony, a bugle call and drum roll sounded from within the Post Office, followed by a fanfare of trumpets and a volley of rifles from the rooftop. As the gathered crowds broke into cheers, a formation of warplanes passed overhead, dipping their wings in salute to the hallowed building and the memory of 1916. Inside the building, de Valera gathered with his ministers and a select audience made up of veterans of the Rising and relatives of the men who had died in the conflict nineteen years earlier. His address, which was broadcast over a speaker outside the building, began by acknowledging that nearly two decades earlier Pearse had proclaimed the Republic of Ireland on the very site where the prime minister now stood. The proclamation was, according to de Valera, "an event that will ever be counted an epoch in our history": "It has been a reproach to us that the spot has remained so long unmarked. Today we remove the reproach. All who enter this hall henceforth will be reminded of the deed enacted here. A beautiful piece of sculpture, the creation of Irish genius, symbolizing the dauntless courage and abiding constancy of our people, will commemorate it modestly, indeed, but fittingly."[10]

10. Quoted in "Mr De Valera Unveils 1916 Memorial," *Irish Times*, Apr. 22, 1935.

With these remarks, de Valera acknowledged the suitability of the Cuculain figure for the purpose of honoring the Irish rebels and identified the role that the ancient warrior had come to occupy, at least for some, in the national imagination. But the prime minister was also cognizant that the statue, notwithstanding its heroic subject, was a rather small gesture for the occasion, something that was only highlighted by the grandeur of its unveiling ceremony.

To be sure, despite the majesty of the parade and the large crowds that had gathered to witness the affair, the dedication ceremony was not without its detractors. De Valera himself, alluding to the partition of the island between North and South, the United Kingdom and the Irish Free State, acknowledged that "the time to raise a proud national monument to the work that was begun here and to those who inspired and participated in it has yet to come."[11] Before the ceremony, the leader of the opposition party, W. T. Cosgrove, had also pointed out that the goal Pearse and his comrades fought for had not yet been realized: "it is not possible," he jibed, "to hide the humiliations of to-day or to cover them with the veil lifted from the statue of Cuchulain."[12] It must be admitted that the choice of the Cuculain statue was to some degree a problematic one because the hero was traditionally associated with Ulster, the six counties still under British rule as the dedication ceremony took place. The *Irish Times*, acknowledging the Unionist perspective, suggested it was "somewhat paradoxical that the warrior who held so long the gap of Ulster against the Southern hordes should now be adopted as a symbol by those whose object it is to bend his native province to their will."[13] Many Republican voices argued that Cuculain, "the Hound of Ulster," was simply not an appropriate symbol

11. Quoted in ibid.

12. Quoted in Yvonne Whelan, "Symbolising the State: the Iconography of O'Connell Street and Environs after Independence (1922)," *Irish Geography* 34, no. 2 (2001): 141.

13. Quoted in John Turpin, "Cúchulainn Lives On," *Circa* 69 (1994): 28.

for 1916 because the six northern counties had yet to be freed from British control. Maud Gonne, Yeats's former friend, lover, and muse, told the *Irish Times* in the week leading up to the ceremony that she "hoped all true Republicans would not go near the General Post Office on Sunday next."[14] Instead, radical Republicans staged their own parade after the official one had ended, heading up O'Connell Street in front of the remaining crowds, making their salute at the General Post Office, and then proceeding to Glasnevin cemetery, where they gathered at the Easter Week plot. There, the marchers were addressed by Maurice Twomey, the chief of staff of the Irish Republican Army, who described "the imposture staged that morning in Dublin's streets . . . as nothing more than a desperate attempt to prevent exposure" because de Valera and Fianna Fáil had failed to live up to the ideals of 1916 and to support the Republican cause effectively into the 1930s.[15]

Installed at the epicenter of the Irish Republican movement, the figure of Cuculain became a lightning rod for competing visions of contemporary Ireland. This focus was sustained well after the crowds had dispersed from O'Connell Street, not just in Yeats's late poem but also in Samuel Beckett's first novel, written within a few months of de Valera's dedication ceremony. In chapter 4 of *Murphy*, set on September 19, 1935, we find one of Beckett's characters in the General Post Office, "contemplating from behind the statue of Cuchulain":

> Neary had bared his head, as though the holy ground meant something to him. Suddenly he flung aside his hat, sprang forward, seized the dying hero by the thighs and began to dash his head against his buttocks, such as they are. The Civic Guard on duty in the building, roused from a tender reverie by the sound of blows, took in the situation at his leisure, disentangled his baton and

14. Quoted in Tracy, "'A Statue's There,'" 213.
15. Quoted in "Demonstration by I.R.A," *Irish Times*, Apr. 22, 1935.

> advanced with measured tread, thinking he had caught a vandal in the act.[16]

What is it that provokes such a response from Neary, who has come to Dublin from Cork in pursuit of a young woman and who has reached a point of exhaustion and despair by the time he wanders into the Post Office? "[T]hat Red Branch Bum was the camel's back," he tells his friend Wylie after he has been pulled from the clutches of the Civic Guard,[17] but his actions are indicative of more than a personal crisis. The startling gesture also suggests a protest against the state, its representative icons and institutions, as well as against the mythohistorical legacy that had granted Cuculain representative status. That Neary focuses his angst on the statue's posterior is part and parcel of Beckett's corrosive humor: recalling in the aftermath of the event that the "deathless rump was trying to stare me down," Neary has been shocked out of his heartbroken withdrawal by this powerful emblem of communal investment.[18] By depicting an assault on this iconic statue, Beckett's novel takes aim precisely at the powerful confluence of governmental authority, monumental art, and cultural tradition that has been put in the service of de Valera's regime.

This is not to say that Neary's attack on the statue is in the name of another political affiliation—whether Unionism or radical Republicanism—but that, in some sense, the action seeks to break the hold of such icons on the present and on the minds of Neary and his contemporaries. Just a year earlier, in an essay titled "Recent Irish Poetry," Beckett had taken the "antiquarians" and "twilighters," especially "Mr Yeats," to task for consistently reverting to conventional themes, including "Cuchulain," "Maeve," and the "Táin Bó Cúailnge," rather than exploring "the new thing that has happened, or the old thing that has happened again, namely the breakdown of the object, whether current, historical, mythical or spook." The

16. Samuel Beckett, *Murphy* (New York: Grove, 1957), 43.
17. Ibid., 46.
18. Ibid., 57.

modernist poets whom Beckett praises in the essay do not fall back on the antiquarian materials of "Sir Samuel Ferguson and Standish O'Grady" but rather stand to face the contemporary moment without the crutches of a solid and coherent tradition.[19] Neary's assault on Cuculain's buttocks, "such as they are," is part of this same break from the past and the power it wields over the present, a break that is not just a matter of aesthetic choices but also of political assertions in a country where art and politics, myth and action, have been so closely linked.[20] Neary's blows, that is, proclaim a break from any ideological continuity stretching from O'Grady to Pearse to de Valera, if only that his story might stimulate the "ruptures in the lines of communication"[21] characteristic of the present, the contemporary, the modern.

Beckett's indictment of Revivalist atavism is in many respects a gross caricature, but it is true that Yeats's writing continued to return to the past in search of an antidote to the fragmentation and degeneration of the present or of a point of origin from which to initiate a new future. In this search, he returned to the greatest of the Knights of the Red Branch yet again in his final play, titled, just like Sheppard's statue, *The Death of Cuchulain*. Written in the autumn of 1938, not long after he composed "The Statues" and not long before he died, the play opens with an "Old Man" who protests the degradation of the modern age and acknowledges that he has been selected to "produce" the play "because I am out of fashion and out of date like the antiquated romantic stuff the play is made of."[22] If the Old Man is a proxy for Yeats, expressive of his situation and sensibility, then the Cuculain of the play is also closely associated with the

19. Samuel Beckett, "Recent Irish Poetry," in *Disjecta: Miscellaneous Writings and a Dramatic Fragment*, ed. Ruby Cohn (New York: Grove, 1984), 71, 70, 76.

20. Beckett, *Murphy*, 42.

21. Beckett, "Recent Irish Poetry," 70.

22. W. B. Yeats, *The Death of Cuchulain*, in *The Collected Works of W. B. Yeats*, vol. 2: *The Plays*, rev. 2nd ed., ed. David R. Clark and Rosalind E. Clark (New York: Simon & Schuster, 2010), 545.

playwright and, especially, his tumultuous love life. Betrayed by his mistresses and already wounded, the hero attempts to fasten himself with a belt to the familiar pillar of stone, only to be bound there by the vengeful Aoife, who announces that she has come to kill him. Cuculain's death, however, comes at the hands of the "Blind Man," reappearing from Yeats's Cuculain play *On Baile's Strand* (1904) and arriving on the scene to sever the warrior's head, with the promise of twelve pennies from Queen Meave in return for the deed. The play closes with a song by three ragged street singers of the type found in Yeats's Dublin, who remark the death of the great hero and then pose a series of adamant questions:

> What stood in the Post Office
> With Pearse and Connolly?
> What comes out of the mountain
> Where men first shed their blood?
> Who thought Cuchulain till it seemed
> He stood where they stood?[23]

If the play undercuts Cuculain's heroism, even writes it off as unfashionable romanticism, the closing song still seeks to understand the power of his example to move men, to shape history, to impose itself on the present. Despite his death, the spirit of Cuculain lives on in the deeds of 1916, but only with the aid of those antiquarians and artists such as O'Grady and Yeats himself, who "thought Cuchulain" until the time for action had come. The song concludes:

> No body like his body
> Has modern woman borne,
> But an old man looking on life
> Images it in scorn.
> A statue's there to mark the place

23. Ibid., 554.

By Oliver Sheppard done.
So ends the tale that the harlot
Sang to the beggar-man.[24]

The singers suggest that the brand of heroism embodied by Cuculain has now passed away from the earth, even if it has left behind a trace, a material legacy, in the form of Sheppard's statue. And the Old Man, an image of Yeats at the end of his career, can only scorn the courage that is beyond him as he looks back at the defeats of his own life, for which the statue seems to serve as a painful reminder. The image of Cuculain taunts him, for he has lived up to neither the ideal of the ancient warrior nor the spirit that had inhabited Pearse and James Connolly in the hour of their heroic deeds.

In light of all this, Sheppard's sculpture is a rather inadequate memorial, but it is all that remains of that heroic spirit in the modern world. It is, no doubt, as much an emblem of what has been lost—in the decidedly unheroic guises of the new state and the Old Man—as an emblem of what Cuculain was said to have embodied in life. If Yeats had dedicated his artistic career, at least in part, to reviving a sense of heroism in the modern world, there is a distinct sense of defeatism in his final play, which itself amounts to little more than "the tale that the harlot / Sang to the beggar-man." The poet-playwright seems to admit that there are limits on the power of myth to extricate us from the "filthy modern tide," limits that disrupt the coherence of communal identity, the force of inherited beliefs, and the authority of national traditions. But he refuses to abandon the Revivalist desire for a sacramental link with a stable, ordered, and unified past. Michael McAteer's essay in this volume calls our attention to the divergent legacies of O'Grady's Cuculain narrative in Pearse's military cult of the hero and Yeats's solitary man of ancient ways. But the ending of Yeats's final play captures a

24. Ibid.

further ambivalence in this ongoing story that pits the past against the present, tradition against modernity, creating an indecisive push and pull between these temporal poles—an ambivalence that is perhaps Cuculain's most salient bequest to Irish cultural nationalism and the dreams of a fully independent Ireland.

Timeline

Glossary

Further Reading

Biographical Notes

Index

Timeline

1846 Standish James O'Grady is born during the initial stages of the Great Famine.

1852 The Great Famine comes to an end.

1858 The Irish Republican Brotherhood is founded.

1861 Eugene O'Curry publishes *Lectures on Manuscript Materials of Ancient Irish History.*

1865 William Butler Yeats is born.

1867 Matthew Arnold publishes *On the Study of Celtic Literature.*

1868 O'Grady graduates from Trinity College, Dublin. James Connolly is born.

1869 Prime Minister William Gladstone disestablishes the Protestant Church in Ireland.

1870 Land Act gives compensation to evicted Catholic tenant farmers.

1873 Issac Butt founds the Home Rule League.

1877 Charles Stewart Parnell becomes president of the Home Rule Confederation.

1878 O'Grady publishes *History of Ireland*, volume 1: *The Heroic Period.*

1879 Michael Davitt founds the Land League, and Parnell becomes its president. Pádraic Pearse is born. The Irish Land War begins.

1880 O'Grady publishes *History of Ireland*, volume 2: *Cuculain and His Contemporaries.*

1881 O'Grady publishes *History of Ireland: Critical and Philosophical.*

1882 James Joyce is born. The Irish Land War comes to an end.

1884 The Gaelic Athletic Association is formed.

1886 The first Home Rule bill fails to pass through the House of Commons. O'Grady publishes *Toryism and Tory Democracy.*

1887 Emily Lawless publishes *The Story of Ireland.*

1889 Parnell is implicated in the divorce proceedings of Captain William O'Shea and Katharine O'Shea. Douglas Hyde publishes *Literary History of Ireland from Earliest Times to the Present.* O'Grady publishes *Red Hugh's Captivity: A Picture of Ireland, Social and Political, in the Reign of Queen Elizabeth.*

1890 The Irish Parliamentary Party splits.

1891 Parnell dies.

1892 The second Irish Home Rule bill is passed in the House of Commons but is defeated in the House of Lords. O'Grady publishes *Finn and His Companions.*

1893 Douglas Hyde founds the Gaelic League to promote the use of the Irish language in Ireland. Connolly founds the Irish Socialist Republican Party. O'Grady publishes *The Bog of Stars and Other Stories and Sketches of Elizabethan Ireland.*

1894 O'Grady publishes *The Coming of Cuculain.*

1898 Eleanor Hull publishes *The Cuchullin Saga in Irish Literature.*

1899 Yeats, Lady Augusta Gregory, George Moore, and Edward Martyn found the Irish Literary Theatre in Dublin.

1900 O'Grady founds the *All-Ireland Review.*

1902 Lady Augusta Gregory publishes *Cuchulain of Muirthemne.*

1904 The Abbey Theatre (National Theatre of Ireland) is founded. Yeats's first Cuchulain play, *On Baile's Strand*, is performed on the opening night.

1905 Arthur Griffith founds the Sinn Féin party.

1906 Samuel Beckett is born.

1908 Pádraic Pearse founds St. Enda's School (Sciol Éanna), an experimental academy for training young Irishmen. O'Grady publishes *The Flight of the Eagle.*

1909 Students at St. Enda's School perform *The Coming of Fionn.*

1910 W. B. Yeats publishes *The Green Helmet.*

1911 Oliver Sheppard creates a plaster cast of his statue *The Death of Cuchulain.*

1912 Unionists found the Ulster Volunteers to thwart Home Rule in Ireland.

1913 Nationalists found the Irish Volunteers to protect the Home Rule movement.

1914 The third Irish Home Rule bill is passed, but its implementation is suspended owing to the outbreak of the First World War.

1916 An armed insurrection known as the Easter Rising takes place in Dublin. Pearse, Connolly, and fourteen other rebel leaders are later executed.

1918 The First World War comes to an end.

1919 Sinn Féin, led by Éamon de Valera, establishes the first Dáil (Parliament) of the Irish Republic. The Irish War of Independence begins with an Irish Republican Army campaign on British forces. Yeats publishes *The Only Jealousy of Emer.*

1920 The British Parliament passes the Government of Ireland Act, establishing a parliament for Northern Ireland and another for the rest of the island.

1921 Anglo-Irish Treaty establishes the Irish Free State, an independent dominion of the British Crown separate from Northern Ireland.

1922 The Dáil ratifies the treaty in opposition to the wishes of de Valera and his allies, leading to the Irish Civil War. James Joyce publishes *Ulysses.*

1923 The Irish Civil War ends. The Irish Free State enters the League of Nations.

1924 Daniel Corkery publishes *Hidden Ireland.*

1926 De Valera founds the Fianna Fáil party with other leaders who had split from Sinn Féin.

1928 O'Grady dies.

1929 Hugh O'Grady publishes a biography of his father, *Standish O'Grady, the Man and the Writer.*

1932 De Valera is appointed president of the Executive Council (prime minister) of the Irish Free State.

1935 De Valera dedicates Oliver Sheppard's statue *The Death of Cuchulain* at the General Post Office, Dublin.

1937 Voters reelect de Valera and ratify the Constitution of Ireland, which replaces the Irish Free State with Éire (Ireland) as a sovereign state.

1938 Douglas Hyde becomes the first president of Éire. Samuel Beckett publishes his first novel, *Murphy.*

1939 World War II begins; Yeats dies shortly after completing his play *The Death of Cuchulain.*

Glossary

Note: Entries are listed using the Anglicized spelling and capitalization that O'Grady uses in the first appearance of a name or term in the selections given in this volume, and all non-English terms listed (including variants) are given in roman type here, whether included in an English dictionary or not. In many entries, variant spellings immediately follow. Works referenced for the definitions or descriptions provided include: Peter Berresford Ellis, *A Dictionary of Irish Mythology* (Boston: Little, Brown, 2005); James MacKillop, *A Dictionary of Celtic Mythology* (Oxford: Oxford Univ. Press, 1998); Patricia Monaghan, *The Encyclopedia of Celtic Mythology and Folklore* (New York: Facts on File, 2004); as well as Standish James O'Grady, *History of Ireland*, vol. 1: *The Heroic Period* (London: Sampson Low, Searle, Marston and Rivington; Dublin: Ponsonby, 1878), *History of Ireland*, vol. 2: *Cuculain and His Contemporaries* (London: Sampson Low, Searle, Marston and Rivington; Dublin: Ponsonby, 1880), and *History of Ireland: Critical and Philosophical*, vol. 1 (London: Sampson Low, Searle, Marston and Rivington; Dublin: Ponsonby, 1881).

Acaill (Achall): According to O'Grady, this figure "was sister of Erc, and deeply attached to the boy. 'Her heart brake nut-wise in her breast' when she heard of his death. He was slain by Conaill Carna revenging Cuculain. As Acaill travelled to Tara they showed her his dissevered head. Her tomb at Skreen is near Tara. That of Erc is near it."

Adamnan (Adamnán, Adhamhnán, Adomnán): The abbot of Iona (679–704), best known as author of *Vita Columbae*, a hagiographic work in Latin on the life of St. Columba.

adze: Ancient cutting tool similar to an ax, with a curved blade fastened at right angles to a wooden handle. It was used chiefly for chopping or shaping wood.

Aileel Mōr (Ailell, Ailill, Aleel, Allil; mac Máta, mac Matach): The most famous of the many mythic heroes and kings bearing the name "Aileel," which means "sprite" or "elf." He was the consort of Queen Meave in the *Táin Bó Cuailnge.*

Aileel Finn (Ailell, Ailill, Aleel, Allil Finn): Mythical king of the Gamanradians, who is preceded by Fiecha Folgra in O'Grady's "royal list of kings of all Ireland." According to various accounts, he ruled for nine or eleven years until he was killed by Airgetmar and succeeded by Eochu.

Alba: The name, derived from Scottish Gaelic and modern Irish, commonly used for Scotland in Irish mythology.

Angus (Áengus, Aonghas, Aonghus, Óengus, Oíngus): The god of beauty and poetry among the Tuátha De Danan, who accompanied Queen Meave on expeditions. According to O'Grady, "in the third century (the old faith then weakening before the stress of Roman Civilization in the adjoining country, and the introduction of Christianity), Cormac Mac Art denied his existence. But the god appeared to him at Tara in the gloaming, having in his hands the traditional tympan."

Αριστεία: Greek for "excellence" or "distinction."

Ard-Druid: A highly ranked druid or member of the Celtic priestly class. Druids, both men and women, played a number of roles in Celtic society, ranging from magician to poet, philosopher, and lawyer.

Ard-Ollav (ard ollam, ollamh, ollave): Highly esteemed bard who was considered equal in dignity to the king in each region or kingdom of ancient Ireland.

Ard-Rie (ard rí, ard rígh, ardríg): The position of high king of Ireland. In many stories of ancient Ireland, the Ard-Rie is portrayed as ruling over the island from Tara, where he is crowned at the inauguration stone.

Ath-a-Luan (Athlone): A town on the River Shannon near Lough Ree (Loch Rí).

ban-ecla: The female courier of Concobar Mac Nessa, who, according to O'Grady, is mentioned as educating Deirdré.

Ban-Shee (banshee, bean sídhe, ben síd, bean sí, ben side, bán síde): A female wraith or fairy in Irish and Scottish Gaelic tradition who is attributed the power to foretell death.

battle-plough: A weapon or "warlike instrument," which, according to O'Grady, "our antiquarians have yet failed to describe."

bauves: The daughters of Ned (Nét), the god of war.

Book of Invasions (*Lebor Gabála Érenn*, *Leabhar Gabhála*): A collection of pseudohistorical texts in poetry and prose, compiled in the eleventh and twelfth century, though some date from much earlier. Informed by Latin learning and biblical commentators, these texts tell the story of six conquests or invasions of Ireland by six different groups of people, beginning with the tribe of Kaesair at the time of the biblical flood and concluding at the time of the Milesians in the Middle Ages.

bratta: A capelike garment, often of bright color and fine cloth, worn by both men and women in ancient Ireland.

Bregia (Breagh, Brega, Bregha, Mag mBreg): The great plain between the Boyne and the Liffey Rivers, which is an important mythological site described in several ancient Irish texts.

Bricrind (Briccirne, Briccriu, Bricne, Bricriu, Bricriu Nemhthenga): The "bitter-tongued" poet, warrior, and troublemaker of the Ulster Cycle. In the epic *Briccriu's Feast*, he goads Cuculain and two other champions to quarrel over the champion's portion, resulting in a great deal of bloodshed. According to O'Grady, this "strange Ultonian . . . seems to have been the Thersites of the Red Branch," though, unlike Thersites, he was rich and powerful. When Cuculain's demise is first reported, Bricrind "more than all the rest had . . . lamented for [the hero], for his patrimony bordered on the kingdom of Cuculain, and no word of the mild hero rankled his mind. Moreover, he was the first to hasten eastward when the cry was raised concerning Cuculain."

bru-fir (Brugh-Fir): The host at a house of hospitality maintained by the king for strangers in his realm.

Brugh-Fir: See "bru-fir."

Cairbré (Cairbri, Carbre, Carbry, Caipre, Carpre, Cairpre, Coirbre, Coirpre, Corpre): A common male name in ancient Ireland borne by many legendary heroes. See "Cairbré Nia-far."

Cairbré Nia-far (Cairbry Nia-far, Cairbre Nia Fer): Ancient king of Tara, celebrated for his twelve beautiful daughters. Although O'Grady later refers to him as "King of all Erin" (p. 150), he notes that Cairbré Nia-far was never put down as such in the "more trustworthy lists." He was a rival to Cuculain before being killed by the hero.

caiseal (caisel): A fort built of stone.

cantred (cantref): A subdivision or spatial unit of land used to describe political boundaries that preexisted the Anglo-Norman invasions.

cath-barr (cath barr): A "battle-top" or helmet (typically made of gold and adorned with precious stones) worn by an Irish king or queen, as in the case of Meave.

cathair: A circular stone fort.

Cathvah: The Ard-Druid, or high priest, of the Ultonian nation.

Cethern Mac Fiontānn (Cethern mac Finntain, mac Fintain): A warrior from the Connaught forces who is known for his generosity, his bravery, and the silver spike he carries as his only weapon.

Clan Dēga (Clann Deda, Dedad): One of the principle warrior tribes or races of ancient Ireland who were likely synonymous with the Érainn people.

Clanna Gædil (Gædil, Gáedel, Gaedhal): A warrior race or tribe who came to Ireland from Spain and were known for their wandering ways.

Clanna Rury (Clanna Rudraige, Clanna Rudraighe): The race or tribe of Irish warriors based in Emain Macha who descended from Rury. Also called the "Ulaid (Ulaidh)," whose name was given to the modern province of Ulster.

colg: Sword.

Conaill Carna (Conall Cearnach, Conall Cernach, Konal Karna): One of the greatest champions of the Ultonian Cycle, known as the most faithful knight of Concobar Mac Nessa and as the foster brother, close friend, and avenger of Cuculain. He was the "fairest and bravest of the Red Branch," according to O'Grady.

Conairey Mōr (Conaire Mór, Conairy Mor; Conare, Conary; Már): Conairey "the Great," a high king of all Ireland and protagonist of *Togail Bruidne Da Derga* (The Destruction of Da Derga's Hostel), who ruled over a peaceful kingdom but was slain by marauders, including members of his own foster family.

Concobar Mac Nessa (Conachar, Conchobhar, Conchubar; mac Nessa): High king of Ulster during the period recounted in the Ulster Cycle. He bears a matronymic derived from his mother, Nessa. Following the death of Concobar's father, the Druid Cathbad, Nessa agrees to take Fergus Mac Roich as a husband if he will temporarily hand over his kingdom to her son, which he does, never to regain it.

Connla (Conla, Conláech, Conlaí, Conlán, Conlaoch, Conle): Son of Cuculain and the warrior woman Eefa, conceived without his father's knowledge and raised in Scotland by his mother. The story of his death at Cuculain's hand is told in W. B. Yeats's play *On Baile's Strand* (1904).

Connla's Well (Cóelrind's Well): An Irish mythological site of uncertain location. Nine hazel trees surround the well and drop nuts, which are then consumed by salmon swimming in its water. It is said that wisdom and inspiration come to anyone who drinks the water or eats the nuts or salmon.

Cormac Conlíngas (Cormac Conn Loingeas, Connloinges, Conloingeas, CondLonges): A great warrior and one of twenty-one sons fathered by Concobar Mac Nessa. According to O'Grady, he was known as the handsomest of Meave's host and the most valiant warrior after Fergus mac Roy and Cet, the son of Maga.

Cormac's Glossary (Sanas Cormaic, Chormaic): A glossary of more than fourteen hundred old and rare Irish words, including the names of many ancient heroes. The earliest version is traditionally ascribed to Cormac mac Cuilennáin (d. 908), king-bishop of Cashel.

Cowshra Mend Macha (Cúscraid, Cúscrid; Mend, Menn, Menn Machae): One of the twenty-one sons fathered by Concobar Mac Nessa, king of Emain Macha, and foster son of the hero Conaill Carna. He plays a central role in *Scéla Mucce meic Da Thó* (The Story of Mac Da Thó's Pig). He receives the nickname "Mend Macha" (Stammerer of Macha) because Cet mac Mátach pierces his throat in a battle.

Crann-tawl (crann-tawl, crann-tabaill, Crave Tawl): A stone-throwing sling weapon made from a long staff of wood and one or more thongs.

Crave Rue (Cráebruad, Cráeb Ruad, Craobh Ruach, Craob Rua, Crave Rua, Crevroe): Irish for "Red Branch," this is the name given to one of Concobar Mac Nessa's three royal residences. The large hall was often a meeting place for warriors, who came to be known as the Knights of the Red Branch and gave the Red Branch Cycle its name.

Crave Tawl: See "Crann-tawl."

Cruaideen (Cruaidín, Cruaidín Catutchenn): The mighty sword of Cuculain.

Cûlairechta: According to O'Grady, the court of appeal where each nation's or kingdom's legal cases were adjudicated.

cumal (cumail): An ancient unit of monetary value, the name of which derives from the Old Irish term for "female slave."

Curoi Mac Dary (Cú Roí mac Dáiri; Cú Raoi, Curroi, Córroí, Cú Ruí): O'Grady identifies him as king of the Ernai or Clan Dēga in Munster, who is slain by Cuculain and the Ultonians before the Táin Bó Cuailnge (Cattle Raid of Cooley) happens.

Daman (Damán): Father of Fardia and sworn brother of Cuculain, he trained with the hero under the Amazonian Scáthach but was then tricked by Meave into fighting against him in the battle for the bull Donn Cooalney (Couailnge).

Dectera (Dectara, Dectora): King of southern Cooley (Cuailnge), he accompanies Curoi Mac Dary on a conquest of the Isle of Man, where they share the affections of the maiden Blana, also beloved of Cuculain.

Deirdre (Deirdré, Derdriu, Deridriu, Deirdriu, Deirdri, Derdrend): A princess of Ulster and daughter of the royal storyteller Fedlimid mac Daill. She is known as "Dierdré of Sorrows" owing to the misfortunes she brings on the warriors of the province, including her lover, Naysi (Naoise). After Naysi's death at the hands of Concobar's men, Dierdré is betrothed to the king, though she takes her own life soon thereafter.

Devorgilla (Dearbhfhorgaill, Derbforgaill, Derbhorgill, Derbforgaille, Devorgill, Dervorgilla, Devorvilla): A mythological princess who endures an unrequited love for Cuculain. She takes the form of a swan in order to seduce him but fails in her efforts; she later marries Cuculain's close friend Lewy Rievenerg but meets an untimely death at the hands of jealous court women.

Dove (Dûbh): A famous bard and female druid who is killed by a slingshot in revenge for drowning her husband's mistress. The city of Dublin (originally "Dubh-linn," or "Pool of Dub") takes its name from a pool in the River Liffey where Dubh falls after being struck.

Dûn (dún): The Irish and Scottish Gaelic term for a fortified place or castle.

Dûn Dalgan (Dûndalgan; Dûn-Dalgan; Dûn-dalgan; Dún Delgan, Delga, Dealgan): The majestic fortress that is Cuculain's residence, near the present-day town of Dundalk.

Dûvac Dæl Ulla (Dubtach Dóeltenga, Dubtach Doél Ulad, Doelliad): The "chafer-tongued" Ulster warrior who is often shunned by his comrades in arms due to his malicious disposition.

Eefa (Aífe, Aoife): A Scottish woman warrior, chieftain, and charioteer known for her great prowess in battle, like her mother, Scáthach. After

Cuculain defeats Eefa in combat, she relents to his advances and conceives a son, Connla, with him.

Eiderkool: A lord of the Clan Farna and son of a noted storyteller in the king's court.

Emain Macha (Eamhain Mhacha, Emhain Macha, Emuin Macha, Emania Macha): The mythical capital of the Ulster in the Ulster Cycle (akin to Camelot in the Arthurian tales), which serves as royal seat of Concobar Mac Nessa.

Emania: Latinized spelling of "Emain Macha."

Erc: A king of Leinster, ally of Queen Meave, and nephew of Cormac Con-língas. He becomes a key opponent of Cuculain after his father, Cairbré Nia-far (Cairbré Nia Fer), king of Tara, is slain by the hero. His name translates as "Salmon" or "Speckled."

eric (éric, éraic): A fine or "honor price" paid as compensation for a violent crime, the amount determined according to the victim's social rank. In the absence of a formal police or court system, erics served to organize legal affairs in ancient Ireland.

Ernai (Earna, Erna): Group of warlike peoples in ancient Ireland who were a division of the mythical race of Fir-bolgs.

Espân: Spain.

Eterskel (Eterskél, Eterscél, Eterscéle, Etarscéle): A high king of Ireland and a father to several royal heirs, including Conairey Mōr.

Fabâne (Fubán): The great shield of Cuculain, embossed with the image of a wild boar's head, his personal symbol.

Fæd-Fia (Faedfia, Faydfia, Fayd-fia): A magical mist or shroud used by the Tuátha De Danan to render themselves invisible.

Fardia (Fer Diad, Ferdia, Ferdiad, Fear Diadh): A warrior of Connacht who trains with his friend and foster brother Cuculain under the warrior woman Scáthach. Later, during the Tân war, he sides with Aileel and Meave but tries to avoid combat with Cuculain.

fasti: The Roman calendar, which indicated dates for festivals, courts, and important events.

Faydfia of Goibneen (Fæd-Fia, Faed Fia, Faedfia, Fayd-fia): The curse or dark emanation of Goibneen (Goibniu), the smith of the gods. One of three divine craftsmen in Irish tradition, Goibneen not only creates lethal weapons but also provides a magical ale and a sacred feast to mortals.

Fenian cycle: One of the four major cycles of early Irish mythology, featuring the legendary hero Finn MacCool (Fionn mac Cumhaill) and his band of warriors, the Fianna Éireann.

Fenians (Feinn, Fena, Fiana, Fianna, Fiantachean, Fingallians): A band of warriors led by the legendary hero Finn MacCool (Fionn mac Cumhaill). The name was later bestowed on members of the fraternal organizations that sought to establish a self-governing Irish republic in the late nineteenth and early twentieth centuries.

Feis (féis, fes): Feast or celebration, especially one in honor of a king.

Fer-lōga (Fer Loga): The royal charioteer of Connaught who serves Aileel and Meave.

Ferrogane: A foster brother of Conairey Mōr, but Ferrogane and his other brothers are banished by the high king after they go marauding through the countryside.

Fergus Mac Lēda (Fergus mac Léide, mac Léte, mac Léti): A mythical king of early Ulster who is probably the same person as Fergus mac Roy.

Fergus mac Roy (Fergus mac Roech, mac Róich, mac Roth, Mac-Roy, MacRoy, Roech, Ro-ech, Roi, Roich, Roigh, Rosa Ruaidh, Rossa, Roth): A great Ulster king and hero who tutors Cuculain before losing his throne to Concobar Mac Nessa. He goes into exile, joins Queen Meave's forces, and later tells the story of the Cattle Raid of Cooley to the poet Seanchán Toirpéist.

Fianna: See "Fenians."

findruiney (findruine, fiondruine, findrina, findrinny, findriny, fionndruine): A bright yellow bronze purportedly of superior beauty to gold that, according to O'Grady, was made by the ancient Irish through a secret process now lost and forgotten.

Fion-Cu: Servant to the high king responsible for summoning the Knights of the Red Branch to war.

Fionscōta: Cuculain's daughter by Emer.

Fir-bolgs (Fir Bholgs, Fir Bolgs, Firbolgs): A mythological race that formed the fourth wave of invaders described in the legendary account of Irish history *Lebor Gabála* (Book of Invasions). Perhaps based on an actual people, they are said to be responsible for dividing Ireland into its five provinces and founding a sacred kingship.

Fir-Mac-Be (Fir-bē): O'Grady writes that he is a "prince of the Olnemacta."

flaut: A flautist in O'Grady's usage. Eiderkool, the flaut, is noted for "shrilling songs" as he marches with his fellow warriors.

Fomorians (Foawr, Fomhoire, Fomhóire, Fomoire, Fomóiri, Fomoraig, Fomhóraigh, Fomor, Fomoré, Fomorii, Fōmoroh, Fomors, Fo-Muir): A race of monstrous deities in Irish mythology, sometimes portrayed as having only one eye, one leg, and one arm, who antagonize the people of ancient Ireland.

Fōmoroh: See "Fomorians."

Forgal Mánah (Forgall Monach, Manach): Father to Cuculain's wife, Emer, whose principle role in the Ulster Cycle is to keep the lovers apart. His surname, which translates as "the Wily One," is appropriate to his role as a taskmaster responsible for setting obstacles in the way of Cuculain's courtship.

foss: A waterfall.

Four Provinces: Ireland has historically been divided into four territories or provinces—Connacht, Leinster, Munster, and Ulster. A fifth province in the middle of the island, Meath, merged with Leinster in the post-Norman period.

Furbey (Furbaide Ferbend, Foirbre, Forbaí, Forbay): A son of Concobar Mac Nessa and nephew of Queen Meave, who is remembered primarily as the assassin of his aunt, the queen, reportedly slaying her with a stone cast from his sling and thus avenging the death of his mother, Clothra, at Meave's hand.

Gæ-Bolg (Gáe Bolg, Gáe Bolga, Gáe Bulg, Gáe Bulga): The fearsome spear of Cuculain, which he received after training with the great woman warrior Scáthach in Scotland. Made with the bones of a sea monster, the spear flies with great speed and inflicts devastating wounds on its victims.

Gæil: See "Gael."

Gael (Gæl, Gæil): The name, which is of disputed provenance, for Gaelic-speaking peoples of Ireland, Scotland, and the Isle of Man.

Galtees (Galty, Na Gaibhlte): A mountain range in the province of Munster.

geise (gæsa, geas, geis, geiss, ges): A magical taboo, prohibition, vow, or pledge, often of great complexity, imposed on kings and heroes in ancient Ireland. In some cases, the *geise* forbids certain actions; in others, it demands certain actions. In most cases, the reasons for the *geise* are not immediately evident but become clear in the course of the narrative.

Glan-na-mōhar: O'Grady translates this place-name as "the dog's glen" but confesses that he does "not know the position of this glen."

greenan (grianan, grianán): A word of disputed usage. O'Grady, who likely follows Eugene O'Curry, uses it to indicate a solarium or similar enclosure within the walls of a palace.

Heber (Éber Finn): A son of Milesius and an important leader of the Milesian invasion of Ireland in the *Lebor Gabála* (Book of Invasions). He is killed in battle with his brother, Herēmon.

Heim: O'Grady notes that, in addition to being a royal bard, Heim "was also a warrior, and fought in the battle of Guara."

Herēmon (Éireamhóin, Erem, Éremón, Eremon, Érimón, Heremhon): The first Milesian king of Ireland, he played an important role in the Milesian conquest of Ireland and established his capital at Tara.

Hound of Emain Macha (Hound of Eamhain Mhacha, Emhain Macha, Emuin Macha, Emania Macha): Sobriquet given to Cuculain.

Hound of Ulla (Hound of Ulster): Sobriquet given to Cuculain.

hurle: Variant of "hurley stick," a wooden bat used to hit a small leather ball in the Irish sport of hurling.

Iar: Son of Milesius, he is shipwrecked on Skellig Michael, an island off the southwest coast of Ireland.

Iarn-glunah: Surname of the Ard-Druid Cathvah, meaning "Iron-Kneed."

Ioldāna: According to O'Grady, "this was the surname of Lu Lam-fada, i.e., Lu the Long-Handed, and indicates the belief that he was the source of the arts. It was he who delivered the gods from Fomorian tyranny." See "Lu Lamfáda."

Ith (Íth): A leader of the Milesians who was killed by the Tuátha De Danan.

Keasair (Ceasair, Cesair): Leader or queen of the first invasion of Ireland in the Mythological Cycle. O'Grady claims a link between the era of Keasair and the "earliest of Irish Gods."

Keating, Geoffrey: Also known as Séathrún Céitinn (ca. 1570–1645). An Irish priest, poet, and author of a much-cited history *Foras Feasa ar Éirinn* (Foundation of Knowledge on Ireland). Born in Tipperary of Norman stock and educated in bardic schools, he worked in Ireland as a parish priest.

keeve: A tub or vat for holding liquid in brewing or bleaching.

Kelkar (Celtar, Celtchair, Celtchar, Keltchar): A leading figure in the Ulster Cycle, often cited in rosters of heroes.

kerd (cerd): An artisan or craftsman.

Kimbay Mac Fiontann (Cimbáeth, Cimbaoth; mac Fionntan, son of Fintan): Legendary king of early Ireland who was thought to have lived around 300 CE.

Konal Karna: See "Conaill Carna."

Læg (Laeg, Láeg): Cuculain's friend, messenger, and charioteer, who is killed by Lewy Mac Conroi at the pillar stone with a spear intended for Cuculain. His brother Id is charioteer to Conaill Carna.

Lægairé Buada (Lóegaire Bern, Búadach, Buadhach): Great Ulster Cycle hero. "Lægairé of the Red Victorious Helmet," O'Grady writes, "chivalrous and noble." He contends with Cuculain for the champion's portion in *Fled Bricrenn* (The Feast of Bricrind).

Lægairey (Lóegaire mac Néill; Laeghire, Láegaire, Laoghaire, Laoire, Leary, Lóeghaire, Lóegure): King of Tara (ca. 427–463) who was converted to Christianity by St. Patrick. Son of Niall Noígiallach (Niall of the Nine Hostages), he is the earliest king of Ireland whose dates can be known with reasonable accuracy.

Lahan: Contemporary Leinster, a province in eastern Ireland.

lath: A thin, narrow strip of wood used as the material of a mock or stage weapon, as in a bow, dagger, or sword of lath.

Leabhar na Huidhré (*Lebor na hUidre*): *Book of the Dun Cow.* The oldest manuscript written entirely in Irish, compiled before 1106 at the great monastic center of Clonmacnoise. The codex contains texts of the Mythological Cycle and the Ulster Cycle, including a version of the epic *Táin Bó Cuailnge* (Cattle Raid of Cooley).

Lear (Lir): A god of the sea (whose name means "Sea") and father of Manannan as well as of the personages of the story "The Children of Lir," from which we learn practically all that is known of him. Ler is the equivalent of the Brythonic Llyr, later immortalized by Shakespeare as King Lear.

lēna (léine): Shirt.

Lewy Mac Conroi (Lewy mac Curoi; Lugaid, Lugaigh, Lúí, Luga; mac Con Roí): Son of Curoi (Cú Roí) Mac Dary in the Ulster Cycle. Taken on by Cuculain after Cuculain kills Lewy's father, Lewy later joins Queen Meave and kills Cuculain.

Lewy mac Curoi: See "Lewy Mac Conroi."

Lewy Mac Neesh (Lugaid, Lugaigh, Lúí, Luga; mac Nóis): A foster brother and "true friend of Cuculain" in the *Táin Bó Cuailnge* (Cattle Raid of Cooley).

Lewy Rievenerg (Lugaid, Lugaidh; Reo-derg, Réoderg, Riab nDerg, Riadhdhearg, Sriab nDerg). "Lewy of the Red Stripes" was, according to O'Grady, "son of the three Finns of Emain, sons of Yeoha the melancholy, father of Queen Meave." He became a close friend or foster brother to Cuculain and married Devorgilla after her attempt to seduce the hero.

Liath Macha: "Grey of Macha." One of the hero Cuculain's two chariot horses, along with Dub Sainglend (Black of Saingliu or "black Shanglan" [p. 66] in *History of Ireland*).

Lir: See "Lear."

liss (lis): The enclosed ground or court of an ancient dwelling, such as a fort. By extension, the term can also mean "ring-fort" or "fairy fort."

Loch-an-Tanaigté: According to O'Grady, a "lake in a district called Raheady, and about two miles from Dundalk, on the road between that town and Louth. After the death of Cuculain it was called Loch an Cladav, the lake of the sword," because Cuculain cast his sword into it.

Lōk Mac Favash: Most potent warrior of the south of Ireland and, according to O'Grady, "King of the Shiel Heber" (p. 88).

Lu: See "Lu Lamfáda."

Lu Lamfáda (Lug, Luga, Lugh; Lámfada, Lámfhada, Lámfhota, Lámhfhada): Celebrated chief of the Tuátha De Danan and central hero of the Mythological Cycle of early Irish literature. A solar deity and the father of Cuculain, he is one of the three great heroes of Irish tradition, along with his son and Finn MacCool (Fionn mac Cumhaill). See also "Ioldāna."

Luprachān (leprechaun, luprachán, luprecan, lúracán, lurgadán, lurikeen): A male, solitary fairy who is a guardian of hidden treasure in Irish literary and oral tradition. In the most famous story featuring this figure, he distracts mortals from obtaining the "pot of gold" he protects.

Lusk (Lusca): A village outside Dublin. The name derives from an old Irish word, *lusca*, "cave" or "underground chamber."

Mac Erc (Eochaid mac Eirc): Husband of the goddess Tailtiu and legendary King of the Fir-bolgs, who ruled over an ideal realm of abundance, justice, and honesty. He resisted the arrival of Tuatha Dé Danann or the but became the first Irish king to be killed with a weapon.

Macha Monga-Rue (Macha Mong Rua, Mong Ruadh, Mongroe): The "red-haired" Ulster war queen who marries her rival, Kimbay Mac Fiontann (Cimbáeth), and dominates him. As the daughter of one of the three kings, Áed Ruad, Díthorba, and Cimbáeth, who agree to serve in successive seven-year reigns, she is heir to the throne.

Mac Manar: "Æd Orphid, or Æd of the golden harp was his real name," O'Grady writes. "Eefeen, a fairy-princess, gave him the harp. He lived at one time at Shee Canuta in Connaught." Cuculain hears him singing, the "harp in his slender hands, all golden."

Magh Ai (Magh Aí, Maghai, Magh-ai, Machaire Connaught, the Maghery): The great plain of Roscommon in central Ireland.

Maineys (Maine, Mainí, the Manes): The seven identically named sons of Queen Meave and Aileel Mōr.

Mananan (Mananān, Manannán mac Lir, Mananaan, Mananaun, Manandán, Monanaun): An Irish god who is the son of Lir (i.e., Son of the Sea) and is associated with the Isle of Man ("Mananan's isle," in O'Grady) in the Irish Sea between Great Britain and Ireland.

Meath (an Mhí): A county west of Dublin.

Meave (Maev, Maeve, Medb, Medbh, Medhbh): Warrior queen of Cruhane (modern Connacht) and leading figure in the Ulster Cycle. According to O'Grady, she is a "famous warrioress, who in after days ruled over all the country west of the Shannon, and who feared not to enter the battle, and to fight with the heroes of Eiré."

Mesgœra (Mesgadhera, Mesgedhera): According to O'Grady, he is "a great Leinster champion, slain by Conail Carna." His brains are mixed with clay and used in a ball that ultimately kills Concobar Mac Nessa.

Mid-luhara (Mid Luachra, Mid-Lúhara): A wilderness in Murthemney.

Milesians: The final mythic invaders of Ireland, said to have come from Spain. Their name derives from Milesius, the line's founder, and they are reputed to have descended from Noah's son Japheth. After a failed attempt to conquer the Tuatha Dé Danann, they retreated, only to return victorious in their "snoring galleys" that run "out into the open sea, bearing the Clan Milith to Inis Fail."

Milesius (Milesius, Míl Espáine, Mílid Espáine, Míl Espáne, Míl Easpáine, Míle Easpáin, Míled, Mílead, Míleadh, Miles, Mille Easpain): "Soldier of Spain," founder of the Milesians, according to the pseudohistory *Lebor Gabála* (Book of Invasions), and fictional ancestor of the Irish people. Though his usual name, Míl Espáine (clearly a title), links him with Spain, descriptions of his earlier career place him in Scythia, an ancient region north of the Black Sea. He dies before reaching Ireland in the invasion, but his kin manage to defeat the Tuátha De Danan.

Milith: The sons of Milesius, king of Spain to whom all the princely families of historic times trace their origin. May also refer to Ith, nephew of Milesius. On hearing of the death of his nephew Ith in Ireland, slain by the De Danan, Milesius sets out to conquer Ireland. See "Milesians" and "Milesius."

Mōr Reega (Mōr-Reega, Mórrígan, Morrígan, Mórrigan, Morríghan, Mór-Ríogain, Morrígu, Morrigu): Great queen but also phantom queen. She is the goddess of war fury in early Irish tradition, usually spoken of with the definite article, as in "*the* Mōr Reega." She is part of a trio of war goddesses, with Bahb and Macha, called the Mórígna. She appears to Meave at her camp just before the battle at Cooley, and under her sanction, O'Grady writes, "shall be conclusion of the great foray, and the prosperous dispersion of the Tân."

mōr-tuath: Great tribe.

Moy Tura (Mag Tuired, Mag Tuirid, Magh Tuireadh, Mag Turach, Moytura, Moytirra, Moy Tureyf, Moytirra): Fabled place-name and site of two battles between the Tuátha De Danan and their enemies, the Firbolg and the Fomorians.

Mugain (Mughain): Wife of Concobar Mac Nessa, king of Ulster, and sister of Meave. She appears to be identical to the better-known Mór Muman. In an often-repeated episode, she and her maidens strip naked before Cuculain as he is returning from battle on his way to Emain Macha.

Murthemney (Mag Muirtheimne, Mag Murthemne): A plain adjacent to the Irish Sea between Dundalk and Drogheda—that is, the mouth of the River Boyne, where Cuculain's fort is located.

Naysi (Noíse, Naoise, Naísi): Son of Usna, lover of Deirdré.

Neara (Neara mac Niadhain, Nera): Hero of the Old Irish narrative *Echtra Nerai* (The Adventure of Nera). His sons are repeatedly mentioned as followers of Meave.

Nectan (Nechta Scéne, Nechtan Scéne): According to O'Grady, he is "renowned amongst the tribes of Meath for valour and strength." A man privileged with the right to visit Connla's Well, over which nine hazel trees drop their nuts, said to impart wisdom. Cuculain uses his spear, Gæ-Bolg, to kill Nectan's three sons, who murdered half the living Ulstermen.

Ned (Nét, Néit): According to O'Grady, "this is the old primæval war-god, Ned = slaughter. He does not seem in the existing heroic literature to be a distinct character, but more of the nature of a pervading personality, though I believe he was different in the more remote lost literature. His wives were Fea and Neman."

Nemedians: Descendants of Nemeth (Nemed), they were mythic invaders of Ireland around 1700 BCE. O'Grady writes that they enslaved the Fomorian giants, who later interrupted the Nemedians' rule. "The word Nemedh means sacred; he himself was the root whence sprang the gods of the historic age, the deities of ethnic Erin." They are also said to be ancestors of the Fir-bolgs.

Nemeth (Nemed, Neimheadh, Nemheadh, Nemedius): Leader of the third mythic conquest of early Ireland, who is descended from both the biblical Noah and the monster god Magog, according to the *Book of Invasions.*

Nial (Niall; Noígiallach, Naígaillach, Naoighiallach): A quasi-historical figure, he is one of the earliest recorded high kings of Ireland and, according to tradition, the leader of ambitious foreign conquests. He is purported to have reigned 379–405 CE.

Nieve (Neeve, Niam, Niamh, Niau, Niav, Niave): Druidess and daughter of Kelkar, "who, above all the women, loved and honoured" Cuculain. In O'Grady's account, she helps protect Cuculain with "some weird spiritual shield against the spiritual foe" (p. 164).

O'Curry, Eugene: Irish philologist and antiquarian (1794–1862). O'Curry wrote widely about the ancient texts and published, among other volumes, *The Manuscript Materials of Ancient Irish History* (1860). This book and *Manners and Customs of the Ancient Irish* (1873) were of vital important for O'Grady's *History* and, later, for Revivalists such as Yeats.

Ogham (ogam, ogum, oghum): An alphabet for the Irish language using groups of one to five strokes, which were represented as notches on the equivalent of a tallystick or on the edges of standing stones or vertical posts.

ollav (ollam, ollamh, ollave): The highest-ranking member of a social group—for example, of *fíli*, an elite class of poets, or of judges and priests.

Ollam Fodla (Ollamh Fodhla, Ollamh Fódhla): According to O'Grady, the "great pre-historic King of Ulster and of all Erin."

osiered: To be furnished, covered, or adorned with osiers (willow trees); twisted or plaited like osiers.

Olnemacia: O'Grady's idiosyncratic variant spelling of "Olnemacta."

Olnemacta (Olnemacia): The name of present-day Connacht in Cuculain's time. When preceded by the definite article, "the Olnemacta," it refers to the tribe of warriors who hailed from that province and fought for Queen Meave.

Partholān (Partholón, Partholon, Parthalán, Parthanán): Mythical invader of Ireland and deified hero from around 2057 BCE. According to O'Grady, he and his descendants are connected with the hill of Tallaght (*támh leacht*, or "plague pit"), ten miles from Dublin, which "was where they were chiefly adored." The Clan Partholān fought against the Fomorians. The Nemedians were a later branch of the Partholānian clan. After flourishing for more than five hundred years, all the Partholānians died of the plague within one week.

rann: A stanza in a bardic poem or song.

rath (ráth, ráith): A fortified dwelling, presumably of an early chieftain or king, surrounded by an earthen wall.

Rath Cruhane (Cruhâne, Crogan, Cruachan, Cruachain, Rathcroghan, Rathcruachain): Meave's fortress in Connacht (in present-day County Roscommon), which serves as the capital of the province and is equivalent to Emain Macha in Ulster.

rechtairé (reachtaire): A steward—for example, one who enacts Cuculain's decrees.

Red Branch (an Chraobh Rua): Also known as "the Clanna Rury." Headquartered at Emain Macha, they were the knights who defended Ulster during Concobar's reign. Their glory, O'Grady writes, "fills the prehistoric world of the bards." They were believed to have been founded by Concobar's grandfather, Ross the Red. Cuculain is the greatest of the Red Branch Knights.

Red Hand of Ulster: The heraldic symbol of the northern (Ultonian) clans.

Riangowra: Læg's father.

Riastarra (ríastrad, ríastradh, ríastarthae): The "warp phase" or "battle rage" that distorts Cuculain's features and gives him superhuman power. O'Grady notes that Cuculain is called by the name "Riastarra" in a story titled "Sick Bed of Cuculain" and that the name "refers to the idea that in battle his stature increased."

Rie-damna: According to O'Grady, "the material of a king, i.e., one powerful and conspicuous enough to be elected, and of royal blood."

Rod (Ruad Rofessa, Ruadh Ró-fesa): One of the principle gods of the Old Irish tradition, who nonetheless has a rather confused set of identities. His name means "lord of great knowledge" and was associated with several figures, including the Dagda, a warrior, artisan, and magician, and Donn, the ruler of the dead and the Celtic Otherworld.

Ros-na-Ree (Rossnaree, Ros na Riogh): "Wood of the kings." According to O'Grady, "Ros-na-Ree was a great Pagan cemetery, on the southern bank of the Boyne," at the site of the present-day village Rossnaree.

Rossa Roe (Mac Rosa Ruaid): The full patronymic of Cairbré Nia-far (Cairbré Nia Fer), king of Tara. See "Cairbré."

Rury Mōr (Rudraige, Rudraighe, Rory): "Rury the Great," founder of Clanna Rury. According to O'Grady, he is "a descendent of Ir, son of Milesius, and the ancestor of the founder of the great Northern Confederacy, the Red Branch of Ulster." He is reputed to be a "son of Fomor, or the Fomorian—this word always representing a supernatural personage."

ruth: Compassion or pity.

Saba (Sāba): In O'Grady's usage, an advisory council to a royal or high personage.

Samhane (Samain, Samhain): A Gaelic festival marking the end of the harvest season and the beginning of winter.

Scathach (Scáth, Scáthach, Scáthach nUaind, Skaáh, Skatha): Amazonian warrioress of Irish legend who lived on the island named for her and who trained Cuculain and other heroes in the martial arts there. Some legends claim that Cuculain attempted to wrest ownership of the island from Scáthach but that he eventually relented after days of strenuous combat.

scythed: With bladed wheels.

Setanta (Sétanta): Birth name of Cuculain, son of Sualtam and Dectera.

shanachie (seanchaí, seanachie): A traditional storyteller and member of a privileged, powerful cast of poets, diviners, and seers in early Ireland.

They are distinguished from the lower-status bards and the *brehon*, whose learning dealt more with law.

Shanglan: Dub Sainglend (Black of Saingliu or "black Shanglan"), one of the hero Cuculain's two chariot horses, along with Liath Macha.

Shee (sídh, sídhe, síodh, sí, síd, síth): A fairy mound and, by implication, the realm beyond the senses, the Otherworld, or, in oral tradition, the fairy world—and thence the fairies themselves. The Milesians drive the Tuátha De Danan underground, where they become the fairies.

Skaáh: See "Scathach."

Slieve Blahma (Sliabh Bladhma, Sliabh-Blama, Sliabh-Blamaht, Slieve Blâma, Slieve Bloom): A mountain range running through the central plain of Ireland in the province of Leinster.

St. Columba: There are thirty-two saints with this name, the most notable of whom is known in Irish and Scottish Gaelic as "Colum Cille" (ca. 521–97 CE). He was an Irish missionary credited with disseminating Christianity throughout Scotland, founded several monasteries associated with manuscript copying, and became the third most celebrated saint in his homeland, after St. Patrick and St. Brigid.

St. Fiech: Probably St. Fiacre. Historical (d. 670? CE) Irish saint, born Fiachra, who was exiled in France. According to O'Grady, in a hymn "in honour of St. Patrick, St. Fiech distinctly states, that in the old times the people *used to worship* the Shee." St. Fiacre is a patron of travelers and gardeners. James Joyce facetiously makes him the patron saint of cabdrivers.

St. Patrick (Patrick, Patricius, Pádraig, Pátraic, Cothraige): Evangelist to and national saint of Ireland who lived in the fifth century CE. Legend records his dialogues with Fenian heroes Oisin and Caílte.

St. Sechnall (St. Seachnall, St. Secundinus): Bishop and confessor (ca. 372–457 CE), he was believed to have accompanied St. Patrick to Ireland in 432.

Sualtam (Sualdam, Sualtam mac Roy, Sualtam mac Róich, Sualtach, Subaltach): The brother of Fergus Mac Roy, he is the mortal father of Cuculain. When Aileel and Meave invade Ulster, Sualtam attempts to raise Concobar Mac Nessa's warriors.

Talkend: A nickname for St. Patrick, referring to his tonsured crown, which also led to the nickname "Adze-head" in his contentious dialogues with the Fenian heroes Oisin and Caílte. O'Grady relates a medieval legend "that a vision of Christ was seen by Cuculain" in which he and his charioteer Læg "announced the coming of the Talkend."

Tân (táin): Cattle raid, as in the title *Táin Bó Cuailnge* (Cattle Raid of Cooley).

Tan-bo-Cooalney (*Táin Bó Cuailnge, Cuálgne, Chualige*): The greatest work of classical Irish literature, which is part of the Ulster Cycle of myths and tells the story of the "cattle raid of Cooley." The narrative of this clash between Queen Maeve and Cuculain was first recorded by Christian monks in the Middle Ages, though the origins of the tale date back to the oral tradition of Celtic Bards centuries earlier.

tanist (tánaiste): King elect; the successor apparent to a Celtic chief, usually the most vigorous adult of his kin, elected during the chief's lifetime.

Tara (Temair, Teamhair, Temuir): A site near Navan in County Meath traditionally associated with the high kings of Ireland. O'Grady notes that Tara hosted a "great central and national feis," or festival, and that the chief Irish king presided there and "enjoyed the reputation and emoluments flowing to him on that account." The prehistoric remains at the site include a Neolithic passage tomb, a fort, and several barrows and fortifications; it is also the site of the Lia Fail, the inauguration stone or pillar.

Tayta Brac: The Red Branch armory.

Tec Mid-cuarta: The chamber in the middle of a palace.

Temair: See "Tara."

Temairian: A native or inhabitant of Tara.

Tierna (Abbot of Clonmacnois or Clonmacnoise): An Irish historian who flourished in the eleventh century and who critically separated the elements of romance and fact in Irish history. Clonmacnois was Ireland's foremost early monastic settlement, founded by St. Ciarán on January 25, 545, in present-day County Offaly.

tuath (*túath*): A tribe or group of people and the land on which they live.

Tuátha De Danan (Tuatha Dé Danann, Tuátha Dē Danā): Tribes of the goddess Danu. According to O'Grady, they are a divine people ("immortal and all powerful") who occupy an "enchanted land." They are the origin of the fairies (áes sídhe), "the final outcome and last development of a mythology which we can see advancing step by step, one divine tribe pushing out another, one family of gods swallowing up another, or perishing under the hands of time and change, to make room for another." They are described as excelling over all peoples of the earth in their proficiency in every art.

Túatha of Erin: See "Tuátha De Danan."

Uath (Uathach): Daughter of the warrior woman Scáthach and guardian of her island fortress (the Isle of Skye). In O'Grady, the chief bard sings of "the contest of Cuculain for the championship of Ulla" from Uath's point of view. In the song, Cuculain asserts his bravery: "Be my name renowned among the nations, / Be my glory sung through all time" (p. 117). Cuculain is reputed to have been Uath's lover as well.

Ulla (Uladh, Ulagh, Ulaidh, Ullin, Ulaid, Ulidia): A tribe in early Ireland who gave their name to the province of Ulster.

Ulster (Ulaid, Ultonia): The ancient province and kingdom covers approximately the same geographic boundaries as present-day Ulster in Northern Ireland. "Ulster was the old Ultonia," O'Grady writes, "the patrimony of the Red Branch Knights." The Red Branch "all but wrested the whole island from the greatest of the English princes." Tradition has dated the decline of this kingdom as a significant power to the time of Cormac Mac Art (254–77 CE).

Ultonian cycle: Usually called the Ulster Cycle or Red Branch Cycle, a series of renowned Irish mythological tales, including the *Táin Bó Cuailnge* (Cattle Raid of Cooley).

Usna (Clanna Usna): The sons of Usna (Naysi, Anly, and Ardan) are prominent Red Branch Knights who appear throughout O'Grady's histories.

viands: Items of food or provisions.

wattled: Made of stakes interlaced with branches or twigs.

Further Reading

Castle, Gregory. "Nobler Forms: Standish James O'Grady's 'Imaginative History' and the Irish Literary Revival." In *Reading Irish History: Text, Contexts, and Memory in Modern Ireland*, edited by Lawrence McBride, 156–77. Dublin: Four Courts Press, 2003.

Curtin, Jeremiah. *Myths and Folk-Lore of Ireland*. London: Sampson Low, 1890. Reprint. New York: Weathervane, 1975.

Deane, Seamus. *Celtic Revivals: Essays in Modern Irish Literature 1880–1980*. Winston-Salem, NC: Wake Forest Univ. Press, 1987.

Duffy, Sir Charles Gavan, George Sigerson, and Douglas Hyde. *The Revival of Irish Literature*. London: T. Fisher Unwin, 1894.

Fallis, Richard. *The Irish Renaissance*. Syracuse, NY: Syracuse Univ. Press, 1977.

Foster, John Wilson. *Fictions of the Irish Literary Revival: A Changeling Art*. Syracuse, NY: Syracuse Univ. Press, 1987.

Gregory, Lady Augusta. *Cuchulain of Muirthemne*. London: John Murray, 1902. Reprint. Gerrards Cross, UK: Colin Smythe, 1973.

Hagan, Edward A. *High Nonsensical Words: A Study of the Works of Standish James O'Grady*. Troy, NY: Whitston, 1986.

Higgins, Geraldine. *Heroic Revivals from Carlyle to Yeats*. New York: Palgrave Macmillan, 2012.

Hull, Eleanor. *The Cuchullin Saga in Irish Literature*. London: Nutt, 1898. Reprint. New York: AMS Press, 1972.

Hyde, Douglas. *A Literary History of Ireland from Earliest Times to the Present*. London: T. Fisher Unwin, 1899. Reprint. London: T. Fisher Unwin, 1906.

Keating, Geoffrey. *The History of Ireland, from the Earliest Period to the English Invasion*. Trans. John O'Mahony. Kansas City, MO: Irish Genealogical Foundation, 1983.

Kelleher, John V. "Early Irish History and Pseudo-History." *Studia Hibernica* 3 (1963): 113–27.

Kiberd, Declan. *Inventing Ireland.* Cambridge, MA: Harvard Univ. Press, 1996.

———. "The Perils of Nostalgia: A Critique of the Revival." In *Literature and the Changing Ireland*, edited by Peter Connolly, 1–24. Totowa, NJ: Barnes and Noble, 1982.

Kiberd, Declan, and P. J. Mathews, eds. *Handbook of the Irish Revival: An Anthology of Irish Cultural and Political Writings 1891–1922.* Dublin: Abbey Theatre Press, 2015.

Lawless, Emily. *The Story of Ireland.* New York: Putnam, 1887. Reprint. London: T. Fisher Unwin, 1891.

MacKillop, James. *Myths and Legends of the Celts.* London: Penguin, 2006.

MacLeod, Sharon Paice. *Celtic Myth and Religion: A Study of Traditional Belief.* Jefferson, NC: McFarland, 2012.

Marcus, Philip L. *Standish O'Grady.* Lewisburg, PA: Bucknell Univ. Press, 1971.

Maume, Patrick. "Standish James O'Grady: Between Imperial Romance and Irish Revival." *Éire-Ireland* 39, nos. 1–2 (2004): 11–35.

McAteer, Michael. "'Ireland and the Hour': Paternalism and Nationality in Standish James O'Grady's *Toryism and the Tory Democracy.*" In *Ireland in the Nineteenth-Century: Regional Identity*, edited by Glenn Hooper and Leon Litvack, 199–214. Dublin: Four Courts Press, 2000.

———. *Standish O'Grady, Æ, and Yeats: History, Politics, Culture.* Dublin: Irish Academic Press, 2002.

McKenna, John R. "The Standish O'Grady Collection at Colby College: A Check List." *Colby Library Quarterly* 4 (1958): 291–303.

Mercier, Vivian. "Standish James O'Grady." *Colby Library Quarterly* 4 (1958): 258–90.

Nolan, Jerry C. M. "Standish James O'Grady's Cultural Nationalism." *Irish Studies Review* 7, no. 3 (1999): 347–57.

Nutt, Kathleen. "Irish Identity and the Writing of History." *Éire-Ireland* 19, no. 2 (1994): 160–72.

O'Curry, Eugene. *Lectures on the Manuscript Materials of Ancient Irish History.* Delivered at the Catholic University of Ireland during the sessions of 1855 and 1856. Dublin: Hinch, 1878.

———. *On the Manners and Customs of the Ancient Irish.* A series of lectures delivered by the late Eugene O'Curry. Edited with an introduction, appendixes, etc., by W. K. Sullivan. London: Williams and Norgate, 1873.

O'Grady, Hugh Art. *Standish James O'Grady, the Man and the Writer: A Memoir by His Son.* Dublin: Talbot Press, 1929.

O'Grady, Standish Hayes, ed. *Silva Gadelica (I–XXXI): A Collection of Tales in Irish with Extracts Illustrating Persons and Places.* London: Williams and Northgate, 1892. Reprint. New York: Lemma, 1970.

O'Grady, Standish James. *All Ireland.* London: Unwin, 1898. Reprint. Poole, UK: Woodstock Books, 1999.

———. *The Bog of Stars, and Other Stories and Sketches of Elizabethan Ireland.* 2nd ed. London: T. Fisher Unwin, 1893.

———. *The Coming of Cuculain.* London: Methuen, 1894. Reprint. Dublin: Talbot Press, 1919.

———. *Cuculain: An Epic.* London: Sampson Low, Searle, Marston & Rivington; Dublin: Ponsonby, 1882.

———. *Finn and His Companions.* Dublin: Talbot Press; London: Unwin, 1921.

———. *The Flight of the Eagle.* Dublin: Sealy, Bryers and Walker, 1908.

———. *In the Gates of the North.* Dublin: Talbot Press; London: Unwin, 1919.

———. *Selected Essays and Passages.* Edited by Ernest A. Boyd. Dublin: Talbot Press, 1918.

———. *The Triumph and Passing of Cuculain.* New York: Stokes, 1919.

O'Halloran, Sylvester. *A General History of Ireland, from the Earliest Accounts to the Close of the Twelfth Century. Collected from the Most Authentic Records.* 2 vols. London: Hamilton, 1778. Republished with additional material as *The Pictorial History of Ireland, from the Landing of the Milesians to the Present Time.* Boston: Murphy & McCarthy, 1884.

Pereira, Lucie. "The Victorian Fathers of the Irish Revival: The Treatment of the Dierdre Myth by Samuel Ferguson and Standish James O'Grady." *Irish Studies Review* 14, no. 1 (Feb. 2006): 69–89.

Sullivan, Daniel J. "Standish James O'Grady's *All-Ireland Review.*" *Studia Hibernica* 9 (1969): 125–36.

Valente, Joseph. *The Myth of Manliness in Irish National Culture, 1880–1922*. Urbana: Univ. of Illinois Press, 2011.

Yeats, W. B. *The Collected Works of W. B. Yeats*. Vol. 1: *The Poems*. Edited by Richard J. Finneran. New York: Macmillan, 1989.

———. *The Collected Works of W. B. Yeats*. Vol. 2: *The Plays*. Edited by David R. Clark and Rosalind E. Clark. New York: Scribner's, 1989.

———. *The Collected Works of W. B. Yeats*. Vol. 4: *Early Essays*. Edited by Richard J. Finneran and George Bornstein. New York: Scribner's, 2007.

———. "Mr. Standish O'Grady's *Flight of the Eagle*." In *The Collected Works of W. B. Yeats*, vol. 9: *Early Articles and Reviews: Uncollected Articles and Reviews Written between 1886 and 1890*, edited by John P. Frayne and Madeleine Marchaterre, 342–45. New York: Scribner's, 2004.

Biographical Notes

STANDISH JAMES O'GRADY (1846–1928)

Standish James O'Grady was born in 1846, during the era of the Great Famine in Ireland. He came from a long line of country squires—to be precise, eight centuries in the Barony of Brough, according to his son and biographer Hugh O'Grady. His father, Thomas O'Grady (d. 1871) of Kilmore, became rector of Castletown Berehaven and married Susan Doe, who came from a planter family with connections to Clan Carty. As the younger O'Grady was growing up, the evangelical movement was in full swing, and he developed a deep knowledge of the Bible. But he was also drawn to the great epic writers Virgil and Homer, who later provided him with a heroic vocabulary for his three-volume work *History of Ireland* and for his later Elizabethan stories. As a boy, he attended Tipperary Grammar School, where he acquired his skills in scholarship and literary writing as well as his habit of painstakingly researching his historical and fictional works.

As a young man at Trinity College, Dublin, O'Grady won a number of awards, including a classics scholarship, the University Silver Medal in Ethics and Psychology, and the Philosophical Society's silver medal in oratory and gold medal in essay writing. Following his mother's wishes, he studied divinity with an eye toward entering the church, but he ultimately found his disbelief to be as powerful as his belief. He decided instead to make a career at the bar in West Cork, where his talents as an orator earned him a lasting reputation. During this period, he also employed his verbal abilities in writing leaders for the Unionist paper the *Daily Express* in Dublin.

While engaged in these activities, O'Grady stumbled upon Sylvester O'Halloran's *General History of Ireland* (1778) and found himself entranced by what he read. He soon began to write on Irish subjects, though he had difficulty placing *History of Ireland* with a publisher and

3. Standish O'Grady, n.d. Unknown photographer, frontispiece to Hugh Art O'Grady, *Standish James O'Grady, the Man and the Writer: A Memoir by His Son* (Dublin: Talbot Press, 1929).

was compelled to have it printed at his own expense. At first, his work was more enthusiastically received in England than in Ireland. After another fortuitous discovery, this time of George Petrie's essay "The Round Towers of Ireland," O'Grady reconceived his subject and rewrote his "sober treatise" in the form of adventure novels with Cuculain as the protagonist.

At this time, in the 1890s, he began to experience greater success as an author and was acknowledged by writers such as W. B. Yeats, George "Æ"

Russell, and T. W. Rolleston. But as literary tastes began to change during the fin de siècle period, O'Grady gradually withdrew from literary circles and turned to Elizabethan history, writing a number of works, fiction and other, on the great Irish families of the era. He also tentatively entered politics, producing pamphlets on Ireland's political and economic experience under British control. His overarching concern was the complacency of Irish landlords, whose wealth and power were built on flimsy claims to the land, though his criticism extended to issues of taxation, which he saw as symptomatic of Britain's betrayal of the Act of Union.

At the end of the decade, finding that journalism in Dublin was not sufficiently remunerative, O'Grady left for Kilkenny, where he edited the *Kilkenny Moderator* and later the *All-Ireland Review*. In these papers, he advocated for a particular form of national unity, with common policies, common aspirations, and a common culture for the Irish people. After the turn of the century, he dedicated himself entirely to the *All-Ireland Review*, which became an important intellectual source for the Irish Literary Revival and was initially praised by Yeats, in a letter to O'Grady, for being "as truly literary as it was truly Irish." But as O'Grady became increasingly estranged from literary matters, the publication turned more and more to social, political, and agricultural concerns. During these years, his book sales continued to grow, and he was awarded a Civil List Pension, which allowed him to retire from editorship of the *All-Ireland Review* in 1908.

O'Grady's health began to decline in the following decade, and he eventually sought a milder climate. He left Ireland in 1918, first for northern France and then for England, staying for a few years in Northamptonshire before moving to London and finally to the Isle of Wight, where he died in 1928.

Based on Hugh Art O'Grady, *Standish James O'Grady, the Man and the Writer: A Memoir by His Son* (Dublin: Talbot Press, 1929).

CONTRIBUTORS

PATRICK BIXBY is associate professor of English in the School of Humanities, Arts, and Cultural Studies and director of graduate studies in the New College of Interdisciplinary Arts and Sciences at Arizona State University. Author of *Samuel Beckett and the Postcolonial Novel* (2009), he has served as assistant to the editors of *The Letters of Samuel Beckett* (4 vols., 2009–) and has published essays on Beckett, Joyce, Yeats, Rushdie, and others. He is currently finishing a book titled "Nietzsche and Irish Modernism" and coediting a collected volume, "A History of Irish Modernism," with Gregory Castle.

GREGORY CASTLE is professor of British and Irish literature at Arizona State University. In addition to essays on Joyce, Yeats, Wilde, Stoker, and other Irish writers, he has published the books *Modernism and the Celtic Revival* (2001), *Reading the Modernist Bildungsroman* (2006), *Guide to Literary Theory* (2007), and *Literary Theory Handbook* (2013). He has also edited *Postcolonial Discourses* (2000), *Encyclopedia of Literary and Cultural Theory*, vol. 1 (2011), and *A History of the Modernist Novel* (2015). His current projects include an edited volume (with Patrick Bixby), "A History of Irish Modernism," and a book project, "Modernism and the Temporalities of Irish Revival."

RENÉE FOX is assistant professor of literature at the University of California, Santa Cruz, where she teaches classes in Irish studies and Victorian studies. She is currently completing a manuscript entitled "Necromantic Victorians: Reanimation and the Historical Imagination in British and Irish Literature," and her published work includes essays on Robert Browning, W. B Yeats, J. Sheridan Le Fanu, and Bram Stoker.

MICHAEL MCATEER is associate professor in the Department of English Literatures and Cultures at Pázmány Péter Catholic University, Budapest, and was formerly lecturer in the Department of English at Queen's University, Belfast. He is the author of *Standish O'Grady, Æ, and Yeats: History, Politics, Culture* (2002) and *Yeats and European Drama* (2010). He has published an extensive range of book chapters and journal essays on modern Irish literature and is the director of the Budapest Centre for Irish Studies.

JOSEPH VALENTE is Distinguished Professor of English and Disability Studies at the State University of New York, Buffalo, and treasurer of the International Yeats Society. He is the author of *James Joyce and the Problem of Justice: Negotiating Sexual and Colonial Difference* (1995), *Dracula's*

Crypt: Bram Stoker, Irishness, and the Question of Blood (2002), and *The Myth of Manliness in Irish National Culture, 1880–1922* (2011). He is also the editor or coeditor of *Quare Joyce* (1998), *Disciplinarity at the Fin de Siècle* (with Amanda Anderson, 2002), *Urban Ireland* (2010), and *Yeats and Afterwords* (with Marjorie Howes, 2014). His current manuscript projects include "Exceptional Subjects: Autism and Moral Authority in Modern Literature," "The Crux of the X: Dispatches from Ireland's War on Children (with Margot Backus), and "Ireland's Complex Revival" (with Marjorie Howes).

Index